turas

a story of strangers in a strange land

turas

a story of strangers in a strange land

colin neill

Matador
5 Weir Road
Kibworth Beauchamp
Leicester LE8 0LQ, UK
Tel: (+44) 116 279 2299
Fax: (+44) 116 279 2277
Email: books@troubador.co.uk
Web: www.troubador.co.uk/matador

ISBN 978 1848766 334

British Library Cataloguing in Publication Data.
A catalogue record for this book is available from the British Library.

Typeset in 11pt ITC Giovanni Std Book by Troubador Publishing Ltd, Leicester, UK

Matador is an imprint of Troubador Publishing Ltd

For Claire, Matt and Suzy

"... I assure you, Christ will take possession of Ireland, and not just of a wee nook of it in the North parts as formerly, but Christ will have Ireland from sea to sea..."

Rev Michael Bruce of Killinchy, preaching on 27 July 1689

Foreword

The inhabitants of the beautiful island of Ireland are a story-telling people. Somewhere buried deep in our lineage, (from wherever you trace it) is a gene that sparks us into lengthy regaling, whether to make a profound point or just to make friends laugh. Or both.

Our problem is that the vast majority of our stories are drawn from the past. Sadly we all know where that particular predisposition has landed us. Add to that a preoccupation with *our* stories to the exclusion of others' and you can see why we are left fractured and defensive.

Rarely does someone summon prophetic imagination to tell a story of our future. Colin Neill has done this in a way that does not forget or erase the past, but honours its memory by reaching forward to provoke our present. And my, does it provoke. On page after page you will be stung and amused by Colin's insightful observations into the paradoxes and joys of Ulster protestant life. You imbibe a complex set of relationships that slip down smoothly with a ring of authenticity. As I read, I began to wonder whether Colin had been secretly carrying a small notebook around for most of his days, scribbling down every idiosyncrasy he spotted. That these behaviours *were* incongruous is easy to see with hindsight, but I simply had to sit in admiration as I realised that Colin spotted that in real time. It is a joy to read words from someone who has obviously had "eyes to see". These eyes have seen beyond the middle-class pretensions and idolatry, but also to the honest pain of those who are products of a culture they had little part in creating.

The characters of *Turas* beautifully mimic many uptight Protestant Northern Irish relationships. Don't dig below the surface. Don't challenge someone else's lifestyle (at least not to their face.) Don't break any stereotypes, or if you do, don't let your family know. Don't let the mask drop. Everything's fine. And above all, avoid conflict at all costs. Don't directly communicate with the person with whom you have a problem. But definitely mention your frustrations to anyone else that will listen. That's "Conflict resolution 101" – Norn Iron style. Watching these characters extricate themselves from lifelong presumptions or resign themselves to them will be a cathartic experience for many.

This is an important book. You may end up laughing, crying, ripping out pages, or throwing it across the room, but that's partly the point. Perspectives that previously came up against a "No entry" or "Do not disturb" sign in your brain or heart might just sneak in to annoy, enlighten, offend and challenge you. But try to remember. It's just a book. Maybe.

Andy Flannagan
London, June 2010

Introduction

My name is Peter Jeremiah McKibbon. I write these words on a blank page, though I believe that no such thing exists. Blank pages are just wishful figments of our imagination – the same delusions as fresh starts and clean breaks. As individuals we never live our lives in the single moment – from cradle to grave every incident and happening is a link in the chain from beginning to end. Actions have consequences, and as the snowballs of our experiences roll down the hill they gather around us more and more character and hurt and joy and defensiveness and vulnerability. On and on and on it goes.

Nobody comes from nowhere. Two lovers who come together may start off by making a life but in the fullness of time they form – for good or bad – people. Think of the son whose insistent pessimism is a draining reminder of the cynicism of his father. Think of the daughter whose through-other unkemptness is a reaction against her mother's propriety. Whether they embrace it or rail against it each person makes a myriad of decisions – knowing and unknowing – in which the past and the present makes them what they'll be in the future. How far and deep does all of this extend: God alone knows who and how many bear the scars and show the virtues of the grandparents and the great grandparents – and way beyond those – that they never even met? There is so much more than heirlooms and the contours of facial features that are passed down.

From my earliest years people would shake their heads and roll their eyes and tell me I was just like my grandfather: Jeremiah Andrew McKibbon – or Sandy as he was known to family and friends. I could tell you who he was but that would say nothing of what he was. What he was, was a dissenter, righteously railing and speaking out about all that he was for and against.

By profession he was a Minister of the Word of God, yet he seemed to approach that Word not as the double edged sword that Scripture self references as, but rather as a blunter weapon. The Apostle Paul called it that as an analogy for his day, and Granddad seemed determined to bring it up to date as an automatic machine gun.

He was ordained into ministry just two years before the outbreak of the Second World War. If the Word of God was his weapon then the pulpit was his trench. What he saw before his eyes he filtered through the words of the Bible and reflected back to the congregation in front of him: they sent the signal and he gave the pictures and sounds. Such an approach earned him a reputation but won few friends. He persevered for 13 years and three callings, and the last time he shook dust off his feet he decided it was time to cast his net as far as a different continent altogether. As his eldest children headed off to university in Scotland so he and my Grandmother went to a new life in South Africa with an idealised desire to preach that in Christ there was neither black nor white. "They can't ignore an outsider like me the way they would one of their own," he said when he was going.

It was in South Africa that my own Father came along – a 'wee late one' as Grandpa referred to him in his mother tongue. Where Granddad was an action man of God, Dad was an academic man of God. Which goes to prove what I said earlier: embrace or reaction; it's always one or the other. He followed his father into ministry, but realising that his heart lay more in his study than the front rooms of his flock, he left congregational life after five years to pursue a Professorship and teach in a Bible College. And that is where he met my mother, who lectured in an adjoining Medical School.

Me: I'm a chip off the old block – I inherited Granddad's love of justice, Dad's love of study, and Mum's love of science. That's how I got to where I am today, researching the links between poverty and nutrition. For the last five years I've been doing research on and off with Queen's University in Belfast and 18 months ago the opportunity arose for me to do an exchange for a year. This of course was more than a busman's holiday: it was a chance to go home and find out more about me and Granddad, see what influenced the not so blank pages all those years ago. It was also a way to catch up with my old friend Adam – he did his elective many years ago in Jo-burg and his and mine was a connection that I think most of us are fortunate if we can achieve even once or twice in a lifetime.

So to paraphrase the saying, I couldn't have gone at a better time – not if I'd tried. For as all of you who read this will know, it was just a year ago that age old division was – apparently – set aside as Ireland was united. What you will read on these pages is the story of who I met, and got to know, and what we all learned together.

In my sphere of study I frequently wrestle with the conflicting influences of nature and nurture: I never fail to marvel at how much of a person's character and experience often seems the consequence of a random chance of birth. Think of the Kamikaze pilot flying his plane into American aircraft carriers off the coast of his homeland. Think of the civil rights marchers thronged behind their banners in the Deep South. Think of the North Koreans who live and then die within such a narrow tunnel of opportunity that oppression is numbed only by their not even knowing how oppressed they are. If God in his providence had set all these people, made in his own image, in another time and place, their lives would have been completely different.

And it is just the same with all whom I met. Nobody met them at the top of a birth canal and asked them to tick a box to say that they wanted to be Ulster Protestants or Irish Catholics. They simply came out and were placed in their mother's arms and took what they were given – as we all do. Yet those mother's arms and those father's influences – as well as the churches and the schools and the politics and the shibboleths and the history and the versions of the history – all of that was what formed them.

The choices that we have in life are – I believe – much fewer than many tell us that we have. You can choose how to react but you often have very little say in what you are reacting to. The men I met and came to call my friends were going on a journey that no one asked them if they wanted to go on. All of them responded in different ways: this is the story of where the journey took them.

1

Willie

It was just another new day and yet a day like none before it. Everything was just the same but everyone knew – really – that so much would never be the same again. Willie Maxwell pottered about the comforting familiarity of his home in the solitude of the day's early hours, faithfully performing the gentle habits of his morning.

The dog still barked eagerly to be let out first thing and answer nature's call, and that done Willie turned to acting out the lovely dullness of spousal intimacy. The kettle was clicked on and he reached into a cupboard for the tea caddy. He arranged the breakfast table just so, little marital geometries, choreographies of pills and tablets, tea pot and tea cosy, and bowls and spoons set out – everything just the way that everything had always been.

Then he went to the back door and let the dog back in, and prepared its breakfast in turn. It ate the same thing at the same time in the same bowl every day but its tail – if not its whole bum – never failed to wag in enthusiasm for the meal clattering into the receptacle. And despite eager eyes and a lolling tongue it would never puts its nose to the job until permission was granted, the crunching of its mouth and the dropping of sloppy debris on the lino now providing a sound of soothing percussion.

The next habit turned to was a breaking of the spell – listening to the morning news would click fingers and expel Willie from the contenting hypnosis of domestic routine. When 'the wireless' was turned on Radio Four was still there. But whilst the *Today* programme was the same the *Today* programme was different. It had always been for him a firm anchor at the start of each day. Every morning aloof politicians and ministers were cut down to size: Tory politicians and Labour ministers –

not *our* politicians, thought Willie, but *our* Government nonetheless. A looking and a listening east to hear of an overnight fire at a block of flats in Barnstaple or fears growing over a missing teenager in Ashbourne, or job losses announced at a factory in Gwent. In most senses not in any way relevant at all but nonetheless a daily reinforcement of identity.

But now as Willie listened the plummy accent told of sombre truths. The newsreader reported that just eight hours ago, at midnight, a short ceremony at Stormont had confirmed the passing of Northern Ireland, and had officially confirmed the birth of a now *32* county Republic of Ireland. The Union Jack had been lowered and the tricolour raised. The Secretary of State had made a short speech, shaken hands, and in the most dignified manner that he could, 'got out'. For him, it was like attending the funeral of an elderly relative who he had only known distantly in his youth: and even then nobody seemed to like her much. He had to be there but the event meant little to him. He would be only a footnote in history but he felt a strangely grubby sort of footnote, and painfully wanted to get back home. Later that day a TV report would reveal the unfortunate way he had kept blowing out his cheeks and checking his watch through the evening. Those little glances seemed to say it all.

Of course they didn't say *this* on Radio Four. This was the BBC and they were too objective to state the obvious. But there was commentary and analysis of every line uttered going on simultaneously in Willie's thoughts. The news in parenthesis: his heart in parenthesis. He was fluent in such translation and as he fussed and shook his head at the reports, it was as if he had earphones on in some international house of legislature. To Willie the polite Englishman's voice was just oral fog in the background and in his own head flowed the truth of the matter. If his wife had been here now, she'd have asked him who he was talking to.

The newsreader said that across the former six counties of 'the North of Ireland' there had been few reports of violence. The unrest *had* been there of course – particularly at the time of the announcement ten months ago – but the majority knew deep down it was a futile gesture that would make no difference.

The referendum had been held three months earlier in the preceding November – 61:39 in favour in the North and 78:22 across the island as a whole. Demographics are like the rolling of the years, pondered Willie: they only move in one direction. The politicians of the remnant made promises that this would happen only over their dead bodies, but the protest rally called immediately for Belfast City Hall attracted only half the crowd anticipated. The bark was willing but the bite had long gone.

Immediately after the governmental agreement, life in the North had been rather less peaceful: both practically and philosophically. Pockets of pessimistic Protestants christened this period 'the last days', and in the first instance that apocalyptic phrase seemed horribly appropriate: buses were burnt; blast bombs blew; shots rang out; and barricades blocked roads.

But none of this made any difference because power is only useful if it can be channelled and directed. Despite the sanguine acceptance demonstrated by some, a portion of the people revved hard, emotions and sheer anger red lining. But the only thing that happened was wheels spinning round and round, with lots of mud flying about the place, and most of it hitting their own faces. A collective people seemed to regress back to toddler status and to no effect. They could scream and kick and holler and huff but they weren't going to get what they wanted. Somebody else had more power and they would have to get to understand the boundaries.

Unionists would get a nation state's mechanisms for protecting minorities: their education preserved; peace money for public housing and business incubation; funding for their community and youth workers. There was even suggestion of there being a Protestant Ombudsman (the 'Ombudsprod' as Willie's wife referred to the role). But these were sweets and biscuits; these were felt tips and stickers: these were not the main prize. That was the colourful flag with red, white and blue flying high in the castle of their hearts and they couldn't have it. That was gone now: lost forever.

And so after the first furious months the tantrum ebbed away and all that was left was a worn out people, still sufficiently proud to scorn affection from any quarter, but despite that show of determination 'beaten and they knew it'. After all the talking, it turned out that it had in fact just been talk. Red cards are not rescinded and instincts of self preservation soon began to take over.

Willie yawned: rubbing some sleep from his eyes he clicked the radio off. He felt tired and had a dull headache starting to brew at the back of his mind. The night before had been a late one, as he and Violet had been to the New Year's Eve Watch Night service. It was often somewhat joyless – as if it was 'the world' that went in for celebration at the New Year and so seriousness was holiness – but last night had been particularly downbeat. Again the analogy of a funeral came back to Willie's thoughts: the congregation had looked wretched at the service and Reverend Houston had struggled to know what tone to strike. If he tried to offer words of comfort and hope, he would seem to be betraying his flock because everyone felt utterly hopeless. He would risk seeming like an apologist for that which was detested. But if he didn't try to offer words of comfort and hope there seemed little point in being there at all, in gathering at a place of worship. Nobody had much conviction anyhow, so he muddled through as best he could.

The Reverend was a man for whom a vocation to Christian Ministry had been centred on mission and outreach. The meat and drink of his life among the people had been repentance and eternity and however much he loved his flock a heart felt conviction was no substitute for pastoral intelligence. He consistently reminded churchgoers of the dreadful realities of damnation but in so doing he further condemned whole swathes of people who collectively now felt condemned anyhow. It hit glazed surfaces in front of the congregation, and their dulled spirits just cleared it like wipers, and he rained more of it at them, and so on and on it went. A preacher forced to be a chaplain to a bereft community, Willie imagined that as his head and body delivered sermons in the pulpit, beneath his legs were peddling a thousand revolutions per minute, just to enable him to stand still.

Willie reached into the medicines cupboard and pressed two paracetamol tablets from their blisters, running the tap until cold for a glass of water and then swallowing his pain relief. He always thought it better to take something for a headache before it got too far ahead of him, a peculiar self diagnosis which the hardier Violet disapproved of. Having got in from church six hours earlier he had then slept dreadfully what with all the thoughts rushing through his head, his heart pumping, mind racing at a million miles per hour. All about the last ten months and what was going to happen now.

Everyone had had choices to make since the end of February. Should we stay or should we go? And if we do go, do we go over there? We wanted for as long as any of us are able to remember to be a part of them, but now we know what we always knew, that they were indifferent to having us. Someone, Willie recalled, once said that it is more important to be accepted than to be loved, and whilst we knew of course the English never *loved* us, their drawing up of plans and timetables to "wash their hands and sell us down the river" had still been a bitter pill to swallow. Everyone knew someone who had gone. Those who went rubbed deeper salt in the wounds and any sense of community broke down further. Ten years ago the village had been full of confidence as ever bigger developments of ever grander homes sprang up: 'Little Protestant Xanadus', Willie called them.

Willie remembered something his grandfather had told him: just over one hundred years ago he said that as grim news arrived in relentless waves from the Somme, no terrace in the village had been left unvisited by dreaded telegraphs. And again in 2020 no development or cul de sac remained untouched. They were pockmarked this time by For Sale signs that saw neighbours and long standing friends put in ply board, notice of their intention to quit. Community was fragmenting: however strong the togetherness might have been it had been overcome by an even keener Protestant instinct, that of the individual and every man standing on his own two feet.

Resignation was pervasive. One neighbour was going to Carlisle where his brother in law ran a haulage company and he'd been told he could get work as a driver. Another, a son of a friend, was going to go to London and retrain as a teacher – he'd been successful in accountancy here but apparently they can't get enough Maths teachers in London. Some would just take their chances because "there's always work for people who want to work". The younger were fitter for change and building a new life: so in the quickening of a ray theirs was a community that would become older, greyer, and frailer. Some elderly felt abandoned, just as certain tribes cast aside the older whose practical worth is no more.

Supply and demand was pushing and pulling too. With every house sold the property market slipped further downwards. And that also hurt because bigger is better had so long been the mindset, work ethic in hock to mortgage repayments. Now equity too was being worn down by the doubt and leaving. However true it is that Godliness with contentment is great gain, many had rather pursued a maxim that Godliness with gain is great contentment.

Willie set his glass aside and ran the tap again, this time filling the kettle and clicking the toggle at the bottom of the jug. And then – like a bolt out of the blue – a different sort of switch tilted inside his mind, and as it did so often now, the anger kicked in. It could kick in when he was washing his hair in the shower, it could kick in when he was mowing the grass in the garden, and it could kick in when he was carrying in the shopping from the boot of the car. Because it was one thing being a victim but another thing being a loser. Emotionally, being a victim had been irrationally satisfying at times: you could be nasty in that parenthesis of heart and mind, and then tell yourself that was ok, because what you were thinking was legitimate righteous anger. But truth be told most of the anger was somewhat unrighteous and deep down he knew that to be the case. Being a loser diminished him to the core of his being.

The other side had won and he hated that. He had made

the speech from a silent husting in his head a thousand times over. *They* bombed and shot us for thirty years. Then *they* got the Good Friday Agreement and the men who had done the bombing and shooting got out early: what justice is there in that? *They* served in Government, with Martin McGuinness – 'bloody Art Garfunkel' as a friend called him – the Deputy First Minister. The Butcher's Boy from Derry who had organised and directed sins and misdemeanours becomes a statesman. Not a bit of wonder he chuckled.

All the watch towers and security fortresses in places *they* had done terrible things were taken down. Then *they* got the police service *they* had killed and maimed, reformed the way *they* wanted it reformed, and *they* had got to serve in it *themselves*. Those who were on the run, some of them for doing the most wicked of deeds – *their* on the runs – got an amnesty and were able to come home. *Their* victims dead and buried never got to come home. *They* even got *their* criminal records, records reflecting abhorrent acts, wiped clean. Clean: some clean. Nothing was ever enough for *them*. Long runs the fox – or so the saying goes – and hadn't Mr Adams been a fantastic Mr Fox. Parenthesis again: whether 'they' was the Republicans or 'them' were the British it was always some they or them against us. It is us now who find ourselves alone.

He held a favourite mug and was about to make Violet a cup of tea, because a cup of tea in her hand always made her start the day by telling him what a lucky wife she was, helped her get the duvet pulled off and get going. He shouldn't be thinking about these things, he said to himself. He should be noticing the robin pecking at the bird table, he should be thinking about his grandchildren's faces later on when they come round for lunch like they always do on New Year's Day.

But having begun the speech he would see it through to a conclusion, as he always did. Where was he? Nothing was ever enough for *them*... no matter what *they* got, *they* always wanted more. *They* moaned and chivvied and lobbied and *they* never gave up. And now *they'd* got what *they* wanted, *their* Holy Grail, *their* Republic! *They* shot and *they* bombed and *they* intimidated and *they* beat and *they* murdered the innocent in pubs and *they* robbed banks, and now *they'd* got their Republic. Dear God, he pondered, what sort of land is it going to be, a land administered by this sort of people? Doesn't it say in the Bible that righteousness exalts a nation: well then what hope is there for us in this place?

For five years in a younger season of his life Willie had lived outside Northern Ireland, serving in Kenya as a missionary teacher. Somebody had commented to him once about the suffering in Africa, the sense of desolation felt by people there who were crushed by the helplessness of poverty and bad leadership, robbed by famine and HIV. In comparison – his friend had remarked – Western Christians in their affluence had no idea what the great biblical cry of 'How long?' meant. For the first time in his life, Willie was suddenly starting to feel inside him a 'How long?' And he knew that 'How long?' is a long time when you're calling it on the very first day.

He reached into the fridge and pulled out the milk, splashing a dash into Violet's mug, and then pouring the boiling water into the pot. He switched the cooker on at the wall and turned a ring to a low setting. It had been a clear and crisp morning but now clouds were beginning to gather. His father always said that when the day starts off sunny and bright, that's never a good sign for what's to come.

Having poured the tea into the cup he slapped gingerly up the stairs to the bedroom, thinking not for the first time that these flip floppy slippers his daughter in law had given him for Christmas were a death trap on the open treads, and maybe he shouldn't wear them there. Then another thought came brooding over him. When Violet came down she'd probably turn the TV on for the Breakfast News she loved to watch – as she put it she "enjoyed Eamonn Holmes on the sofa every morning." (Violet was the rather more outgoing personality in this relationship: it was not without reason that friends affectionately called her 'Shrinking').

He normally didn't mind her watching TV news over breakfast, but today could not bear the thought of it. *They* would be all over the news having celebrations: night time street parties and fireworks being let off in Andersonstown and the Falls, Ardoyne and Poleglass. Adams and McGuinness *et al* fêted as heroes. Huge plasma screens and crowds waving tricolours, chanting down the final seconds in unison in Irish. (He struggled to imagine every detail of this as he momentarily wondered what counting down to zero sounds like in Irish). And when they hit zero Unionism's temple curtain would be torn in two.

Violet sleepily plumped her pillow and sat up against it to receive her morning brew. "Thanks dear" she said. "You're a star, that's just what I wanted". And he pulled her Bible off the dressing table at the far end of the room and gave it to her with the quarter's new notes. Now it was Quiet Time.

Willie headed back down the stairs: down was actually worse than up so instead of mincing precariously he just took his slippers off and carried them, an exercise which gave temporary distraction to his mood: what's the point of slippers that you carry? He would have to devise a strategy, he would have to have one set of slippers for most of the time, and then be able to pull the 'slip-per hazard pair' (as Violet called them) out when his daughter in law came round. He padded into the kitchen and pulled his Bible from the place where it resided in the plate rack.

He picked up his notes but then another little switch flicked in his brain and he just as quickly set them down again. Sitting at the kitchen table he lifted his Bible and then sighed and held it a while, the headache and the intensity of the morning catching up on him. He thought he must turn down the central heating. The kitchen was silent and his head silent and he looked into quiet mid-air and sat still as a statue. After just a minute or two – though it felt like much longer – he opened the Bible and decided that for once he would do it on his own this morning, set the notes to one side.

As he started to thumb for his book of choice he felt shame, knowing what he was about to do was abuse of the Word of God. What he was taught to do is read the Scriptures and open his heart to let God speak to him. But he didn't want that this morning: it was a viciously special day and he deserved to indulge himself. He was a faithful follower hammered by the present and fearful for the future so deserved today for the Good Book to reinforce his feelings, to make him feel sorrier for himself. He did not want God to honestly speak to him: he wanted God to tell him it was quite alright to feel the way he did. He was sure God understood that.

So Willie reached for Lamentations, which he knew he could read but still feel he was doing his Christian duty. But he also reckoned that reading it would make him feel bad, and today making him feel bad would in turn make him feel good. Lamentations is all about a people betrayed, a whole nation bereft, and that is exactly how he felt, so that would do well then. When he found it he did something which was worse again. He was running out of time now, because Violet would be well through by this stage and coming down shortly for her All Bran with chopped banana, so he'd have to get a move on. He dug deeper into indulgence. Not only would he dip into Lamentations just to make himself feel bad, but now he would scan the book to find a particularly mournful bit and that would be him done. That would be God talking terribly into a terrible state of affairs.

As he read a parallel conversation was occurring. Scripture was talking to him, but he was talking back to Scripture. He was talking about God rather than to God, in sheepish questions that made him somewhat embarrassed because obviously he believed God could hear him anyway.

"Is it nothing to you, all you who pass by?
That could be the English, couldn't it, all you who pass by.
Look around and see.
Is any suffering like my suffering that was inflicted on me, that the Lord brought on me in the day of his fierce anger?
That the Lord brought on me. Not so sure about that bit. Why would the Lord be behind all of this? Why would a righteous God want to see them in control, them rulers and leaders in any land? No, the Lord hasn't brought this on. Or has He?

"From on high he sent fire, sent it down into my bones.

He spread a net for my feet and turned me back.

He made me desolate, faint all the day long.

"My sins have been bound into a yoke; by his hands they were woven together.

They have come upon my neck and the Lord has sapped my strength.

He has handed me over to those I cannot withstand.

I'm not so sure about the sins bit, *they're* a darn sight worse than we are, but he has certainly handed us over to those we can't withstand. Dear God, He's done that. Handed us over? Would He? Why?

"The Lord has rejected all the warriors in my midst; he has summoned an army against me to crush my young men.

In his winepress the Lord has trampled the Virgin Daughter of Judah.

"This is why I weep and my eyes overflow with tears.

No one is near to comfort me, no one to restore my spirit.

My children are destitute because the enemy has prevailed."

Zion stretches out her hands, but there is no one to comfort her.

The Lord has decreed for Jacob that his neighbours become his foes;

Jerusalem has become an unclean thing among them.

The words of loneliness, of a people having no one to comfort them seemed all too real. Ireland crowed and England shifted uneasily but when Ulster reached out her hands… nothing. And yet he had discernment enough to realise that this was not as simple as he thought it. He knew deep down that God isn't fickle to a nation state, that history can be consequences of earlier history. According to this good book you reap what you sow, and that in effect made it all worse. Then he scanned on to realise that amidst all this condemnation were also words of comfort and solace.

Because of the Lord's great love, we are not consumed, for his compassions never fail.

They are new every morning; great is your faithfulness.

I say to myself, "The Lord is my portion; therefore I will wait for him.

This is the Word of God, he thought. I can't argue with the Word of God. But right now I don't feel this way at all. Should my faith be truer in some valley I don't want than on a mountain top looking down on my six counties? Why is that?

The Lord is good to those whose hope is in him, to the one who seeks him;

It is good to wait quietly for the salvation of the Lord.

It is good for a young man to bear the yoke while he is young.

Let him sit alone in silence, for the Lord has laid it on him.

Let him bury his face in the dust – there may yet be hope.

Let him offer his cheek to one who would strike him, and let him be filled with disgrace.

For men are not cast off by the Lord forever.

Though he brings grief, he will show compassion, so great is his unfailing love.

For he does not willingly bring affliction or grief to the children of men.

So God can give me compassion. OK, then, but he can't turn back the clock, can He? He can't influence the past: not even God can do that. Not even for all His being the same yesterday, today and forever.

To crush underfoot all prisoners in the land, to deny a man his rights before the Most High, to deprive a man of justice – would not the Lord see such things?

Who can speak and have it happen if the Lord has not decreed it?

Is it not from the mouth of the Most High that both calamities and good things come?

Why should any living man complain when punished for his sins?

Let us examine our ways and test them, and let us return to the Lord.

"Let us lift up our hearts and our hands to God in Heaven, and say: We have sinned and rebelled and you have not forgiven.

"You have covered yourself with anger and pursued us; you have slain without pity.

You have covered yourself with a cloud so that no prayer can get through.

You have made us scum and refuse among the nations.
"All our enemies have opened their mouths against us.
We have suffered terror and pitfalls, ruin and destruction.
Streams of tears flow from my eyes because my people are destroyed.

He'd have to stop now. He tried to tell himself he was stopping because Violet would come down for breakfast, but the reality was that his reading was driving him crazy. He had snatched at the Word of God, used the double edged sword like a lucky dip, and realised how dangerous that was. Where he thought there would be consolation, there was only confusion. What if this was God's will? What if God would make it that his wee country was scum amongst the nations? He checked again – those words are in the Bible – "scum and refuse."

He couldn't pick and choose with the will of God. He couldn't say that it was God's will for him to go to Lamentations this morning but not God's will when he didn't like what Lamentations was saying! And all the sin stuff: is that right? Are we being punished for our sin – look at all that's happened. How in God's name are we not more sinned against than sinning?

The dog's feet scuffed on the floor as it turned to lie in a more comfortable position. But Willie was spiritually paralysed by what he'd been reading and thinking. And then some steps started on the stairs above him and a voice he loved called out: "Can we still get Radio Two for Chris Evans?"

2

Strangers in a Strange Land

On a Tuesday evening at five minutes to eight, as was religiously his custom, Willie eased himself into his car and drove the short distance to the home of his friend Jim Scott. Willie's car was one of those that could be described only as overwhelming in its brownness. The outside was a kind of coppery-cum-coffee-brown, the seats a pale brown crushed velour, and the dashboard a slightly nauseating shade of dark brown – as if moulded plastic is not meant to be brown and this was the best effect that dyes and chemicals could achieve. Altogether, all very brown, and broken only by the cubed box of tissues that sat on the parcel shelf where no one could possibly reach it if the need of a wipe or a blow were to arise.

Tuesday night was 'House Group Night', which meant by definition that in the evening a group would meet in a home for prayer and Bible study. It was something started by the church many years ago: some all male; some all female; some young; some old; some rather more eclectic than others but those ones few and far between, the believers inevitably gravitating to those most like themselves.

The group Willie attended was held in the home of Jim Scott. If you met Jim at a party what he would like most of all would be for you to ask him what he *did*, because what he did was what he most liked. It was what gave him his identity. Jim was the Managing Director of a local food manufacturer: the narrative of his life had produced not a story but a balance sheet.

Willie often thought there was something a little odd about Jim, something he struggled to pin down. Jim was one of those businessmen who never passed up an opportunity to tell others how *he* lived in the 'real world'. The real world was commerce and deals. Those not in business and therefore not subject to financial justification – nurses, teachers, ministers of religion etc – were most definitely not "in the real world". All of this was despite the fact that Jim had never emptied a bed pan or taught a class of five year olds or conducted a funeral… Willie always felt that when Jim was talking to him after church on a Sunday morning he was only a stopgap: that Jim's eyes were always scanning the floor for someone more interesting or important.

Anyhow, Willie rang the doorbell and waited for a response. There were no other cars in the driveway yet: he was the first one here. Willie was surprised that Jim hadn't gone: Jim seemed successful; big in his field; what was he still doing here?

"Willie, come in sir. That's a cold night. You know where to go, just in there, first on the right."

'The purpose of the groups is to meet together, study the Bible, pray together, and get to know one another more'. That was the stated vision several years ago when the initiative started in the congregation. *'The purpose of the groups is to meet together, study the Bible, pray together, and get to know one another more'.* In general what they did was just that, and everyone was by and large content. But always unspoken was a sense of being under-whelmed, a sense of 'Is that it?' A divine discontent that wanted to go further: but always a private discontent and never voiced.

For example: when John, who led this band of brothers, asked at the end of the evening if there was anything anyone wanted to pray about the responses were always in the safe middle-distance of the public domain.

"It would be good to remember Alfie Arbuckle coming up to the anniversary of Winnie's death".

"Miss McCandless – she's a wee woman sits at the back on the left hand side, you'd know her if you saw her – she always wears a tea cosy hat – they're hopeful she might be getting out of hospital this week, and it won't be easy for her."

In the spirituality of these men little walls and fences abounded. If you were up to your neck in credit card debt, or you couldn't stop having fantasies about your sister in law, or you'd come unimaginably close over the last weekend to wanting to hit your wife, you were hardly going to mention it here.

But even if everyone felt that there should be a sense of going deeper nothing would ever happen as it could not be articulated: other than on very rare occasions no one had actually gone deeper so there was no proper sense of what or where deeper was and what it was they missed out on. So they just met twice a month and went curiously deep enough. Which was undoubtedly polite and holy up to a point and nobody could dispute that it had drawn together some bond of friendship in the past four years.

John – the leader – was the next to arrive. He was tall, fit and distinguished, always well presented, in a seemingly dressed by his wife sort of way: and he looked like the leader of a group. Except that he never looked particularly happy – this was a drawback when this group ought to have been about life and life in all its fullness. Violet used to comment that she didn't see John smile that often, which was a pity as he had such an attractive smile.

But life had dealt this man some hard blows and his manner was not without reason. John Todd had seen much and done much: here was a man who knew that real world well. He had retired four years previously after 30 years of service, first with the Royal Ulster Constabulary, and then with the Police Service of Northern Ireland. While he had left the police, the police and all the experiences contained therein, had not left him and never could.

Policing for John transcended everything. He had been on the scene soon after colleagues had been blown up and limbs were scattered, the smell of flesh and cordite filling the air. He had been on the scene when Orange crowds were pushing forward and baying with indignation and ten feet away a figure snarled at him and shouted with menace his name and address. He had been on the scene at a checkpoint in Belfast when a well known Republican mocked him and laughed: "Sure, won't that uniform look good on me when I get to wear it."

His hurts were genuine and real, and the environment around him – one of District Policing Partnerships, Historical Enquiry Teams and Community Policing Initiatives – was one of rain and sunshine and fertiliser that grew and cultivated everything inside John. He wanted to be free from the oppression of his feelings and yet simultaneously held on to them and kept them fresh and real. So much had been taken away: he owed it to his values and former colleagues not to betray them, not to give an emotional inch.

"Good Christmas, John?" Willie asked.

"Oh, good enough, Willie, all things considered. We'd a nice couple of days with the wee ones and the presents and all, but Peter and Ruth and the kids went back the day after Boxing Day – Peter had to work over the Hogmanay you see – and it leaves the house awful empty, you know. It's very hard on Gillian. She misses them so badly – I think women do miss them more. What about you?"

"Oh we'd an alright Christmas. But it's much the same every year. Violet likes the films and her Christmas TV so I just do as I'm told and watch with mother."

There was a few moments pause. Willie felt he had to break the silence. "I'm sure *you* miss them too. How are they settling into school and all?"

John's son and daughter in law had 'got out' and moved to Scotland six months earlier. "Well it's more Gillian talks to Ruth about that. I think they're doing ok. I suppose you underestimate how resilient kids are and how much they can take, but they get teased a lot about their accents and all. Peter took Ross to see Rangers there a few Saturdays ago and he loved that: thought it was brilliant."

He shifted uneasily in his seat and continued. "But sure it'll be the best decision they ever made Willie. Sure the way this country's going to go now, it isn't the sort of place you'd want to be bringing up kids in."

John looked at his lap and fidgeted some preparation to distract himself. He opened his Bible, opened his notebook, and opened the study guide. Every New Year was the same: the group would diligently work through the whole book of bible studies. Other groups tended to go off at tangents and wore it as a badge of pride that they never got near to finishing their studies but John liked to crack on and keep things moving. His group *always* completed the course.

John liked to adapt the studies – "customise them" he said – which generally meant omitting the questions he thought wouldn't play well with the other men. That often included the first question: those 'way-ins' always drew a blank response. They were meant to be tone-setters to the discussion, things like:

How do people today try to gloss over and avoid the reality of death?

How have you handled habits or addictions that have a hold over you?

Think of a time when you defended yourself in a strained relationship. What did you do?

'We come together to read God's words, not for group therapy. If I asked these questions', Jim thought to himself, 'I'm only going to end up with awkward silence. And then there's Adam and his past: me asking questions like these would put him in a very embarrassing position…' And then there were the closing questions.

Think about the most precious relationships you enjoy with God and other people? What can you do to make them stronger?

What is there about Jesus in this passage that makes you want to tell other people about him?

In what areas of your life are you most in need of Godly sorrow?

These were ignored as well. The material was designed to be topped and tailed with direct impact upon a walk with God: but how these men opened and closed was all intrinsic to the going deeper they did not do. The Word of God met a Victorian Gentleman's Smoking Room where some things were fit to be shared and some things not. It was privacy borne not of pride but of a mix of middle class civility and Christian decorum. Many years ago, John recalled reading an interview with an actor who said that sometimes when he was sad and frightened he would cry out to God about why he would have to die some day and God would say 'No! Stop! Don't you realise I have Chinese people yelling at me.' Whilst they were men of self containment his charges were also men of modesty. To say that you *were* up to your neck in debt or that you *did* in fact fantasise about your sister in law would be hanging out the dirtiest of washing. What would people say and think: not to mention where would they look?

A sense of propriety and proportion said that one's own problems did not matter when God was to be mindful of Mr Arbuckle and Miss McCandless and all the Chinese, Palestinian, and African people yelling at Him. Inasmuch as Jesus had a point to make when He said "Come unto me all you who are weary and are heavy laden and I will give you rest" they preferred to forsake truth for half truth such as "God helps those who help themselves" and "The devil makes work for idle hands" and "you've got to be cruel to be kind."

In the context of such experience of faith it was not unremarkable that Bible Study together assumed the gentle rhythm of question-verse answer, question-verse-answer. Eschewing the tawdriness and vulnerability of habits and addictions that have a hold over one, or discussing difficult and strained relationships, they preferred to focus on the three things Jesus tells the Pharisees in verses 16 to 18, or ponder whether once saved meant always saved, or speculate on why it was that Samson finally snapped at *that* moment and let Delilah in on the secret. Safe ground was better than holy ground.

Another set of headlights momentarily lit up the black winter window and the doorbell rang again. The next member to arrive was Dr Adam Cupples, who somehow stood out in the group despite the fact that there was nothing of any note to make him stand out. Maybe it was his quiet manner, his kindly features: Violet once said she thought he had a pastoral face. There seemed to be a lot going on inside this man but little was vocalised. Here was a man who was humble and gentle: a likeable person by whom acquaintances in turn wanted to be liked. He was pushing 50, and was an experienced A&E doctor who everybody could imagine must have a lovely bedside manner.

"So were you on much over Christmas, Adam?" Willie asked.

"Not too bad, Willie – I actually did Christmas Eve and Christmas Day but they were surprisingly quiet, and then I had the next few days off after that, so I can't complain."

"Good stuff" Jim said. "No jolly fat men in red outfits getting stuck down chimneys then!"

They all chuckled: what nobody said but most of them thought was that this was a welcome distraction from whatever else Adam had done at Christmas. Because Adam was separated from his wife and lived apart from his three children and worse still everybody knew that these were circumstances all of his own making. An awful state of affairs that further demonstrated how much the fruit of the Spirit was discretion, but that did not stop these past events from colouring the thoughts of every member of the congregation who knew Adam. The truth and half-truth was that whilst Christ had rubbed Adam's slate clean, he had nonetheless made his bed and would have to lie in it. His Bathsheba moment was a brief tryst with a Junior House Doctor: even recently one person cruelly rued the doctor's 'bedroom manner'.

"We're low in numbers tonight" Willie said. "Is this all we've got?"

Just at that the doorbell rang and within a few flurried seconds of doors opening, and a coat being unzipped, in bounced a younger man entirely unapologetic for his lateness, with a quip in a faux Irish accent of "Sorry I'm late lads, sure I'm just sort of getting into all this Southern not rushing about thing, so I am so."

For a few seconds that seemed like minutes nobody spoke.

John just stared down at his Bible.

You could hear the clock tick.

Jim looked as if someone had just tooted a little wind and he was unsure where to look.

Willie shifted as if to say 'I can't believe he just said that' and the just arrived Alan Mackey momentarily looked as if he might even say something else –

– But he didn't.

John blew out very gently and whispered: "Do you know is Mike coming, Alan, or should we make a start?"

"Aye he texted me earlier, he's definitely coming." This was Alan Mackey – in maturity a hybrid of a teenager and a 35 year old man – a peculiarly Christian cad and bounder. Or so it seemed. For there was much, *much* more to this man than wise cracking and the latest clothes and gadgets: more than the surface level of things. Alan was a graphic designer and a talented one at that: to some of the others that seemed to suit Alan well because it did not seem a grown up sort of job. If you saw him at work you would see hours of craft and talent poured into his vocation. But then if you saw him at church with yet another pretty young thing on his arm you would stop and think: "what is this guy on?"

The current girl on the scene was Grace: and from a distance it was clear that if you liked girls you would like Grace. She was blond, tall, slim, and altogether attractive: an individual of value and meaning in her own right, but to those in the know just the latest in a long line of holy but interchangeable dolly birds.

'He shouldn't be messing those girls around like that' was what Violet would say. 'Women get to an age like that and start going out with a man like him, and they're bound to be thinking 'is he the one?' He shouldn't be playing games with people'. Alan was a man to whom the chase seemed better than the conquest, the menu better than the meal. 'You know' he quipped to Violet one night, his attitude a cocktail of the blasé and the proud: 'commitment has been a problem for me all my life'. He thought he couldn't help all this: he prayed sometimes for change, but there was no real desire to be any different.

Not that Alan was stupid. Whilst he could *never* resist the joke of the moment he regretted that with such behaviour he undermined himself. His bachelor lifestyle afforded him time to think and read, and on that basis he had plenty to say that was worth listening to. He would want to be taken seriously but then a funny thought would enter his mind and he'd be off again…

That mind was *always* working and no camera could capture what was going on behind his eyes. Jim's lounge was a menagerie of china, canvas and cushions. Once Alan had sat stiffly upon a sofa and discreetly flicked his eyes and cricked his neck to census the pruck and the comfort. He counted slender Doulton figurines, pictures big and small including dried flowers, one cut glass slipper with pot pourri in it, homes and cottages from Lilliput Lane, crystal that was backlit in plated glass cabinets, and certainly more than one mirror. A porcelain cat was menacingly poised just inches from a porcelain mouse. There were 38 items, 38 'bits' as he thought of them (the cat and the mouse counted as two). But he never completed the census. Because he could never look properly at the wall behind him: there was no unobvious way of doing that. He would have to face that last wall in the course of asking to use the toilet or of getting his coat to go home and then he could complete. And then someone would say "Alan looks like a man who could do with going to his bed" and he would be arrested from his wanderings. He *never* remembered to finish that survey.

The last member to arrive was Mike Matthews, a man who always looked as if he really could do with going to his bed. The doorbell rang a final time and a harassed Mike swept in. He sat down quickly and then frantically stood up again, taking off his coat and frisking himself for the pen and study notes he had forgotten. He stood up a second time, found his mobile phone and turned it off, and then sat down a last time.

"Sorry guys – thought Sophie would never go down tonight. Sorry Jim – I'm holding you all back." And then he sat at peace, looking as if he already wished the study was over. Sophie was two years old. Sophie was a porcelain terror.

"Is she not settling down any Mike?" Willie asked.

"Oh crikey, no! It's like putting a stick of dynamite in pink pyjamas, and reading it a bedtime story." he said, with his cheek cradled in the palm of his hand. Sophie was just one high maintenance aspect of Mike Matthews's high maintenance world. A world of a tired and irritable wife, three children under five, long hours, and the biggest mortgage he could stretch to.

For a living Mike sold cars, something he had simply stumbled into. A barrow boy patter belied boredom and long sufferance. He had dropped out of university after one year because he wanted some fast cash and the History degree he had chosen was not what he had expected. Selling cars was only ever intended to be a stop gap but one thing led to another and now he'd been doing it for 16 years: 16 years of finance and special editions and part exchanges; 16 years of shaking hands with one person and pacifying another; 16 years of people like Mr Morris.

Mr Morris was a dapper and quiet old gentleman, probably now in his late seventies – the sort of man who could use his shoes as a mirror and looked like he probably wore a tie in bed with his pyjamas. Mr Morris did 6,000 miles a year and changed his car every January. Always silver, always automatic, always petrol and always a saloon – the four doors were essential for taking Auntie Edith on runs to the seaside. Mrs Morris always came with him, a quaintly glum yet contented looking lady who only ever spoke to say "Thank You" when Mike gave her flowers and the new car was picked up. Mr Morris had taken delivery of this year's new motor that morning and when Mike gave him the keys and Mrs Morris her flowers, he felt like his whole life was ebbing away. Then Mr Morris had got quite agitated because the number plates were not right on the new car and Mike had to point out that they *were* right because this was the new country and back number plates wouldn't be yellow anymore.

As the years went by he was getting ever guiltier about selling Mr Morris his new car. But someone had to look after the wife and the children and the mortgage. Mike did not like the idea of the land he now lived in and a further source of tension had been the case he tried to prosecute for starting out afresh across the Irish Sea. On this occasion he couldn't close the sale. 'Oh yeh, that would be a great life for me. Stuck in the house all day in some place where I don't know anyone, with three kids gurning at me and you never there. That would be super – when can we go?' And that was that then. Those who knew Mike at a distance thought he had a lot going for him but inside he felt himself not in control.

"You're all right Mike. Sure we'll make a start now…"

Jim took orders for tea and coffee and returned minutes later pushing a fancy hostess trolley that seemed inappropriate in the same way that a large man walking a small dog does. There were no mugs in this house it seemed – only the best of china. Alan and Mike referred to this privately as the 'if Jesus came to my house' crockery.

Just as John was finally going to begin the study Adam chipped in to say something. "Sorry, John, just before you do get started, I just wanted to mention something. I've a friend from South Africa – his name is Peter – someone I met years ago when I was doing my elective out there. He's a guy I really clicked with and we've stayed in touch over the years. He lectures in Health Sciences at the University of Johannesburg. Anyhow, I got an email just before Christmas from him to say that he's coming over here for a year on an exchange to do research work at Queen's. So he's actually going to be staying with me and I was thinking it would be nice to have him along to the group here, if nobody objects."

Five heads nodded and there was a collective man-mumble of approval.

"That will be interesting" John said. "It'll be nice to be able to say we have an international dimension to our group… so… what part of Africa, or South Africa… what bit or, eh…"

"He's black" Adam said.

"Oh right" John replied. "A black South African: well that'll be interesting. Anyway we're going to be studying Jeremiah this year. I was talking to Rev Houston and his thinking was, well we've done a gospel, and we've done some Psalms, and we've done a letter, so it would be good to do a prophet. So we'll turn to the end of Galatians in a moment but before we do that, sure I'll open in prayer.

Lord we thank You for the opportunity to gather here together and study Your word tonight. We thank you that however much there may be change all around us, Your word tells us that You never change. Lord, however much sinful men may sneer and triumph, yet help us to be faithful Lord, for Your word tells us 'Vengeance is mine, and I will repay says the Lord.'

And so Father we pray that You would touch our land powerfully, that even yet justice would be done. And so Lord we ask that as we study Your word together this evening, that You would present Yourself among us by Your Spirit and speak to each and every one of us. And all this we pray in Jesus name. Amen."

And so God's word was opened and the Spirit *did* move. The earth did not shake and the mountains did not tremble but the Bible was read and questions asked of the passage and the God it talked of. Nobody poured out their heart and no scales fell from their eyes as they read together. But everyone left the house that night a little nearer to God than when they went in, and they all felt inside themselves that they had done a good thing.

3

Willie

In the familiar sanctity of their front room, Willie and Violet viewed apostasy. They watched as a small private jet serenely glided to a graceful touch down at Knock Airport in County Mayo. On the runway was an excited gaggle of the great and good, the welcoming party headed by the recently invested President Adams. They were awaiting the arrival of a *very* very important person: for the first time in nearly 40 years the Holy Father was visiting Ireland; a new Holy Father, Pope Paul VII.

It was now the middle of the morning and the TV had been on for just over an hour. As 'good Protestants' they were not sure why they were watching this at all: neither of them was saying much and they were viewing in a strange mood of intent fascination mingled with voyeuristic shiftiness. They were not at all a part of this and yet found it strangely compelling. Fifteen minutes ago Willie had got up to answer a call of nature and asked Violet to call him immediately should anything actually happen.

The oddness of their fixation was compounded all the more by the fact that so far nothing *had* happened other than layer upon layer of vacuous live TV build up, comment and analysis laid on a foundation of no story to date. A helicopter hovered over the airport as throngs of the faithful and the fickle gathered for the visit. Then the coverage would cut to people like the Dooley family from Cork who had arrived three days earlier and camped out since then so that they could be a part of this event.

"Aw sure you know I think it's just a great thing that he's taken the time to come and a great thing for Ireland for him to be here, and like in the year that Ireland's all one again, sure that makes it even more special. And sure something this big doesn't happen very often

so we really wanted the kids and all to be able to see it, to be able to say like, and be able to tell their kids and grand-kids that they saw Pope Paul when he came to Ireland."

And at that the editor would cut back to the studio where an anchorman would invite a correspondent to tell everyone a little banal detail of all that was involved in the itinerary for this first day of the visit: such as the menu that had leaked of the dinner Richard Corrigan would cook for the visitor that evening. 'And if you're watching at home why not text us or email us to tell us what the new Pope's visit to Ireland means to you?'

"I could you tell you what it means to me" Willie muttered "but I doubt you'd put that on."

Eventually the plane touched down and after endless more minutes of taxiing and parking and steps for the plane being readied the door at last opened. And there he was: Pope Paul VII appeared at the top of the steps to smile beatifically and give a little rotation of the wrist for a wave. Paul was nearing the end of the first year of his papacy: he was the first Italian pope for several decades, a swarthy and attractive man approaching his sixtieth year. As he stared down from the transcendence of the plane door to the frenzied crowds Violet was the first to speak:

"He's sort of funny looking isn't he" she said.

"Yessss…" Willie replied, not removing his attention from the screen, and only half-listening to his wife.

"I mean he's not funny in a funny ha-ha type of way, don't get me wrong. But he's a grown man and he's wearing these strange robes and… and it's all so peculiar. I think it's the way we see him: he doesn't seem to say very much and so it's as if there's these throngs going bananas on account of some silent movie vicar. Do you know what I mean?"

"Yes, I do, yes I know what you mean."

Paul was now elegantly sweeping down the steps and President Adams was taking his first steps forward, alongside an ageing Cardinal Brady, to welcome the Pontiff to Ireland. "I think" Violet said "there's just something very sad about it all.

Is the Pope not a bit of an anachronism in this day and age? If you were an atheist or agnostic, what would you make of that?"

The President bowed his head slightly and then extended his right hand to shake the Pontiff's own right hand, simultaneously and deftly placing his left palm on the Pope's right shoulder whilst turning just enough for the cameras to catch both their faces.

Willie could not believe what he was seeing. The Pope was one thing: a bogeyman certainly, but what power did he really wield in this day and age – particularly in Ireland after the scandal it had been through? But Adams was different – he loathed and despised Adams – he truly thought the President beyond the pale. The Sermon on the Mount, he often reflected, is one of the toughest sections in the whole of Scripture with its commands to love our enemies and pray for those who persecute us, its instruction that hating someone is just like murdering them. Willie was away again: off again on a pyrrhic stream of bile fuelled thought.

He thought about Protestant workmen innocently killed at Teebane, ordinary 'men on the street' labourers blown to smithereens for no other reason than doing an honest day's work at an army camp. He thought about all those statements denying links between Sinn Fein and the IRA and this man who seemed to lie like other people breathe. He thought about what had happened to the disappeared, the cruelty of that poor lady torn away from her family and murdered for the crime of simply coming to the aid of a wounded British soldier. He thought about the Warrenpoint murders and how the second bomb that day had been callously timed to maim those taking cover after the first bomb went off. He thought about all those self righteous speeches when this man with so much blood on his hands would implore people to think imaginatively, boldly and creatively about achieving peace in Ireland. He thought of the soldiers dragged from their cars and shot dead after they drove into an IRA funeral in Andersonstown. He thought so much about the cruelty this man's movement had designed and could hardly bear to watch him glad hand the Pope of Rome and be fêted as a statesman.

As Paul began to drive off the runway Violet arrested Willie from his despondency as only she could. "I wonder how he goes to the toilet in that cassock and all. He's not exactly in the first flush of youth, is he? I mean, if he's anything like you dear, he must have to run often enough."

He looked at her and they both laughed. "Maybe" he said "holy water doesn't run through you quite as quickly as the stuff we mere mortals drink. I expect it's more prostrate than prostate problems that the Pope has."

"What's that then? Prostrate trouble."

"Well I don't know" he chuckled: "maybe he just can't help himself and he's suddenly seized by his prostrate problem and without any warning spreads himself out flat. I suppose that's what it would be."

The election of Paul VII was in some ways a reactionary act: he had been voted into office as much for what he wasn't as for what he was. And he wasn't another Benedict. Where John Paul had been a high profile Pope visible to the people and voracious in his appetite for travel, Benedict in his elderly frame had seemingly retired from public view after just a few years to concentrate on being an administrating CEO of his church. Whilst the rarity of his public appearances in part leant him an air of saintly mystery, latterly the public perception of his papacy was dominated by frustration from the people that they could not see and have more of their Vicar of Christ.

The Papal cavalcade was now creeping its way towards the huge basilica that dominated the Knock complex. There, Paul would be the celebrant of an enormous Mass, conducted from the steps of the chapel which were flanked each side by giant screens, as if this were the stage for a rock concert. But if it were a show then it was one they had struggled to put on.

Because this was a Catholic church down on numbers and down on its fortunes. Scandal and pluralism and an unwillingness to blindly accept and obey – without questioning – the instructions of those in authority, meant that the heyday of 'Rome Rule' in De Valera's Ireland now seemed a bygone day that was centuries rather than decades old. The shepherds had seemed more concerned with looking after the other shepherds rather than the sheep, and now that had come back to bite them.

There had been stories in the media about retired priests, and ex-patriot priests from England and beyond, being called upon to help them deliver this occasion. On the day itself that seemed to detract from the spectacle. Whilst John Paul's visit in 1979 had been ignited by the greeting "young people of Ireland – I love you", the festival aspects of this Mass were strangely juxtaposed with the white hair and wrinkled complexion of many of those making it happen. The old appeared dotted as diffident sepia amongst the colour of the carnival.

The truth of this occasion was that for all too many of the congregation their motivation for being there was less the celebrant than the celebrity. No longer did the television stations have to make do on Papal stories with speculative zoom shots closing in from the broad expanse of the Vatican to one window where the infirm Benedict may or may not have been. Now they had Paul and Paul was the real thing: a Pope who liked to spend time among people as well as in his study. A Pope who had already been received at both the White House and the Kremlin in his sensational first year. A Pope who loved cars of whom there were pictures shown of him wearing sunglasses and driving a convertible. A Pope who had joined U2 on stage and did not look much older than they were, as they brought down the curtains at a youth festival in Massachusetts. A Pope who planned to visit the new superpowers of India and China before this year was out. A mega-Pope!

What did any of this mean in terms of modern spirituality? Some clutched at straws that these were green shoots of a spring time for the old church. Just as when Benedict had been chosen so the white smoke that greeted Paul's election had been received by huge crowds who chanted and clapped in unison until he appeared and they exploded in frenzy. Commentators read between the lines of this and discerned a groundswell of resurgent Catholicism: Paul was a Pope who could truly reconnect with people, a man under whose tutelage many of the disaffected on the outer reaches might return.

But such people were unwitting false prophets: so desperate for the church that they loved to reenergise that they dimly mistook passing enthusiasm as something akin to their own more genuine devotion. 24 hour news channels had pipe fed the new Pope's ordination and Rome was gridlocked by it for days but the fireworks of fervour burnt white hot briefly and then quickly died. People might have thought Paul to be a 'really cool' and interesting new Pope but that didn't make them any more inclined to want to go to Mass or Confession or say their Rosaries or Hail Marys.

This was an interesting sideshow but for modern Ireland jobs and houses and cars and shopping centres and travel and restaurants and second homes and the hurling and the football and all the craic were where it was at. For the majority of people worship was occasional and when it did happen was fitted in after washing the car and buying the Sunday Times, and before going to the carvery and county minors match. That was all. "They're just like the English or French" John Todd would snap dismissively. "They're an utterly irreligious people. Sure you've only to look at the way a whole lot of them go to Mass on Saturday night so it doesn't get in the way of their Sunday! What sort of faith is that?"

From a spiritual perspective there were three different Irelands. There were the old Northern counties where the Protestants had year upon year slipped away from their historical highs of faithfulness. But despite the often elderly, traditional and decaying nature of their congregations the six counties continued to boast the best attended reformed churches in Western Europe. Also in the North there was a Roman Catholic grouping that had maintained a strong sense of identity through the divided nature of the country and their minority and historically disadvantaged status: this had engendered a powerful sense of togetherness.

It often crossed Willie's mind that Protestants lay too much store on the individual. Every man had to make his own personal decision for Christ which was right and proper: but every man also stood a better chance of having to plough his own furrow when things started to go wrong. He noticed that when he went to do messages down 'the other end of town' there seemed to be more buzz and more smiles on faces. People sharing and catching up and pleased to see one another: folks in no hurry to get their business done. From small talk big relationships grow: this was called community and in its most basic sense it was something that – so it seemed to him – Protestants all too often did badly.

The second Ireland – spiritually speaking – had its centre in Dublin and made its reach felt North, West and South through the new, ugly black motorways that led to uniform cul-de-sacs of detached housing. Such homes dominated commuter towns where an everyman's chapel had a *Sky* dish off the side of it rather than a cross off the top of it. This was the Ireland John had referred to when he swept his generalisation: for many years a prosperous Ireland characterised by premium brands and brightly lit convenience stores where they bought TV dinners after working the long hours necessary to keep the legs of the Celtic tiger running. This Ireland was fast moving and did not suffer fools and was impoverished by its choosing 'me' over the collective, Mammon over Mass.

But it was a long time now since the tiger had seen days like that: now its body was saggy and its coat had lost its sheen. The wise men who speculated on property had in fact been the foolish men, spaced out on a drug of greed that the growth would never end, insecure that everyone else was at it and you had to be on the inside and not the outside. And all of it overseen by politicians whose cronyism and 'on the make' cuteness would have made the likes of Amos and Jeremiah wince. That subvention from the British to help make the unification affordable would come in very handy in paying down the debt owed to the international money markets.

And then there was a third Ireland, one that stretched down the Western coast from Donegal through Sligo, Mayo, and

Clare and beyond to the outposts of Cork and Kerry, an Ireland also seen in the drive through towns of the Midlands. This was an Ireland watched over by roadside Blessed Virgin Marys, where old ladies hobbled faithfully to chapel every morning, an Ireland of Mass cards, apple tarts and general stores. Increasingly the second Ireland was coming to the third: sprawling new developments had taken over land that traditionally belonged to potatoes and dairy herds. From such houses you could drive just a short distance to the seven to eleven shops where the spuds themselves were washed and bagged for you and had never been cheaper.

Meanwhile on TV the Pope was now parading solemnly into the chapel, with pedestrian outriders flanking him, an assorted host of men in black, white, and crimson, some carrying nothing, some carrying holy poles or books or incense. "There's plenty of smells and bells there" Violet said, breaking the silence. And at that, as if her comment were a cue, the doorbell rang. They momentarily sat each one in their armchair and played chicken before Violet said "You get the door there dear, while you're on your feet."

As Willie grumped out of the lounge Violet lurched forward in her seat and was momentarily overcome by panic. *Who on earth was at the door? Who could it be that might come in and stumble upon her and Willie watching the Pope on TV?* It could be nothing. It could just be the lady from the gospel hall with this year's calendars: the ones that told you Christ died for the sins of all men on a picture of a kitten playing with a ball of wool. Or that Polish man who keeps calling trying to sell sketches of horses. But equally it could be the Rev Houston or someone like their florid and curmudgeonly elder Bertie Robinson who Willie once described in rare exasperation as being "as tight as a duck's arse." Imagine if one of them came in and the Pope was doing transubstantiation from the widescreen in the corner!

Willie was undoing the front door latch and she now felt more than flustered. She'd turn it off: better to turn it off. But the remote control was on Willie's chair! She was more or less equidistant between the chair and the TV – which direction should she go in? Her stomach sank below her knees as she whirled around the room in a way she'd rarely done since barn dances at Glarryford 40 years ago: turning off the TV; thrusting a newspaper onto Willie's recliner; pulling her knitting and the pattern from the bag beside her chair.

Her husband was clearly on the same wavelength as her because it was more than hospitable good manners that lead him to shout ahead from the hall to his wife: "it's Adam from church dear: I'm just going to make a pot of tea; do you want a cup?"

"Oh yes, love, that would be wonderful. You must be reading my mind! Thanks." And she noticed that her knitting pattern was upside down and started briefly into deep breathing exercises.

Adam

A few minutes later Willie and Adam joined Violet with a tray of tea and some of her favourite Tunnock's Tea Cakes. Adam smiled at Violet as he bit into the white fluffy marshmallow.

"This is the last thing I should be doing because I was behind before I even started. I'm round with the forms for the Gift Aid on the freewill offering: I've about ten houses to do and you're just the first. But I'd turned on the TV earlier and the Pope's visit was on and I sort of got sucked into watching it. I don't know why."

"Aye, we had a wee look at it ourselves" Violet confessed. "Some crowds aren't there. You'd wonder how they fit them all in. I mean Knock isn't that big a place: is it?"

"There's not an awful lot in it really, other than the big chapel complex. Have you ever been?"

"Oh no" Violet replied, shaking her head for reinforcement.

"Angela and I went there once about twenty years ago. We used to like taking wee breaks down at Achill Island in Mayo and when we were driving back on one occasion we saw a sign for Knock and thought we'd go and have a look. The chapel itself was quite attractive as I recall and then there were all sorts of tea rooms and gift shops like you get in all these places. The shops were a lot of old tat: Mary's picture in a faux gold picture frame for three ninety nine; the Pope on a tea towel, that type of thing."

"They seem to be very into that sort of stuff" Violet said. "Don't they: all their pruck and all".

"Yes" Adam replied. "The thing I remember is the holy water. I remember that along the side of the coach car park there was this low wall with a small row of taps coming out of it and a sign saying 'Knock Holy Water'. And if you wanted some holy water you'd go into a shop and buy a container – like a two litre *Ballygowan* bottle – for one Euro fifty and go and fill it at the wall." And he raised his eyebrows in disbelief.

"Really" Violet said. "I mean, how can any sort of intelligent person believe these things?"

"I don't know" Adam said. "I simply don't know. We have a girl works on our reception and she'd be very devout, you know, never misses chapel on their special days, and wears Ash on Ash Wednesday and so forth. She would know I'm involved in our church: 'good living' she calls me. And I remember her coming into my consulting room one day and I was in a flap looking for some lost file or other. 'Have you lost something Doctor' she said. 'Say 'Jesus is lost, Jesus is found' three times and it'll turn up, that's what my Mummy always says.' And I said to her 'Sinead – I'd like to think Jesus has bigger things to worry about than my lost file.' It's sort of stuck in my mind that… I felt afterwards I had put her down and I regretted that. But the weirdness of it stuck in my mind."

One story said so much and given time and a relaxation of sensibilities they could have talked all day about *all* the things they did not understand. About Mary: Mother of God. About Papal infallibility. About Rosary Beads: what do they *do* with them anyway? About places like Lourdes and Fatima and Knock: visiting shrines and holy places. About priests reverently called 'Father' and the seemingly unreasonable demands of celibacy. About making saints of the best of their dead people: about praying for the repose of their dead peoples' souls. About places like Croagh Patrick and Lough Derg: crawling up hills on your hands and knees and walking round and round all night; what's all that about? About hierarchies of cardinals and nuncios, about corridors of power and all that goes on in the Vatican. About lighting candles and going to confession and saying so many Hail Marys. They were theologically another world away.

"The thing I find hard about wee Sinead is the whole taking the name of the Lord in vain thing. I mean she's a lovely girl but every spilt cup of tea or record that's input wrong is 'Sacred Heart this' or 'Mother of God that'. And I mean that to us is such anathema: but she thinks nothing of it. She can get up early any number of mornings to go and receive His body and blood but she's no problem using His name as a swear word. I just don't get that. But anyway, who am I to judge?"

"Well" Willie muttered: "I'm sure there's plenty we do that they don't get or understand."

This for Adam was faith like a child. As a teenager his parents had once taken him on a trip to the city of Armagh. They pottered, shopped and pic-nicked. And they went to the two cathedrals, to educate their children and enjoy some quiet moments in the beauty of holiness. But Adam, then just 14 years old – and full of *all* the certainty and priggishness of a 14 year old evangelical – knew best where to draw the line that summer day. He stood in the porch of the Catholic Cathedral in solitude from his family: for he would not go in. He knew the truth and that place would spoil and sully him.

The sadness was that however adult and grown up he now was, like the majority of his peers there remained a great portion of ignorance in his Christian faith. Just over half the people in the North were Catholics – faithful or lapsed – and over 80% of all on the island were Catholics. But Adam could neither define nor contest Catholicism. He had no true friend who was a Catholic. His understanding of Catholic faith reduced their theology to that of the Reformed Church's enemy. He *might* have been able to find a surprising amount in common with Catholic friends and neighbours but he hadn't wanted to know enough. Like most of his fellow evangelicals he'd sold himself terribly short. They'd stayed outside in the porch of the chapel and they and the other community were diminished for it.

While they were chatting Violet reached for the remote control and sneaked the TV back on. "Do you ever" she said "look at it all and think: haven't we really come such a long way from Jesus and 12 disciples running around Galilee doing miracles and good turns? What must he make of it all?"

Adam realised that if he did not move the conversation on he would never get out the door. "Now, last year you gave £1,040 to the church, and as it was all given last year – in 2019 – the British Exchequer is still obliged to pay back on that offering, which means…"

Willie

… "The thing that gets me about them" Willie interrupted "is Sinn Fein". Willie had been brooding on this through the morning and didn't want to let the direction of the conversation drop now. "I mean, it's all very well going to Mass and Confession and all those things, but how many of them voted for Sinn Fein? Look at who they are and where they came from and think that there must be one in two Catholic people – at least – voting for them in the North, and ask yourself what that tells you about their community."

Adam didn't look up – he wanted to get a move on – but he did concede that: "well, that thought has struck me myself from time to time. I'm sure it's struck a lot of Protestants."

But Willie was on a roll. "Sure Sinn Fein is nothing but a bunch of gangsters and paramilitaries. Does that mean that at least half the people at that big Mass think it was ok to rob banks and kill innocent men in pubs and cover it up, never mind murder policemen and soldiers? Does that mean that for every ten Catholics I know, five of them would happily see me dead for the sake of their united Ireland?"

He was only verbalising what he had often thought and was

now thinking more and more. The Republican movement seemed so abhorrent to him but they clearly had a powerbase when it came to the polls. More and more he found himself looking at the Catholic people he knew and wondering about them... they seemed reasonable and moderate people who would surely vote for a middle ground... but maybe not? Maybe in the secrecy of the ballot box these respectable neighbours were happy to endorse what the killing machine had come to be. After all – somebody must be voting for them – it could easily enough be his acquaintances.

"Were half the Catholic doctors in your place quite happy if they got some blown up British soldier coming in? What does that tell you about the spiritual state of Roman Catholic people in Northern Ireland? The great big Pope of Rome didn't have an awful lot to say about that, did he?"

Violet and Adam seemed embarrassed at this outburst but Willie was unapologetic. "Well I'm only saying what a whole lot of people must be thinking. Aren't I?"

Nobody replied. "Aren't I?"

"You are Willie" Adam nodded. "And may God give us the serenity to accept the things we cannot change."

4

Alan

There was uncomfortable silence in the car, as Mike drove his friend Alan to the second House Group of the New Year. Alan part funded an addiction to fashion and technology by foregoing the small matter of having his own vehicle. Mike once pointed out to him that he could instant message from any corner of the globe and yet could not drive to the corner shop for a pint of milk.

But Alan generally managed to avoid inconvenience through negotiation techniques that traded to profitable effect in banter and goodwill. He still borrowed his mother's car on a regular basis, even if the small people-carrier she was now driving sat uncomfortably with his image. And it helped that Grace too – like most of his girlfriends – had her own little runabout, even if he felt a little emasculated sitting in its passenger seat: he just couldn't be doing with teddies on dashboards.

Mike began to think that his friend was more than quiet: he smelt a rat.

"Is it not about time you changed the habit of a lifetime and got yourself your own set of wheels? You know what your problem is: you're all fur coat and no knickers."

"Um – I suppose so. I even have a friend who works in cars. I could ask him to be on the lookout for something for me."

"Nah, you don't want to do that: I hear he's a bit of a rip-off merchant. Come on though: it's hardly in keeping with your man about town image to be having to cadge lifts off a young fogey like me? Upwardly mobile is the only way you are mobile. I mean, I don't mind myself, but does the fair Grace not give you a hard time about it?"

"Oh yeh she does – but I suppose that's all a bit academic now. I was looking for a way to tell you there: Grace and I are off mate. Finito: no longer an item. It only happened on Sunday night, after church."

"Well there you go: there's a surprise. Sure the two of you seemed all very happy and touchy-feely together."

"I know" Alan replied: "that's just what she said as well. I tell you: she really took it badly – cried all over me and said she didn't have an inkling it was coming and all of that. What made it worse was that I thought she was playing all blonde and dumb to make it harder for me. So I spelt it all out a bit… well, maybe a bit blunt and straight down the line. And then she really let rip and there was water works and Kleenex *everywhere*. I mean, it's not an easy thing to do in the first place, but they sure don't make it any easier for you."

Mike lifted a hand off the steering wheel to jab a finger in time with his words. "So if she didn't have a notion it was coming and you spelt it out, it was obviously you then."

"Oh yes: I just – well – I just didn't think it was going anywhere."

"It so rarely does with you."

"I'd been thinking about it for a while. She's a really nice girl but – well – how do you say that to her? Girls used to knock me back with that line. 'I'm sorry Alan; you're a really nice boy': and then you knew the 'but' was coming. I try and use just the same kind principles back in reverse but I never seem to sound anything other than so – callous."

"It's the way you tell 'em."

"I just feel really wick about it all. And I prayed about it as well before I did it, but that never seems to make it go any better either."

"How does that work then? 'Dear God please help me to be a complete-B and show your grace and kindness all at the same time?'"

"That's unfair. That's *so* unfair. And then her wee sister – you know the single one who's a bit of a space cadet."

"The one *you* tried to put Rodney on a blind date with."

"Aye her – he was better off out of that. If all you knew of her was you saw her walking out of church some Sunday night you'd say to yourself 'there's a nice girl – eight out of ten there'.

But I'm telling you: just not the full shilling. She posted all this really nasty stuff about me on Facebook. I tell you, if you knew what some people think about you, you wouldn't get out of bed in the morning."

"How long was it you were going out with Grace then?"

"Oh I don't know. It was Easter last year, wasn't it? Was Easter early or late last year? And then to top it all I got my bloody credit card bill this morning."

"And *what* sort of a credit card would that be?"

"Oh don't you start. I got the bloody credit card bill and of course there was £400 of Christmas presents that I got her on it. I tell you, if I'd known then what I know now I wouldn't have spent anything like *that* much on her. But that sort of salves my conscience that I wasn't premeditated in what I did."

"Which obviously makes it alright then?"

"I should have thought about it: I should have known there was some… strange… compensatory motive going on inside me when I spent *so* much on her at the first Christmas… Oh well, I suppose finding £400 – or however many sodding Euros it'll be – will be like a kind of penance. 'Say three Hail Marys and pay the Bank of Scotland £400 by the end of next month.'"

Mike thought there wasn't a great deal you could say to that, which was fortunate because they had arrived at Jim's house. He liked his friend but he knew it was wrong to vindicate all of this. He privately thought Grace a shallow woman but he didn't think she deserved this. He parked the car and the silence was punctuated only by the click of his seatbelt coming undone and the engine turning off. He opened the car door to get out so that his friend had no option but to get out himself. And it was deliberate that only at the last moment as they approached the front door did he say anything. He was careful to be casual because he knew that casual would be hurtful.

"Oh well: sure as you've said yourself so many times: there's plenty more fish in the sea. Or as Grace's sister might say to her: plenty more germs in the toilet."

* * * * * *

41

"Well Peter, you're very welcome here, and we hope you enjoy our little fellowship. Perhaps as our newest recruit you'd like to read the passage tonight. I'm not sure what translation you use but we generally use the NIV – or the Northern Ireland Version as we call it."

Grown men blushed and the newcomer smiled politely with a quizzical look on his face. Adam was not quite as discreet: he caught his friend's eye with a look that said 'It's a local thing, I'll tell you later.'

The passage was Jeremiah chapter one and verses four to sixteen. The room was calmed momentarily with the lovely whisper of thick set hands fingering and thumbing wispy pages. And then an alien voice filled the silence.

"The word of the LORD came to me, saying,
"Before I formed you in the womb, I knew you,
before you were born I set you apart;
I appointed you as a prophet to the nations."
"Ah, Sovereign LORD," I said, "I do not know how to speak; I
am only a child."
But the LORD said to me, "Do not say, 'I am only a child.' You
must go to everyone I send you to and say whatever I command
you. Do not be afraid of them, for I am with you and will rescue
you," declares the LORD.
Then the LORD reached out his hand and touched my mouth
and said to me, "Now, I have put my words in your mouth. See,
today I appoint you over nations and kingdoms to uproot and
tear down, to destroy and overthrow, to build and to plant."
The word of the LORD came to me: 'What do you see, Jeremiah?"
"I see the branch of an almond tree," I replied.
The LORD said to me, "You have seen correctly, for I am
watching to see that my word is fulfilled."
The word of the LORD came to me again: "What do you see?"
"I see a boiling pot, tilting away from the north," I answered.
The LORD said to me, "From the north disaster will be poured
out on all who live in the land. I am about to summon all the

peoples of the northern kingdoms," declares the LORD.
"Their kings will come and set up their thrones
in the entrance of the gates of Jerusalem;
they will come against all her surrounding walls
and against all the towns of Judah.
I will pronounce my judgments on my people
because of their wickedness in forsaking me,
in burning incense to other gods
and in worshiping what their hands have made."

"Thank you Peter." John said.

"RSV" Alan interrupted, as if he had something important to say. "What?"

"RSV" Alan replied. "That's what we'll have to start reading now. RSV: as in Republican-State-Version."

John chose to ignore the younger man with studied insouciance. "So the first question that we come to is 'Summarise the dialogue between the Lord and Jeremiah in this chapter.'"

The question was met with silence. The questions were always met with initial silence. Nobody ever 'baled in' as they would have put it themselves. The general form was to sit tight and let someone else kick off, see what direction they went in and follow the leader. (John always had a set of answers prepared himself so that he could give the whole thing a push start if required). On this occasion however it didn't go as he was expecting as Peter was the first to speak.

"Eh, sorry, that's not the first question in my book – eh, have I got a different version from the rest of you gentlemen?" John said that he was sure Peter hadn't and there were a few brief moments of mumbling whilst everyone looked at their book and that of their neighbour, comparing the covers and leaning over to check the layout of the inside copy. Everyone concurred that Peter had the same book but Peter contradicted that when he said the first question he had was "Think of a time when someone asked you to do something you thought was over your head. What feelings did you have about attempting the task?"

John often liked to say that 'like the hymn writer' he believed in 'letting his ordered life confess the beauty of Christ's peace'. The downside of that was that he could not cope with any deviation from his planned order. But in this case he had no option other than to go with the emerging flow. "Oh sorry" he said. "Sorry, I – eh – I must have missed that one. So the first question is – yes – about doing new things where we are out of our depth and how we felt about that. Sorry – I don't know how I missed that."

A flustered John unconsciously felt for the comfort of stroking his ear lobe. After some initial moments the ice melted. Jim got the ball rolling with a discussion about the first time he had to organise and chair a sales conference. Willie talked about being asked to take church services when he first went to Kenya, how he'd gone out there to teach Geography to missionary children and had felt out of his depth suddenly having to do pulpit supply. It was more than he could manage to preach for 20 minutes and of course they were happy to listen to you for hours on end, but he got into the way of it after a while.

Adam then made his contribution: they were not a group used to the candid and their senses were alerted by this story. This was particularly so as it was obviously not plucked from the easily accessible recesses of memory: it was something they had never heard Adam talk about before.

It was the story of the first time he had broken the news of a death to a patient's relative. She was a little girl just eight years old who was out cycling on a towpath with the rest of her family: the surface was broken and uneven and she hit a rut and came off the bike, her head by some terrible chance hitting the ground in the worst place possible. He and his colleagues had worked with her frantically when she was brought in, her parents cruelly shut behind doors in the frenzy of the admission. But little could be done and she passed away in the early part of a late summer evening. It was down to Adam to tell the parents. The mother wailed: "which sounds like me being melodramatic but that's just what it was like: a human being shrieking in a way I wouldn't have imagined possible". The father just looked totally shocked: dazed and as if he should have had little cartoon stars spinning around him. They glazed over and didn't initially comfort each other, and Adam said he had never felt as inadequate as he did at that moment. It was like grief from a TV drama being transposed into real life: it was other worldly to him. He had since given such news many times and it never got any easier.

And then they went on to summarise the dialogue between the Lord and Jeremiah in the passage they had read. Their reflecting of the passage back to John subtly belied the change around them. God knew Jeremiah and had plans for him even before the prophet was conceived. In years gone by that could have led to an enjoyable tangent debating foreknowledge and predestination: the irrelevant was always more interesting than it should have been. The legs of glasses could have been sucked and the bible furiously flicked for supporting arguments, text plucked from context. Does the setting apart of Jeremiah reinforce the foundational elements of Calvinism? Are we similarly set apart or was this an unusual anointing as is seen in the lives of other Old Testament characters such as Abraham and Saul? Saul lost his anointing: could we lose ours – what about the perseverance of the saints?

But the world was different now. So much had changed and nobody felt quite so clever: nobody felt like such a small expert with such a big bible. Jeremiah felt inadequate and said he wasn't up to the task. But God told him not to be afraid and reached out to touch his mouth: God was appointing him over nations to uproot and tear down, to destroy and overthrow, to build and to plant. Jeremiah saw an almond tree and then he saw a boiling pot, tilting away from the north. In the first instance God explained that he would watch to see that his word was fulfilled. In the second instance God was going to pour out his judgments on people on account of their wickedness in forsaking him. This was what the passage said. This was all there was to say.

They moved through the questions in the book, John

reading each one word for word. "We too are good at pleading inadequacy in order to avoid living at the best God calls us to. What reasons do you use to resist God's call on your life?"

"I think" Alan said "a lot of it is to do with belief. Not just belief in God but belief in ourselves as well. Sometimes I think when I look at the people around me that success is not so much about the amount of ability they have but rather it's more to do with *belief* in their ability."

"There might be something in that" Jim agreed. "I've certainly seen it in my career. The theory that so many companies are disastrously run, because everyone eventually reaches a level where they've been promoted beyond their competence."

"That's an interesting point" Peter said. Everyone looked at Peter: the purpose of being at the group was to make a contribution, but it seemed flash of him to be making a contribution so early. John thought this man was not backward about being forward.

"I guess the Christian life is often about the upside down Kingdom. I've come across lots of people who have more belief than they have ability. But all too often in the church we place the emphasis on ability and we don't have belief: we judge ourselves by very human measures and standards."

"There's a phrase sticks out for me when I hear you say that" Willie said. "It was an expression an old minister I knew used to use and he didn't use it very kindly: 'Jesus loves a little wallflower.' This guy worked really hard and used to complain that nothing moved in the congregation without him giving it a great big shove. He had a real thing about people who every time he asked them to do something said that just wasn't their gift."

"Well it might not have been" Jim mumbled.

"He said that contrary to 1 Corinthians 12 he used to think he had a church that was full of people whose only gift was to be able to pray for others in their front rooms. A wee bit like Jeremiah. And they would plead inadequacy if they were asked to do anything more than that. So he called them 'Jesus loves a little wallflower' Christians. I think he had a point but I suppose you'll always have people who are that bit nervy or cautious."

Peter spoke again. "Are you guys nervy and cautious?" *Are you guys nervy and cautious?* If one of the four Doulton ladies with sun umbrellas on the mantelpiece had done a little jig, it would have been no less of a shock.

"Are you not nervy and cautious?" he continued. "I mean you must be, mustn't you? It's kind of tough for you all. You're living here and you don't really want to be here: at least you don't want to be here now, after it has changed the way it has. That must be *so* difficult. How do you cope with it all?"

They all looked down, staring at their open bibles in the hope that somebody else would speak first. Out of the corner of his eye Mike winked at Alan and his friend returned the gesture with a comically affected frown.

Adam spoke. "I suppose there's just this sense of being a minority now and that's not going to go away. Sometimes it's as if we've been abandoned: I mean in a very obvious way the British have abandoned us – they've done it democratically but the net effect is still the same – but then so many kith and kin have gone too, and that makes it all the harder for those of us who have stayed."

The others seemed to relax as he continued to speak.

"I mean there's no doubt that probably for the last 25 years Republicanism had the wind in its sails whilst we were pushing water uphill but nothing really prepared us for the way it climaxed. I've never known someone closely who is terminally ill but that's what I imagine it might be like: a kind of cancer. You know that eventually it's going to take your friend so you just try as best you can to block out the end and all thoughts of that. But now it's happened. Nervy and cautious: yes, I suppose we are. But before that we were just in denial."

"I think" continued Mike "it's not as benign as being nervous or cautious. I would call it fear. I mean how do you begin to explain what it feels like to go from living in a land where you make up 50% of the population –"

"We weren't 50% of the population Mike. We haven't been

50% of the population for years. That's why we are where we are" interrupted Adam.

"To only being about 10-15% of the population. And I mean it's not just that. It's things like Gerry Adams being President even though he's – he's – well, we all know what he is… It's things like reading in the paper that if Sinn Fein get enough votes in the General Election to be part of a coalition, then they'll be pushing for McGuinness as Foreign Affairs Minister. Imagine having *that* representing your country abroad."

Peter shrugged his shoulders. "But don't you have to accept that making peace is a dirty business."

"*Some* peace: I mean, we might have democracy but sure there's so few of us now we can't make it count for anything. Voting just becomes a futile gesture. The sort of people who are ruling us now: that isn't nervy – that to me is real fear. You could take that wee china cat there and throw it hard against the wall and that's just like what's happened to our wee country."

Jim looked alarmed.

"Don't worry. I'm not actually going to."

"But" Peter said "there are persecuted Christians in this world who couldn't even begin to imagine what it would be like to be as much as 10-15% of their population, to have that strength in numbers. You have rights and freedoms that other people can't even dream of. It's a big world out there…"

"Well that might be the case" Mike replied. "But they're not us!"

"I know the point you're trying to make" Jim said. "But try telling my niece that. She's 17 and she should be doing her A-levels in a good Protestant grammar school but instead she's surrounded by them because the school has been taken over in the same way that they take everything over. That's what they do, you know: they come in and they take things over. Try telling that to a wee girl called Jenny who's the only one in a class where she's surrounded by Orla and Ciara and Mary. I suppose you'd tell her to be thankful she doesn't have nuns running about her…"

"Don't be afraid guys" Peter interrupted, cutting right across

Jim. "Don't be afraid – you know, I read somewhere once that the phrase 'don't be afraid' was the most commonly used expression by Jesus in the Gospels. I believe if Jesus were here now that's what he'd be saying to you guys. But men, you can't force yourselves not to feel afraid. You can't make yourselves think that you're not afraid. You've just got to trust God and be it. You've just got to *be* not afraid. Jesus wouldn't have said it if it wasn't possible."

Peter knew it was time to ease off then: so he looked at John as if to say 'maybe you should ask another question then'.

"God showed Jeremiah two visions in this dialogue. What is the significance of the vision in verses 13-16?"

Jim pondered the page in front of him, took off his glasses and looked up. Mild dread came over the rest of the men: Jim appeared on the verge of one of his 'Bible Code' type moments. "Do you think" he said as his eyebrows rose for emphasis "there's anything in the fact that the boiling pot tilts *away* from – the *north*?"

The rest of the group looked at him in misunderstanding but in a way that willed a big cog inside Jim's head to crank round further and better explain himself. "Is there some sort of message for us in that? Are *we* as Protestants from Ulster to be an instrument of judgment upon Roman Catholic people? Or is there going to be some judgment of God upon this land but the pot will tilt *away* from the North because of our faithfulness and we will be spared?"

"I suppose" Peter said "it depends on how you view the prophets. I think people are sometimes too prone to look at some of the more apocalyptic elements of books like Ezekiel and Daniel and think that the prophets were kind of wacky Nostradamus type figures: and so people would come out with all sorts of weird and wonderful interpretations of the prophets that they were speaking about Russia and America in the 1960s, for example. But no way! Jeremiah lived and prophesied in Jerusalem in the years leading up to the fall of the city and he continued to prophesy to God's people in the midst of the exile. That was the context God had placed him in and that was the situation he spoke God's voice into. I'm sorry to disappoint you – eh, sorry, what's your name?"

"Jim."

"Jim – I'm sorry to disappoint you Jim, but I don't think Jeremiah was the slightest bit concerned about some place called Ireland on the western fringes of some continent called Europe 2,600 years hence."

Jim winced: a curveball had never been batted back quite so ruthlessly before. Adam tried to rescue the situation for him. "I think you're right Peter but I still think Jeremiah has an enormous amount to say to us – today. It might have been a different time and place in the details but many of the principles still hold true."

"Absolutely" Peter said. "One of the most interesting things for me is the whole aspect of God and how he relates to the people of Israel. As modern Christians we tend to be terribly preoccupied with God dealing with individuals: *I*, Peter, must decide what *I* am going to do with Jesus. *I* have to make a personal decision. There's certainly a strong basis for that in the New Testament but we have an Old Testament as well and much of the story of the Old Testament is about God dealing with states and whole groups of people."

"But God doesn't do that today" John contested. "The only group he's concerned with today is the church."

"I'm not so sure about that. Much of the Old Testament is played out among Kings and their courts, on battlefields with shifting territories. Modern Christians are very good at saying that God is the same yesterday, today and forever and if that is the case, and if we really do believe that God is sovereign and in control, then Jim's suggestion is valid up to a point because God is surely working out his plans and purposes in, for example, the unification of this land."

John looked perturbed and was all the more concerned as all around him seemed to be hanging on every word uttered by Peter. *These guys are going to lap up everything this man says: I could end up with some sort of personality cult on my hands.* But the visitor was on a roll.

"I mean you only have to look at passages of rebuke that we see in Scripture. In the New Testament they're targeted at errant individuals or wayward groups within churches and so we confine preoccupation with truth mainly to the church and examination of the ways that Christian people are living. But in the Old Testament when God speaks rebuke and judgment He's almost always addressing a nation, collective groups defined by borders."

"The thing you said" – Alan tried to interrupt but failed to get a word in.

"When we think of confession we think of ourselves as individuals kneeling down beside our beds and telling God the bad things we have done today. But in the Old Testament we see examples of confession that are about great swathes of nation people coming and pleading to God for forgiveness and mercy. The New Testament might have been about something different but God surely hadn't changed. I believe God is always at work – He might not be at work on your terms or the way you want Him to be – but God is sovereign and He is at work"

Now Alan spoke. "That thing you said about God being at work – not necessarily on our terms – but God is at work: that's so true. I don't know why it's coming into my head now but, you know, I remember many a time being at prayer meetings and people would pray those verses from 2 Chronicles – what were they?"

"If my people?" Willie asked?

"That's it" Alan said.

Willie filled in the rest for him. "'If my people, who are called by my name, will humble themselves and pray and seek my face and turn from their wicked ways, then will I hear from heaven and will forgive their sin and will heal their land.'"

Alan continued. "That's it exactly. And people used to pray that – and I used to pray that – but I used to think to myself: what are we really asking for when we pray that?"

"You kept that to yourself" John muttered.

"I mean it sounded very mighty to use those verses in prayer but I think deep down what we were all thinking about was God moving on our terms. 'Well God what would be really good for this land would be if there were a great revival and lots of the Catholic people would be saved, and sure when they're saved they'll come round to our way of thinking politically too, and then we'll all live happily in the six counties: Catholics saved and Union saved. Everything saved.' Maybe God is going to heal our land but He just isn't doing it on our terms: maybe He's got to cut us real deep in the very place that hurts the most before the healing can be properly meaningful."

Mike broke in. "Oh wise up Alan, it's a bit more than a cut! A loving God deals with his people by stabbing them in the back and then gives them a good kicking when they're down! So that makes Gerry Adams an instrument of God? Does that mean God is working out his purposes through David Milliband? Hardly: get real!"

"Mike, I'm just saying – no – you know that's not what I'm saying…"

As nobody could see the wood for the trees an oak of righteousness intervened.

"It doesn't make any sense to me either, Alan" Willie said. "I don't understand what's happening here and I suppose we have to accept that as long as we're mere mortals on this earth we see through a glass darkly. There will always be things we don't like but Peter has hit the nail on the head: God is sovereign and we simply have to trust and believe that He is in control: just because He isn't moving the way we want Him to, doesn't mean He isn't moving."

"Your friend is right" Peter continued. "There's huge pain for you men in this and I don't discount the reality of that. But part of the story of Jeremiah is about a prophet who speaks truth even when it hurts. I think one of the lessons in the book is that it would be so easy for your leaders in the church here to pastor you and sanctify all your self pity…"

"I think it's more than self-pity" snapped Mike. "Correct me if I'm wrong but there is such a thing as victims, isn't there."

"True: and victims can choose whether they wallow or don't wallow."

"Oh come on" John complained. But Peter was not to be put off.

"Jeremiah doesn't do that: he speaks hard truth into a hard situation. Just because bad things have happened to us doesn't mean we can shirk our responsibilities of self-examination and confession. The wrongs of your enemies don't automatically make you right. Maybe it's easy for me, because I come at this as an outsider..."

John saw a moment. The conversation was bouncing around him like a superball in a squash court: every time he thought he could catch and control it, it veered off in a different direction. "Gentlemen, talking of tough questions maybe we should move on to the next one in the book. 'In what ways has God communicated reassurance that he will help you to become the person you are called to be – even in the face of opposition?'"

Mike sighed. "What a question? Who writes these questions?"

But Alan answered. "I don't know if it's a helpful analogy or not, but one of the things I think of is drink – drink as in alcohol. I remember when I went to university in my first year I – eh – I went off the rails a bit: I went through a phase of going out and getting hammered a lot and it really affected my faith."

"Funnily enough" Jim muttered.

"The thing was: everyone had told me that drink was bad but nobody told me *how* not to drink. There was no discipleship to help me know how I should react when drink was put in front of me. I suppose you could argue that I shouldn't have been there in the first place, but hey – I was only 18 and hindsight is a wonderful thing. My faith then started to crumble. Going and getting wasted just seemed like the worst thing a good young Christian could do: how could God forgive me and how could I carry on after that. Here I was in this difficult new situation and the church and my Christian experience had given me no framework for how to cope with it. When I failed in the situation, my faith began to fail me."

"And the point is?" Mike asked.

"Well what I'm trying to say – and maybe I'm not saying it very well – is that maybe we don't have any sense of God's reassurance in this situation because just like with me and the alcohol, our faith hasn't given us any framework for coping with it. When I think about it, as I grew up there was just never any sermons on The Troubles and the way the country is and how we should respond to that.

I mean – in fairness – I sat under some great teaching which has helped me in many ways and for that I'm grateful. But when you think about it in the context of what Peter was saying about the Old Testament it becomes really striking. We lived in this really divided community: separate schools; different parts of towns; two different identities and national aspirations for the two communities. And it was *never* mentioned in church: it was absolutely *never* mentioned! It's amazing isn't it? How can we cope or have any sense of assurance when we've never been challenged or helped to integrate our faith into this context?"

"I think" said Mike "it's nearly more profound than trying to know *how* to do Christian faith in the context of a United Ireland. It's about... just generally *how* to do Christian faith when you despair. We're so false and polite so much of the time. We sing so much bubble and squeak feel-good... crap... about God wrapping his arms around us, and soaring on wings like eagles and all that. And yet here we are and it's just... awful. I must admit that I don't feel any assurance in this current situation... I don't feel any assurance."

John snapped his Bible shut to say to the group that you don't always have to finish and they had done enough for tonight.

Peter spoke in a gentle whisper. "I suppose the great thing about this passage is that it's not all doom and gloom. When God is commissioning Jeremiah, He talks about uprooting and tearing down: He talks about destroying and overthrowing. And that's the way it seems to be for you now..."

"Yes, yes, point made Peter" Adam said.

"I wouldn't dream of telling you all that I have some idea exactly how you feel because that would just be so patronising:

I can't imagine it. But look carefully and God also says He's going to build and plant. I'm not much of a handyman and I don't like gardening either but I know that building and planting are both about making new things. There's mess and rubble and then there is fresh paint and shining windows. There's muck and weeds and then there are flowers.

I'm not saying I've any great insight for you all. I could sit here for the next five minutes and wax lyrical about building and planting: but I don't know what the future holds for you so to do that would be – well, manipulative – trying to make the text say the thing we want to have God say. But we can't deny it's in there. And we can't deny that God is ultimately a good and loving God and He is in the business of making new things. Can I pray for you all?

Lord, thank you tonight for every head bowed here. Thank you for the wonder that I am thousands of miles away from home in a strange and far off land, and that in the midst of a storm there is always a rainbow. Father we confess that for many of us gathered here these are sad and difficult times.

Lord we are anxious; we are confused; and we are often angry and bitter. And we do not know what to do. But Lord into this situation we ask that you will speak your voice, and we thank you that tonight you have begun to do so. We thank you that because you are the light of the world there can never be total darkness.

And we thank you that you build and plant and that is truth. And we ask that as we go forward in this land you will do just that: build and plant. And not just in our land, but in all our lives. And so Lord: help us each one to live well and live obediently in all those places where you have lead us. Amen."

Outside as they parted it was a cold and crisp night. There was going to be a hard frost and in the morning they would be clearing ice off their cars and being wary of treacherous conditions under foot. But that would be then: just now the air felt perfectly chill and fresh. Above seven friends the moon was clear and a thousand stars glistened in the night sky: and for just one moment the possibilities seemed endless.

5

Behind every man…

"Who does he look like?" Violet said. "Does he look much like you or John?"

"Well, that's the thing of course" Gillian replied: "he doesn't much look like anyone, does he? Well, that's not quite true – he's obviously like his mother."

"Oh gosh, yes, I suppose he doesn't. Oh I'm sorry, me putting my big foot in as usual."

"Oh don't be ridiculous, you're fine. I mean he's gorgeous – different certainly, but gorgeous all the same."

Gillian – John's wife – had met Violet for a cup of tea and a chat to catch-up, but share particularly the news of her latest grandchild. As was her habit Violet had knitted a large blanket for the baby: "they throw up so much, you can never have enough."

Hurry sickness had never been a malaise to afflict Violet and a friend visiting for a cup of tea remained a major operation involving the deployment of a range of instruments: tea cups and saucers; a tea pot; a tea cosy; a trivet for the tea pot; the tea bags; milk and a jug for the milk; sugar and spoons for the sugar; and of course the cooker to let the tea sit on a ring for a moment. But time did not matter because there was so much to talk about. Violet did not share her view that small babies don't actually look like *anyone* other than generic small babies and Gillian unpacked her burdens and her joy.

The child had been born over 60 miles away on the North Coast in Coleraine. Its father was David, John and Gillian's youngest son, and its mother was Vicki. David was the 'black sheep of the family': anyone who knew the Todds could have told you that he had always been difficult. He was never a bad child but was nonetheless gifted with an ability to attract trouble. He was ferociously strong willed: as Gillian would say "you know where he gets that from". The boy's interest in faith fizzled out in his early teens when he gradually withdrew inside a surly shell. There were rows in the house and John's voice would be raised and David would scowl and walk away indifferently. Nobody or nothing seemed to stir him from ambivalence, until fellow fifth form pupil Vicki Tsang came along.

Vicki was the daughter of the local Chinese takeaway's owners and loved David for the respite he gave her from the claustrophobia and conformity demanded of family ties and the family business. The Tsangs didn't like David and John didn't much like Vicki: or rather didn't like the idea of Vicki. He did not mind her as a person but her 'sort' would never have been his preferred category of daughter in law, if he had a choice.

Gillian though took a longer view, a length borne of pragmatism and a trust in God. Vicki had no interest in faith – or 'the things of God' as John put it. But Gillian believed that to see this girl's indifference – she suspected Vicki believed in nothing but could not be sure – as a universally bad influence upon her son was nonsense. David was not rushing out to church or going off to youth fellowship weekends but neither was he, by any means, off the rails.

Vicki was undoubtedly a 'cutey': John could see in more enlightened moments why his son loved her so. Long black hair, perfect white teeth, lots of personality, and bags of enthusiasm. And terribly polite as those from her culture seemed to be. When he saw this little gem walk hand in hand with his loping son he would often say "there they go again, the sweet and the sour."

The relationship flourished despite the odds against it. Twice the Tsangs refused to pay protection money for their business. Twice the takeaway had its front window put in, and three times the bins behind the shop were set on fire. (Strangely, since the unification, it was as quiet on that front as the Tsangs could remember for years). Young-hard-tough men at the local school would ask David if there were not enough good girls of his own sort: why did he need to go out with a 'chinky'?

Vicki's disinterest in the Christian faith was not helped by the basic equation that was calculated in her mind. Born-again Christians are all Protestants and Protestants all too often equal loyalists – at least, all loyalists are Protestants, aren't they? What was For God and Ulster on those putrid summer evenings of bands and marching all about? What was the faith of David's parents all about? Those lads in shell suits and uniforms who poured into the takeaway after their parades for curry chips to be washed down with cheap drink: was that what it all meant? Was that what David's parents believed in?

The Union Jack to which these angry young men held allegiance was the same flag that she saw flying from some of the churches in the marching season. And some of their marches on Sundays went to church and they went to the churches themselves despite being – what they seemed to be – big strong men expressing their identity but with little becoming about them when they looked down their noses at you to place an order at eleven o'clock on a Saturday night. Kick the pope bands "walking down the Falls and kicking Fenian balls" – was that what her boyfriend believed in deep down? She did not think about these things a great deal, but when she did, these were her readings of it all.

David and Vicki went up the North Coast to study when they left school: they wanted to get away from it all; wanted a clean break. David studied Mechanical Engineering and was now a Production Manager in a small components company; Vicki did Nursing and worked in the very hospital where their child was born. They bought a house and married just as soon as they could after graduating. Their values and careers testified to a constructive combination of Protestant and migrant work ethic but in the most general sense they both wanted 'an easy life' and that is what they made together.

To them the unification had not mattered much. They were post modern pluralists who said themselves that they believed in nothing. Their creed was one of live and let live, of getting on with their own lives and not bothering other people. They believed in their relationship and the life they wanted to share together and were one another's orientation. And now they were three.

The baby was born on a Sunday evening at the end of February: John and Gillian travelled north to see the new 'family' early the next morning. Vicki and Gillian had always got on well together and as any Granny would, Gillian delighted to hold the baby in her arms. She heard inside herself the words "how sweet to hold a newborn baby, and feel the peace and joy it gives, but greater still the calm assurance…" – but she wasn't the sort of person to recite the words of hymns aloud and anyway, it wouldn't have meant anything to the child's parents. She prayed inwardly just then, and made a little prayer go a long way.

But things were stiffer between the men; they shook hands where the women hugged; they stood apart where the women sat close. John nursed the child and tears seemed to well up in his eyes. He looked at the child longingly: he didn't avert his gaze and look up at the others because he couldn't be sure of retaining his composure and wanted very much to contain himself. He was proud in the end, very proud indeed.

The baby was to be called John Patrick – or JP for short. John was after his paternal grandfather: an olive branch of simple love that bore testimony to unspoken respect. Patrick was in there for historical significance: this was a big year for Ireland and a big year for little JP and it would seem remiss not to mark that in the naming of the child. And when you put them together you had JP. And JP seemed quite Catholic: it would help him blend in for future years, wasn't too conspicuous and that couldn't harm his chances. Neither David nor Vicki felt an inclination to Protestant sensibilities: calling the child William or Stephen or whatever wouldn't do him any favours so what was the point in that?

"JP Todd" Violet said. And then she said it again to further help her decide what she thought of it. "JP Todd – it's quite nice really, isn't it?"

"It's really starting to grow on me" Gillian replied. "John

59

wasn't so sure of course. I think he was quite touched by the whole thing of his grandson being called after him, but then he complained that JP was a 'fenian' name: you know John. But as I rolled it over I pointed out that JP Todd sounds quite holy and reformed in its own way: you know, a bit like J C Ryle or R T Kendall or something like that. And then he comes back into the room about half an hour later and says – as if he's announcing some great revelation – wait till you hear this – that the name does have 'a certain evangelical grandeur'. Men: what would you do with them?"

* * * * * *

John

Whilst their better halves were chatting over tea Willie and John were at the church to do a long deferred piece of DIY: fixing the tiny metal brackets that were used for empty communion cups. The meeting room would not normally be occupied during a Tuesday morning and yet for some reason the heat was almost enough to knock the two friends over, bubbling radiators too hot to touch. What was it with the church and heat? John complained of his occasional disbelief at the capacity of elderly people who gathered here for worship to sit through entire services in winter coats and somehow not pass out.

Violet had packed a flask and some jam tarts and they broke off for some sustenance mid-morning. Willie knew about the new baby but was also aware of all the issues with David – the tension and distance between father and son. He resolved he would enquire no more than John volunteered.

"They're calling him JP you know" John said. "I wasn't struck on it at the start, but then I thought – JP Todd, well in its own way that's quite – how could I put it – grandly evangelical. It's sort of grown on me quite a bit since then." Willie smiled agreeably and John continued.

"I didn't want to say anything the other night at Jim's house but that bible study got me thinking in a few ways." Willie didn't engage in any way that encouraged there to be more, but John's conversation was uncharacteristically needy and he carried on, his words helping him to distil his thoughts.

"I couldn't help but think about David and this wee unborn baby whenever we were reading the passage and God was speaking to Jeremiah about knowing him even before he was formed in his mother's womb. I tend to be very even-keeled in terms of what goes on inside me but I must admit I've been feeling quite up and down these last few days. I looked at that wee baby so small and fragile and looking up all quizzical when I nursed him, his eyes and ears and hands and all so tiny. And I thought about Jeremiah and how here's this child and how God's got its life all mapped out for it even before it was born. But then I thought about David, and I thought how the same thing could have been said for him, and sure look at how he's turned out. Not that twenty-six years of age is how he's ultimately turned out – you never know what the future holds – but you know what I mean."

"I do John, but sure he's got the whole of the rest of his life in front of him."

"And then I had one of those terrible moments when I think that maybe my son just isn't going to be a Christian, those prayers over new-born children are ones which won't be answered, and I find *that* a terrifying thought so I just had to bury it and move on. And then I thought to myself that I should catch myself on: David's a good lad and Vicki's lovely really. You could have an awful lot worse for a son and a daughter in law. Many people do."

"They do indeed."

"Who am I to say that God can't break into their lives? And I thought about this sermon I heard once about Abraham. It was all about Abraham's call and the fact that he lived in this desperately pagan and Godless society and yet God just burst into all that and took Abraham to be a father for His plans. Do you never think that there's got to be more to Christianity than the seeming thing of nice respectable Christian families having nice respectable Christian children who 'give their lives to the

Lord' when they're four years old? That's just what I'm thinking. Is that alright?"

Willie had realised he had got some jam off a tart on his trousers and had been anxiously working at it, dividing his attention between John and his leg. He had started by licking a finger and rubbing the jam furiously and then resorted to pinching up the trouser leg in one hand and picking keenly at the mark with a finger nail. None of which improved matters. They were only clean on: Violet would go in and out through him. "John, I don't think you have to apologise just for telling a friend what you're thinking. You carry on."

"Her parents haven't even visited them yet, did I tell you that?"

"No, you didn't say that – they – they"

"– haven't been near them." John rolled his eyes to say he didn't know what was going on there. "The life of a newborn baby is a blank page which is a dreadful cliché but it's true, isn't it? And it just seems that at the moment, more than ever, a blank page is a very exciting thing but also quite frightening. And then I got to thinking about Ireland and the direction of this land and the sort of place it's going to be to bring up a child. Peter and Ruth decided they'd be better off out of it and I wouldn't disagree with them. I really miss them and the boys but then that means JP's going to be my only grandchild here and I'll definitely make more effort to see him because of that. That could be God moving in mysterious ways, couldn't it?"

Willie nodded.

"And as that wee boy grows up – as long as he's loved and fed and clothed and kept warm – it really won't matter where he lives. And I know that – deep down I do. I know that where he lives doesn't matter, as long as he knows the Lord as his Saviour: since I held him in my arms that's been especially clear. But this land – sometimes I think that even if God himself were to appear at the bottom of my bed in the middle of the night and tell me to let go of it all I'd argue with the Almighty. That's how hard I find it all."

Willie replied softly. "I remember many years ago having a

few problems with someone and being firmly given this advice by another person that I 'just had to move on' from all that stuff. But really John, that was just a rather unkind way of telling me to pull myself together: as if there is a set and determined time within which you should reconcile yourself to some given circumstance. If you're finding all this hard, then what's wrong with that? Lots of us are finding it hard. Seek God and find it hard. Don't try to force yourself to draw some line under this. It will all come right, but don't ever believe a lie that the Godly thing to do is deny the way you feel."

And so the two friends bobbed among the pews: screwing and mending; talking and listening; and all the time making communion possible.

* * * * * *

Adam

For Adam and his recently arrived house-mate a takeaway from Tsang's Hot Food Bar was becoming a too frequent occurrence. But it was like a kind of rite – a sacrament of companionship. Adam was enjoying *sharing* meals on a regular basis again and pushed his plate into the detritus of rice, cartons, sauces and paper, feeling satisfied at more than a physical level.

Peter held up a prawn cracker as he began to make a point, holding it before him for a moment as if toasting his fellow diner. And while doing so he raised something preying on his thoughts.

"There's something that's been on my mind Adam."

"Really: tell me about it."

"Well – the thing is – it's really striking the way you and your friends' talk whenever the subject of Sinn Fein comes up. The tone of how you all talk about '*Adams and McGuinness*': I mean it's as if you can almost – smell the disdain. It's like – no maybe I shouldn't say that –"

"It's like what? I'll not be offended: you know me. It's like what?"

"It's like – not that I've ever heard this but I'm using my imagination here – you know it could almost be Jewish people talking about Hitler or Eichmann and villains of their ilk. That's how strong you seem to feel about the attitudes and behaviour you associate with these men. They're hate figures to people to whom Christ has given an instruction that we're not to hate our enemies – and – and – I'm sorry: I don't seem to be expressing myself very well."

"Yeh" Adam said. "What can you say? They mark this land: them and their cohorts. Their sin stains it."

He walked to the sink to fill the kettle with water and reached for mugs from an adjacent cupboard. It was clear he was going to say more.

"History is history and we are where we are. And they mark this land. Terrible things have been done in this country – by people on all sides, not just them. But I think it's what was done in the name of Republicanism coupled with the fact that there never seems to have been any sniff or hint of remorse. They don't seem to regret any of it: at least not publicly. Maybe they do privately – I'd like to think they do – but I suppose like all politicians they have their fronts to put on."

"Well, how do you ever know what's going on inside people?"

"I think it's a very sad thing in any man's life when he says he doesn't have regrets: God knows I have plenty. Maybe things would be different if they couldn't look into a camera straight on: if they looked down; if they seemed ashamed. But there seems to be such a conviction of rightness within modern Irish republicanism. So I hardly think that's going to happen. So history is history and we are where we are. But I often think that things could have been so different: and if events had taken one course instead of another, how much more content could Protestants have been to be part of a United Ireland? How many more Protestants might have stayed to make a go of it in a United Ireland?"

"How so? Tell me about it."

"What if how things have happened is scenario A? And we

can describe scenario A as the dreadful discrimination against Catholics which seeps into civil rights which is wrongly resisted by some Protestants and dreadfully managed by local and Westminster politicians. And you have the emergence of the Provisional IRA and British soldiers are on the street and by the mid seventies Protestants have taken up their arms as well and this mess ensues for the next twenty years. And there's the ballot box going hand in hand with the armalite and Republicanism apparently has the wind in its sails. Are you with me?"

Peter nodded.

"There's the Good Friday Agreement but the people who are perceived by my community to be the movers and shakers behind so much bloodshed are the ones who have this irresistible political momentum about them. They seem to ring concession after concession out of the process: they get their prisoners out; then they see the police force they attacked so much, reconstituted in a way that gives more credence to their opinions than to those who served in that force. They stoke up the marching issue and of course Protestants walk dimly into that trap and the net effect is yet more diminishing of Unionist status and morale. They believe their 'on the runs' should come home but the same amnesty should not apply to British forces: breathtaking standards of one law for us and another for them.

And this course of events plays on and plays out and here we are in a United Ireland. They win, we lose. But look at how they won. They win the game and the result can't be disputed but how has it happened: how could good and moral people be happy with that? That's scenario A."

"That's scenario A my friend" affirmed Peter. "That's what actually happened: at least that's *your people's* take on what happened. And no doubt an Irish Nationalist would tell that very differently…"

"– No doubt they would Peter. And listen, you know me; you know where I come from. They have their story too and you know I'm sympathetic to many aspects of that. There's two sides to every story – but anyway – that's scenario A."

"So tell me scenario B" Peter said.

"Scenario B goes right back to the same time and place where scenario A started with the discrimination and the civil rights. But a lid somehow stays on the violence: somehow – someway – why did God not keep a lid on it all in the first place I often ask myself? But anyway: it all went down a better road instead. The troops work and are accepted by both sides. No need for armed struggle, no cack-handed policy of internment. A different boat but it's still them has the wind in their sails.

The housing and the jobs discrimination and the social inequality are dealt with because they just must be tackled. Gerry Fitt and the SDLP becomes a meaningful power base and democracy and reasonableness says the Protestants just have to share government. And all the while there's demographic shifts going on: every year the percentage points edging a little more in favour of Nationalism. There's no revolution towards a United Ireland: no glorious rivers of blood flowing for the 32 counties. Just gentle and plodding revolution. Protestants could say they've almost sleepwalked into this but they can't call it a nightmare. What if scenario B was history? What if democratic momentum that we could all see coming was how it had happened?"

"What if?" said Peter. "How do you believe that would have made such a difference?"

"What I'm trying to say" Adam replied "is that we're all convinced we hate this United Ireland. We detest the fact that we're Irish rather than British. But do we *really*? Is this in itself so bad? If it all had happened the way I described in scenario B I don't think we'd be anything like as discontent: sure we'd feel strangers in a strange land to some degree. But we couldn't find it objectionable if we'd found it fair.

But that's not how we feel. The modern Republican movement was what brought about the unification. 'It was terrorism what won it.' In the end moderate Nationalism became a minority to a movement that was all about the armalite and the ballot box hand in hand. Good God fearing people find those events – scenario A – terribly hard to live with. Forget the very first line of the Psalms that tells us how blessed the man is who does *not* walk in the counsel of the wicked or stand in the way of sinners. The sinners and the wicked seemed to turn out the most blessed people of all. I think we can unify ourselves in our minds to Ireland being united but how can we find peace with the idea of the people who made it come about? How do we do that Peter? That's the question. That's the rub."

* * * * *

Alan

Football was on TV the same night as Wendy went to 'Shake-it-Firm-it-Tone-it' which afforded Mike the opportunity to enjoy a takeaway and watch a match with a friend. His wife was heading out the front door just as Alan was coming in. This was unfortunate because there was a thinly veiled tension between Mike's wife and best friend. Alan liked to revel in puzzlement about why Wendy had it in for him and what it was that he had ever done to her. But secretly he disliked her every bit as much as she did him.

"Well here he comes" she said: "the oldest teenager in town."

"Aw Wendy, have a bit of pity. My sofa's barely cold and that's all you have to say to me."

"Oh sorry" she replied. "Your singleness has touched my heart. Sure when I think about where I'm going tonight, there's no reason why I couldn't be on the look out for a new squeeze for you. 15 year old man, GSOH – well, seems to *think* he's quite funny – would like to meet bible bashing and attractive female for transient snogs and friendship."

"Well now – that's very kind of you – but I have a picture in my head of what your class would be like Wendy, and I wouldn't really want a girl at the thicker end of the scale now. Size 14 or below if you get my drift."

Mike winced as Alan said this: his friend had sown the wind but it would be him who would reap the whirlwind. His wife was so pointed as to be almost steel tipped.

"I'll be back about ten. I'll be switching my mobile off, so you're on your own boys."

With Wendy gone the atmosphere improved, and the men soon got themselves settled.

"What have I ever done to your wife and look at the way she talks to me? I bumped into Adam when I was in getting the Chinese" Alan said. "He seems to live in there. You'd think being a doctor and all he'd take better care of himself. Anyway, have you got the goggle-box on?"

The Euro 2020 championships were rolling round: the Northern and Southern teams had played out the qualifying groups in their own right and pundits observed it could have been the first time that two teams represented one country at such a tournament. But it wasn't to be: Northern Ireland went out with more of a whimper than a bang whilst the Republic missed out on a runner-up's place in their group only on goal difference. And tonight Ireland – new Ireland – all Ireland – were playing Italy at Lansdowne Road, a glamour friendly and golden Hello for the united football team. Mike and Alan had determined that they would give it their best shot. Get the food in, get the feet up and make the most of what you've got. The joint guests of honour at the match were a septuagenarian Pat Jennings and the current Celtic manager Roy Keane.

"Gosh" Mike said. "Big Pat's still wearing his hair like two floppy ears on a dog. He's amazing: wouldn't you think his wife or someone would tell him to catch himself on."

Large screens in the corner of the ground jumped from the glories of Gerry Armstrong in 1982 to David O'Leary's penalty in 1990. A harp sat upon the Celtic cross that had once been the emblem of Northern Ireland football. Everybody seemed to be trying very hard to make the poorer relative feel welcome. But it wasn't how it had been. No pitiful Railway Stand behind the goal being attacked in the first half. No 'No Surrender' chorus amidst the instrumental bridge in the National Anthem. No 'Stand up for the Ulstermen.'

It had been a long and tedious day at work and low level moaning for another cup of milk could be heard from Sophie's room. A slow pace to the opening of the match wasn't helping Mike's mood as he sat in row A of his lounge front room. "Who's he?" he said ten minutes in, as the ball trickled back to the Irish number one.

"He's Ian McLoughlan" Alan replied. "He's their keeper. Sorry: *our* keeper."

"Oh. Do *we* have anyone playing?" Mike complained.

"Who? Liverpool? Course we don't – wise up man! Sure there's no Irishmen at Liverpool – how would we?"

"*No, not Liverpool. Northern Ireland.* Does Northern Ireland not have anyone playing?"

"Eh – well – we've Chris Casement at centre half, and Corey Evans and – and – I think that's it. We've two playing."

"So why are we watching it then?"

"Because it's on" Alan suggested limply. "Because it's what we're going to have to watch now. They're *our* team. This is it now."

"Says who?"

"Well…says me because I *certainly* don't want to watch Fair-bloody-City! Content yourself. Look: we're attacking here."

Another couple of minutes passed before Mike had an idea. "Who says we have to watch *Ireland* playing Italy? And who says we have to watch Fair City?"

A harassed reply came back. "I'm not watching Red Dwarf, Mike. I'll go home and watch this in my own house if you're going to get Red Dwarf out."

"No, not Red Dwarf – but there's nothing wrong with Red Dwarf." For the first time that evening there was some skip and dance in Mike's voice. "You came round here for a good feed and good football and I'll give you football as good as it gets."

"Right. Go on then. I'm waiting for it."

"Northern-Ireland-one-England-nil. Windsor Park: 7th September 2005. What about it big lad? Will I get the old DVD player going?

It didn't take a pause of more than half a second for an unhesitant rally back across the room: "Aye, go on!"

In only the time it took to open a DVD case and press some remotes, sugar coated memories were taking away the bitterness of foul reality. Choruses of 'who are you?' at Beckham as he took corners in front of the North Stand. Rooney mouthing back at Beckham, and looking for a few glorious moments like he would lose it altogether. Megastars rattled amidst the 'they don't like it up em' hostility of Windsor Park.

And then that moment of all moments when David Healy left Ashley Cole for dust and buried the ball past Paul Robinson: every time he saw that goal Alan could never fail to remember the screaming delirium like nothing he'd experienced before or since and how the normally restrained Mike had turned to him that night and hysterically yelled "it's better than sex" to him.

The past was a better country: the past on that night was a beautiful place to go. Two little boys were lost in a time spun spell: they could hardly do this every time Ireland played a football match but why not do it tonight? Why expose yourself to the chill of the present when you can bury yourself in the warmth of the past?

The DVD captured not just the glory of the match but also the revelry afterwards: the eleven heroes coming back out from the dressing room to dance and parade and soak up the adulation that rained down from the terraces. Sweet Caroline belted out by a choir of ten thousand men. Alan and Mike sat there, chins in hands, poised on the edge of the sofa: they didn't want it to stop that night in Mike's lounge any more than they had wanted it to stop on the night itself.

Windsor Park was filled with booming choruses that wanted for polish but sparkled with passion. As the cameras captured the players, the microphones picked up loyal fans singing "I'm Ulster till I die, I'm Ulster till I die, I know I am, I'm sure I am, I'm Ulster till I die" carried on by the chorus two or three times in the natural manner of a crowd's repeat to fade.

6

Peter

The words had been on the wall for as long as anyone could remember: *'For God so loved the world that he gave his only begotten son, that whosoever believes in Him, might not perish but have everlasting life. John 3v16'.*

To most people they were just part of the town's wallpaper, but an outsider's attention was more likely to be arrested by them. Which was the case with Peter: he remarked on it to Adam as they drove past one morning.

"What's with the words on that wall Adam? Where did they come from?"

"Couldn't tell you, to be honest. They've been there as long as I can remember: like the wall itself."

"Pretty cool words, eh? I wonder do your friends get them?"

"Course they get them" Adam grouched. "Men like that: they'd have been getting *those* words when they were knee high to a daisy."

"Well yes I know that" Peter said, in a languid manner that sat uncomfortably with what he was saying. "I know they get the bulk of it: the believing and the not perishing and the having everlasting life. Sure isn't that what salvation is to lots of people: heaven and hell and the one way ticket to ride. But what about the rest of it?"

"The rest of it?"

"God so loved the world. I was thinking back to our study the other evening, and something has just been nagging at me. Everything was so narrow: it's as if those guys think God's as hung up on Ireland and Northern Ireland as they are."

"Seems fair enough to me Peter. I'd like to think He is too."

"Yeh but something's missing in their perspective Adam. It's all kind of 'you in your small corner and I in mine'. God loves the world. God loves the whole world. He doesn't just love certain bits of it in particular and He certainly doesn't love some of it more than others."

"I don't think any of them – my friends – I don't think any of them would say that."

"You so sure about that? Did you hear Jim coming out with that crap about pots tilting from the North and could that be Ulster and all of that? What a pile of tosh."

"Oh that's just Jim: I wouldn't be reading too much into that if I were you. He was a big man for the Da Vinci code when it came out, and he likes to wow us all with notions of numerology you know: he has these ideas but he gets over things. Just thank God we're not studying Daniel."

"Maybe I shouldn't go digging too deep then" Peter shrugged. "But it's been on my mind. It's been on my mind and there's been one particular line of Scripture on my mind too."

"What's that then?"

"The line that talks about God appointing Jeremiah a prophet to the nations. Jeremiah didn't prophesy solely about Israel and Israel alone. He'd things to say about lots of Israel's neighbours as well. So if God sent a prophet here and now to Ireland, I reckon he wouldn't just be a prophet for all Ireland, he'd be a prophet to the nations in this age too. Because God's interested in all the Nations: God's interested in the entire world."

"Absolutely: He's even got it in his hands."

"Indeed, He's got it in his... oh very clever. People wouldn't see prophets as prophets if they came today anyway, would they? They'd just see them as grouches and critics."

"Maybe, maybe not: you seem grouchy enough."

"I'm not grouchy Adam: I'm just honest. I just happen to think it's a big wide world out there. A big wide world full of opportunity and a damn sight more suffering than some of your friends realise. And God loves it all: they need to get out there and see a bit more of it."

7

Alan

It had started off as 'a wee job': and small it would have been had the requisite effort been applied. All Mike had to do was kanga hammer the dowdy concrete corner of the back garden, dig it out, remove the rubble and fill it with bark chip. And the result would be a safe and secure play area for his children. But in matters like these he was a better starter than a finisher: and he would have been better not starting at all than creating such a mess that no child could be allowed out to the back garden. It hardly helped to oil the wheels of marital bliss and every time he went outside to put something in the bin, or check the level of oil in the tank, he felt this morass of masonry was taunting and teasing him. Wendy suggested unhelpfully that at this rate of going Sophie would not get to enjoy her wedding reception in the back garden, never mind a plastic slide. If he couldn't pull his finger out then he should get help. So he called in his friend Alan: Alan was touchingly handless in such matters but that was fine because Mike needed a body more than a brain.

This heap of debris had been in the garden since the previous autumn, and in apparently clever testimony to the aforementioned rubble Mike's friend had taken to calling him 'Barney'. He continued in this vein on the Saturday morning when he came round to lend a hand. He put on an imbecilic voice and said things like "Whaddaya want me to do with this Barney" and "Where'd you want your wheelbarrow Barney" and "Do you think we'll find any dinosaur eggs Barney?" It was an ineffective impression but he went on and on and on at it, in infantile curiosity to see how far he could push it. Mike did not once return the compliment or stoop to address his friend as 'Fred'.

It got to the point in the day where they were ready to go to the DIY store to buy the bark chip. As they were driving over in the van Mike had borrowed from his work – totally without warning – Alan dropped the Flintstones and came over all serious.

"You know mate, sometimes I feel a bit jealous of Adam."

"Right –" Mike said, feeling intrigued but saying nothing, waiting to see where this was going.

"Sometimes I feel a bit jealous of Adam and his having a black friend."

"Right – eh" Mike thought this odd and yet sensed it was serious.

"I was thinking about this the other night. I couldn't get to sleep and I was thinking about different things and this sort of came into my head. I thought to myself: I wish I had a black friend like Adam Cupples has a black friend."

"And other than the irrationality of the night, do you think there was any reason for this thought? Was your guilty conscience keeping you awake?"

"Nothing irrational about it at all mate: in fact I would say things are often much clearer in the middle of the night. I thought to myself: I wish I had a black friend. And this went on some more and I thought: I wish I had a Moslem friend. I wish I had a black friend and I wish I had a Moslem friend and I wish I had a gay friend."

"Is this like Granny goes shopping?" Mike asked. "Are you going to put me over all these friends of yours and ask me to recite them in the right order?"

"No, no, not at all: I'm being perfectly serious here. And then I thought, I wish I had a Catholic friend, and I wish I had a Polish friend or a Latvian friend – you know: someone from one of those migrant worker communities. And an atheist friend: that would be good too. I wish I had one of those as well. A real stroppy and belligerent atheist."

"You'd of got on well with Sammy Davis Junior, wouldn't you?" Mike said. "He was black and he was Jewish – not that you're necessarily looking for a Jew – and he was very small as well and I *think* – but don't quote me on this – I think he only had one good eye or only one of something, which technically made him disabled. He'd have killed a brave number of birds with one stone."

"The point I'm trying to make is that there must be a sort of enriching quality about having a friend like Peter. He's from a different background, a different culture, a different place – and that's very refreshing from all of your friends being – well – being people like you are. It's bound to open your eyes and open your mind in some ways. It's got to. I mean take the gay thing for instance."

"I'd rather not…"

"Between you and I – well, I think you know where we both stand on it – I've got a very straight laced view of homosexuality. Sure you've only to look at the plumbing that men and women have to see that men go with women and that's just the natural way of things. But then I think that no matter how right I am up, I've also got to admit to myself that I'm – well I'm downright homophobic. And a lot of that is probably because I don't actually *know* any gay people."

"Maybe you do" Mike replied, raising his eyebrows suggestively. "Maybe it's the ones you least suspect – maybe Peter and Adam are like Eric and Ernie and they sit up in bed together and talk in their button-up pyjamas."

"Oh be serious. You see, gay people are just an abstract concept to me. If I truly called a poof a friend what impact would that have on me? Nothing is personalised. It's the same with Moslems. What if I had a Moslem friend who supported a football team like me, and liked gadgets like me, and liked the same clothes I like, but he also believed that Sharia law should come to Ireland and thought all white girls were sluts? Then views like that wouldn't just be 'what Moslem people think': they'd be the living, breathing views of *my friend* and I'd have to really confront all my own views and prejudices and all."

"Hmmm" Alan muttered. "Would you have them all round at the same time for diversity dinner parties or would you just see them individually? You could have them all round at the house and lead them in a chorus of 'I'd like to teach the world to sing'. Are you going soft?"

"I'm not going soft" he replied. "I've just been thinking: that's all. It's not always a good idea, is it?"

"I think I preferred you when you were Fred Flintstone."

"I mean the worst one is Catholics, isn't it? You know, I can't think of a genuine friend of mine who is a Roman Catholic. Isn't that terrible? What hope is there of a new future for this country if people like me don't have any Catholic friends? I went to the chip shop last night for my tea on the way home. This woman called Nadia served me. She asked me whether I wanted salt and vinegar on my chips in this very Slavic accent."

"Sort of like a Bond Girl?"

"That type of thing: you've no idea how sexy 'do you want salt or vinegar on this' can be when it's said in the right way. And there was a sort of sultry disdain about it all – or maybe I just imagined that. And anyhow – I sort of felt pity for her: she's come all the way from some Baltic state and she's probably a teacher or a social worker or something and she's serving me chips. And then I thought about her again when I couldn't sleep and I thought: that person who served me chips is a far rounder person than me in many ways, because she's gone and made a whole new life for herself in a new culture. She's really *done* something. She was lovely looking by the way – a real foxy piece of stuff. There must be something special about a girl who works in a chip shop but has a complexion like *that*. I could hardly see me serving chips in Warsaw."

"No I could hardly see you serving chips in Warsaw either. Or dumplings or whatever it is they eat there."

"I wish I'd gone away you know. I really wish I'd got out of here for a few years. I didn't even go away to University like some people did. I mean – don't get me wrong – I love here, and I'd definitely have come back. But I wish I'd gone away for a bit."

"Tell me about it. You don't know what it is to wish you'd gone away."

"The thing is" Alan said "right, this sounds odd, but the problem is that it's as if all my friends – *all* my friends – are – crisps. OK? They're all crisps. I'm a crisp and you're a crisp and so are they. There's cheese and onion and there's salt and vinegar and there's prawn cocktail and so on. Ordinary good people: salt and vinegar of the earth, so to speak – if you'll excuse the pun. Dozer would be a cheese and onion crisp: a solid kind of guy but – you know what I mean; he's just cheese and onion. But then you have people like Rodney: the way he travels; the books he reads; the music he listens to; into his Radio Four – more like Radio Bore I think – and really good at table quizzes and all. He'd be a sweet Thai chilli or a sea salt and black pepper. He's a really interesting Prod: but he's still a crisp.

Everyone I know is a crisp. To me a person I know who is 'really interesting' is actually someone just like me but only a little broader minded. Crisps, crisps, and crisps: and there's this whole world out there of onion bhajis and samosas and spring rolls and poppadums that is all just passing me by."

Mike only wanted to get bark chips and get the job done. He hadn't bargained for this. But he felt the need to respond encouragingly to his friend's philosophising.

"Well why don't you do something about it?" he suggested. "Why don't you ask this babe – we'll call her chip shop girl – out for a date?"

"Oh don't be stupid: who knows what she is? Poland: I suppose she'd be a Catholic. Sure there are plenty of them here."

"Good wee Irish catholic girls. Ave Maria and away you go! I wouldn't say there's too many of them now."

"I'd end up yoked to an unbeliever. That would be bad enough: never mind an unbeliever who cries all the time for Warsaw and wants to take me there every summer to spend my holidays in a one-bedroom flat with her mother and eight younger brothers. And a Granny in the corner with no teeth who says nothing but just stares me out: I bet she'd have a Granny who just sits there covered in a big Polish shawl."

"Flip, you've changed your tune quick enough. What were you saying about meeting different people and broadening your mind? Anyhow, would you not be eating the dumplings over a candlelit table for two, with you beaming and saying all dreamily: 'and tell me Chip Shop Girl, *how* exactly do you make these?' There'd maybe be an age old recipe passed down by that very Granny in the shawl. Sure you could always witness to her."

Alan exaggerated an elongated sigh and sat deflated for a few moments. "I could always witness to her" he said, sounding as if that would be the last thing he would want to do. "That's another thing about us, isn't it? Everything is saving people and converting them and so on. Why could I not just like her for her mind and her culture?"

"And her looks."

"Why could I not just value her for who she is rather than making some holy target board out of her? Well – I suppose if I really did love her, I'd want to see her saved, wouldn't I? But I'd fancy an opportunity to snog her as much as anything!"

They were almost at their destination. Mike tore into the car park and flung the van into an available space with an abandon he thought might lift his friend. "Yabba-dabba-doo big lad. Come on and load some bark chips, and I'll buy you a packet of crisps."

8

Peter

As a large tray of tea, crockery and cutlery was set on the table in the middle of the men, Alan did the needful and distributed the tools of the job. The Thursday just past had been St Patrick's Day: most of them had taken Friday off as well and were now communing for breakfast on the Saturday morning at Wee Florrie's café on High Street.

"So then guys, what did you all get up to on St Patrick's Day?" Peter enthused. He was almost knocked back by the indifference. Mike shrugged his shoulders but was polite enough to answer the stranger.

"Good question. What *do* you do on St Patrick's Day? Play with the kids? Do those DIY jobs you're getting nagged about forever and a day? You tell us. What did you get up to on St Patrick's Day Peter?"

"Well I did what I would have thought was a pretty natural thing to do. I got in my car and went to the St Patrick's Day parade in Down*patrick*."

John coughed so hard on his cup of tea that some of it ended up his nose.

"Hey guys. Why would I not have done?"

"Why would you Peter?" Mike asked. "The St Patrick's Day Parade! I'm sure that was great craic. Did you see any snakes being smite?"

Large plates of big food were now being dispersed; knives and forks unwrapped in readiness for an attack. Alan chipped into the debate. "My mum was a teacher and whenever I think of St Patrick's Day I always think of her subbing in this school in a really loyalist area and it was the day before the holiday and this wee fella says 'Miss, sure why *do* we do get St Patrick's Day off: he was a fenian anyway?'"

They all laughed with the exception of Peter.

"So what did your Mum say to this lad?" Adam asked.

"Oh she just told him not to worry about that. Sure wasn't he getting a day off school, whatever St Patrick was?"

"So tell us" John said: "what is a St Patrick's Day in Downpatrick actually like?"

"Well it was a fairly eclectic mix of the tasteful and the tacky. A bit of Christianity and more than a bit of secular carnival all thrown in to the pot. You have Saint Patrick himself walking along and then a few minutes later you have Postman Pat! There were all sorts of dancers: there were people juggling and spinning plates; there was an old VW campervan done up like Scooby Doo's Mystery Machine; and there were people walking along on stilts in strange costumes. I have to say the people were very friendly but it looked to me as if spiritually it could do with being all shook up."

He stopped and looked at his plate. "Eh, what's this soggy thing I have on my breakfast: kind of like a misshapen Frisbee or something?"

Alan looked over. "Oh that" he said: "that's a soda farl."

"A what?"

"Soda farl: it's a type of bread. Eat up: they're great."

"I suppose what I was really struck by was that from what I've read Ireland was very much a Pagan country when Patrick came over in the fifth century: his legacy was that in the midst of this paganism he evangelised and turned people to Christian faith. I mean there were other aspects of legacy as well, but really Christianity is it. So it seemed strange that there was rather more of the pagan – and *pagan* is perhaps too strong a word but you know what I mean – than there was of the Christian in that festival."

Alan interrupted his flow. "If you don't want that soda farl, I'll eat it."

Peter continued. "The strange thing is guys; you don't take St Patrick or want him. But I reckon you're all missing a tremendous example who's sitting right under your nose. He's so wonderfully obvious I can't believe you don't see it."

Mike wasn't in the mood for this. "Are those magic mushrooms mate, because mine seem pretty ordinary?"

This irritated Peter who was on a roll. "Oh come on guys, don't you get it? Think about it! Who was St Patrick? What was his story? Patrick was a young British boy who was captured by the Irish on a raid they made in Britain: they snatched him and took him back as a slave to Ireland. Can you imagine the pain of that? To be a young boy taken away from all you know in terms of culture and friends and family and lose all of that security. To be thrown into the shock and coarseness of slavery in a different place with a different language and nothing that is familiar."

"I fancy more tea" said Jim. "Does anyone else want more tea?" Without waiting for a response he waved over to the waitress.

"The point is: would Patrick have wanted to be here? Hell No! And let's face it – do you guys want to be here?"

"Give me your soda farl there" Alan said, and without an answer, he stretched his arm across Willie's face and lifted his quarry from Peter's plate.

Not sure how to respond to being mugged for a piece of bread, Peter carried on. "From a lot of what you say I wouldn't say you definitely don't want to be here but let's be honest: you're hardly chuffed either! St Patrick wouldn't have wanted to be here and you don't want to be here. But despite the fact that he couldn't have been content with the cruel providence of God that twisted and turned him to Ireland look at the legacy he left."

The waitress had arrived now. "Eh – another two pots of tea please" said Jim.

"St Patrick could have so easily gone to pieces: no reasonable man could have criticised him if he'd lost his faith. But instead he embraced adversity and by the grace of God he rose to the challenge. He wouldn't have chosen to be here but God used him to bring Christianity to Ireland: in terms of a man 'making his mark' I wouldn't say it gets much bigger than that."

"I'll eat those mushrooms as well if you're not having them"

Alan said, reaching his plate over and gesturing to Peter to slide the mushrooms on to it.

"When you think about it like that I reckon it's ridiculous that the way you folks think of St Patrick's Day is about washing cars and laying floors. If *anyone* should be celebrating and embracing St Patrick in this New Ireland it's people like you. He brought Christianity to this island and we're sitting in this coffee shop talking about him 1,600 years after he walked this land. Just like you he didn't want to be here: so what are you going to do to follow his example and be like him?"

* * * * *

It was a fresh winter's morning and the town's generously expansive park was just a short walk from the cafe. Nobody was in a hurry to get away and they were soon revisiting their earlier conversation in the breezy environs of the park's tree lined avenue. There was momentary quiet among the group as their assorted conversations seemed to pause in harmony. Peter seized the opportunity to revisit the themes he had been unpacking earlier.

"The interesting thing about Patrick is that I was doing my bible reading on Thursday evening and it hit me straight between the eyes that here was this biblical character that had tremendous parallels with your saint. It was the first chapter of Daniel. Nebuchadnezzar besieged Jerusalem and in the same way that Patrick was taken back to slavery in Ireland so some of the best young Jewish men were taken back to Babylon to serve in the royal household.

There are some great lessons from Daniel about how to live well in a place where you don't want to be: like Daniel's perspective – he had a clear sense of what mattered and what to let go. Daniel and his friends said yes to things as well as saying no: no matter how strong your convictions are, you need to realise that saying no to *everything* is simply not an option. So they said yes to changing their names and to learning the language and literature of Babylon but they drew the line at eating defiled food."

Adam wasn't paying close attention to his friend's ramblings, as he was distracted by Jim's behaviour. "Are you alright Jim?" he asked. "Do you want to sit down or take a wee break?"

"Oh I'm fine" Jim responded, rolling his eyes and rubbing his chest. "Fries in the morning don't seem to agree with me anymore. I feel like I've eaten defiled food myself: they give me awful heartburn. I've more repeats on me than BBC1."

"The question for you guys is: what truly matters? There's a lot of symbolic stuff that it's so easy to get worked up about: like currency and flags and street signs in the Irish language. In the grand scheme of things how much do any of those *really* matter? But then there are other things that fundamentally should be problems for you."

"Aye" John complained. "Like the Catholic practice of Mass on a Saturday night to free up Sunday for other things. That's not right: Sunday should be a separate day of worship to God."

Peter grimaced. "Well, that's not really the sort of thing I was thinking of. But Sunday is really being rolled back to be a day just like any other in terms of shopping and sport and so on. Maybe that's a way where you should take your stand. Or maybe take your stand is the wrong way of putting it: maybe that's where you try to set a better example and be different from those around you."

"I'm coming under more and more pressure to work on a Sunday" Mike said. "It's getting harder and harder to say no."

"Is the fair Stella on her high horse about it?" Alan asked.

"More like her broomstick."

Jim butted in: "Is that really such a bad thing: mass on a Saturday night. Sure didn't the Jewish Sabbath start at sunset on a Friday? Is it really so bad if they start their Sunday on the evening of the day before: sure mustn't Jesus have done the same thing."

"What about education?" Mike asked. "I mean historically, there was always a clear division between Protestant and Catholic schools. We would have had our RE and the local ministers coming in to do assemblies and all those things. But obviously the mix of numbers has changed and the education system is being put together, yet I'd still like to see *some* of those connections between our traditions and schools maintained. I don't want to have to explain to my five year old why it's such a big tickle that 'wee Bridget' is having her first communion. Why should she have to deal with that at her age?"

"But take it one step back" Peter said. "Roll back to where you were a minute ago. Why can't your child be educated with those other kids and not still have her own identity? How can you help them to be different without being separate? You can be among people but not conformed to them."

John and Willie were starting to lag behind. John whispered to Willie. "I wish to hell he would give us all a break and go and be separate from us. He's starting to get on my nerves."

Peter was oblivious to this. "Another interesting aspect of Daniel's character is that as well as having good discernment he had good *attitude*. When you read on into the second chapter and Nebuchadnezzar is losing the plot and decreeing that all the magicians and astrologers are for the chop – because he's had an awful dream and wants it interpreted but they can't even tell him the dream – we're told that Daniel responded to the situation with 'wisdom and tact'.

In the first chapter when Daniel and his friends want to eat good vegetables instead of the supposedly fine but defiled Babylonian food, he obviously has sufficient relationships to extract that concession. Spiritual intelligence is all very well but it isn't much use if we don't have emotional intelligence. You're in a minority now and tact will benefit you more than bloody mindedness. And that doesn't mean that you become a doormat community because it's obvious that Daniel was very adept at retaining his identity. So a good attitude matters too."

John snorted in indignation at this point. "I'm sure what you're saying is very worthy but it's all hypothetical, isn't it? I mean we don't have much choice: it's not as if we can be anything other than tactful. The horse has bolted and is several miles down the road: we're hardly going to dig our heels in *now* and insist that Ulster says 'No'. And I'd remind you Peter that it also tells us in the Bible to be shrewd as snakes and innocent as doves. High principle is all very well but you need to be realistic about the world we're living in."

"Point taken John" Peter said. "But Daniel wasn't some cardboard cut out figure in a 'gentle Jesus meek and mild' fairy tale. He was mixing it in circumstances that are as tough as it gets. He was right in there and sticking his neck out in the court of a despot: Nebuchadnezzar was a head-case. And tact was part of how Daniel dealt with this King and his minions. Another aspect of Daniel's example is the friendships he had. Maybe I'm overdoing things here and getting into too much speculation..."

"Maybe you are" John said.

"But part of their capacity to cope must have been drawn from their relationships with one another. Later on in the book three of the friends are confronted by the prospect of the fiery furnace on account of their refusal to worship a gold image commissioned by Nebuchadnezzar. *All* three of them stand together when they face the king and *all* three of them are together as they go into the furnace. You're a group of six so think how much *you* can support each other."

They were walking past the expanse of the park's lake and the calm of the waters and the seeming contentedness of swimming ducks prompted them to stop for a break. The ducks ambled through the water and quacked hopefully but there was no sustenance on offer. "Every time I see ducks" Alan said "it reminds me of one of my favourite lines from a song: how on earth does a man duck tell his wife from all the other ducks? Or something to that effect: epic line".

"Funny thing about ducks" Mike said "is the difference between the husbands and the wives. I mean there's not many animals, is there – and you can include us in this – where the man is so damn better looking than the woman."

"Maybe" Alan suggested "you tell your husband by the gait of his waddle or the pitch of his quack or something like that."

Mike glanced at his watch and in an instance his face turned to horror: "Hey lads: enough of ducks and Daniel; I'm going to be a dead duck if I don't get myself home pronto."

And with a spring in their step they started heading back to their cars. "The other interesting thing I noticed about Daniel" Peter said "is the extent to which he and his friends started off with the disadvantaged status of prisoners and ended up being men of enormous power in Babylon. At the end of the second chapter when Daniel's stock has risen so dramatically, he requests that Shadrach, Meshach and Abednego should also be given positions of responsibility. Instead of wringing their hands at the nature of this regime and sitting in judgement on it, these young men have the opportunity and then the guts to influence from the inside. That's the equivalent of talented young 'Unionists' being prepared to sit in government with Sinn Fein. You guys are always going on about 'Adams and McGuinness' but Nebuchadnezzar was hardly pure as the driven snow."

"Hmmm" Alan said. "Maybe Big Ian got it all wrong then: maybe Ulster says No and all the years of never-never-never wasn't such a good idea. Though he fairly changed his tune in his twilight years."

"Well he hardly had much choice, or so he said" Mike replied. "Though I tell you what, he must have made Trimble sick as a dog: all the abuse he gave the UUP and then he turned round and jumped into bed with the Shinners himself when it suited him."

"Now that's very simplistic: Ian Paisley was a wonderful man" Jim announced.

"History is gone and you cannot influence the past" Peter said. "But never-never-never makes no sense at all. Look at how some of your politicians got on. Would Daniel have done the same? I bet Daniel sat with Nebuchadnezzar, I bet he shook Nebuchadnezzar's hand: he would certainly have shaken Gerry Adams' hand: it's far more courageous to engage with a threat head on than stick your head in the sand."

They were back at the cars now. Mike took Alan with him and they scorched out of the swimming pool gates and sped off to make peace. The others leant back on the boots of cars to let the sunshine gently lick their faces. The calm of the moment invited Peter to make his final point.

"Do you know what I reckon the most fundamental thing about Daniel was? His faith. I accept that we're not all gifted to be men of great learning and hold our own in corridors of power, and we're certainly not all gifted to discern and interpret dreams. But we can all have faith. And hey: some faith.

He was a Jew. He worshiped Yahweh, the great I am. He worshiped the God of Abraham, Isaac and Jacob: the God who showed Abraham stars in the heavens that mirrored how numerous his descendants would be; the God who took his people out of Egypt and into the Promised Land. The God who helped a small boy defeat a giant with just five small stones. The story of his faith wasn't just about Abraham and Moses and David though: it was about Israel, about the story of a whole nation. And now Israel was gone – and he kept on believing – he had faith. We can all have a bit of that Daniel faith: we can even call it Patrick faith cause it seems to me like it all came out of the same bottle."

Across the car park a harassed family had frantically found a parking space and eager toddlers were piling out to swim. A small girl with bunches gave one hand to her mother and gripped her Cinderella rucksack with the other.

"Look at that" Adam said. "Life goes on. Good things still happen, don't they?" And he looked upwards and seemed to speak to himself then, as much as he spoke to the others. "The sky is still there and it hasn't fallen in. The sky is still there and good things still happen."

9

Mike

Mike Matthews was in a twist. He had had a truly awful day at work. He didn't like his boss and was convinced she didn't like him. (He was right). But he was 'good living' so had to be civil and self-controlled with her. His temperament was not entirely fruit and his heart had very little spirit. He actually thought the woman was a cow; a battleaxe; a witch; a dragon. He couldn't say any of this and his faith did not technically allow him to think it either. But think it he did. Mike's boss was an abject defeat to him every time he went to work.

Today he had scuffed a car against a bollard whilst manoeuvring it on to the forecourt, and had to face 'Stepford Stella' and tell her what he had done. (This is how she was referred to when he was at home. It was a high risk way of letting off steam: he knew it was only a matter of time before one of the children met her and called her this to her face).

Worse than facing her with this bad news were the seemingly endless minutes that it took him to find her. These were spent rehearsing the mealy words he would serve to her and predicting her smashes and volleys back. As it happened she was surprisingly reasonable about it all. Which was good because she could have been so nasty; but bad because he was forced to momentarily adjust his view of her and lessen his victim status.

When he got home he had a dull headache forming behind his eyes, and a tense neck and shoulders. His headlights lit up the front of the house when he steered into the driveway and his view was dominated by three toddlers excitedly pressing their hands and faces to the lounge window. It was 6.33 and he wondered if anything interesting had happened in football today. So he let the car and himself idle for a few minutes and listened to the headlines.

A look of daggers greeted him when he got in, and a smell of disinfectant nearly overpowered him. Where had he been? Sophie had been cleaning the bathroom. With the toilet brush: and with the water from the toilet. She did a thorough job: the floor; the sink; the bath; and some of the tiles. She had been helping.

After a frenzied hour of tea and tantrums, baths and books, he found himself slumped in an armchair, his mind masticating on a newspaper. There were slams coming from the kitchen and he felt tangibly alone. His head was really thumping now. There was Champions League football on the box and it was kicking off in ten minutes but away seemed a better prospect than home. The house group would get him out: anything was better than this. He squeezed his wife from behind and whispered that he was sorry, because he knew he had to, and because he really was. And he picked up his Bible and found his coat and drove out of Egypt to visit the wandering in the desert.

Strangers in a strange land

Mike was – as always – the last one there. Alan called it MST: Matthews' Standard Time. "Here he comes, bang on the dot. Eight o'clock MST. Have you had a bad day, big lad? You're looking rough."

"Oh you know how it is – well, you don't actually" Mike replied. "I'm not too bad. There's no point complaining: sure nobody would listen anyway." His friend made a chorus of those last words he uttered, chuckling carelessly.

"The reading" said John – who had paused as Mike came in – "is from Jeremiah chapter seven and verses one to fifteen. Listen for the word of God:

This is the word that came to Jeremiah from the LORD: "Stand at the gate of the LORD'S house and there proclaim this message:

"'Hear the word of the LORD, all you people of Judah who come through these gates to worship the LORD. This is what the LORD Almighty, the God of Israel says: Reform your ways and your actions,

and I will let you live in this place. Do not trust in deceptive words and say, "This is the temple of the LORD, the temple of the LORD, the temple of the LORD!" If you really change your ways and your actions and deal with each other justly, if you do not oppress the alien, the fatherless or the widow and do not shed innocent blood in this place, and if you do not follow other gods to your own harm, then I will let you live in this place, in the land I gave your forefathers for ever and ever. But look, you are trusting in deceptive words that are worthless.

" 'Will you steal and murder, commit adultery and perjury, burn incense to Baal and follow other gods you have not known, and then come and stand before me in this house, which bears my Name, and say, "We are safe" – safe to do all these detestable things? Has this house, which bears my Name, become a den of robbers to you? But I have been watching! declares the LORD.

"'Go now to the place in Shiloh where I first made a dwelling for my Name, and see what I did to it because of the wickedness of my people Israel. While you were doing all these things, declares the LORD, I spoke to you again and again, but you did not listen; I called you, but you did not answer. Therefore, what I did to Shiloh I will now do to the house that bears my Name, the temple you trust in, the place I gave to you and your fathers. I will thrust you from my presence, just as I did all your brothers, the people of Ephraim."

John opened the study in the manner that he always did: verbatim and a little faltering and looking at the book rather than the group. It was a rat-a-tat-tat of four questions in a row. "What was the attitude of the Israelites as they approached worship? What deceptive words were the Israelites using? Why were they appealing? In what ways might your church be clinging to deceptive words? Well gentlemen: there's certainly plenty to keep us going there."

The attitude of the Israelites was relatively straightforward to deduce. But the words of the prophet were stark and direct: extracting the obvious did not have the tick box simplicity they often found in such exercises. The trust of the children of Israel had been in the rituals and formalities of temple worship rather than an authentic worship of God through right living that honoured justice and gave Him His proper place.

Reading it twice over or even a third time showed that there was more to it than even that. A 'more to it' that was deeply uncomfortable because there appeared to be a deal on the table for the people of God. If you don't change your act and start living the way God expects then you will not continue to live in this land. If you don't believe Him, go and look at Shiloh. And it's not as if this is the first time God has warned you. You are foolish enough to believe that just by conforming to certain religious mores you can get away with this behaviour. You are taking God for granted and God commands – in the most serious terms imaginable – that you wake up and smell the coffee. But whilst the clock might be ticking down to midnight it's not yet too late: it is absolutely in your gifting to change the course the future will take.

"I wonder" Jim said "how consciously sinful these people were. God is telling them to change and they were evidently falling short of what He expected. Did they think of the temple as a means of wiping God's eye or was it all less deliberate than that? Were they just going about their everyday business and taking their eye off the ball – a kind of falling short in percentages – or was it more fundamental than that?"

Peter requested that the questions be read again. And read again they were: with pauses for emphasis and digestion.

"What was the *attitude* of the Israelites as they approached worship? …*What* deceptive words were the Israelites using? … *Why* were they appealing? …In what ways might *your* church be clinging to deceptive words?"

"It's just like last time, isn't it?" Alan said. "I can only speak for myself. I'm scared that if I approach this from the context of our situation then I'm reading something into it that isn't there. But in being so rational I could miss the point altogether. Did we put our trust in wrong words? Things like 'Ulster says No' and 'No surrender' and 'For God and Ulster'. Were those deceptive words? But does that have anything to do with God and religion?"

"I suppose" Adam suggested "it depends on how you view

the word deceiving. They weren't deceiving in the sense that they were uttered in good faith. But we deceived ourselves – or certainly a large proportion of our community – deceived ourselves when we stuck to those words as kinds of mantra instead of forming a more constructive vision of the future. And of course there are different views of words and why words are *appealing*. Words can be appealing in an intellectual sense: they have a form and reason that leads from A to D with logic for why B and C are in there. But ours were more about a forceful appeal: shout it loud enough and often enough and no one can doubt your passion and you make yourself feel strong. But we were misguided in believing our own publicity."

"But is that *really* the same as in this passage?" Jim asked. "The people of Israel were trusting in false words and that was religion gone wrong: that was all about their relationship with God. Which – I think anyway – is different to our situation. One is religious and one is political."

"But can you separate them" Adam replied. "I mean, let's be honest, in Northern Ireland the political and the religious were deeply entwined. There was this unspoken maxim that if you were a Protestant then you were a Unionist – and by extension of that you were also a Conservative and generally right of centre in your entire political orientation – you wanted tax cuts – you weren't too fussed on immigration – you read the Daily Mail. You only had to look at the DUP: it had its own religious wing called the Free Presbyterian Church."

"So what does that mean then?" Jim said. "If Ireland being united is a punishment from God then what is he punishing..."

"...*I'm* not saying it's a punishment..."

"...If – I said *if*" Jim snapped, the colour in his face rising. "If Ireland being united is a punishment then what's being punished? Is it a political thing because we put our trust in second-rate politicians or is it a religious thing because we weren't up to the mark? And if it is political then we're back to the thing of why would he punish us over the other lot? And if it's a spiritual thing, then why would God punish an entire community simply because the religious portion of it underperformed? God is just and that's not just."

"I don't know" Adam said, defensively. "How do I know? What about how many angels dance on a pinhead: that might be easier? Is it right that we view everything in terms of us, them, and God? Maybe part of the challenge is that we've just got to exclude them from our thinking and confine ourselves to worrying about us and God.

Maybe one of our problems over the last forty to fifty years is that we made the errors of Catholicism and what we think are the sins of Republicans our moral compass. Maybe that was the deceit. Have you never heard the phrase 'monopoly of truth': we think because we have sounder doctrine that makes us in some way spiritually superior to them when the reality is that we may have guarded our doctrine closely but our behaviour has let us down a bucketful."

"Well we do have sounder doctrine" said Jim.

"I agree Jim. You know what? I think Catholics are totally up the left in some of what they believe but that's no reason for me to be arrogant. My assurance should come from what Jesus has done for me, not from what other people don't happen to believe." He jabbed his finger at his own chest for emphasis.

"Maybe the grand lie we told ourselves was judging ourselves against crooked plumb lines rather than the real holiness we read about in the Bible. I once heard someone say that the problem with evangelicals is that they ought to be the most radical people in society yet we're probably amongst the least radical. What about big houses and expensive cars? What about fancy clothes even if we are virtuous and don't drink or smoke or do the lottery? What about all the petty nonsense we get caught up in within churches, instead of going out there and engaging with people and getting our hands dirty?"

"I think we get your drift" Mike said.

Alan took up the baton. "I think the interesting thing about the passage is what it suggests about how history happens. I'm no philosopher but I suppose a question to ask is: how does history work? Is history something that just happens to me and carries me along, or is history something that I help to make happen?

A good example is the way that Christians talk whenever they're applying for jobs. 'If you're not in you can't win.' 'If it's for you it won't go past you.' 'I'm just going to push the door and see if it happens.' The basic attitude is that if I pray about it then whatever way it works out must be the will of God. I call it 'Christian fatalism': God just carries me along and whatever will be will be. The effort I put into preparing for the job interview – trying to anticipate questions and finding out about the employer – are nothing to do with it: I'm absolved of responsibility because it's all down to God."

"I'm not so sure about that" Willie said. "I think it depends where people are. I think some people view the future as something very much in their own hands when they're looking into it. But when they look back at the past they – well they don't romanticise it – but they spiritualise it. 'Oh I can see now why we didn't get that house and so on.' They're pragmatic in the present but holy in hindsight. "

Jim raised his eyebrows: "I know who holds the future and He guides it with His hands..."

"Ok" Alan said. "I know I'm generalising a bit. But evangelicals – well, most of them – are very into 'the providence of God' and 'the sovereignty of God'." He made a serious face to emphasise the outlook of his peers. "That kind of makes us puppets on a string so that we have no say at all in whether Ireland is united. We're all just chess pieces with God moving us about the board. Is there a relationship between the convictions some people have about Calvinism and predestination and the fact that so many Protestants have such a victim mindset about the unification? And yet common sense says we obviously have free will and can determine actions and consequences: our politicians made bad calls and theirs outsmarted us and that's part of why all this has happened."

"But you're throwing the baby out with the bath water" John argued. "You're practically saying that God doesn't come into it at all."

"I'm not. I can't define how it all works but I believe that

God is sovereign and yet our own actions help to determine the course that events take."

"So you want to have your cake and eat it" rebutted John.

"But that's what the passage says. The Israelites' free will to trust in the wrong things and God's sovereignty to guide the consequences of that combine. Whether it's a punishment or not both we and God have had a hand in Ireland being united."

He heaved a sigh. "And now it is *my* free will that I need another caramel square. The body is the temple of the Lord so why not put on an extension?" And he reached out a hand.

John saw his chance. "I suppose we've been kind of talking about this anyway but the next question asks 'In what ways did the Israelites need to change? What is the connection between worship and how we live our lives?'"

Peter had been uncharacteristically quiet. "Well it's quite straightforward isn't it? The question almost contains the answer. The point is that there *is* a connection between worship and how we live our lives. It can't be worship on a Sunday and then carte blanche to live as we want to the rest of the week."

"Tell me about it" Jim said. "I remember going to a funeral years ago of this guy I worked for. That man made my life hell. Turned out he was a great man for the church. I have this recollection of being about half way through the sermon and wanting to look at the order of service to make sure I hadn't got the wrong church!"

"Some people" Peter continued "are very into the notion of intention in the Christian faith. That much of the way you live is about being intentional: every event and every day present a series of choices in which we can decide to engage and act as a Christian ought to. Spiritual transformation is all about being conscious of God, and making the right decisions. Which ties into what Alan said about free will, and whether we're hapless bystanders in our own lives, or we really have the power to shape and influence."

Adam developed this thought. "Which goes back to what I was saying earlier: evangelicals should be the most radical members of society but are actually amongst the least radical.

We may not be philosophically conformed to the values of the world, but we're very conformed to its standards when it comes to things like cars and houses and clothes and so on."

"Yes" John said. "I think we got that earlier."

"But even behavioural things too: how truly different is a Christian when it comes to gossip around the coffee station at work? How different is a Christian when it comes to covering his ass or passing the buck? You know, I've always been fascinated by the difference between goodness and holiness. I truly believe I live well, but holy, well that's another matter…"

He leaned back and scratched his stomach – as if he had more to say.

"But this" Alan said "makes me go back to something I know I've said here before. When I look back at my upbringing and consider my memories of how the church was, there was no effort to connect worship to how we live our lives in a Northern Ireland context. We were living in one of the most divided parts of Western Europe, and yet there was little or no effort to link our faith to our – what would you call it – our environment. That was alright for those lefty-woolly people at Corrymeela and ECONI and the like – the beards and Moses sandals brigade – whilst the rest of us sat on our high horses and looked down our noses on them and preached about *truth*…"

And Mike cut in with his sore head that had been winding up all night and raised his voice to say "Will you all give over and listen to yourselves. Guys, I have had nothing but *shit* all day."

Jim tried to catch Willie's eye to see if it would meet his in embarrassment but for some reason Willie didn't seem bothered at what had just been said.

"And now I have to sit and listen to – to – all this clever dick historical revisionism – and flagellating – what awful people Ulster Protestants were and how they did this and they didn't do that. Listen to yourselves! Do you know who Ulster Protestants are and were? People like you and me. Give over passing judgement because – you know – we may have ballsed up a few things and not been perfect holy Joes and all – but you'd think we were collaborators in France or Fascists in Italy the way you're all talking. I mean – just – just don't get your knickers all in such a twist. Alright."

Adam came straight back with a raised voice:

"But that's the point! That's exactly the point. That's what I mean when I talk about the difference between good and holy. Of course we're not like Vichy France or Mussolini's Italy: but our moral compass is not collaborators or Fascists. And look, what are you really saying? Yes, I agree we're not bad people: we're not bad people in the sense that IRA bombers and UVF gunmen were bad people. But nobody is bad compared to them. If you think about – 'and what does the Lord require of you? To act justly and to love mercy and to walk humbly with your God?' – if you think about that, then most of us are bad Mike. I think most of us are pretty bad. And I'm not God and I can't make sense of it all but that might have something to do with how we've got to where we're at."

"Bad people!" Mike said. "Bad people? Am I hearing you right? Adam, if you want bad people I'll show you bad people. I'll take you up the Falls Road to Connolly House and show you bad people. If God is God and He's going to judge me then that's fair enough but I'll tell you this for free: He'll judge them a damn site harder because there's no fire too hot for some of that filth. Are you telling me that God is rewarding them – *them* – just so he can punish us?"

"Mike, I'm not telling you anything. I'm just saying that God is not a relativist. The judgement day isn't going to be a case of giving us all a score for what sort of people we were and the top ten per cent will get in. It's not a transfer test to Heaven. Look: you're not asking anything new, are you? I mean there must have been angry young Jews who questioned what on earth God was playing at when the Babylonians were marching them into captivity"

"Adam" Jim said "just to put you over this again – to be sure I'm picking you up right – do you really believe it is God's will for Ireland to be united?"

"Jim" Adam replied quick as a flash: "to be sure I'm picking you up right? Do you really believe that God is sovereign?"

"Yes, it's all very well saying that" Jim said "and it's very clever to answer a question with a question. But you and Alan want it both ways. You want to pin it all on God because He is sovereign and you want to pin it all on us because we're not up to the mark: you're hedging your bets, aren't you? Would history have been different then if there had been some great revival and we had all turned to God? If God had found fifty righteous people in Belfast would he have spared the whole place for their sake?"

Adam uncrossed his legs, and rapidly crossed them again in the opposite direction, as if to stop himself from stamping his feet in temper.

"Jim – grow up! Ireland has been unified. Sodom and Gomorrah were destroyed. You're comparing apples and oranges and you know you are."

Willie weighed in with a slow pace to his voice. "It's not A-B-C-D is it?"

"What?" Peter asked.

"It's not A-B-C-D: A – accept; B – believe; C – consider; D – do. I've been sitting and listening to you here and there's been all sorts of interesting points made. But I think one of our biggest problems – and Mike, this isn't a bad thing – is that we like things to be certain. If you accept Christ to be your Saviour then you're going to Heaven, and if you don't then you're going to Hell.

We like things to be certain. As long as I can remember we've enjoyed a genuine assuredness as Protestants in terms of our convictions and our moral superiority to Republicanism. But all this talk about free will and the way our actions determine consequences make me ask who God is. Faith is being sure of what we hope for and certain of what we do not see. I do believe in Jesus: I know Him but until I pass into Glory I think I know Him in limited ways. The Bible is full of truth but it is not the whole story.

As long as I am a mere mortal on earth I know God in limited ways and part of that is the narrative of this island. Gentlemen: how can we ever be ultimately certain of God's view on Ireland as long as earthly bodies and limitations of his word confine us? We don't know. We can't know. God forgive all the people who put union jacks on the front of churches because we never knew enough to do that."

"You're right" Peter said. "You're so right. We think we see the world as God sees it but the truth is we don't. It was the same in my own land: many people I knew made it out that God was a black man. We need to recognise that part of faith is mystery. Much of what we generally call suffering is mystery: why do some people get cancer; why do some couples endure childlessness; why did Ireland go one way and not another? They're mysteries and we can do no more than speculate on these things. And of course like so many mysteries, even if you did know the truth behind it all, would you feel any better anyway? Remember how dismayed Adam and Eve were after they ate from the tree of knowledge."

Mike

When Mike arrived home that night the house was quiet with only the kitchen light on to guide him through the back garden. The floor remained awash with the flotsam of small children and the table had been set for next morning's breakfast.

Sophie had been painting earlier and now one of her works was blu-tacked above the table at the place where he sat: he recalled her telling him at bedtime that she had painted him a picture. And there it was now: random splashes of spontaneity with some bursts of shape and recognition among it. A head, a smile, and the wheels of a car. And in the top right hand corner words had been scribed with a bold black felt-tip in kind and round female writing: "Daddy likes reading the bible with all his friends." Two hugs and two kisses were added for good effect.

He felt a little touched and he felt a little torn. Something deep inside him made him regret that he could not just enjoy the innocence of the moment. And he remembered how dismayed Adam and Eve were after they ate from the tree of knowledge.

10

Peter

"So what was it like then?" Adam asked. "How did you find it?"

"With great difficulty" Peter replied. "Funnily enough, a black man stopping his car in the middle of nowhere in North East Ulster and asking an old woman where he would find some church seemed to leave her remarkably nonplussed."

Peter had spent his Sunday making an effort to go back to the start. This had taken him 60 miles away to the North Antrim coast and morning worship at the congregation where his Grandfather's Irish ministry had concluded over fifty years earlier.

He was subdued: not his normal self. "I don't know what I expected to find, but it was…" A look of regret crept across his face: "maybe the saddest thing is that I doubt it was very different from when Granddad was there. It felt like stepping back in time. I expect most of the people there today probably sat in those pews and heard him preach: there was hardly a head that wasn't grey at best."

"So it was quite dead then?"

"What?"

"So it was pretty dead?"

"What on earth does that mean? How can something be quite dead? Gee whizz: you're a doctor, aren't you. There's hardly degrees of deadness, is there?"

"Well, I suppose not…"

"I don't know how you'd describe it. Probably like most of the people in it: still going but on their last legs."

"And did you reveal yourself? Did you show your hand: you must have stood out like a sore finger?"

"No." It wasn't like Peter to be so peremptory.

"Why not?"

"Why not? What do you mean 'why not?' I was hardly going to make a scene: do a Dustin Hoffman at the end of The Graduate." He shrugged his shoulders. "I didn't go there for them. I went there for myself: I wanted to – I don't know – I just wanted to see what it was like."

It was a cold evening and the central heating had only just kicked in. Peter lowered his head into the neck of the fleece he was wearing and pulled the zip as far up as it would go. "What a vision of the church. Light of the world: more like some old torch with the battery about to give up the ghost. Granddad was right about them: I thought I might react to it all smugly and think to myself 'he told you so', but there's no pleasure in seeing a church like that."

Adam didn't know what to say: whether to try to change the subject or encourage his friend to talk more. "What was it actually happened? How did he go – I mean, what was it that made him go?"

Peter had his fist clenched to his mouth and sighed against it.

Adam back-peddled. "I mean… not… don't tell me if you don't want to go into it."

"No it's fine" Peter replied. "I mean there's not a whole lot to say. But he certainly went out with a bang more than a whimper."

"As is the family style."

"He was always a visual kind of man, Granddad – one for props and artefacts and a bit of theatre in the pulpit. And one day… well one day he went too far."

"How so?"

"Well he wanted to make a certain point: and he made the point so sharp he practically impaled himself on it. You know, Martin Luther King once said that a man one step ahead of the people was a leader but a man ten steps ahead of the people was a martyr. Granddad was about 15 steps ahead of his people: ahead of the people and ahead of his time. All this history you're going through now…" he said, raising his eyebrows.

Adam nodded.

"…Granddad could see it coming. He saw it coming like most Christians see the second coming of Christ: didn't know whether it's ten years or a hundred years off but believed it was a certain reality and was going to happen one day. They were tough sheep, his flock: stubborn as mules. And he was always falling out with them: flags; orange services in the church; reproaching bigotry. You know, the local priest went into a hardware shop one day and stood two hours before walking out when no one would serve him. And the owner of the shop was one of Granddad's elders."

Adam shook his head.

"Granddad wasn't one to miss and hit the wall. So one Sunday he gets into the pulpit and he has in his hand a figurine of William of Orange riding resplendent on his horse. He holds it up and out in front of the congregation and he says to them: 'God wants to ask you a question this morning: does this matter more to you than I matter to you?' Then he threw it up and caught it in one hand. 'And God has the answer to the question as well.' And at that he held it out beyond the pulpit and let it drop ten or 12 feet or whatever it was where it hit the floor and smashed into tiny pieces.'

Adam winced at the thought of it.

Peter saw what his friend was thinking. "I know" he said: "I shudder at it too. And then he finished. 'Fix your eyes and hearts on what is eternal: on what will never perish, spoil or fade. For God says that by your grandchildren's generation this Union will pass away, but my words will never fade away.'" He rubbed his right hand across his eyes.

"What a way to cook your goose" Adam said.

"Roasted" Peter responded. "Well and truly frazzled. But that was my Granddad for you: he believed that if God was saying something to him then it was better out than in." He got up and started walking out of the room, remarking as he went – as much to himself as to Adam: "I suppose I think that too…"

11

Alan

'There's plenty more fish in the sea'. That's what his friend had said to him: 'plenty more fish in the sea'. Here stood Alan Mackey: ready to go fishing again. And no better place, he thought, than the fish and chip shop. In the confines of his own imagination he liked that: the romantic circularity of it all gave him a good feeling. 'One man's coincidence' he reflected 'is another man's serendipity'.

He had continued to think about *that* girl in the chip shop: she did not depart his mind and indeed seemed to visit there with increasing frequency. He was now popping into the *Frying Saucer* at least once a week and altering routes and creating errands to walk past it. The little flutters in his stomach said she wasn't going away.

He had managed to catch her eyes a few times and liked what he saw. Her smile, he thought, was an absolute knockout, and he noticed she had plain but carefully kept nails when she wrapped his chips on one occasion. All in all there seemed to be something fantastically straightforward about her. He knew all about those sort of smiles: he knew it was about more than customer service and enjoy your fish supper. It had often struck him as he rode the ups and downs of his romantic entrepreneurship that he was good at making women laugh, but he wished he'd wrung more smiles from them. And all these thoughts swirled in the grease and heat of a chip shop: she looked like someone who didn't have to try to be a pleasure to be with, and a girl who need make no effort to look pretty either. She seemed a breeze: aprons had never looked so good. Surely this would be a woman worth getting to know more.

For no rational reason he also decided that she seemed to be a person who would have no agenda, and that, he felt, could only be a good thing. One of the things that had needled him about Grace, at the end, was that he thought she bossed him a little, took him for granted. She had acted like a wife with aspirations of being a girlfriend but what he wanted was a girlfriend – and one with no aspirations whatsoever. 'Strings' he told Grace 'just aren't my things'.

That the girl in the chip shop had a certain mystery about her was not, however, without its disadvantages. The most obvious conundrum was that she might be taken already. Who was to say that there wasn't a Gregor or a Stanislav whose eyes – he imagined them sunken – she wistfully stared into every evening: whether you're Irish or Polish a good looking woman is still a good looking woman. But if he thought about that too much then he would end up doing nothing. The sort of love he liked was not a thing prone to paralysis by analysis, and what, after all, was the worse that could happen? She could only say no.

But if this was what dominated his mind for the most part, some things gnawed away at the back of it. He rehearsed this relationship and thought it bound to be one where he could only have the upper hand. For a start, he would be speaking in his mother tongue but his would always be her second language. He had lived here all his life but it was a strange country to her. How much would all those elements of the foreign translate into control for him, and how much did that bother him? And if it didn't bother him, how much should that in and of itself bother him? Was he running to someone or was he running away from something? Enough, he thought. Life was too short and you could drive yourself crazy thinking such things: better to do and to botch than never to have done at all.

The Catholic thing needled at him too. As Mike had said, if she was Eastern European she was almost certainly Catholic: she hardly worshipped weekly at First Warsaw Presbyterian. That was bound to make things hot and heavy: deep was something he could like in a woman but complicated he could live without. This was where he had to see the cup as half full instead of half empty. If he was articulate enough with his own sort, how could he not – in the kindest possible way – run rings around a girl like this? He knew he had a way with words and he knew he had a way with women. There was no reason why that couldn't get around religion and the charisma of a romantic could not be the persuasion of an evangelist. In fact never mind getting around religion. It didn't need to be an obstacle; with the Spirit in his sales he convinced himself he could hurdle right over this.

His mind wandered once or twice to that thing he'd seen done in Scripture Unions and Youth Fellowships. One person stands on the table and the other on the floor and how much easier it is for the person on the floor to drag the other down, than it is to drag the heathen up on to the table. That was nice easy imagery but he knew himself made of sterner stuff than the illustration implied: what he felt in his mind and heart was far more significant than any passing notion of gut or groin. If all went as well as it could he would be the best thing that had happened to her for eternity and beyond. But if it didn't work out, no harm would come to him.

Church was not beyond the vision of how he saw this working. Different scenes and acts played out in his mind. There were no rings or aisles or prams – there never were – but he imagined himself going to church and coffee shops with her, introducing her to his friends. There was no doubt that this woman would be edgy – and indeed controversial – in a way that no girlfriend had ever been before, and he would enjoy that. He liked to play devil's advocate and challenge conventions and she could be a living 'Totem Pole' of all of those ideas. 'Totem Pole': he liked that – it alone nearly made him have to ask the question. It was just like he'd said to Mike: if he knew her that would make him think differently about things, and it would make all his friends think differently as well. Why was all this pouring through his head: he didn't even know her name?

In the midst of his mind's meandering he panicked occasionally that he did not imagine himself on his own with her at any time. He tried to forbid the cosy stuff from his mind's eye for obvious reasons, but he had not thought of tables for two with her or what it would be like talking together on long walks on a Sunday afternoon. That should have been a warning light to him, but he wasn't much of a man for warning lights. Having weighed it all up he was sure that he should go for it. There was more than a hint of mischief about how people would see all this and he liked that. But he was sure he liked her more. He was settled in his mind that given a choice he found the woman more attractive than the idea of the woman. He believed his motives were pure and he had no reason to reproach himself: just about; on balance.

That being the case there then remained the practical problem of how he was going to initiate this. Love at first sight was all very well but not without its inconveniences. He was used to nods and winks and propositions that were worked up to: but this was unknown territory, like a stranger on a train liaison.

He settled on the idea that he would write her a little letter. He'd go into the shop, place his order, get his order number, and whilst placing the requisite cash into her hand, give her the note as well. She might think this a little peculiar but a knowing raise of his eyebrows would overcome that. He had convinced himself there was a little chemistry to work with.

The method being decided upon, he settled down to compose the note: he didn't do gushy or mushy well so decided to go for humour. Such an approach might be perceived as flippant – and humour could be so cultural which made it an unknown quantity – but he thought it in keeping with the way he was going out on a limb here. He doodled down some options to see what he could make of them.

'Chips' and 'hips' was what came to him quickest: he liked that but you had to know a girl to raise the matter of her hips – she might have some peculiar aversion to her own hips – it wasn't a way of making an introduction. Fried chicken brought him on to all the breast and thigh jokes: up his street but bound to give a smutty impression to someone who didn't know him. He smirked at these thoughts but they wouldn't do.

'Fish' and 'wish' were quite obvious. He liked that and would definitely get it in somewhere. He jotted down 'frying' and 'sizzling' because he could see potential in the imagery that went with that. Beside those he noted the words 'frisson of sexual energy' with two exclamation marks. And then he scored the frisson bit out. 'Would you like to come round to my plaice?' was good but silly. 'Pizza the action' was noted down but quickly eliminated as they didn't do pizza and she'd think him some one trick pony obsessed with junk food, the route to his heart being through his stomach. But he soon decided to be done with worthy notions of over-crafting the thing and just have a go at it.

When I see you fry your fish
I close my eyes and make a wish
And in my mind there is a dream
Where I am chips and you are bream
I'm incomplete and all at sea
So salt and vinegar and season me
I think we'd make a lovely match
And long for you to be my catch
Maybe if you feel the same
You'd throw this fisherman a line
By texting back your mermaid's name
And we could meet and you'd be mine

At the bottom he put his name and mobile number. In the end it took him only three minutes to get it down: he wished that skills that were so useless did not come to him so effortlessly. No woman – he was convinced – could fail to be intrigued by this. It had to be worth a punt. He wasn't sure about the bream bit so he looked that up in a dictionary: apparently they were silvery – which he thought fitting with the mermaid line and silvery implied that she was precious – so he kept it in. 'Fish' said Mike. *'There's plenty more fish in the sea.'*

It all fell down a little when he went to perform the act. When he first went in she was behind the fryers and rather than walk in and walk out again he felt obliged to give his order, sans note, to a thin and gaunt man behind the till who he had heard being called Roman on several occasions (he looked anything but). But she did see him and he got *that* smile.

The second time he went in he decided that she didn't necessarily have to be serving to get the letter. If she was wrapping that would do as well. But he could only catch a glimpse of her in the back: she seemed to be on the peeling machine. 'Those hands' he thought: 'she must go through a mighty amount of *Atrixo*'.

This was starting to seem ill-conceived. Apart from anything, if he kept coming in this often he was going to come across as lardy and spotty which is hardly a way to woo a woman. He wanted the chips to seem a thing of convenience in a fast paced and stylish life: not his staple diet. So he had to leave gaps of at least a week in between his visits: and all the time the clock was ticking with little elements of doubt creeping in whilst he built her up bigger and bigger in his mind.

But the third time he went in she was taking the orders and it came off. He was careful to make eye contact from the off.

"Cowboy supper and a bottle of Coke please".

"Seven Euros ninety."

In for a penny, in for a pound, in with a ten Euro note. This was it. She looked startled and went to return him this scrap of paper. But he smiled hopefully: she gave it enough of a glance to determine the content before smiling back and giving him his change, quickly stashing the correspondence in the pocket of her apron.

"And two and ten makes ten Euros: your order number is 169."

He felt convinced that her hand touched his more than incidentally in dropping the change into it. That was something to hold on to.

Five minutes later he walked out of the chip shop, round the corner and put the cowboy supper in the bin: he had to be at his Mother's at half-six for tea, and would never make it at this rate of going.

* * * * *

He was just settling down to watch the ten o'clock news when the call came. She was giggly and upbeat and would be delighted to see him. Her name was Nadia. He was less jaunty than he had expected to be, and felt a strange sense of delight but anti-climax as he put the phone down. But they were on for the cinema on Friday night.

12

Peter

It was a clear and bright morning. A coat was needed – because it was only six-fifteen and still the middle of April – but there was neither wind nor rain and all agreed it was unseasonably pleasant. The company was good too: about two hundred had made the effort which was more than most years, an encouraging mix of faces and a wide array of ages. And then came the moment they had all been waiting for when the congregation was called to order with a joyous greeting of 'The Lord has risen' and all cried back in one voice: 'He is risen indeed' before bursting into applause. A short service of celebration followed before sharing a breakfast barbeque of sausages and bacon.

Adam had given Peter a lift to the Easter morning daybreak service. He was fond of his friend even if sometimes he would have liked more self-containment in the privacy of his home, and on occasions like these. He felt they were becoming tolerated as 'the odd couple' of the church, and that was what they were as they drove the twenty miles back to town. They talked about the people that Peter had got to know in the last few months. Adam set him right on the matching of spouses and corrected occasional confusion about who went with who. What was it about some couples, they asked? How is it that some very friendly men seem to be married to some very unfriendly women, and likewise some gregarious women had husbands who appeared remote and sullen?

It was coming up to eight o'clock as they tore past a tractor that had been holding them up on a windy stretch of road. As Adam moved up through the gears he reached for the radio to hear what was happening in the world that morning. RTE news advised listeners that in Dublin the finishing touches were being put to preparations for the Easter Rising Commemoration in O'Connell Street – historians estimated this would be among the largest public gatherings in the history of Dublin. Hundreds of thousands of people were expected to line the streets of the city for a parade by the Irish Army with the President Gerry Adams receiving the walk past and being flanked by Taoiseach Bertie Ahern on one side ("flip, Bertie is some survivor" muttered Adam) and on the other by a grandson of Eamon de Valera.

In the corridors of power and the airwaves of the media, there had been much debate and soul searching about the nature of this event. The Irish Army were hardly the most prestigious fighting force in the world, the action it had seen limited to occasional sorties as members of UN peace keeping forces. The army seemed to be battalions of irony given the state's long standing policy of neutrality, but the new Government had feared the appropriation of the occasion by retired Republican Volunteers, which would not play well on an international stage. The march of the army who had done absolutely nothing to bring about the unity was symbolically confusing and messy in the way that most compromises are.

The newsreader explained that in addition to the main celebration in Dublin there would be commemorations in other towns and cities including Belfast, Cork, Derry, Galway, Limerick, Newry and Waterford. In the afternoon it was expected that hundreds of street parties would be held in towns and villages throughout Ireland.

Adam sighed. "If it wasn't Easter I'd say it's another St Patrick's Day. Another day to wash the car or lay a floor." Their mood had been bright when they got into the car but now it dimmed: Adam turned the radio off and there was silence for some miles.

Then he spoke again. "I just can't relate to it at all: it doesn't stir a single bone in my body. I'm sure when I say that I must sound terribly self-righteous. Church is the place to be today, isn't it? The Risen Christ is the one who should be worshipped today. I wonder what that's a reflection of. Is it a Protestant thing or is it a me-thing?"

"Maybe it's a contentment thing" Peter suggested. "Maybe it's as simple as your focus being on the right things."

"Yeh, but sometimes I wonder if I would have been more patriotically aroused had I been born to a different time or place. I'm a unionist with a small 'u' – I was always politically nonplussed. Would it have been different if I'd grown up as a Palestinian living in Gaza or a black man in Alabama? But then I think: well, in the grand scheme of things how much did Irish republicans suffer? Was theirs the anger of genuine loss or was it a romantic and idealistic anger picked up on their grandparent's laps? I mean your people were radicalised by apartheid but I can understand that: anyone can see why that would happen."

Peter frowned for a split second as he processed the question. "I suppose it's the difference between needs and wants, isn't it? 'Coloureds' as we were referred to in South Africa were treated dreadfully: apartheid was manifestly unjust and we had to rise up against it. I'm not an Irish Republican but it seems to me that whilst they were apart from what they longed for emotionally, nonetheless for the last 20 or 30 years they had very acceptable standards of equality and healthcare and education and the like. A united Irish state was an important aspiration for them and they *wanted* it, but there's no reasonable way in which you can say they *needed* it. But then I passionately believe salvation is a need rather than a want and there's not that many people respond to Jesus Christ, so you may very well ask me how much I know."

* * * * *

The minister's sermon that morning conformed to the usual pulpit norm of three points. He was a typical Presbyterian pedagogue: everything – from prophets to miracles, from psalms to letters – could be reduced to treble truth. He spoke to the congregation of the risen Christ who brought reassurance to his disciples in three ways. He brought to them a word of peace: "peace" he said "be with you". This was a ragtag collection of men who had more or less forsaken Christ in their Master's most desperate hour of need: they were wracked with guilt; they were in need of forgiveness. Christ did not hold what had happened against the disciples. He also gave the disciples a gesture of encouragement, eating a piece of fish among them as evidence that he was not a mere apparition but was in fact a physical person. He concluded by showing the congregation how Christ had given the disciples some gentle teaching to place everything in context: all of what had happened was in order to fulfil what was written in the Law of Moses, the Prophets and the Psalms. In teaching in this way Rev Houston blatantly ignored the wider events around him that Easter: he was a man of considered caution when it came to weaving the word and the world.

Afterwards a large proportion of the congregation retired as they usually did, to the hall for tea and biscuits together. Despite this being Easter the topics of conversation differed little from that of most Sundays. Are you busy this weather? What about yesterday's results in the football? How is your mother keeping after her operation? Are you off the whole week?

There was no atmosphere of vibrancy in the hall, for the majority of these churchgoers were people of a great and strange evenness. As it is true that God is the same yesterday, today and forever, so most of them had adopted an approach to God that was the same in spring, summer, autumn and winter. To Peter's amazement there had been no services during the preceding Holy Week. Whilst he was enjoying 'doing' Christianity in a different place he had complained to Adam of the most un-Easter like Good Friday he could ever remember. He couldn't put his finger on it but it seemed that these were Christian people of unusual plainness. There had been no slow build up of anticipation to Easter so it was of little surprise that Easter Sunday itself had no sense of climax. Having now been among them three months Peter privately thought them to be hearty people: meat and two veg Christians who had many virtues.

Their sensibility had much to commend it but he concluded they did not do peaks and troughs well.

* * * * *

The odd couple expanded at lunchtime to a ménage-a-trois as Alan was invited for lunch. Peter had pledged to make a chilli and had been grandstanding for several days with a promise that he would blow his guests' heads off. Soon the conversation turned to the great post-church ritual of dissecting the sermon.

"Isn't talking about a sermon a strange thing" Adam said. "I've always noticed in our church that if you ask someone what they made of the service all they'll do is critique the sermon. And even at that the discussion of it is usually narrowed down to 'was he good'? It's always the head and never the heart."

While Adam stacked his dishwasher, Peter put finishing touches to his pudding. Alan loitered: he loved to peruse the books and music on other people's shelves – you could tell so much by doing that.

"Housty did kind of cop out today, didn't he?" Alan said. "I mean there's so much he could have said but he just evaded it all. Peter must have an opinion. Let me put you on the spot big fella: what would you have preached on if it had been you in that pulpit?"

Adam groaned. "What does that achieve? I mean, how is that helpful?"

"It doesn't achieve anything" Alan shrugged. "But just because it doesn't achieve anything doesn't mean it isn't enjoyable."

Peter gave a bemused look of false modesty, stroked his chin a little, and said he would need to think about this, buying time whilst cutting slices of his chocolate tart. After he had blobbed cream on his own portion he proceeded.

"I suppose one obvious angle you could go down is the concept of sacrifice. Those who commemorate the Easter rising are recognising the sacrifice of men who gave themselves for the cause of Ireland being liberated from the English. That could be compared with Jesus Christ who gave himself to suffer on the cross as a redeeming sacrifice for the sins of all men."

"Allow me to pick a hole in that" Alan said.

"You're not meant to be picking holes" Adam interrupted. "You're meant to be sitting humbly in a pew and receiving the message."

"I can't help myself" Alan replied. "Surely the sacrifice of Christ was very different from the volunteers in 1916. Christ knew what He was getting into: He went into the cross knowing the pain and suffering with which it would all end. I don't think the proponents of the Easter Rising went into that event in the willing expectation of martyrdom."

"How do you know that?" Adam asked? "You were hardly there yourself."

"I wasn't there when they crucified our Lord, as the song goes. You don't have to be somewhere to know what it means. I can never understand that hymn – I used to sing it as a wee boy and think: no, of course I wasn't there. It was two thousand years ago, how stupid is that? The Easter rising lot ended up dying because their plan was ill-conceived: it was always going to fail."

"Well that's arguable" Peter said. "But set aside your black cap for the purposes of this conversation: we're only generating ideas. So I would contrast the sacrifice between the Republicans who died for Ireland and Christ who died for the sins of the world. That then takes you into a whole other set of questions. Very rarely will anyone die for a righteous man, though for a good man someone might possibly dare to die. Christ demonstrated his love in dying for sinners, but the Irishmen chose to die for something totally different: a free Irish state. What – ultimately – is worth dying for?"

"You know" Adam continued "that then begs *another* question. Because what is worth dying for is inextricably linked to what is worth worshipping. We all judge. We know we shouldn't but we can't help it – well, maybe it's too easy to say we can't help it but you all know what I mean. Anyway, when we come to judge Republicans – and I suppose Loyalists as well – we judge most immediately against the standard of 'you shall not murder'. But when we look at events like today and the way that people are getting on in Dublin, then I think we have to judge against the standards of 'you shall have no other gods before me'. Patriotism as a subject has always fascinated me. When do you reach the point of too much patriotism: when does patriotism become false religion?"

"Look at 'God bless America'" Alan suggested, dabbing his finger and rolling it round his plate to mop up the best of the remaining crumbs. "Even worse: look at 'For God and Ulster'".

Peter continued. "I suppose patriotism is one thing but worship is another, and as you say Adam, where does one stop and the other start? If you wanted to, you could compare the nature of patriotism with the nature of love. True love – I believe – is not uncritical. If you really love someone you'll be realistic about seeing their weaknesses and wanting them to change. Patriotism at its most extreme can fail to have a moral and a critical faculty, and that's where Christians should have real problems with it. We can't make windows into the souls of the people who are celebrating the Easter Rising. But if their approach to it all is one of romanticised nationalism: if they're approaching it all in selective ignorance of shared history and they fail to acknowledge the terror they and their forefathers inflicted on other people to achieve their goal, then frankly that seems to me to like a false religion."

Peter lay back in his chair, and raised his eyebrows to his friends in satisfaction at his argument. "In fact" he carried on, leaning forward with renewed enthusiasm "if you want false religion you've only to look at the Easter story itself and ask with whom those celebrating in Dublin have most in common. The answer is those who lauded the Messiah when he rode into Jerusalem on Palm Sunday. Because that carnival atmosphere had very little to do with religion: that was all about Nationalistic fervour and their hope that Jesus would be the figurehead of some uprising against the Romans. His failure to meet that ideal was the earthly tipping point that began the events that ended up with Christ hanging on the cross. That's rich food for thought. There was an Easter rising in Dublin, and certain Jews would have loved the very first Easter itself to be all about uprising. The spirit that wanted Barabbas set free and chanted 'Crucify Him' is the same sort of spirit that gathers at rallies to honour volunteers. How about that for the Bible still being relevant today?"

"I'd never thought about Easter that way" Adam reflected. "But hey: maybe we're getting a bit carried away here. Sure the worst excesses of our community were just as bad: it's not as if they have a monopoly on it. But what are we talking about here: we seem to have come a long way from the cross and the resurrection."

"Not that far really" disputed Alan. "It's like the spiritual equivalent of one of those association things you see in newspapers." He paused for thought. "It's like going from carrots to heaven in six steps."

"What?"

"From carrots to heaven. Let me think: carrots make you think of Bugs Bunny. Bugs Bunny is doctors – doctors as in 'What's up doc?' Doctors work with nurses and nurses are like angels and angels are found in heaven. From carrots to heaven: easy. Anyway: what about another sermon?"

"One more certainly" Peter responded. "Another way to approach the subject is the angle of symbolism. The cross of Christ is the most powerful logo the world has ever known. The cross symbolises the means by which Almighty God gave his son to die as the world's saviour.

And in the case of Irish Republicanism, the Easter rising is also of great significance. The sacrifice of volunteers, who so burned with a desire for liberation that they laid down their lives for their cause. That event set out a stall and by 1921 they had reached – at least in part – the object of *their* faith: the formation of the Irish Free State. On the surface level both are symbols but on closer examination one is seen to be just that – only a symbol – whilst the other one actually *was* of enormous significance. You could say that the Easter Rising was all hype and no substance: glorified in hindsight but in practical terms it was a shambles. An under-resourced attempt at revolution that was doomed from the outset. But the cross is more than just a symbol: the cross means life and life in all its fullness."

"And I suppose an extension of that" Alan continued "is that whilst both seem historical, on closer examination one actually has the power to be very contemporary. The Easter Rising can only ever be stuck in 1916 and it can't get out of there. But the resurrection of Christ and his rising can still mean something today, right at this very moment."

Whilst Peter and Alan locked horns in conversation, Adam – still sitting in his chair – had seemed to go off to some other place. Divorced from the last few minutes he picked up quietly where neither of his companions had left off. "Or you could just not preach at all. Why do we *always* have to be preaching and teaching? Why do we *always* have to be learning? Death is defeated so why do we need to analyse all this? Even Jesus himself didn't do a whole pile of teaching when he rose from the grave: he seemed to spend most of his time just hanging out with the people who meant most to him. Why could we not just revel in the wonder of it all: God help us all if a Protestant heaven is going to be nothing other than long sermons."

13

Behind every man…

Nobody could say it was the greatest story ever told of friendship conquering barriers, but the relationship Gillian Todd had with Siobhan McAleese was so counter to her culture that it was a secret to many she was close to. That secrecy was something that often led Gillian to feelings of guilt: it seemed a betrayal that she should not disclose her friend, and she knew that being a friend was something a person should never need to justify.

Gillian had given up her teaching job many years ago when the pitter-patter of tiny Todds had come along: John worked difficult shifts and it had not been possible to juggle raising a small family and the two of them work as well. On hearing that she had been a teacher the first thing that generally surprised listeners would want to know was what she had taught. History had been her chosen specialist subject. "I tended to do the Tudors mainly. Although Irish history really interested me I always thought it best to stay away from it because the Catholic schools do it *so* well. Plus you never know what your own sort might say, and then if they get the likes of some priest marking their paper, and he takes against them, well…"

When her children got to the point of leaving and cleaving it was an opportunity for Gillian to return to her vocation and get back to the classroom. But that did not work out because as it happened there was now a limited demand for modern History teachers, and even less for those who were ring rusty to the tune of twenty years. But then an unexpected door opened for Gillian in the form of Hospital and Home Teaching. The thought of trying to educate the 'can't go to schools' and the 'don't want to go to schools' did not appeal to her, but she supposed she had nothing to lose and should give it a go.

And so it was that five years previously Gillian had taken up her first assignment, which much to her distaste was in the 'wrong' end of town: the 'wrong' end and the 'other' end. And if that wasn't bad enough it was also in the middle of Kilgallon, a sink estate typical of the deep seated deprivation that characterised pockets of the Province.

Gillian was to teach a fifteen year old called Shauna who had broken her leg whilst playing football: on receiving her brief she was shocked to find welling up inside her less than generous assumptions about the character and appearance of a teenage girl who plays GAA. "You'd think she'd be the butch and bruising type" John said. But the reality was very different.

Shauna, it transpired, was a bright and bubbly girl and an enthusiastic pupil. She enjoyed meeting new people – particularly adults – and was approaching her influx of teachers with gusto and relish. She had just one older brother – Kevin, who was 18 – and again Gillian was surprised at there only being two of them. "They breed like rabbits" John said: "that's the problem you see – Protestants just aren't willing to have piles of kids the way they are. All these nice gentlemen's families that people have these days: stopping with your wee boy and your wee girl is all very well, but sure all you're doing is replacing yourself. That doesn't do the Unionist cause much good."

Kevin was a quiet and gauche adolescent: he looked down more than he looked up and mumbled more than he talked. There didn't seem to be a man about the house but – these sort of people – this sort of place – what did Gillian expect? The two kids – who was to say they even had the same father? She reproached herself and prayed forgiveness for her snobbery, but this was no less than she expected.

The house was clean and orderly: not plush but bearing the definite evidence of those who are proud of what they have. The garden was neat and tidy and the pavement outside even bore the appearance of one that had been brushed. John commented that it was a very Protestant looking property. When she saw it Gillian could not help but feel sorry for this

120

hopeful beacon of orderliness amidst the surrounding detritus of murals, tricolours and painted kerbstones.

John bet Gillian that it was a lot less Protestant when you got inside: he asked if there was a picture of the Pope or a saint or even one of those dreadful portraits with Jesus and a glowing red light in the middle of it. Gillian said there were none of these things except for a rather noticeable – or certainly noticeable to her – crucifix in the front room. It struck Gillian as a rather sobering thing: having *that* there could surely not help but focus the mind. But John replied that this was typical of them and reminded Gillian that Jesus wasn't on the cross any more but had been raised from death and was seated at the right hand of the Father.

Gillian was flushed with guilt when she learned the truth behind this family. The absent father was in fact a dead father: he was the childhood sweetheart of Siobhan and had been a loving daddy. Only 18 months after the arrival of Shauna he had passed away: 'taken' by leukaemia. Gillian only learnt this on the occasion of her fourth visit for a lesson: and when she did everything made sense very quickly, in the rapid manner of the way the last pieces of a jigsaw fit. And yet this woman was so positive – *so* positive – and something ran through Gillian's mind about suffering producing perseverance, and perseverance producing character, and character producing hope.

From there on the barriers seemed to come down and there was a clicking of a sort that Gillian found inexplicable. One day they started talking and it carried on from there. It was humbling for Gillian because at first she found herself doing rather more listening than she did speaking. This was surprising because Gillian was the evangelical equivalent of a *sassy* woman: one generally regarded as in control, one to which others would come for advice. And yet here she was receiving light from such an unexpected quarter.

When she got light from her own quarters it was because someone was virtuous and wise and worthy of a pedestal. But this woman she was with now was just an ordinary person yakking in her kitchen: she wasn't even trying to be a light –

would not have thought of herself that way – and yet she was irresistibly luminescent. However weather beaten Siobhan was by all that life had rained on her, nonetheless she was inspiring. There was no false pretence or going through the motions.

From their unfamiliarity came an inevitable freedom. Gillian often thought it ironic that in the long conversations that developed in Siobhan's kitchen, there was almost a quality of going into the confessional. Not that it was like that exactly: she didn't disclose her numbered sins and misdemeanours. But they could be frank one with another because those mugs of tea at that kitchen table were the single point at which their worlds touched. Siobhan didn't know John or David or Vicki or Violet or Rev Houston. Siobhan knew nothing of the life that Gillian lived except for the cups in the kitchen and the lessons in the lounge. It was not that Gillian would bitch or let off steam or anything like that because she knew nothing would get back – but Siobhan was a lady who lovingly made instant coffee and produced wrapped chocolate biscuits from a plastic barrel, and such hospitality was utterly refreshing. She wasn't entertaining a guest: she was serving a friend.

This was the pleasure of disparate lives touching one another. Gillian soon realised that every time she mentioned a pre-communion service or elders or home bible studies or prayer triplets, that would require a stripping down of explanation which in her own mind begat exploration. And there was take as well as give, as Siobhan would describe the importance to her of Mass and the Rosary and Mary and so on and on it went. Gillian always limited Siobhan's words to description and discussion: she would never make her justify because she was scared of what that would do to what they had.

Not that Gillian left her critical faculty at home when she met Siobhan. She would not be argumentative or confrontational but she would think long and hard on the conversations they had. It seemed to her that this new friend had a very genuine faith: her routines and practices were evidently the skeleton upon which she had fleshed her existence.

"She trusts" John said "but lots of people trust. The question is: does she trust in the right things? Plenty of people have faith but what's faith – it's got to be faith in Christ."

Whenever John made comments like that it showed Gillian so eloquently how the monopoly of truth could be reduced to the level of a game. Gillian knew he had a point but she hated the point. Everything and everyone that Gillian knew had taught her she should be superior to this lady, but now she was faced with flesh and blood she could not believe that to be the case. The faith that this lady had was evidently genuine: Gillian would not for one minute want to trade the reformation for the ritual, but whilst Siobhan did not have *the* real deal, she certainly seemed to have *a* real deal. After all that this lady had been through and after all that she had taught her – not that Siobhan had ever set out to teach – Gillian just could not bring herself to judge.

14

Peter

Mike was embarrassed: it was not how he had envisaged this. "Lazy wee skitter" he raged under his breath. "Needs to get off his lazy fat arse and get outside. Get outside and get a life." It wasn't the first time – it was a perennial parental problem. His eldest child – Michael – liked the idea of doing things more than the actual doing.

His mother in law had whisked 'the fair Wendy' away for a 'Pamper Day'. So Mike was left looking after the kids – or babysitting as he put it, though Wendy insisted it could hardly be called that when they were his own children.

("Pamper as in treat yourself" he had explained to Alan: "nothing to do with nappies. No nappies involved at all: that's the point of it."

"They could nearly have called it a No-Pamper day then."

"I suppose they could, but it hardly rolls off the tongue the same way").

Peter had said he would give Mike a help out if he wanted. He wasn't good with small children but he would happily take Michael to the park if that would help: kick a ball about; shoot the breeze. Two weeks ago when this was put to Michael he had loved the idea – Wendy said that with his dad working such awkward hours his son didn't get enough male company – so an arrangement was made. But now the appointed Saturday had come and Michael was sullenly lodged in the sofa, apparently not for shifting.

"I don't want to-oo" he whined. "It's too cold. Why can't Peter play with me on the Xbox?" His coat flew across the room and landed on his lap, and seconds later his hat and gloves hit him in rapid succession. He drew his feet on to the sofa and turned his back to adopt a foetal pose of defiance.

"It's cool" Peter said to Mike. "Don't push it: if he doesn't want to go, he doesn't want to go." Then he spoke over to the ball of indolence. "Tell you what Michael: why don't you pick two teams and play a game on your Xbox? See what the score is: then we can hit the park and see if we get the same result."

The boy turned round with a glum scowl that indicated half-hearted agreement to this plan.

"That's a deal then. Your dad and I will get a cup of tea and then we'll head out."

The two men disappeared into the kitchen.

"Sorry" Mike said – both hands out in front of him and chopping the air for emphasis. "I'm sorry: boy he really knows how to wind me up."

"It's fine" Peter said. "Relax: let him get it out of his system. You've nothing to be sorry about."

* * * * *

"Do you know what that child's like?" Peter asked Adam later in the day.

"A spoilt brat?"

"No – I'm not talking about *him*. It's what he's *like*. He's like the church."

"Sorry?"

"He's like the church. He's just the way that so much of the church has been here this last forty or fifty years."

The lines on Adam's forehead scrunched together: it was the way Peter said these things in such a matter of fact way.

Peter continued: "he loves football. He loves to watch it on TV and read about it in football comics and play it on a console. But he's only eight and already he's an armchair fan: he doesn't want to be out there on a pitch and running and heading and tackling and passing and shooting. He loves the game and yet he doesn't love playing it."

"Which has got what exactly to do with the church?"

"What was it Jesus said" Peter asked – not even giving his friend time to answer the question. "Blessed are the peace makers. Not, blessed are the peace *lovers*. Blessed are the peace *makers*. The church in this country – I reckon it was just like Mike's son.

So many people: they loved to sit in their pews and hear sermons about peace. They loved to go to seminars and workshops about peace. They loved to read books about peace and have people coming from other places and give testimonies about working peace and forgiveness out in their lives. They loved peace: but they didn't want to get off their butts and go out and get their hands dirty and love their enemy and make peace.

Michael's not a bad kid – and hey, the people in the church – they're not bad either. But you can already see the sort of adult he's going to be. He'll always be a fan: but that child hasn't a hope in hell of being a footballer. Not a hope."

15

Alan

Alan Mackey was not a happy camper. 'What on earth is a man like me doing in a place like this of a Friday night' was the prevalent thought that clattered through his mind. Love had turned his head and clouded his judgment. And so it was that he found himself, at the end of a week at the end of April, driving to the St John of God Parish Centre to see the local drama group on their first night's performance of *The Sound of Music*.

It was Nadia's idea and it was amongst their first big dates: in such circumstances he didn't want to refuse. She said she'd got her ticket weeks ago and was unsure if she could still get one for him: he feigned disappointment but stoically insisted that she must go, even if she couldn't wangle a seat for him. But in the end, the said ticket came through. He thought of crying off with a headache or a dodgy stomach but concluded that endeavour was the better part of valour. As Mike put it to him: 'that which does not kill you makes you stronger'. He would fight manfully onward. He was resolutely uncomfortable with the whole idea but how could he explain such feelings? How do you get across to a blow in like Nadia why a man like him might not be so welcome at an amateur dramatic performance of a Friday night?

As he walked into the auditorium he felt himself reproaching the bigotry in his own mind. 'You're mad' Mike had said to him. 'You might as well be going in with a great big flashing 'I'm a Protestant' light on your head. They'll be giving you that look that says 'you don't come from round these parts''. But as Alan sat down to take his seat he wasn't sure which of his attitudes was the worst. Yes, the spiritual snobbery was bad but he had also fallen victim to self-centredness as well. The blunt reality was that the people of St John's Parish Centre were about as interested in Alan Mackey, as Alan Mackey was interested in the people of St John's Parish Centre. He wasn't being noticed – at least not in *that* sense.

Everyone turned out to be much friendlier than he had expected. People were saying hello to him and Nadia, nodding to the couple, exchanging small talk pleasantries as they brushed past them to take up their seats. He noticed how many of them were personally greeting Nadia, how they seemed to have made an effort to make her feel at home among them. And that brought home to him one guilty notion: up to this point, he had held off from inviting Nadia to a service at his own church. There were a range of reasons for this, but one of them was that – whatever her creed, colour, or country of origin – he had very little confidence in the propensity of his brethren to welcome warmly the stranger in their midst. Sitting with the shoe on the other foot made him uncomfortable.

In between discussing the events of his day with Nadia, he flicked through the programme for the show. Even though he had no interest in the pending performance, for some strange reason he found the programme compelling. It was a window to a world for him. He noticed that Father Artur – the Polish curate who Nadia had mentioned several times – was playing Rolf. If the picture was any way accurate the man appeared to be only about 12 years old. In fact there were two priests in the musical, because an older cleric called Gerry Byrne was playing Uncle Max: according to his mug shot this man looked too dour to be playing the spivvy agent. Two priests were good, Alan thought: it would help him ham up the story of the night. To that end, he was disappointed that there were to be no *bona fide* nuns on stage.

The evening ran with military precision and as stated on the tickets the show commenced on the stroke of eight o'clock, the audience being requested in firm but friendly tone to take their seats and settle down for the performance. Alan had to give it to them: it was all much better than he in any way anticipated – so good in fact that he checked his watch only three times during the first half. This was obviously not amateur dramatics of the thrown together variety: time, effort, and – dare he say it – talent, were all parts of the equation. He did feel for the woman playing the Mother Superior – who the programme would later tell him was a local hairdresser called Philomena – however much she gave it her best shot he reckoned she just didn't have it when it came to hitting the highest peaks of Climb Every Mountain. A further criticism – if anyone were asking him – would be that Von Trap children just don't look right with frizzy ginger hair.

His one disadvantage as the interval approached was that he had dressed inappropriately for the occasion. Dashing in from work he had a short interval to turn himself around before heading out again, and in changing he had grabbed the nearest clothes that came to hand. He threw an old Northern Ireland shirt on and stuck a fleece over it. He was too warm with the fleece but too cold without it, and not knowing what the hall would be like, had erred on the side of caution.

It was a crisp but cold April evening: the sort that is more enjoyable to look at than be out in. But in the glass sided auditorium the combination of dramatic lighting, black curtains and sunlight against the windows was doing him no favours. He was being slowly cooked and suffering for the sake of art. He started to shift uncomfortably from side to side, desperate to take the fleece off but convinced that he ought not to. Beads of perspiration formed in a mass across his forehead, and as Maria sang the song of The Lonely Goat Herd he could feel the sweat gathered in his armpits trickle in disarming rivulets down each side of his chest and stomach.

At the interval the old man beside Alan started making conversation with him – this elderly patron was clearly delighted with his evening's entertainment. He was a plump and highly coloured man with baldness attended to by number one hair clippers all over. He wore a zipped up and patterned cardigan that seemed to belie the ambient temperature around him. Alan cheered himself up by imagining what sort of a shirt *he* might have on underneath, and wondered if he got his head clipped by the Mother Superior.

With great relish his septuagenarian friend insistently offered Alan a cinnamon lozenge which Alan politely refused: seemingly unable to comprehend how anyone could fail to want a cinnamon lozenge the pensioner simply tore one from the packet anyhow and forced it into his hand. He felt Nadia kick his ankle hard in an admonishing instruction that he was to do the polite thing. The greater part of Alan didn't give a damn: he'd never met this man before and had no intention of ever clapping eyes on him again. But he was here to build rather than to burn bridges, and soon his mouth was stoked to the same heat as the rest of his body.

The veteran theatre goer gushed in praise of all aspects of the performance, stammering with excitement and enthusiasm as he declared that Brigeen McAtamney – who was playing Maria – was every bit as talented as Julie Andrews or Connie Fisher. He dribbled slightly as he concluded his point. Alan simply agreed with him as this was a time to traverse the path of least resistance.

As the second half wore on Alan began to wilt somewhat, his enjoyment increasingly overcome by an aching longing for the whole thing to draw to a close. He was perked up however by the sudden way that one of the Von Trap girls burst into a five minute solo of Irish dancing in the middle of the family's virtuoso performance at the Salzburg festival. He was no expert when it came to the minutiae of The Sound of Music but was pretty certain there were no jigs and reels in the original. It was good to know that the insistence of power parenting was alive and well.

With the performance drawing to a close he glanced at Nadia's face. She had held his hand the whole way through the show, and as the cast reprised the highlights of the musical and took their bow to the audience, she leaned into his shoulder, her face beaming with satisfaction. Here was his girlfriend who had left all her foundations of family and community behind when she departed Poland, and perhaps here she could experience something approaching that. A lot of those around him knew Nadia, knew who she was. His own sort would never have given her this level of attention.

What grabbed Alan most as he walked out was not so much the standard of the performance as the very idea of doing such a show itself. Where on his side of the fence would you get people giving up their spare time and pooling all their talents to do something like for this – all for no other motivation than the fun and the craic of putting on a show and catching up with friends and neighbours. As they eked up the aisles towards the door it seemed that everybody knew somebody. The whole throng buzzed with gossip and laughter: it was all 'Seamy this' and 'Mary that' and 'Patsy, how are you?' There seemed lightness in these spirits that he didn't recognise among his own community.

At the door on the way out, Father Byrne was meeting and greeting, receiving the accolades of the audience and asking after his parishioners. "Well, Nadia, did you enjoy that then?"

"Brilliant" – she replied – "brilliant, Father, it was absolutely brilliant."

"That's good now. And who's this fine young man you've got with you, Nadia?"

"Oh – this is Alan."

"Alan? Well there you go – I don't think we know you Alan, do we?"

"Eh – no – you wouldn't" Alan replied blankly, shaking his head.

Father Byrne looked him up and down briefly and Alan felt the sweat starting to form on his forehead again.

"Well" the cleric concluded. "I'm glad you both had such a lovely time now."

16

John

The forbidding and official looking letter dropped through the door just after nine o'clock. The brown envelope; the franc; the window; and the warning that its content was 'strictly private and confidential': it had it all. Fortunately Gillian was in the bathroom and John had no problem getting to it first. Did nobody ever think than when you send this sort of menace out on a Friday it lands on a hall carpet on a Saturday, and has all of its ruinous impact through somebody's weekend? Maybe – he thought – that was the point: maybe they did it deliberately.

Dread welled up inside him as soon as he saw it. He picked it off the floor as if it was live with electricity and stared at it in momentary paralysis. 'Oh dear Lord' he muttered in a hybrid of prayer and cursing. He heard the electric shower click off and when the water stopped he heard Gillian stepping on to the bath mat, enthusiastically singing some song of God's goodness as she did so.

'Lord of mercy you have heard my cry…'

He knew this was coming but hadn't prepared himself for the moment. He'd been dealing with it in the best manly manner by not dealing with it: and now crashing through the front door with all its attendant weight came the elephant in the room. It had hit him but he felt like he had hit it: it was like running hard into a brick wall and struggling in a daze to pick oneself up.

'…in the storm you're the beacon, my comfort in the night…'

They were meant to meet friends for coffee at Marks & Spencer in less than an hour and were well behind schedule. Gillian would not be lingering. This called for the sort of snap decision making in a moment he was meant to be so good at.

'…singing what a faithful God have I…'

He ripped it open in gut wrenching expectation and scanned it with the efficiency that comes from panic. The title – the first paragraph – the last paragraph – who it was from – then the content in the middle. Later he would reread it several times. Get the lines that were in it and the bits that were left out and read the bits between the lines as well. But for now he understood: he got the gist of it. The gist was bloody awful.

'...*faithful in every way'.*

He looked up in dread and in the hope that someone was in turn looking down, and then he looked around him. The singing had stopped and his wife was coming. And in an instant it came to him that the best thing to do was what he had been doing already. Standing on the polished wooden floor he leant down, picked up the brightly coloured rug that greeted visitors to their home, and threw the envelope and the letter beneath it.

* * * * * *

Adam

Adam loved to walk: it often struck him that a well worn phrase from the lexicon of Christian sub-culture was that of having a 'walk with God', and on a practical level lots of his walks were 'with God'. When he left his home and left the boundaries of the town behind to enter quieter country lanes, this was a gait that lent itself to prayer and thinking.

Finding himself with a welcome afternoon off in the middle of the week, he had chosen his favourite company of all: his own. When Adam confined himself to the house or tried to sit still he found it difficult to concentrate. He was a person who found it hard to relax and that carried through to his spiritual life. But when out on a good pounding of rural roads many things seemed less puzzling and perplexing: because he was unwinding his mind could see *round* things more, whereas in the house – sitting in a chair – he would feel the need to put his intellect right *through* the things that perplexed, and all would break down and only mess would be left.

He got to thinking as he strode that afternoon about Ireland – all that had gone on and what was happening now – and it struck him that in a strange sense God could not win. He knew that many if they heard that thought would think it heretical, but he thought it perfectly reasonable. God – for all of His omniscience and omnipresence – could not win when it came to Ireland.

He extended this hypothesis a little further to test its worthiness. A good Protestant could come to God in the tidiness of their front room in the middle of the morning some day and long in earnest prayer that God would not break the Union. They could petition Him that the land that they treasure would not lose the identity they cling to. But at the same time an equally righteous and faithful Catholic Christian could be sitting in the Chapel and lighting a little candle and asking God how long it would be before they could have the identity they so aspire to: before they could be simply an Irishman living in Ireland.

One community wants one thing and another community in the same land wants another – and yet the two aspirations are mutually exclusive. Maybe it was ever so: a family pray on their holiday that they'll have sunny weather and the farmer in the next field is petitioning that the rain would fall. God made squares and God made circles but even God can't square the circles.

What can a God of justice do when both longings are in their own way just? God is perfectly capable of giving us whatever it is that we ask for in His name but he plainly can't give two people in the same time and place two things that are diametrically opposed. Someone has to be disappointed. That Ireland was united didn't mean that God doesn't answer prayer thought Adam: it just meant that God hadn't answered some of his prayers. And he – and others in his community – would have to accept that God knew best and this did not make Him in any way a lesser God.

17

Strangers in a strange land

Three solid lines of forward slashes marked the place in the email where the dead man had suddenly slumped. Jim Scott had been feeling peaky but resilient as he composed an electronic missive to chastise those members of his sales force who the tables and graphs of his analysis showed were underperforming. The rebuke would leave his outbox before seven thirty in the morning. As a strong ache made his left bicep almost unbearably painful, his last laugh undeliverable was to copy the Group Managing Director in Reading: this would reinforce fear to the feckless whilst the sent time could not fail to impress the superior. Upward and downward: all bases covered.

But only seconds before he would have depressed a finger just a millimetre to left click his mouse and send, a searing pain ripped across his chest as his head crashed into the laptop. His morning habit was to work in a zone of uninterrupted focus for an hour and a half, and when his PA arrived for work the first thing she would do would be to bring Jim a strong mug of tea. She was served an awful image that would be lodged in her mind forever when she went there that morning. The accompaniment of his mobile ringing whilst she entered made it like a scene from the very cheapest of horror films. (Two impatient voicemail messages were left between the time of death and the discovery of the body).

A macabre friend later remarked wryly that sending an email had been a good way for Jim to go: it seemed a black observation 'but sure didn't he die doing what he loved most and wouldn't we all want to go that way.' The jungle drums of bad news soon began to beat around his friends and colleagues: on reflection it was agreed to be something of a shock but nothing of a surprise. He'd been working as hard as ever but had looked very tired of late. He could walk the golf course as well as any man but had noticeably put on weight.

Violet said she thought he had looked a bad colour at church the previous Sunday: "yellow" she said "but not a good yellow." So paunchy had he become that Mike had privately been referring to him as 'Slim Scott', jauntily declaring that 'He's more chins than a Peking phonebook'. He now felt prangs of guilt about this but assuaged his conscience by telling himself that you'd never give anyone a nickname like that if you *knew* they were going to die in the next few months. If life were based on such morbid assumptions you'd have no fun at all.

Much of the compassion and conversation over tea tables that evening focused on Jim's wife Thelma and what she would do now. John and Gillian called for Willie and Violet after tea and together they gave one another strength in numbers as they 'went to the house'. It was all rather awkward because as they agreed in the car on the way there, they all felt that they were a friend – though none of them a close friend – of Jim, and yet none of them would say that they knew Thelma very much at all. But they got through the evening and felt relief blot out anxiety as they left: Thelma seemed remarkably composed given what a dreadful day it must have been, and they were all glad they had gone.

John had felt a strange and otherworldly quality about the room they sat in. He was used to it being a place of sober study of the Word of God. But after the wave of shock there had been that day, he found himself beached in Jim's lounge and having to try to be the Word of God to a widow he barely knew. He was the leader of her dead husband's house group: he should be full of mighty-man spiritual strength and deep wisdom yet he felt nothing but inadequacy. Fortunately Gillian had a sensitive intuition for punctuating talk about small things with listening about big things and it served her and her husband well in circumstances such as these.

As for Adam he was working that night but would not shirk from doing the right thing and would certainly go at some stage. Alan and Mike on the other hand rang each other and had a long conversation which concluded in mutual justification of why – on balance and taking all things into consideration – they would tilt towards not going. They were never sure what to do in such situations. Their relationship with Jim was judged to rank high enough that the funeral was a certainty but low enough to eliminate a need to visit the house.

* * * * *

Torrential rain bounced outside the entrance to the church as the mourners made their way to the door: Willie always said the only thing worse than a dry funeral is a wet one. He was feeling conspicuous in his black tie: he had told Violet that very few people seem to wear black ties to funerals these days and 'after all I'm not family': but nonetheless she insisted that he should wear it.

When the Maxwells and Todds had agreed that neither of them were close friends of the deceased they also remarked that they did not associate Jim and Thelma with having *any* close friends in the church. The sad reality was that this couple had focused their energies mainly on building networks rather than relationships. But on the day itself there was a tanned and expensive looking couple no one had seen before called Frank and Georgie who stood strong and beside Thelma. It was good to see that Thelma had them.

Willie nudged Violet as she rummaged in her handbag for funereal soft-mints and muttered that John was now talking to the stranger who was 'dressed like a sore finger'. Frank had introduced himself to John and – huddled underneath a much pattered upon umbrella – said that he had heard of John and how Jim had talked fondly of the house group and the times they had together. He asked John if the entire group had made it to the funeral that day and John had already made sufficient mental notes to affirm that they had. Frank then wondered if – that being the case – the men would mind giving the coffin a lift as they were going to walk a little after the service. John said that would not be a problem.

Another of Willie's stock funeral reflections came to him as he went inside the church and looked around: such services are strangely enjoyable insofar as you have the opportunity to catch up with people you haven't met for months or even years. Indeed there was a man who lived over the road from Violet and him who never missed a chance to go to a good funeral: no association was too tenuous to pass up donning his best suit and overcoat. This man's wife seemed somewhat foreboding and Willie thought he was probably glad of chances to get out of the house: he had reached a stage in life where funerals appeared to be an important social outlet. He approached them in the same spirit that a restaurant critic appreciates a good meal: after each one he would stand at his driveway gate with Willie and give the reportage and analysis of a funereal connoisseur.

As the huddled mass of those paying their respect shook their sodden selves down and the organist piped a hymn as slowly and quietly as it is possible to play a musical instrument, Violet shared her default complaint. "He's only dead *two* days and here we are at his funeral: it's more being banged to rest than laid to rest. What is it about this country that we have to bury people with such indecent haste? If I go before you I want you to wait *at least* three days."

The Rev Houston was on a week's study leave and the minister on call was the Rev McNally, a retired bastion of the local district. Rev McNally was a single-minded man who had set himself apart from gentleness and kindness to be a stern and sober figure of authority. Thus – despite him being a clergyman of peculiar unfriendliness – there was unspoken consensus that he was a 'great' man as far as his sphere of influence extended and someone to be looked up to. Privately there were very few people who actively liked him but nobody would dare vocalise such a heresy.

Retirement had not dimmed his menace in the pulpit and on the occasion of Jim Scott's funeral he failed to disappoint.

The sermon majored on eternity and everlasting rest but did not omit the importance of wheat and chaff: 'for chaff – loved ones – is burned'. He retained his habit of leaning close into the pulpit – with both hands spread upon it like an eagle's talons – and delivering the most crucial points with a frank whisper and a matter of fact frown. Willie's neighbour across the road had once complained in empurpled bitterness after a funeral that if Harry McNally was the sort of man who went to heaven then he himself would sooner go to hell.

Willie, Violet, John and Gillian sat together in a pew. They knew each other well enough to run a mentally recorded book on one crucial aspect of the proceedings: "I wonder how long it will actually take McNally to mention Jim by name: other than in his opening comments of course but that doesn't really count. I'll bet you it's seven or eight minutes anyway." John wasn't far off: the first meaningful reference was on eight minutes and 40 seconds, half way through the opening prayer and after the first hymn as Rev McNally supplicated 'God who calls himself the defender of widows to draw close to Jim's loving wife Thelma.'

One modern aspect of funerals that even the rod of McNally could not expunge was the now near habitual event of the family tribute. This was given by Jim's only brother who as Violet said looked as white as a sheet and obviously could barely believe he was in this place and doing this thing. He shared recollections of childhood and growing up together and the reasons why Jim would always be special to him: he started falteringly but grew in strength as he got into his stride but then broke down near the end just as he realised he was on the verge of nearly getting through it all.

Violet remarked that this 'phenomena' as she described it 'of people having to give these eulogies at family member's funerals was just an absolute nonsense'. If it was palpably clear to her that not everyone is up to the ordeal of speaking at such a service, then why could other people not see that? Violet would not expect anyone to speak at her funeral.

"Will you stop going on about your own funeral so much"

Willie whispered. "You're starting to make me feel ill the way you're going on."

"Well we've got to talk about these things" she muttered back. "We're only burying our heads in the sand otherwise."

But at least the severity of Rev McNally and his reminder to the congregation that Jim like all of us was 'a sinner' and 'dust' had offset that other contemporary funereal habit of 'so avoiding speaking ill of the dead that we swing the other way and canonise them before they're cold.' Violet further reminded Willie that when she died she would go to Glory but she would not become another star in the night sky, or an angel in the celestial choir, and would not expect to be eulogised in such tones.

The consensus was that the sermon wasn't bad but that if you'd never met Jim it would not have helped you get to know him. The closing rendition of Amazing Grace was both rousing and moving (even if Violet could never understand why they had to sing it to *that* tune). The weather had changed in the forty five minutes that they had been inside: as the group members congregated there was clear blue sky overhead even if the next downpour didn't seem far away.

The undertakers ghosted around the conscripted pallbearers and organised them with typically discreet efficiency. They loitered in pairs and were taken as they stood: Willie and John; Adam and Peter; and Mike and Alan.

Willie regretted that he had spent time comparing himself to Jim that he should have spent trying to get to know him. John inwardly muttered prayers to God for strength in this moment and tried to focus his mind on the enormity of carrying a dead man's body.

Peter marvelled at the bonds of faith that found him bearing on his shoulders the casket of a near stranger with a band of brothers most of whom he hadn't known a few months ago. Adam felt like something of a fraud and had pangs of guilt that perhaps this man he was carrying felt more for him than he had ever particularly felt the other way.

Mike thought there was 'nothing bloody slim about him'

and wondered how far they were going to have to go. Alan was chilled by his own mortality and the certainty of death on his shoulders but cheered when he thought of Jim's niece who had done the bible reading: he had never once doubted that a long skirt with a slit is sophisticatedly much sexier than a short skirt.

As unseasonal wind-chill tore across the cemetery. Harry McNally's robes blustered like a Holy Ghost wind-sock and a stony-faced undertaker held down the pages of his folder as he barked out the sure truth of 'Get them at the graveside' evangelism. Jim was with God which was better by far but those who have not made that choice for Christ ought not to ignore this moment of salvation for life is but a vapour that blows momentarily and then is gone.

* * * * *

Peter

When the committal was over the mourners returned to the church hall where kind hospitality – "a cup of tea will be provided by the ladies" – was laid on for them. The women of the church hovered round their guests from all directions, every angle worked as a front to be attacked with sandwiches and sausage rolls, traybakes and tea.

Some were sitting and some were standing, and Willie chivalrously ensured that Violet had the nearest available seat. As he stood with a plate in one hand and a cup and saucer in the other and nowhere to put either he reflected that he couldn't actually enjoy either the food or the beverage unless he had the trunk of an elephant. He had often thought that to meaningfully eat at such occasions a person would need to be 'tridextrous', but whether you had hands or paws the good Lord only provided such tools in units of twos or fours.

The members of the group were initially dispersed throughout the hall but as the supper progressed they gradually gravitated towards one another.

"Well gentlemen: here's to Jim" John said as he self-consciously raised a cup of tea to the departed. "He was a good man. He obviously set great store by the principle that anything he did he would do well. Jim was a man of integrity."

"A man of integrity *in his own way*?" Adam added: "do you remember that one?" There was some shaking of heads: not everyone knew this anecdote. "Hmmm… well I suppose it's going back over twenty years so not all of you would remember it – I'm showing my age a bit here. I remember there was a funeral of a loyalist leader who had been gunned down and in the sermon the pastor described him as 'a man of integrity in his own way'. If you stepped out of line on his patch you'd get a bullet in the head but he would gladly help your Granny cross the road. You could say anyone is a person of integrity in their own way. Osama Bin Laden was a man of integrity 'in his own way'."

"I think legacy is an incredible concept" Peter said. "Funerals always get me thinking about it. I wonder to what extent it's a particularly spiritual concept. I'm not convinced the average man in the street gives it much thought. I fully respect those who believe that everyone has a yearning God shaped hole inside them, but it seems to me there's lots of people going to hell in a handcart as they live for the here and now. What exactly is the legacy of a man's life?"

"It's not something I've ever given a lot of thought to" John continued, "but I think there's a distinction between what I would call small legacy and big legacy, and every man has to have a certain amount of both. Small legacy is all about the tiny details of how you treat people. You were a good husband who remembered anniversaries and occasionally bought flowers for no reason at all. You were a good colleague who everyone thought highly of: always nice for a wee chat at the tea station.

And yet I think it's easy to have an over-romanticised view of small legacy and say that it alone is enough. Because you could have a lot of small legacy without ever having stretched or striven to make a mark and do the very best with all God has given you. Even the tax collectors have a small legacy, to use a biblical turn of phrase."

"'Jesus loves a little wallflower Christians'" Willie interrupted.

"Exactly" John agreed. "'And yet you could be a great Christian in wee things but timid about greater callings. We all need to have a big legacy of God having given us our ten talents and us making at least twenty talents back."

Adam eagerly developed his point for him. "But in terms of all this big and small stuff there's no point having one if you don't have the other. Look at McNally there" he said, lowering his commentary to a whisper. "He's a 'great man of God' in terms of his single-mindedness in pursuing what it is that he believes God has called him to. But in terms of small legacy, there's no other way of putting it: he's just horrible. What damage has he done for the kingdom on account of sheer rudeness?"

"Personally" Peter said "I've never seen the man before but what struck me about his message was the preoccupation with the after-life. When Jesus defined eternal life he said it was about knowing the only true God and Jesus Christ whom He had sent. And yet we think of eternal life almost exclusively in terms of heaven and hell. Shouldn't we be more concerned with the values of 'the Kingdom of God' in the here and now than with what comes afterwards?"

There was blank dumbness in the faces in front of him. "Maybe I'm not making myself very clear. What I'm trying to say is that sometimes at funerals the predominant message is all about the life afterwards: 'eternal life'. But maybe that emphasis is all wrong: maybe instead the focus should be on... well Jim has had his time and Jim is gone. But I still have my time and when I see how suddenly the time can be taken away from me, I should redouble my efforts – or *make* an effort never mind redoubling – to do the very best I can with what I have been given."

"Salt and light" Mike said.

"I guess so" Peter agreed: "that certainly puts it pretty succinctly. I love the analogy of the Christian life being a journey. But if you place too much emphasis on heaven and hell then you're overly focused on the end destination and you miss the pleasure of the travelling. If eternal significance is the only significance then the Christian life as a journey might as well be an autobahn: just travel in the most efficient way possible to the end of the road. Heaven and hell are realities of enormous proportions and we've got to be frank about saying 'How will we die?' but we need to be equally candid about 'How will we live?'"

He was becoming excited and he beckoned his friends closer to himself.

"I mean, think about it guys. Who are you? You're the minority living in the first year of a new country unified contrary to your wishes. You're people who proclaim faithfulness to God but live in a continent that has almost overwhelmingly chosen the secular rather than the sacred. In thirty years or fifty years or one hundred years time historians are going to pore over your community and they will be fascinated to analyse how it was you prospered. Did they stand up for their God and their principles and live radical counter-cultural lives in the pluralistic-Roman Catholic hybrid of this New Ireland? Or did they just blend in and live out little days in callow conformity? That's legacy: what about that for legacy?"

"Oh button it" Mike snapped. "This is neither the time nor the place: where do you ever get off? You've obviously had the pleasure of being at the top of mountains I haven't been on. What time is it?" He snatched a look at his watch. "Ten to two: I'd better be off then; I'll see you all on Sunday no doubt."

And so the numbers lowered one by one. As each man or couple parted he or they were sure to do their dutiful turn: complementing Thelma on what a lovely service it had been and assuring her of their thoughts and prayers. Some more practical matters were attended to on the way out such as Willie's habitual visit to the gents: Violet often teased him that he lived as if he ran the risk that he would never get to a toilet again. By the time he had got in and out of there Violet had become locked in earnest chit-chat with Gillian, so Willie fell into conversation with John.

"One thing struck me about that funeral" John confided. "Not once was the nationality of the deceased mentioned. I'm not all up myself like yer man Peter but this is going to sound like the sort of thing that he would say.

I suppose when you get to the end of your days maybe that isn't a matter of great importance: I mean it is for – say freedom fighters or really patriotic people who suffered for a cause. But it's no big deal for the average five-eighths man, is it? Your wife and your children and the way you treated people and the things you did are what matters. Legacy is what is truly important and there isn't much legacy – be it small or big – in living all your life in the place where you were born as a random act. Where we lived is much less important in the grand scheme of things than how we lived."

But before Willie could respond to this point Violet broke off her conversation with Gillian and pointed her voice to the two husbands. "Well, Gillian, I suppose we'd better be heading, because those two old women there would gas all day if you gave them half a chance."

* * * * *

Mike

A lovely peace had descended on Mike's home as he and his wife rested in easy chairs: the children had settled to sleep and if you listened closely you could hear the gentle rhythm of their somnolent breathing. With it being such a cold day Wendy had decided to 'spontaneously combust' the hearth and put a fire on. On account of the wind outside it had taken well: they had a homely blaze without needing to resort to Mike's preferred method of ignition, that being at least half a packet of firelighters.

(In early married life they had coincidentally discovered in some random conversation that they had both watched – or at least heard of, they weren't sure if they had watched it – some documentary about people who spontaneously combusted. It was probably on BBC2 but they couldn't agree on that and it didn't matter anyway. The point was they had both seen this programme about these people, and they spontaneously combusted in their bed at night: bhooosshhh – up in flames and that's them gone.

And as good evangelical eight year olds – well catechised and Sunday Schooled – this had freaked them out: it quite literally put the fear of God into them. What if I spontaneously combusted tonight: who would miss me and what would happen to me and where would I go? But now they were both older and wiser and had the presence of mind to realise that it would never happen. They could laugh about it and refer to lighting a fire as "the hearth has spontaneously combusted").

It was rare that they got an opportunity to have such a night together. Mike's work meant he was often out in evenings: then there was the church routine of house groups and Rainbows and Boys' Brigade and so on, that more often than not seemed to split the family up. They sat side by side on the sofa – she with her girly book and he a newspaper – and he worked hard at pretending that he was comfortable with silence and comfortable with her company. The girly book seemed to hold her in a trance but having read the sport section and got half way through the news, Mike's concentration was wilting. He asked her if she wanted hot chocolate and was disappointed by the apparent indifference of "whatever, only if you're having one."

He made the hot chocolate – proper stuff with milk, and he managed not to burn the hob – and whilst grateful, Wendy nonetheless remained in the grip of this hip new writer called Honey Flynn. He furtively cocked his head to an angle that allowed him to read the back of the book: it was about a girl called Orla who thinks she is happy with Ronan until one day an old flame called Conor – who she was sure she was over – surprisingly moves into the house next door with Sorcha and her whole world is turned upside down. 'Fenian chick lit' he thought to himself: 'you can't get away from them'.

He went back to the newspaper but it held his mind only

until he had drained his mug of its fluffy dregs. He rested the paper on his lap and stared ahead and it was then that he began to be arrested by deeper and unwelcome thoughts. He fixed on the fire and clarity seemed to suddenly enter his thinking that could not be diverted. It had been lit for several hours now and was pushing out intense heat: red hot with the embers orange and every now and again there would be a little movement or collapse of coal and you would see bits that there were bright orange like lava. The thought of hell entered his head and then he could think of nothing else. Nothing at all. He thought of people he loved and he liked and how they must be going there – family, friends and neighbours – and now he was terrified.

He thought of Jim and carrying the coffin that day, and felt dreadful remorse at his callous ambivalence when it was on his shoulders. What was in that casket had once been a man: but now it was only dead matter and tissue, and where was the man? Death is real, he thought – death is so real – and I am probably half way through my three score year and ten and it will come to me. It and taxes: the two great certainties. And he believed in God and he believed in Jesus and Heaven and Everything but he was so damn sure that he didn't want to find out too quickly what any of it is like. He loved God but he loved being alive every bit as much. What actually happens when you – whatever – cross to the other side? What actually happens? He had become scared now: darkly, deeply scared.

He thought he could talk to Wendy and that would help matters but when he turned his head he saw she had dozed off and her book had slumped on her chest. He felt a churning in the pit of his stomach and a realisation that it is lonelier to be with someone sleeping at a time like this, than it would be to have no one at all. Death is real, he thought, and what have I done with it all?

And then his mind jolted on: it jolted because it felt like his soul was being taken on a helter-skelter ride of its most stripped down anxieties. The next drop was legacy and all that stuff that they had talked about after the funeral. What difference had he ever made to anybody? This had frequently troubled him in private moments: he did not believe that he had ever helped to save one soul and if he let it, that thought could crush him with guilt and inadequacy. People would talk about being links in the chain but what had he done. What had he ever done, really?

Why had this happened now? Why had this happened tonight? He had had no inkling that this was coming: funerals always unsettled him a little but he had never expected to feel this way now when he sat down with a cup of tea at the beginning of the evening. Now Wendy's chest was heaving steadily in rhymes of sleep: he knew that if he woke her and told her it all she would comfort him, but this was his time and God's time and he realised he shouldn't let her in.

And so he did what was most unnatural to him and stole silently off the sofa and fell on his knees on the floor. Thoughts and prayers tumbled sheepishly and incoherently out of him as he wanted to tell God how it was but didn't want to get caught like *this* by Wendy. What on earth would she think?

He told God he was sorry and he would try harder. He pleaded that people he loved would go to heaven and not to the fire, and that he would be able to talk to them about these things, and if not him then someone else – just somebody – would talk to them. He asked for passion for prayer and for God's Word and asked that God would help him to use the time he had left to good effect. He wanted more and wanted to be better but realised he couldn't do that on his own.

He would stop now: he wasn't quite sure how much of this prayer would be enough to make a difference but he would stop now. He sneaked back up on to the sofa and looked straight at Wendy to make sure she was still asleep. He wouldn't say he felt peace like a river but there was certainly a stream of something running through the lounge. He woke Wendy gently and she was surprised to realise she had even been asleep, and he said she was obviously exhausted and they should really be getting to bed now if that was the case.

18

Strangers in a strange land

A new pattern and order was to be found as they met for the first time since Jim's death. Over time it had been established that, for example, Alan and Mike would sit together on the sofa: subtly befitting their friendship and a youth that did not yet merit the demi-statesmanlike comfort of individual armchairs. John sat in a large reclining chair that sometimes caught him out and tried to gobble him up if he moved the wrong way, but by its size seemed to emphasise authority, like a metaphorical headdress.

But now they were at John's house: the sensibilities were the same but the setting was different. After a short opening prayer to clear their minds and gather their thoughts, Alan did the bible reading "which is taken from Jeremiah chapter eighteen, and verses one to eighteen.

This is the word that came to Jeremiah from the LORD. "Go down to the potter's house, and there I will give you my message." So I went down to the potter's house, and I saw him working at the wheel. But the pot he was shaping from the clay was marred in his hands; so the potter formed it into another pot, shaping it as seemed best to him.

Then the word of the LORD came to me: "O house of Israel, can I not do with you as the potter does?" declares the LORD. "Like clay in the hand of the potter, so are you in my hand, O house of Israel. If at any time I announce that a nation or kingdom is to be uprooted, torn down and destroyed, and if that nation I warned repents of its evil, then I will relent and not inflict on it the disaster I had planned. And if at another time I announce that a nation or kingdom is to be built up and planted, and if it does evil in my sight and does not obey me, then I will reconsider the good I had intended to do for it.

Now therefore say to the people of Judah and those living in

Jerusalem, 'This is what the LORD says: Look! I am preparing a disaster for you and devising a plan against you. So turn from your evil ways, each one of you, and reform your ways and your actions.' But they will reply, 'It's no use. We will continue with our own plans: each of us will follow the stubbornness of his evil heart.'"

Therefore this is what the LORD says: "Inquire among the nations: Who has ever heard anything like this? A most horrible thing has been done by Virgin Israel. Does the snow of Lebanon ever vanish from its rocky slopes? Do its cool waters from distant sources ever cease to flow? Yet my people have forgotten me; they burn incense to worthless idols, which made them stumble in their ways and in the ancient paths. They made them walk in bypaths and on roads not built up. Their land will be laid waste, an object of lasting scorn; all who pass by will be appalled and will shake their heads. Like a wind from the east, I will scatter them before their enemies; I will show them my back and not my face in the day of their disaster."

They said, "Come, let's make plans against Jeremiah; for the teaching of the law by the priest will not be lost, nor will counsel from the wise, nor the word from the prophets. So come, let's attack him with our tongues and pay no attention to anything he says."

"Well the first question in the book is fairly straightforward" John said. "'What words would you use to describe God's feelings about the nation of Israel in this passage?'

"Well" Adam began "I suppose whatever words describe God's attitude; they wouldn't be words of consolation. One thing that comes across is that God is straight-talking, and yet he's also fair. If God says that He is going to punish a nation and then the nation reforms itself in terms of behaviour and so on, then God will relent. Equally if a nation that is in receipt of a promise that it will be built up and prospered deviates from God's will and behaves contrary to His demands, then God can reconsider the good He had intended. We ought not to predict the nature of God and take what will happen for granted."

"That's all very well but to what extent does any of this apply *now*?" Alan asked. "Do we get too hung up on all this *stuff* about God moving in the lives of nations? I mean, surely we're modern New Testament Christians and if God still moves among a collective group of people then it's the church we should be worrying about."

"Ah, but" Peter said "remember that the whole bible hangs together in the round. What we are reading is the words of a Jewish prophet and we have to realise that the Christian faith is intimately linked to the Jewish faith. God didn't start all over when He sent his son to this earth: He did amazing new things and he did them on existing Jewish foundations. Sacrifice still existed but now there would be a once and for all perfect sacrifice. Jesus did not come to abolish the law: He came to fulfil it.

I accept what you're saying about the church but when He sent His Son to earth God didn't have a clean sheet of paper. This is our heritage and there are lessons we can draw from it. We can't be selective about the bible: we can't say we want to take Old Testament comfort and wisdom out of the Psalms and Proverbs but we don't want to take anger and judgment from the prophets."

"There are a few more words to describe God's feelings" Adam said – he had been further scanning the passage. "There's anger and revulsion as He sees He's been forgotten by His own people. 'Forgotten' is a dreadful word: the indifference that it implies – like 'I'm so sorry I forgot it was your birthday.' And look at that bit there – there's a phrase that speaks of total disgust – 'I will show them my back and not my face in the day of their disaster.' It's as if God has just had enough and is washing his hands of the whole lot of them."

Peter's eyes were also gliding eagerly over the text and he continued straight on the heels of Adam. "Isn't it fascinating to think of the idea that God will relent. I know we've talked about this before but that to me reinforces the sense that whilst God is the God of history, nonetheless we're not just passive bystanders to whom history happens. Is it the case that if we behave a certain way, then God will change the course of action He is set on?

Look at verse eight there: 'if that nation I warned repents of its evil, then I will *relent* and not inflict on it the disaster I had planned'. An interpretation you could take out of this text as you reflect on the recent history of Ireland is, was there a time when a particular choice stood before you and you could have gone down a certain road so that God did not relent? Because if God *can* relent then it might have been in our power – *your* power even – for things to have been different. If God can relent then there hasn't necessarily been some irresistible progress towards unity that was always going to turn out that way. To use a phrase that was very *en vogue* a few years ago: was there a spiritual 'tipping point' or 'tipping season'? A time when it all tipped one way but could so easily have tipped the other?"

This idea was met with silence. Some looked at their laps and bibles and some looked at the ceiling: one glanced at his watch but no one looked at Peter. Then Adam spoke, developing the thought but doing so cautiously.

"I suppose – depending on how spiritual a filter you choose to view history through – there might have been a number of tipping points. The late sixties and the civil rights movement could have been one: should there have been a stronger moral leadership from Christian people and the Protestant churches to stand up for the Catholic minority? Roll on another thirty years and was the Good Friday agreement another such moment? There was – what – seventy odd per cent of people voted for the agreement. At that time the Catholic community made a choice to almost overwhelmingly back this horse for a way forward, but just over half the Prods said they wouldn't endorse such consensual principles. If both communities had overwhelmingly backed that accommodation *within* Northern Ireland, would Ireland be united now?"

"Now hold your horses there" cut in John. "No harm to you, I think you're gilding the lily somewhat the way you're portraying things. The Good Friday Agreement involved power sharing with a terrorist party who were giving no undertakings about what they would do with their private army, and it also meant large swathes of… scum prisoners – for whom life should have meant life for a whole lot of them if you ask me – getting early release. Have you got some Holy dementia about what our land was actually like and the things that really happened?"

"I don't know John. I'm not a historian and there's an awful lot of 'what ifs' here. I just have a pile of questions like the rest of us. I mean, what about the election in 2005, was that a turning point? I'm not sure how historians will judge Trimble but he was a man I'd a great deal of time for: and I know some of you wouldn't agree with that. It seems a dreadful shame that more people didn't recognise as he did that the best prospects for unionism were to make with the British and the Irish and the Nationalists the best deal they could, rather than have an even less palatable deal imposed on us from without. Was that a tipping point when the God of history could have relented, but He chose instead to turn His back on a community when they themselves turned their back on a visionary leader to choose instead to follow naysayers?

But then the die-hards changed their minds. Look at the way our leaders conducted themselves. One group sought moderation whilst the self-styled defenders of the Union crowed betrayal and weakness and didn't get their hands dirty by any means. Then when they'd trounced the moderates in the polls they seemed quite happy to take the power and trappings of accommodation they'd been condemning just a year or two earlier. Talk about letting someone else do the dirty work and then you take all the glory. I think that was the right thing to do, but I don't think they did it for the right reasons. That's all very political – and judgmental – but it is in effect what you're saying Peter: isn't it?"

"It is, yes" Peter said: "it's just the sort of thing I was getting at."

John had to make a point. "It seems to you a dreadful shame Adam. I tell you, it seems to me a dreadful shame that Trimble was ever elected leader of the Ulster Unionist party in the first place. If that excuse for a leader – that so called politician – hadn't done what he did we wouldn't be in this hole now. That's my two pence worth – or two cents – or whatever it is…"

"No, that's ok" Alan confirmed dumbly. "It would be two cents now."

Willie sat like a sponge taking all this in, and whilst he had not said anything he was certainly thinking. "The thing about that theory is – and the thing about a whole lot of this if you want to apply it to Ireland – is where was the warning? If you look carefully at Jeremiah and delve into so much that the prophets said, there's lots and lots of warnings. God doesn't seem to just burst in on people and take them by surprise. It's as plain as day in this passage here: 'This is what the LORD says: Look! I am preparing a disaster for you and devising a plan against you. So turn from your evil ways, each one of you, and reform your ways and your actions.'

And there's the same sort of stuff in other passages we've read together. The last study was all about 'the Temple of the Lord, the Temple of the Lord, the Temple of the Lord'. There was that warning that they mustn't trust in deceptive words and needed to change how they were treating the oppressed. If God is behind our unification, then for Him to be just and fair, ought He not to have given a warning?"

"That's not something I've ever thought about before" Adam said. "I suppose there were pockets of strong leadership but not much more than that. Sometimes at the top of the hierarchy you'd have had Bishops or Moderators who spoke out at times when there were retaliatory cycles or flurries of unrest. But there was *never* a really overarching sense of a warning from God to the whole community. *Never! Never!*" He made a cross face and a bad stab at Ian Paisley's voice. "Now there's the word – from Dr No himself. Though I suppose he changed in his twilight years – whatever that was about."

Willie shook his head and at that particular moment looked elderly as he did so. "But the church was weak. Really, the church was weak. You had congregations in some interface areas like North Belfast who were tremendously earthy and engaged in issues on the ground. And then there were some middle class churches in the likes of South Belfast, who were kind of doing ecumenical stuff: 'building bridges' as they'd put it and all of that.

But for the most part the Protestant congregations were a bit like one of the churches at the start of Revelation: neither hot nor cold on the issues springing from conflict. I know young Alan has talked about this before, but the average minister on the average Sunday in the average pulpit would never touch on the Troubles. Take the Sermon on the Mount and read right through it week by week, but never challenge me to deal with my bigotry or get to know my Roman Catholic neighbour."

"But then, would we have listened anyway, even if the message had been set in front of us?" questioned Alan. "Jeremiah spoke to these people – and hey, he was the real deal, wasn't he – but it's no use because they say 'We will continue with our own plans; each of us will follow the stubbornness of his evil heart.' Part of the downfall of these people is that they're *so* stubborn and yet if you looked at our community – the Ulster Prods, as we were – stubbornness is something we all held on to as a kind of virtue.

I remember coming across a similar passage in Ezekiel where God accuses the people of being obstinate and stubborn. If you'd said that to Protestants in Northern Ireland they'd probably have been quite chuffed. God says it's a sin but we see it as a virtue. 'Never, never, never: we will not be moved'. 'We will not sit down at the same table as Sinn Fein'. 'We will not recognise the authority of the parades commission'. Was stubbornness part of our downfall?"

"Thran" Willie said.

"What?" Peter asked.

"Thran" Alan answered, butting in. "It's a Norn Iron word for stubborn or crooked people. Like Wee Bertie – Bertie's a thran man – he's practically thran incarnate."

John intervened in nervy embarrassment at the mention of an elder's name. "Gentlemen, time is marching on. Let's take the next two questions together or we'll never get through this. In what ways did the nation of Israel resist being moulded by God? What was God's response to their resistance?"

"Sorry John" Peter piped up "but before we go on to those questions can I just mention something I've been thinking of?" He didn't wait for permission to be given. "Willie asks if there was ever a sense of warning, and Alan has talked about what he thinks of stubbornness, but maybe Willie – or maybe anybody – wants to pick up on a point I think relates to the subject of warning. What should follow after a warning is a turning: did that ever happen? Was there ever a powerful sense of the Protestant people – or at least the evangelicals among them – seeking God's will for their situation?"

"No" Adam said, regretful that he didn't need to think about this. "No – hand on heart – I don't think so. I don't believe there was ever a time when Protestants in this land collectively turned to God and sought His will for their future. I don't know: is that fair?"

The rest of the group mumbled and shook their heads. Adam carried on.

"What you have to appreciate Peter is that the kinds of issues we're wrestling with here have over the last forty to fifty years been seen as optional add ons to the core of the Christian faith which is about worship and witness and prayer and bible study and so on. There were always some people who had cross-community orientations, which was fine for *them*, but it was always a fringy, fuzzy, lefty sort of thing. Social justice and reconciliation and all the issues of the Troubles was quite simply never mainstream in the lives of most congregations up and down this land. Many of the churches were like an opposite of Saddam's Iraq."

"What!" Mike said. "Where did that come from?"

"Well stick with me. It sounds absurd but let me explain. I remember reading a newspaper article about Iraq once. Saddam was a secular dictator who allowed a surprising amount of religious freedom: his attitude was that as long as your political life conformed to what he wanted, he wasn't terribly bothered about what you got up to spiritually. The counter to that is that a lot of the evangelical churches in this country seemed to take the view that as long as you were religiously 'good living' and involved in the church, then they weren't concerned about what you got up to politically.

But I suppose a lot of clergy were choosing the path of least resistance – Protestantism was angry and many of them would have been afraid of the destabilising impact it would have had on their ministries if they confronted these issues. And understandably so: it's a hard enough job without splitting your church down the middle as DUP on one side and UUP on the other."

"Hey" Peter added "don't we only need to look at the passage that's right under our noses. Look at the flack Jeremiah has to take for his stand: 'come, let's make plans against Jeremiah… come let's attack him with our tongues and pay no attention to anything he says.'"

Willie gave a long and plaintive sigh. "Dear Lord: and to think some regard the bible as outdated and having nothing to say to us today. Sure that could be straight from the mouth of someone in this country. Couldn't it? 'I don't like the man next door or the church next door so I'll attack them with my gossipy wee tongue and pay no attention to anything they say'. Except that we wouldn't be secure enough to pay no attention to it: we would have to dissect it and biblically prove all the faults in it to argue why it's not worth any attention! Take heed and all of that.

Everything is so factional. Look at those dreadful petty letters you used to get in the Belfast Telegraph: one theme of vindictive doctrine scoring could have gone on for weeks and weeks. If some God anointed prophet – a Jeremiah of our time – had stood up and laid it all on the line for us on a Monday there would have been at least ten points of correction for him in the Belly Telly by the Wednesday. People in this country would be more interested in debating with him than being humbled by him. I think that's something very frightening about this land: that you can live through the likes of the last forty or fifty years and be so breathtakingly arrogant that you fail to be taught and you fail to change. You just fundamentally fail to 'get it'."

"Sorry, sorry" John said "all good stuff but could we even just *try* and look a wee bit at this last question: What are some of the ways that people today, especially Christians, resist being moulded by God?"

They looked to the text in front of them expecting an answer to leap from the pages. And then Peter spoke: but tentatively by his own standards. "You know friends, there is one thing that – it may be too strong to say it has *bothered* me – but I've certainly been aware of it since I came here.

The thing is – and it's not necessarily a question of resistance to God but it is striking – the thing is… money. I'm reasonably travelled – I've not spoken to anyone about this before, not even Adam – but something I've been very conscious of since I came here is money. Not even money itself but just – some things. Like the houses. Some of your houses are just *so* big. And there seem to be so many of them: great big developments of these huge hulking houses sitting on the edge of every town. And it's not like it's just the town mayor or the doctors or the lawyers who live in them – so many of you seem to live in these big enormous houses. Why?

And then there are the cars. Gosh: the cars. I've never been aware of so many new BMWs, and Audis, and Mercedes, and so on since I came to Ireland. Not even the quantity of them but so many of them are *so* new and *so* big, all the latest models. And it's not like there's this huge ascetic chasm between the Christians and the non Christians: you go into your church car park on a Sunday morning and – well – there's a fair number of these big fancy cars. It's really kind of taboo and awkward to talk about money with people you call your friends. And don't think I'm saying it's a sin: I'm not for one minute calling it a sin. But just – why?"

There was a gap as he collected his thoughts, before carrying on in the same vein.

"I mean I'm not at all suggesting that you can't be a Christian *and* have nice things: I'm not saying that at all. I mean, look at Job with his hundreds and thousands of sheep and cows and all, and how much he loved the Lord. But if you look at the

New Testament and the things that Jesus had to say there's this clear link between having money and that being an obstacle to a walk with God and spiritual development.

And I look at so many of these people who I've met – and I think – they're clearly good people and they obviously love God – and yet there seems to be some sort of need or want there for good stuff and the best of stuff. Are many of us going to end up apart from God but that will be ok because we lived in big houses and drove fancy cars along the way? Gain the world and lose your soul?"

A collective squirming and murmuring was apparent.

"I'm not sure that I can see how it's any way justifiable. But then as Willie said people here are the sort of Christians who can justify anything to themselves: God is to be explained rather than experienced. Why is it so important to some of you?"

19

Strangers in a strange land

There seemed to be something inappropriately clinical about saying that a church was no longer viable. Fifty years ago the Methodist Church at the top end – the Protestant end – of the town's Main Street had been a vibrant spinning top of Christian life. There were Sunday services and there were missions; there were 'Midweeks' and there were prayer meetings; there were packed Sunday schools – both morning and afternoon – and a flurry of activity for 'young people' from uniformed organisations through to youth clubs and youth fellowships.

(Alan loved the way churches referred to a certain set of people as 'the young people'. It was a curiously evangelical way of speaking and he particularly liked the ill-defined nature of what a 'young person' was. When, he asked himself, did you stop being a 'young person'? Was it about marrying and settling down? Was it about having children? He had often thought it curious that nine years old was the cut-off age where you were no longer able to go to 'children's church' but rather had to sit through the main service and sermon. What was the rationale for nine being an age of enlightenment: was there a similar point for stopping being a 'young person'?

It could also be a pejorative phrase: it was meant as a damning criticism when certain others would say things like "the problem is the young people don't seem to appreciate how dear these hymns we grew up with are" – or "if only the young people were prepared to commit and get involved." It was a demographic definition exclusive to churches: around and about society streamlined classifications such as toddler and child, tween and teen, adolescents and early twenties etc abounded. But the church did not streamline as the world did: rather it clumped and opted for 'young people').

As for the local Methodists, the decline of this once active family of God's people could be traced to a range of factors typical of so many congregations across the North of Ireland. The leadership of the church had failed to catch a vision. Although large numbers had flocked to this place Sunday after Sunday, that had been evidence more of social mores and respectability than it had been fruit of the Spirit.

The church became inward looking, with a pettiness that verged on the stifling. There were debates about future direction that at times were so ill-spirited they would have been out of place at a golf club or rugby club, never mind a church. There was too much looking in and not enough looking out, and tradition and worship were inevitable sources of tension. When one lobby pointed out that Saint Paul did not read his hymns off a screen, the counter-argument would be made that Saint Paul did not go to church in a Toyota Avensis. "And I'd further point out to you that in the reformed tradition we are *all* saints."

Decline crept up on the congregation from behind rather than ambushing it: and just as there were fewer heads among the pews week by week so more of those that were there would be grey and white. As age wearied people and the pace of life grew faster so there was less time and bodies to feed the creaking monster that the church calendar had become.

And so by the time they had realised the imperative to change, the mountain had become too high to climb. Mike recalled that only two or three years ago he had gone to an evening service at the Methodists with his father-in-law. An energetic minister from a thriving Belfast congregation had sought to charge the people with conviction about what *they* were going to do to grapple with the local community and get involved with it. As Mike relayed it to Alan it had been almost pitiful: all these septuagenarians and octogenarians who looked fit to grapple with nothing but milky coffee and digestive biscuits, with this futile enthusiasm bubbling in front of them.

"I suppose" Alan said "you could trace it back though, couldn't you?"

"What do you mean" Mike replied, with a puzzled look.

"Well – when you think about it – when we see these churches declining we tend to come at it from a very – I hate to use this word: 'worldly' point of view. You know: we tend to analyse it the way you would analyse a business that has failed and look for all the underlying causes.

But then you look at the start of Revelation and the letters to the churches there and it makes you think that every church has a story to be told to it. You wonder what Jesus would have written to that congregation or what he would say to our place if he was still doing that sort of thing today. We tend to come at it from an angle of them not doing enough outreach work or they called the wrong minister or they stuck with a choir and organist for too long – combinations of very predictable things. But when Jesus looked at churches he approached it in terms like being lukewarm instead of hot; forsaking their first love; having a reputation for being alive but actually being dead. Who are we to say why things have worked out this way or that way?"

Around and about these people of God the world had changed and moved on: and God's people failed to move on with it. Those who had been pillars in the church had become columns in the evening paper. And so their numbers dwindled to the point where that awful word 'viability' did indeed enter into the scheme of things.

They didn't go out with a whimper but they didn't go out with a bang either. To commemorate the heritage of their witness there was a last hurrah of worship to God. Those with both long standing and loose connections were invited back: the likes of sons and daughters of former ministers; the likes of men and women who had grown up there but now moved on – some of course as recently as in the past year. And so for one last time the walls of the sanctuary shook to singing voices as air expelled from lungs to blow out the dust and cobwebs from among the loved ones. Everyone remembered what had been and regretted what might have been and the doors were shut and the railings locked for the very last time.

Few passers by noticed that anything had changed, until the

large 'For Sale' sign appeared on the property. It was a prime site on the street and rumour had it that a Dublin developer had snapped it up. Violet commented that if it were renovated sympathetically it would be the sort of building that would make a lovely 'thingy' shop: "you know, a shop that sells cards and candles and scented things and all sorts of stuff – thingies – that nobody actually needs". Willie thought it would be nice to see a bookshop though he doubted if there would be much demand for such a business in a town this size.

There was a moderate sense of panic when it emerged that a local entrepreneur called Davy Kyle had bought the building: Kyle had a number of bars and clubs in the surrounding area but the grapevine attempted to salve anxiety with assumed reassurances that he surely wouldn't do a project like *that* with a church building. He would more than likely do something like a restaurant where he could recover the sort of investment he'd need to gut and refurbish such an old building. But little did they know.

* * * * *

Willie

Willie nearly went into the back of the car in front as he drove up the town.

"For goodness sake: watch where you're going. Are you trying to get us both killed?" Violet asked.

"No – I'm sorry. I was looking at *that* – look – at *that* over there."

Violet's mouth gaped in incapacitated astonishment as she read the large sign that as if from nowhere had appeared on the front of the Methodist Church. Amidst a bevy of generously proportioned and scantily clad blondes and brunettes were the words: *Coming Soon: The Happy Slappy Church – Where Every Day is Funday!*

"Did you ever in all your born days see such a thing?" Violet said.

"What on earth is the world coming to?" Willie asked. "He surely can't do such a thing – I mean you'd – you'd think there'd be covenants or something on a building like that."

But when they got home and opened the local paper they found themselves very much mistaken: there was a spread announcing the arrival of the town's soon to be newest and raciest attraction. Kyle himself had sported robes and a dog collar for the photo and with a large black bible in his hand he was sporting a faux pose of admonition towards a suitably lascivious looking young lady.

The gist of the article was that he was extremely excited about his new project. He understood that some people would be offended by what he was planning but such people are killjoys and they had to appreciate that this was just a bit of fun. Times changed and the town was crying out for an attraction such as this.

'If singing old hymns and getting hell fire and brimstone shoved down your neck is your idea of a good night out then there's still plenty of places to go here. Needless to say, we think we're offering something different. We're going to put some fun into Sunday and we're going to put some fun into every other day of the week. And you know: holier than thou people might look down their noses at what we're doing here, but I can guarantee I'll have a lot more people going through those doors than the old proprietors did.'

"It's just so shameless" Violet said.

The local churchgoers in the town were suitably appalled. How could it be that a thing like that was happening in a place like this? They talked among each other and recalled in shock their memories of that place: weddings, funerals and baptisms they had been to in the church. It seemed so flagrant: it didn't even attempt to hide its disrespect for them and their values, for heritage and decency. Everyone agreed that something ought to be done to object to such a scandal: and everyone sat on their hands and waited for someone else to do the doing.

20

Alan

It had seemed like a good idea at the time. Alan had noticed some pounds beginning to pile on and realised he was getting to a point in life where a trim waist could no longer be taken for granted. Mike suggested that he join a gym but Alan said he wasn't ready for that yet. "There'd be all these toned and honed bodies and then me in the middle of it all like Mr Muscle meets the Michelin Man. They'd all be looking at me from behind their towels: you can't join a gym until you get fit."

However he was aware that Peter was into running and thought this might provide a cheap and easy option for getting started at exercise. It only involved putting one foot in front of the other in rapid succession: anybody could do that if they put their mind to it. He mentioned his plans to Peter who said he'd be welcome to join him – he ran in the park three evenings a week at tea-time. 'Penalty kick' thought Alan to himself: he must easily have 15 years on me. No matter how bad I am, I'd be able to keep up with him.

They met on a Wednesday evening. Alan was a firm believer in looking the part for anything he did and had invested in a new pair of running shoes to complement the coming season's Liverpool top and last year's holiday's shorts. Peter had texted him to say he was running late – Alan wondered if that's where the phrase came from – so he took the opportunity to grab a few minutes rest on a park bench. He got up and started a bit of running on the spot when he saw Peter pacing purposefully towards him.

"Sorry" Peter said. "Just give me a few moments to warm up here. Have you stretched already?"

Alan nodded unconvincingly. "Oh I'm fine."

Peter didn't argue, before proceeding to turn, pull and twist his body in the manner of some life-sized Morph.

"You ready then?" Peter asked.

Alan didn't like the sound of this – the lack of small talk was beginning to alarm him. "Oh absolutely. Ready when you are."

"Great – a circuit of the park is two miles. I normally go round two or three times, but sure you see how you get on. You're welcome to dip out as we come round again."

And off they went. The first thing Alan noticed was the noise: Peter seemed to go instantly from standing start to cruise with no process of acceleration discernible, and was almost inaudible as he glided along. Alan however was particularly conscious in the early evening quiet, of the inelegant thumping of his trainers on the ground. And Peter was so focused too: like a Dalek in a track suit. Alan looked down and realised that Peter had those types of remarkably spindly but muscular legs he associated with certain breeds of athlete: he had seen more substantial legs hanging out of birds' nests, but they didn't seem to have any problem propelling his friend along.

The effortlessness of Peter's performance became more apparent as he began to engage his younger running mate in conversation. "How was your day" he asked Alan, with no discernible impact on stride or breath."

"Oh… you know… how it is… nothing strange… or startling."

As they moved up a hill that was both gradual curve and incline, Alan became increasingly aware of his left nipple rubbing against the Liverpool crest. The building agony of this was matched only by the flesh eroding friction of his heels in the new shoes. He noticed ahead of him that three 'feral youths' – as he would later describe them to Mike – were lolling up the path ahead of them. Two of them were wearing Rangers tops and all carried bags of cheap alcohol: as the runners got closer to them, Alan caught the smell of cigarettes in the air. But he was nonetheless relieved that with the narrowness of the path at this point – and it being closed in by trees on both sides – the pace of this unholy trinity would buy him some breathing space.

As Peter and Alan closed in behind the boys and slowed to a walking pace, sniggers could be heard in front of them.

"Excuse me" Peter said.

He was obviously ignored.

"Excuse me" Peter said a second time – louder and more impatiently.

One of the three laughed. Peter stepped off the path and brushed against the scrub and shrubs in an effort to get past. But the boy on the left hand side simply moved over to block him.

"Come on now Stevie" said the middle lad. "Let Barack Obama past."

"I'm only doing him a wee favour Jinky: sure he looks like he needs a break."

"I'd whip your ass round here any day." Peter replied.

The boy on the left – Stevie – blew out a snort of derision. "I'd like to see you try."

Peter stopped jogging. "Fine then – where are we going to race to?"

Stevie was not expecting this – but wasn't about to lose face in front of his friends. Before he could reply though, Peter made a suggestion. "What about the gate at the end of the lake? I reckon that's about three quarters of a mile from here: should be no problem for a young fellow like you."

Stevie reached out his bag of booze but neither friend volunteered to take it off him. "It's fine" Peter said: "Alan here will caddy for you. You ready?"

Stevie scowled at Peter. "Are you going to set us on our way then Alan?" Peter asked.

The two lined up beside each other.

"On your marks. Get set. Go!"

Stevie hared away with whoops of encouragement from Jinky to "put the pedal to the metal". Peter followed after him; his opponent was building distance between himself and the older runner, but Peter was by no means hanging around and was exhibiting greater rhythm. As they disappeared into the distance, Alan began a lumbering jog behind with the bag of drink banging against his knees, the other teenagers following with him.

There were a range of bends and twists and so the race was out of view for most of the next six to seven minutes. As Alan came round the corner approaching the back gate, he saw ahead of him the two competitors. As he got closer he noticed that Peter was leaning back against one of the two pillars with a distinctly satisfied look on his face, whilst Stevie was on the grass, looking flushed and angry as he leaned back with his arms behind him.

Around two minutes later Jinky and the third amigo arrived. The sound of panting filled the air and their bags were tossed to the ground as they leant forward to recover with the palms of their hands on their thighs. Alan was pacing stiffly like an elderly animal in its zoo enclosure.

"Is this it?" Peter said, surveying the near-carnage arising from a mere mile of effort. "Are you lot the future of the Protestant people? Because God help them if you guys are it. I tell you lads: 'if you have raced with men on foot and they have worn you out, how can you compete with horses? If you stumble in safe country, how will you manage in the thickets by the Jordan?'"

"What the hell are you talking about now?" Alan asked.

"It's from Jeremiah. It means if your faith is of no importance to you even when all is fine and dandy in the garden, how do you expect it to be any kind of help when there's rain and frost and weeds about you? At the time when troubles come and things aren't going your way: at times like now."

Peter looked down at his watch. "Nice to meet you Stevie" he said, holding out his hand for a shake and a peace offering. "Now I'm going to go and get a few more miles in."

21

John

John could not get his head round the promise of the train taking the strain: travelling seemed tiring these days, no matter what way he did it. But then he never was much of a one for the catchy slogans of marketing types: that was all gloss and polish if you asked him. As he leant his head back now, he could feel involuntary pulsing sensations beneath his eyes when he closed them. He knew whenever those started it was a sure-fire sign that he was running on empty.

He had not enjoyed Dublin today: he had never liked the city and indeed loathed it now more than ever. It was all fast and busy and full of bustle. Everyone had a purpose about them and seemed too focused on their day's goal to be any way aware of the humanity around them competing for space on the pavement. And they all clutched these cups of coffee in their hands as they hurtled to their destinations: he was sure the human body was not designed to properly digest hot liquids whilst moving at such a pace.

Maybe it was unfamiliarity or maybe it was age catching up on him – or perhaps just the anxiety of the day's events – but for the first time in his life he felt nervous as he walked the streets of a city alone. He just didn't get Dublin: it was just another greedy modern metropolis; nothing 'diddly-dee' or 'fair city' about it. And barrow boys were just wide boys in his estimation. (Though he did notice that some of the girls 'were so pretty' and it troubled him that no matter how much older he got this never seemed to get less apparent).

He tried reading a book but could not concentrate – although the cradling of the object in his hands gave him something to hold on to, at least in the physical sense. He tried reading the paper that he had picked up at Connolly Station when he'd got back there half an hour before his train was due to depart. But it was full of Irish affairs that he neither cared for nor understood: what did it matter to him if schools were closing in Athlone or hospital waiting lists were rising in Ennis?

And then he startled as he saw the back of a familiar head going up the middle of the train and glancing around for a seat: he was sure it was Mackey. There was something telltale about the long-legged gait with which he strode everywhere with great purpose. And a wee giveaway was that he had one of those fey manbags slung over his shoulders that so many young men seemed to mince about with these days. It was one thing to wonder what your wife has in her handbag: another thing altogether to imagine what might be in Mackey's manbag...

Mackey had earphones plugged into him as well. John didn't get that either: he might have many problems weighing on his mind but he contented himself that at least he could sit at peace in the silence of his own company. Earphones were just a form of running away. His book was in his rucksack and the paper was now crumpled beside him: if distractions wouldn't work that was a pity but not a problem for he told himself that he was old enough and wise enough to not need distractions. Just staring into thin air was rather a waste of time, but nonetheless it gave him space he could be doing with.

Mackey kept on striding up the carriage. His work – or whatever way it was that he put his day in – must have taken him to Dublin. He must have felt at home down there, what with his wee Catholic girl and everything. But now John's worry was starting to subside – he felt sure he had not been seen.

It came to the stop one before his home town and so John rose to his feet to get off the train. He'd be careful to head back down the carriage: even if it gave him a little further to walk it would reduce his chances of being spied by his so-called friend. The train moved away from the platform and John hung back from the crowd; walking behind it was the best way of glancing over it to be sure that no familiar faces were gathered up among it. And content with his rudimentary reconnoitring he wandered slowly to the car park. There he opened his boot and pulled out a large black suit carrier. He had gone to the car with sufficient sloth as to be almost alone now. Glancing around him he put the suit carrier over his shoulder and locked his car before heading back to the station and the convenience of its gentlemen's toilets.

A few minutes later he returned to his car attired in the sweater and trousers of a day's round of golf. He would tell Gillian how good it had been to catch up with all the old boys and get a few hours of walking and fresh air to boot. He would relate to her their reminiscences and how Bobby Murray who'd been his Inspector in North Belfast had lost some weight, but if you saw wee Sergeant McCloskey now you'd hardly know him because he's just like an old man. Gillian might ask him what exactly it was that they had talked about all day but if she did he'd simply say 'Oh nothing'. That infuriated her because she would then say that nobody could spend a whole day talking about nothing, but he knew that it would be enough anyhow. It was not, all in all, a very elaborate plot but then it did not have to be, for John knew he was married to a trusting woman.

* * * * *

Alan

Alan had also noticed John on the train: he wondered what it was that he was doing there, but the inner feelings of antipathy were mutual. A streak of him was nosy enough to want to enquire, but such curiosity was soon struck down by the fact that if he spoke to John he'd feel obliged to sit beside him the whole way back. There are needs and there are wants but Alan viewed John as an altogether negative two for the price of one: he neither needed to speak to him nor wanted to. John was alright in a group but he was hard work on his own. Alan likened talking to him as being akin to making conversation in a foreign language: all the time that he was prattling on, Alan would be scratching about and straining his mind to rehearse whatever he could find to talk about next.

He was careful not to break stride as he paced up the train, and consciously did not look back until he had reached the safety of the next carriage. He needed to be alone: Nadia was weighing heavily upon him. It seemed that the one as beautiful as a rose was becoming a thorn in both his flesh and mind.

Women were truly a wonderful thing – whether making them laugh; or engaging their minds in his cerebral conundrums; or having a plain good roll on a sofa – he enjoyed their company more than that of men. But love brings its own share of problems. Earlier in the day he'd gone into a Starbucks in St Stephen's Green, to fuel up with coffee and kill some time before the presentation he had travelled down to deliver. The woman who served him – Svetlana according to her badge – was tired looking and appeared nervous and harried. He was careful in how he executed his transaction with her, making eye contact and deliberately saying 'Thank You'. She appeared to be almost startled by this. Three months ago he wouldn't have done that: three months ago she'd just have been a body to take his cash and coin and provide a service.

A good looking woman was to him a good thing. A good looking woman with a great personality to boot was an excellent thing. But to be in love was a special thing. And such as his epiphany in Starbucks is what it did to him: he saw things – some things anyway – differently now. He wore 'what would Jesus do' on a scruffy little bracelet but now he reflected too on the matter of 'what would Nadia think'. The colleague under pressure with a deadline; the wee boy across the road who didn't seem to have a Dad; the old man next door who lived on his own. He had a heightened awareness of all of them now. She was an outsider and loving her made him alert to all such on the periphery: he was softening and changing. 'In so much as you do it to the least of these you do it unto me': there was a fundamental rightness about this, but how had it taken her to make him see that?

It was not just her being about and him loving her that struck Alan – there was also the way that she lived her life. Nadia knew God and she lived according to who she knew. Her

English was better than most of her peers, and on one evening off, she had announced she couldn't see him until after nine because a friend of a friend of a friend was struggling to fill in forms to resolve a landlord problem, and she felt she had to help. Two afternoons a week she would sit patiently over disheartened boys and girls at a homework club for academically lagging children. A choice between spending thirty Euros on a new top and sending more money home to Granny was a no-brainer.

He noticed that he had lots and lots of *belief* but perhaps it was the case that she had more *faith* and that made him jealous. The study group was just another example of that – sure all they did was talk. Was that just some small microcosm of the effectiveness of their faith? She might think a lot of stuff he didn't agree with but she was at least a doer and that much he could not deny. Faith without works is dead, so did that make her more living than he and all his righteous friends were?

When Alan had started out on all of this he hadn't thought it through to the point of such a dilemma. There were times when he was riddled with doubt and could happily have had the phone in his hand: 'let's call the whole thing off'. And yet there were other times when it had such rightness about it, more right than anyone or anything that had gone before. There were, however, no signs of her changing: there was no hint that he was heroically dragging her up to his level on the table above her, to his elevated plane of truth and knowledge. He thought that Catholicism was just a 'Dick and Dora' sort of faith: simple, easy stuff of liturgy and ritual where you left your mind outside the chapel and went inside for all the mass and going through the motions. But it turned out that she was anything but a simple sort of girl, and yet she believed all this and held to it every bit as much as he did to the orthodoxies of his tradition.

They had rows about it – huge rows. He quite enjoyed a good swing of theological gymnastics and picking apart Catholicism in the company of another Prod, but he hadn't bargained for the challenge of such a conversation with his own girlfriend. He thought these discussions would be like picking up a Bible and all he had been brought up to believe, and going bowling with it. But when he flung his Bible with weight and speed that seemed certain to demolish her beliefs, he was perturbed that at best he could only dent and spin a few peripheral pins around her edges, with the rest left standing firm.

She persisted in going to confession and he insisted that she didn't need to do that. If you've done something wrong just say it straight to God. And there's no penances needed: nothing you can do can make God love you any less, and nothing you can do can make God love you any more, so what are you doing wasting time with your Hail Marys and all that malarkey? Ok, so there is that bit in John where Jesus says to the disciples that if they forgive someone, they're forgiven. Well if that's where you're getting it from, said Alan, sure tell me what your sins are, and I'll forgive you: you don't need to go into some man in a box for absolution. He quoted to her that there was one God and there was one mediator between God and the human race – Jesus Christ. Priests are an Old Testament thing, you know: if you're going to priests to get the nod that you're all clear with God then you might as well be sacrificing a few goats here and there as well.

She in turn told him that was absurd, that it was nothing like that, and he knew it was nothing like that. It's about being honest – it's about being sorry and facing up to all your shortcomings and actually being prepared to make an admission of that to someone. Externalise the internal and it's so much harder to pretend about what's on the inside. And then the penances are just a way of making that contrition tangible. One is saying sorry and the other is showing that you mean it. What was so wrong with that?

He looked out of the train and at the countryside whirring by in a blur, and thought that it was all very well agreeing to disagree, but you couldn't base an entire relationship on such a principle. How could he have been so dumb as to be blithely attracted to the nature of her character, and yet not bargain for the strength of that character? Glancing at his watch, he wondered if they were over the border yet, and then he remembered that Dundalk to Newry was now just another town to town stretch on the track. A further complication was that it wasn't just about him and her: family and friends had been difficult too, more so than he wanted to admit to himself.

Aunt Agnes was his Granny's spinster sister who lived in a terraced side street off the Donegal Road. She was bluff and loyal and orange to the core – outspan in both body and mind – the proverbial Big Aggy from Sandy Row. He generally only saw Aunt Agnes on family occasions of hatching and dispatching, but she had generously persisted year upon year in sending him birthday cards. She seemed in something of a time warp insofar as they were always of the cheap and nasty variety that had a painted racing car or footballer on the front, and always with a ten pound note enclosed. He appeared to have stopped in her mind at something around the age thirteen. Perhaps he sometimes wondered, Aunt Agnes had had some Miss Havisham type experience, unbeknown to all the family – that would have explained a lot.

But this year there was a card only and no ten pound note. And inside the card, beneath the words 'may today this special boy, have birthday wishes filled with joy' was a terse note that explained that she wasn't giving him ten pounds this year, and he knew why, and 'you should be bloody well ashamed of yourself. One of the problems of the Protestant people was that we failed to replace ourselves at their rate of knots – it's bad enough you've not married and done your bit, and now you're taking up with one of them. You have no backbone'. He had chewed that over a few times in his mind – the not married bit seemed a bit rich coming from Aunt Agnes, but for all the frequency with which he saw her, he could live without her favour. It was mates like Dozer cutting and running that he found harder to take.

Dozer was a 'Free P' friend who had given him a nasty little tract entitled 'The Devil Scented lure of Popery' – on the cover of it was an image of rosary beads beside a bowl of pot-pourri.

He had laughed when it was given to him, and in so doing only made the moment worse. On the back of the booklet was a PO Box number you could write to for more such material, which would be posted to you free of charge, with correspondence courses also available. Now Dozer was being distinctly stand-offish with him, and on the one occasion he'd met Nadia had been downright rude.

He looked out the window again. So much was now uncertain, but what contributed to all the knots and tangles was that one of the few things he could be sure of was that she loved him – it was stormy at times but it was no game to her. And compared to 'his own sort' and girlfriends who had gone before, there were ways in which where she came from gave her such an innocence. She was an immaterial girl to whom trophies and trinkets were not important. There was no constant checking of balances of giving and receiving with her: she seemed to treasure most of all his time and his company and being with him.

Nadia was different. She believed in the wrong things, but yet she believed in them more strongly than all the previous women who believed in the right things. It seemed to him now that they could take or leave their faith, but Nadia had taken it thousands of miles and it remained the centre of her life. Maybe he was being hard on Grace and others – he was hardly Mr. Virtuous himself and perhaps this was just a reflection of the type that he had 'gone for'. Nadia was challenging and changing him more than anyone who had gone before.

The previous Saturday they had gone to the North Coast for the day. It was sunny and warm but as they walked on the coastline itself a strong wind blew in from the Atlantic. Nearing the cliff edge at Mussenden he had stopped to tie his lace and she had walked on a few feet ahead of him. When he stood up again he looked ahead and viewed her from a distance. With her back to him but her arms out wide she was standing in the wind and the sun and soaking in the rough beauty before her.

He stayed where he was so that she could be the centre of his view, and make the pleasure of his moment complete. She could have been the statue of Christ in Rio, he thought. She could have been the lady herself in Manhattan Harbour – holding her torch out to the migrants and mendicants, just as she herself was a migrant. He looked at her that moment and thought that she must be the one. He could happily have run to her and gone down on bended knee. And yet another part of him could just as easily have run past her to the edge of that cliff and thrown himself off it. What had he got himself into? He thought of that line from the book by Charles Dickens, whatever it was. This was the best of relationships but it was the worst of relationships: certainly she was the least complicated of girls but the most complicated of girlfriends.

The apostle John said that Jesus Christ had come from the Father full of grace and truth. That was all very well, thought Alan, but what do you do when you have to make a choice between the two? Grace seemed like it could only pull him in one direction and that direction was one person. But truth made him want to turn the other way and put as much distance as he could between Nadia and himself. Grace and truth was the son of God the Father but grace and truth – as he saw it now – was one almighty mess.

22

Adam

"More than anything" Adam said "I feel a strange sense of; I don't know – sadness – or maybe loss. And yet loss is hardly the right word either because it's not as if it meant a lot to me at the time. I mean – there became a lot that was wrong with it – but then there was a great deal about it that was harmless too. I suppose on balance it's a shame that it's gone."

It was the morning of the twelfth of July and Adam was decorating his lounge with Peter. In a sense that was entirely normal because to people like him that was what the twelfth of July was for. For many years Adam had experienced it as a peculiar holiday: grateful to Orangeism that its celebration gave him two restful days of statutory leave; and yet irked that it left him so constrained, that assorted shops and swimming pools and amenities weren't open and so there was relatively little you could *do*.

It had been to Adam not so much the 'glorious twelfth' as the 'useful twelfth': not a time to march but a time to potter. Around dinner tables and office kitchens Adam had, like so many, adopted – post Drumcree especially – a sniffy and dismissive view of the Orange institutions. 'The marching season is a wonderful thing: half the country ships out on holiday and the other half stays at home to wreck the place.' He occasionally felt pangs of guilt about this when, for example, he looked contentedly at the fruit of a day's gardening on a twelfth evening: he felt a little grubby, like an atheist pulling a Christmas cracker and unwrapping his presents.

Somebody had once said that Englishmen generally had a disinterest in the Church of England: no inclination to go along each Sunday and worship God – but nonetheless it was oddly nice to know that the Church of England was *there*. Is that, he pondered, how he felt about the Orange Order? That they were in some sense priestly people who were doing high-Unionism and making up for people like him who absented themselves from such committed patriotism. In some deeper recess of his attitudes had it always been good to know that even if he wasn't interested, there were people like that *there* – people 'to do it' for all of them?

How 'to do' the marching season was a challenge to the New Ireland. Who had the greater right: the minority with their prerogative to march and express themselves; or the majority who didn't want the inconvenience of this group – who if they did march would be raking up history and proclaiming allegiance to something other than the new land?

But such lofty debates dwarfed the meagre reality on the ground: anything the Orange Order did put on would not be on a scale that anyone could find offensive. When you took away those who had left for England and Scotland, and then considered those too disheartened or anxious to march, you were left with a decidedly tiny remnant. And so what you saw was what you got: something proud and determined but nonetheless small and insignificant. Where once one hundred thousand marched, there was now at best only ten to fifteen per cent of that number: a big enough parade in Belfast and parts of Antrim and North Down but very little anywhere else. The crowds were small too: where once there had been thousands clapping and cheering from the pavements, waving their union jacks beneath a sky pock-marked with bunting, now people would just stop casually for a little look whilst they went up to the shop for their paper. It was the sort of sideways glance you would have given when the circus came to town.

Some couldn't help but think back to the scenes in O'Connell Street on Easter Sunday. This was all wrong: in the best colloquial sense Prods did some things better; things like marching and rallies. Protestants were superior at pomp and circumstance: this stemmed from their innate Britishness. And Catholics did some things better: the GAA was what most obviously sprung to mind. Local soccer and cricket couldn't hold a candle to the community significance of the Gaelic games. They were good at culture with their fiddly-diddly music and their Irish dancing. And murals too: Catholics were much better at murals. But now the tables were turned and the Protestants couldn't even march better: look at the Catholics putting on a march that in scale and fervour towers over anything the Protestants could manage.

They had started out hundreds of years ago standing up for Protestantism and civil and religious liberties. People would have died for this cause and all their determination was to fear God, honour the King, and love the brotherhood. But who cared today for principles like that – who cared today for principles at all? Now in their distinctive regalia of black suits, sashes, and bowler hats, would a modern and secular state reduce their traditions to the quaint moral equivalent of those English people who roll big cheeses down hills, or those Spaniards who madly run around the streets of their town happily throwing tomatoes at one another?

"Did you ever go to the marches?" Peter asked.

"No" Adam replied. "Well maybe once or twice when I was very little but I can hardly remember it. All I can recall is the sense of – well – boredom, really. Unless you were looking out for your Grandpa or your Dad's friend or someone like that, there wasn't really much to see. The thing that used to fascinate me later was how you actually got into it. Dad took us to see them but he wasn't one of them and I wondered why that was. Did you just go along to a lodge and say you believed in this and you wanted to be in it? Or did you wait for some patriarchal elder statesman of the church to sidle him up to you some night and tap you on the shoulder and mutter that you seemed a fine lad, and we've noticed what you're like, and would you like to be in our wee club? But of course that was hardly going to happen to me because I was always on the lefty-woolly side of the church.

You see, Protestantism worked in concentric circles of commitment. There were those in the middle who were in the Orange Order and faithful to the core: marching in bands and flying the Union Jack from their house at the right time of the year. Then there were those in the next circle out: not in the order but committed supporters and very certain in their politics and the sanctity of the Union. And we were probably in the outer circle: we were soft Unionists who definitely hated Republicanism and wanted to be part of the UK, but socially and all we weren't terribly interested in the activities of the inner group. We probably thought ourselves a bit above that."

"It's not dissimilar to the St Patrick's Day thing, is it?" Peter suggested.

"I've never thought about that" Adam replied "but you may have a point. St Patrick is our patron saint yet you were able to come along and teach me things about him because Protestants have largely chosen to ignore Patrick. And the Orange Order is also a fundamental part of Protestant culture and heritage and yet I could tell you very little about it either."

"Well, I'm afraid I can't help you out with that one."

"Gosh Peter: I'm sure I've said this before but I feel terribly ignorant. I don't know how you actually get to be in the Orange Order. I know nothing about their structures and how they organise themselves. I know it has an association with Loughall but I don't know the real history of how it came to be formed. Some of the stuff you see on arches is really weird – snakes and ladders and compasses and the like – it looks a bit Masonic to me. I certainly haven't a clue about what the difference is between the Orange and the Black. You could join that –"

Peter chuckled and Adam continued.

"Whether it's Patrick on one side or the Orangemen on the other, maybe that's one of the problems with this country: the people in the middle have in the main opted out of heritage. They – we even – I – me and people like me – we chose to take our identity far more from things like class, consumerism and professions than we ever did from culture and community. Maybe if I'd to do it all again that's something I'd do differently Peter. Maybe I'd of got stuck in more: maybe I'd of joined the Ulster Unionists and gone along to the local lodge."

"What: and tried to be a voice of reason? And tried to light a candle instead of cursing the darkness and all of that?"

"No – no, not at all. You see I don't think that's fair Peter. What you're getting into is one of those really ironic things where broad minded people are all superior about who they think are narrow minded people: which makes them narrow minded themselves. And that's a lot of the problem in the way so many people viewed the Orangemen. I remember when my own kids were small they *never* saw a march because Carolyn was adamant that she didn't want them near that sort of thing. But that was throwing the baby out with the bathwater.

Maybe the Orangemen were to a degree the victims of a modern society where anyone who believes very strongly in anything is viewed as being a bit loony. Of course Drumcree had an awful lot to do with that. And don't for one minute get me wrong: Drumcree and some of the things they did and they let happen were truly dreadful. They made the most enormous mess out of it all. But did we – and by we I mean the ordinary Christian people of middle-Northern Ireland – did we make enough of an effort to understand all of that? There is nothing I would want to do less on a hot July afternoon than walk down the middle of a road behind some banners, to the accompaniment of a pipe band. It would bore the pants off me. But for other people that was *their* world: that was dear and precious to them and it mattered to them.

Drumcree was grim – but there were too many people who responded to what happened in a really unthinking type of way. And I was one of them. You know, I can actually remember, in the midst of one of the blockades at a road, rolling down my window and shouting at the guys manning this barricade – in fact yelling it at the top of my voice – 'FASC...ISTS...!!' Not that I had the courage to do it at very close distance. But *I* did that Peter: that was *my* response at the time."

"Yeh but come on Adam: you couldn't excuse it. The things they did were awful. I mean think about the three little boys burned alive in their house: how did that happen at the turn of the twenty-first century in a civilised country?"

"Yeh, yeh: I know that Peter. You're absolutely right. They

were really badly led and they got sucked into a dreadful cycle of two wrongs make a right morality. It was inexcusable: I'm not saying it was right – I don't know what I'm saying – I just think that some of us – and certainly me – should have tried to understand it better."

"You're surprising me man" Peter said. "What exactly is there to understand about the difference between right and wrong?"

"Yeh but – are you not confusing sympathy with understanding? It's not that I'm necessarily sympathising with the Orangemen or agreeing with all that they stood for. I don't. But I have no right to view it all from some untouchable position of self righteousness. Was that not the story of this country? The Protestants fail to make accommodation for the Catholics' point of view, and the Catholics fail to make allowance for the Protestants' point of view, and then somewhere in the middle you have the moderates sitting on the moral high ground and failing to connect with the standpoint of those on the extremes: like it's somehow beneath them. People who live in pompous ghettoes of the mind.

There are people in this society who view a right to walk down a road as sacred and non-negotiable. I don't agree with that but I think me and people like me need to deal with that in a more sophisticated way than the moral equivalence of sending a naughty child to their bedroom to have a long hard think about what they've done. They certainly do need to do a lot of thinking but maybe some of the thinking is down to me as well. Putting a child on a naughty step punishes behaviour but it doesn't necessarily address the frustration or whatever that lay behind it. Drumcree was a sin and shame but it gives me no right to regard a portion of my community as pariahs."

"But Adam, come on, if you follow these arguments through to a natural conclusion you could justify anything. You can argue black is white if you're clever enough."

"Yeh – I know that – and I'm thinking on the hoof here Peter. But go back to that analogy of punishing a child. Sometimes when my kids were small there were cries from another room and when I got in I'd hear that one person had pinched or scrabbed the other and the other had pulled hair back. And faced with no evidence but just two grumpy children I'd jump to a conclusion based on nothing other than gut-instinct. Who looked guiltier?

How did Drumcree and Dunloy and Ormeau Road and so on come about? Did all those Resident's Groups just magically appear? I'm really not a savvy man of street wise sense but there must have been a pre-meditated effort by Republicans to attack this aspect of the Unionist community and to go looking for confrontation. That's the opposite of peace making: that's discord making.

A small minority of Orangemen were and undoubtedly are bad news: yobs and rabble rousers. But the majority of them were essentially harmless. For every hooligan Orangeman I'm sure there was also a couple of elderly gentleman for whom the lodge was an important social outlet and perhaps a link to the past: his father and his grandfather had been a member and walked the same routes before him."

"But Adam, you know as well as I do that there are two sides to every story."

"I do indeed Peter and that's where I'm going to get to. Terrible things happened and it seems to be that many Orangemen weren't able to come up with anything more constructive in response than 'they started it first'. A lot of the routes for parades were clearly problematic and were throwbacks to previous times. What sensible Orangeman would derive pleasure from walking through some Nationalist area?

The bands were a big problem too. However inoffensive some of the Orangemen may have been, the bands didn't seem to be policed very well and all too often they looked and sounded aggressive. Sometimes I would see them congregating at corners or filling stations waiting for their bus for wherever they were going and they were – well, let's just say they weren't the sort of young men you'd be delighted for your daughter to bring home. And when that sort of influence got in – and an organisation lacking in leadership – well, that was always going to be a recipe for disaster.

The worse bit was the civil unrest… I mean when you look back on it and think about it – the blocked roads and the intimidation and – yes the three wee boys in Ballymoney. To think that an organisation rooted in biblical Christianity descended to all of that. I remember John telling me – he was in the RUC you know – about being at Drumcree and having Orangemen pointing at him and colleagues and yelling at them and shouting out their names and addresses. It actually became a kind of ritual to go home from morning worship on numerous Drumcree Sundays to turn on the TV and see the live feed of scenes outside this church. How surreal was that?"

"So where does that leave you and your views then?"

Adam sighed deeply "Oh Peter – I don't know – I hardly know what my views are. Northern Ireland is a very complicated place. Spiritually it is extremely untidy. Nothing here is simple, so nothing here should be approached simplistically."

* * * * *

Peter

"You see" Adam said "you might find it hard to believe, but we wouldn't have been able to do that on the Twelfth ten years ago."

They had run out of the apple white that was the mainstay of their decorating and had nipped to the local DIY store for replenishments.

"Gosh I needed that –" Adam reflected, talking in the main to himself. "Paint starts to get to you after a while: it doesn't half go to your head."

"That's your story and you're sticking to it" Peter retorted. "What do you think would have happened if there had been no Drumcree: if it had never happened? Where would the Orange Order have been in that case?"

"I don't know: is there any point asking questions like that? You can't extend reality."

185

"Well you can't, but it's still interesting, isn't it?"

"Well, I don't know about the Orange Order. I suppose like a lot of tradition based organisations it would just have fizzled out. The thing about Drumcree is that whilst it set the Orange Order off in a very misguided direction, it nonetheless gave it tremendous momentum in that direction. It energised it: people actually flocked to join the Order after those disputes though you might well ask what their motives were.

I mean if you think of a comparison, how many children today want to go off to Boys Brigade and go on camps and do drills and get their badges and all of that stuff? It's all very worthy but it's also outdated: people in church have a tendency to wring their hands when there are only four boys and two leaders going to the BB on a Tuesday night but I think it's just the course of progress. Things change and everything ends. In my less reasonable moments I suppose I'd say the Orange Order was just like a uniformed organisation for grown-up boys and it would be fading out and going the way the other organisations are. I mean let's be honest Peter. Grown men in dark suits, sashes and bowler hats parading along a road behind a piped band are a bit of an anachronism in the year 2020."

"But that makes it all sound very harmless. There's more to it than that Adam, is there not?"

"Oh absolutely. Drumcree was a truly desperate advert for Unionism around the world. Look at the sort of messages that it sent out. Unionists barricading roads and burning cars and then policemen wade in with batons to clear the way for them to get up the Garvaghy Road. This was the image of our community that was being flashed around the globe at the end of the twentieth century. It was an absolute PR disaster. And if 'brassed off from Bolsover' was sitting in their home in middle England watching that you could hardly blame them for wondering why exactly the United Kingdom bothered having anything to do with us.

But as Christians I think we've also been too quick to forget that all those scenes were played out in front of a church: in front of a place of worship. That got lost in the midst of all the passion and anger that was raining around on all sides. There's the age old expression about not being able to see the wood for the trees: at Drumcree you couldn't see God for the religion.

I've never considered it this way before but think about this. In the first half of the first decade of the twenty first century Moslems remonstrated with public opinion about things like veils and niqabs and cartoons of the prophet. They seemed to lose any sense of reasonableness and sections of their community became incapable of hearing any kind of criticism against them. A down to earth and decent man from Northern Ireland would look at radicalised Moslems outside a place like the Finsbury Park Mosque and shake his head and mutter something like 'sure how would you even begin to reason with people like that?' And yet less than ten years earlier there were Christian men gathered outside a church in Portadown throwing bricks and stones and blast bombs at the police. When you get too close to these situations you lose the rational perspective that sees how crazy all of it was."

"But in fairness Adam" Peter said: "there's a big difference between an Orangeman at Drumcree and the mindset that's happy to blow themselves up for the cause they believe in. It's a big leap that gets you from that A to that B."

"Mmmm, I suppose so" agreed Adam glumly. "Say what you will about the Ulster Prod but when he's lobbed his bricks and barricaded his roads he'll still want to get home to his creature comforts. There's just too much conservatism and self-interest in him to be truly 'radical'. Whereas your average Moslem radical has done a really good day's work if he *never* goes home but ends up in a body bag. What an utterly depressing conversation."

"Eh yes Adam, it is rather."

"But the thing is that God was so caught up in it: the very signature of the organisation was 'For God and Ulster'. I mean don't get me wrong: I wouldn't instantly take a big fat pen and put a line straight through that. But I think for a lot of people the Orange Order was far more about how committed you were to the Union than how much you were committed to God.

Just to link the two together is plain wrong. It's as if being for God meant you had to be for Ulster as well. They would never have said so publicly but I think some Protestants had a barmy notion that God looked upon Ulster as having some marked specialness, like a kind of anointed Old Testament Israel come to Western Europe. That is utterly fatuous: the Ulster Protestant way is by no means the God way. Why not for God and Ireland? God is not an Ulster sympathising deity who places the rights of one community above another. Heaven will be a great place Peter, because there'll be no flags there. Heaven will be fantastic."

23

Peter

You can't have a carnival atmosphere without kids, thought Peter. That was the problem: where were the kids? There was no shortage of serious and elderly faces, scrunched up against the sunlight as they sucked ice cream cones through lips and gums. There was the odd smattering of young parents and small children, but the old were in the majority. He had come with Adam to the Sham Fight in Scarva, and the muted crowd was awaiting the annual stand-off between King William and James II.

"But the fight wasn't here, was it?" Peter asked. "Surely the fight was the Battle of the Boyne. Isn't that down in the Midlands?"

"Absolutely" Adam replied. "This was the training ground though – William had an army of 30,000 and they camped and prepared here before going on to the Boyne."

The main event took centre stage. There was huffing and puffing, to-ing and fro-ing, and a flurried crossing of swords. Yet as the crowd cheered, William's victory, in this new island, was as hollow as any win can be in such a wide open space.

"Is that it?" Peter asked.

"That's it."

"It's not exactly the rumble in the jungle, is it?"

"Well what do you want?" Adam replied. "It's a more than three hundred year old action replay. It's bound to be a bit predictable."

They turned and began to walk away.

"It's a bit of metaphor, isn't it?" Peter suggested.

"How so?" Adam asked.

"Well it's just like the Protestant people, isn't it? It's stuck in the past."

"You what?"

"You know Adam, I've heard so much guff since I've come here about Priests and Catholicism and the heresies of Rome and the wickedness of Sinn Fein and the IRA. But lots of that stuff is just like those two actors out there: it's yesterday's battles. But maybe history is comforting if it helps you not to have to cope with today."

"It's just a tradition" Adam said defensively. "It's part of their heritage: it's good for things to be passed down."

"That's fine as long as it's just a sideshow. But your people's religion is of no relevance to the battles that need to be fought today. Being able to argue Catholic doctrine inside out has nothing to do with secularism or materialism or agnosticism or post-modernism. The swords and muskets are fine for fighting swords and muskets, but the devil has gone on to heat seeking missiles."

"I'm not sure that's fair."

"It's not nice but it doesn't mean it's not fair. It's just my advantage: I see things from the outside. Sham religion is no use: you go to church and you get salvation preached to you when at least 90 out of 100 are saved anyhow. You get told that you're the good people and the ones outside are the bad people. Which makes you feel good but doesn't matter a damn to the bad people because…"

He looked at Adam in a way that made clear he expected his friend to finish his sentence.

"They're on the outside."

"Exactly: and the outside seems far more real and exciting and here and now than what's going to happen in Heaven or Hell any number of years from now. Sham religion makes you feel good when you go to the service but it's like this sham here – enjoyable while you watch it, but now that it's over they've all got to face up to the fact that they're the defeated and the minority in this present age."

Peter stopped and looked all around him – then he looked at Adam.

"Don't get me wrong, Adam. This is great – in its own way,

it's all perfectly harmless. But these are people who seem convinced that their best days are behind them. Forgive me for saying so, but your up and coming generation don't seem to be tripping over themselves to be here, do they?

This is not real – nothing about it is real. When your idea of a community celebration is reaching over three hundred years into the past – when the best of your church history is revivals that happened over a century and a half ago – then it seems to me that there's more than a few things wrong, and you're a people who need to ask hard questions about the direction you're heading in."

24

Strangers in a strange land

"I'm ashamed to say it" Willie said. "I take my hat off to your wife, John. If you want to get something done, you want to get a woman on the job."

"Oh don't talk to me. I tell you: once she gets an idea into her head it's practically impossible to dissuade her." He blew out a long and worn down sigh. "It looks lovely today but it's nippy enough when you're standing on the one spot."

The Happy Slappy Church was due to open in two weeks time, and the men of the cell group found themselves amongst the most reluctant activists in all Ireland. The congregation and its leadership had dithered in inertia for the past month until Gillian had door-stepped the Reverend Houston on the way out of church one night, and asked him directly what the leadership proposed to do about this. He suggested falteringly that perhaps she might like to put together a little paper for the elders – but before he could conclude the formalities of this invitation, she asserted that this needed action rather than words. "When Jesus saw the moneylenders in the Temple he didn't write the Father a little paper!"

And so the date was set: on the morning of the last Saturday in September church members were mobilised to gather outside the former Methodist meeting house to protest, and stand up for their principles and beliefs. Gillian did in the end prepare a paper but it was not what the Reverend Houston had in mind. Instead she had written and was distributing a ten point bulletin on why the town's pending new attraction should be opposed.

Mike and Alan stood in the back row, lending scale to the protest but doing little else: their hands were plunged into their pockets and they looked as half-hearted as they felt. "Are the two of us just going to stand here for the next two hours? Is anything actually going to happen?" Mike asked.

"I know. You'd think we should be doing something: singing a song or holding a banner or whatever. Like wee Bertie there."

"Gosh, look at Bertie alright."

A poker faced Bertie Robinson was standing in the gap of the front line with a large placard that simply read 'SHUN FILTH!!'

Mike also noticed for the first time – he supposed he didn't see him much beyond a church context – that wee Bertie was one of those sweaters and slacks men who had a mobile phone clipped improbably to the belt of his trousers. Would someone ring him here and now? Was this to field the wave after wave of texts that were consistently hitting his inbox? What on earth was the point of that?

"Look at the size of his sign: it's nearly as big as he is."

"Aye – and look – he has a wee fishy lapel badge on."

"So he has – I haven't seen one of those in years. Good man Bertie: you're wearing a wee Jeffrey Donaldson badge. I tell you what – it's cold. As they say in Tokyo 'there's a wee nip in the air'. We don't have a banner: what would we sing then?"

"I don't know" Alan replied. "Blowing in the wind? We shall overcome? I'm not very up on protest songs but those don't seem right: I suppose we'd have to adapt the words to the occasion."

"Could you do that?"

"I probably could if I wanted to. But I don't feel terribly inspired this morning."

"Go on: try."

Alan plunged his hands deep into his pockets and furrowed his brow in thoughtfulness. There was a few moments pause and then a snigger came across his face. "Eh – what about this: now it's hard to whisper and sing at the same time, but I'll give it a go."

"Right big lad: what's the tune?"

"'Mine eyes have seen the glory of the coming of the Lord': are you ready? I'd better be careful I don't start too high…

193

Oh this club is very filthy and this club is very wrong
And we are very righteous and that's why we sing this song
Oh may Davy Kyle be smote with piles
If he still goes along
With his Hap-py Slap-py Church…"

"Very good brother: very good. I like it. May he be smote with piles – piles like something out of the book of Job. It's not the most exciting protest there's ever been is it? I mean it doesn't look as if wee Bertie's suddenly going to go off his head and start throwing Chick publications at the peelers."

As a self congratulatory titter went up from the cheap seats in the back row Bertie Robinson glanced round with a florid glare.

"Fair's fair" said Adam to Peter. "Gillian's done a great job: I mean we're not exactly bringing the street to a standstill but there must be a hundred, or a hundred and fifty of us, which in this day and age is some achievement. You know, I'm sure this is a terrible indictment of all my middle class sensibilities, but I think this is the first time in my life I've *ever* protested about anything."

"Really? You want to come from the place I come from."

"And if I'm honest I'm probably here as much because of what other people will think of me if I'm not here, as much as what I think about the club. The problem is the way that people perceive the religious nowadays. Society has become so agnostic: it's all pluralism and post-modernism and anything goes. Any*one* who actually believes in any*thing* is regarded as being some sort of crack pot."

It was from their vantage point of the back row that Alan and Mike first noticed the crowd of people who seemed to be coming in their direction from the bottom end of the Main Street: the *other* end of the town. As they got closer this movement towards them became more and more obvious to the gaggle of protesters and murmurs of speculation began to spread among them. Then somebody noticed that at the front of the gathering march – striding purposely – was a man dressed all in black, the black broken only by a dog collar. He was getting closer and there seemed to be sixty or seventy people with him.

It was obvious that they were heading for the Methodist Church. "Who's that there clergyman?" Willie muttered to John.

"Willie, don't quote me on this" he said in a clandestine manner "but I think that's the parish priest – is it Byrne you call him? You'd see his picture in the paper: I'm nearly sure that's who it is."

Gillian looked at the approaching solidarity and she too distinguished Father Byrne's identity by pictures she had seen of him. The mumble of conversation amongst the Protestants was now softening to a palpable silence. Gillian also recognised the woman walking alongside Father Byrne: it was her friend, Siobhan McAleese.

As Siobhan approached, Gillian faltered: she hesitated just for a second, but not so much that anyone would have noticed. And then she could not contain her spontaneity: she stood proud of the crowd and embraced her friend. She could feel tears welling up too but clenched her fists hard and managed to hold those back.

"We had to come" Siobhan said. "I thought about it and I thought about it. The conversation we had the other week. And I thought 'she's right – Gillian is so right'. And I spoke to the Father here about what you were doing – because we've been talking amongst ourselves like, about the club and all, and how wrong the whole thing is. And then I noticed that you'd got the wee bit of press in the paper about it, and I thought, well why wouldn't we come? I really admire you Gillian: I think it's fantastic that you've done this."

Father Byrne was a man of around sixty years: pale and thin with ginger hair that had whitened. He was known among his community as awkward, but determined: as not chatty, but clear minded.

(Violet later commented tangentially that it was a pity he was a priest because black was *so* not his colour – as far as she could see it seemed to show up a wee dandruff or dry scalp problem. It was a shame he hadn't got up to one of the purples or reds).

He strode to the Rev Houston and he held out his hand. "Father Gerry Byrne sir. Pleased to meet you. Isn't it great to give something but not give anything away? We wanted to stand with you today; there's no theology in decency, now is there?"

The Rev Houston found himself on the spot. Every eye seemed to be looking at him. He knew that he was damned if he did and damned if he didn't: but for the sake of grace he chose damnation. He stretched out his own hand and he shook strongly. "Noel Houston: pleased to meet you too."

And at that there was a near touchable lifting of the tension. Siobhan took some of Gillian's leaflets and distributed them among her own people. They stood side by side and did not particularly mix among one another, an electric current of God's Spirit in the air. Most felt excited at the sudden moment but some could not be. All Bertie Robinson's best sensibilities were offended: he had dropped his sign where he stood, and the thunderous look on his face showed that he would interpret people as making a clear choice in whether they stayed or walked with him. Some – half a dozen to a dozen – went: Noel Houston thought he saw his ministry among these people evaporating before his eyes, and yet felt also an immense sense of liberation.

The crowd mixed and matched a little in the hour or so that followed: men talked with men, and women with women. Sport and weather and plans for the balance of the day were discussed: and of course the now notorious establishment behind them also gave some common ground. And so it seemed natural for the Reverend Houston to say as noon approached that the Presbyterians would now be retiring to their hall for a bread and cheese lunch, and their friends were most welcome to join them.

* * * * *

At the end of the lunch, Peter was helping to clear away tables and chairs when he noticed that somebody had left behind their glasses. "There are some spectacles here" he said to Alan: "I wonder who they belong to: whether they're one of the visitors."

"Oh that's easy enough. I mean, you can tell just by looking at them, whether they're a Protestant or Catholic pair of glasses."

Peter was both appalled and bewildered. Alan lifted the glasses. "Yes, yes" he reflected "that's a really Protestant pair of glasses. The frame is a real giveaway: there's at least an inch between the two lenses. Whereas the Catholic glasses: well you'd be doing well to get as much as half an inch of a space. It's their eyes, you see – their eyes are a dead giveaway – *their* eyes are a lot closer together." And he put on the glasses and gave Peter a cheeky wink.

Ireland was changing and Ireland was morphing. That part in the North which had been a bastion of traditional and biblical values was withering. Much of the new nation wanted nothing to do with Christianity, be it of the traditional or the reformed kind. Catholicism was in places becoming irrelevant and elderly: the notion of a land plagued by priests and nuns was a nonsensical fantasy perpetrated by people who had been left behind by all of society – north and south. The hymn writer had the modern Ireland down to a tee: this was a case of change and decay in everything. There were things that drove the communities apart and yet there were things that could pull them together. In one sense it didn't matter whether Jesus was on the cross or off it: Christian values were declining and soldiers of Christ needed to stand together. Secularism was the new enemy. Nobody compromised in any way and no doctrine was diminished by social action or by faithful conviction.

25

Alan

After an evening out at the cinema – "that was pretty good for something with a three on the end of it" – they sat in Alan's Mum's car, his mind curious and expectant about just how soon the evening might end.

"Here – I've got a great joke for you" he said to Nadia. "You'll like this. In fact you'll more than like this: you'll love it."

"Ok. Go on then."

"Jesus is going down this street…"

"Jesus?"

"Yeh, Jesus. That a problem?"

"Well…"

"Jesus is going down this street with his disciples one day and all of a sudden he comes across this crowd. And there's a real sense of tension in the air – you could cut the atmosphere with a knife – and then he sees why.

There's this woman in the middle of them all and it turns out she's been playing away from home – so to speak – caught in adultery. And this Pharisee is standing there holding her by the scruff of the neck and some of the mob standing about have taken up stones and bricks and they're about to let rip at this doll.

And Jesus steps into the midst of them all – and there's a kind of a hushed drama about the crowd because some of them recognise Him and know who He is. And Jesus puts up His hands to calm them and there's a silence as they realise He's going to say something.

'Let him who is without sin cast the first stone.'

And the mob: well they all go a bit coy and reproached and sort of one by one start dropping their bricks and skulking away, the oldest ones first, then the younger ones follow their elders.

But suddenly this wee old woman shuffles through the middle of them all with a great big ignorant rock in her hand. And she takes it up and aims it and she fires it straight at the girl caught in adultery and it flails through the air and catches her right between the eyes and knocks her over. Stone cold; out like a light.

And Jesus turns round and looks at the old woman and says "aw Mum, for goodness sake, *how* many times have I told you?""

Nadia didn't laugh. Normally when he told a joke and someone didn't get it he found it no more than irritating. It was unfortunate but no more than that: it generally worked that they were the stupid ones because they didn't get it, but him who ended up looking foolish. But this was something more: she was staring at him in a manner that suggested he had said the wrong thing.

"What?" she said.

"Well – you know – it's Mary isn't it? Mary's without sin – according to what you lot believe anyway – the whole Mother of God thing and all that. So she takes up the stone..."

Nadia was stern: there was not even the trace of a smile on her face. He tried to be light hearted in the face of adversity.

"That's supposed to be funny."

"Well yeah – I thought so – it's only a joke."

"What do you mean it's 'only a joke?' I don't find jokes about Mary funny. And I certainly don't find jokes about Jesus funny. Surely you get that at least."

"Aw Naddy: lighten up. I was only having a laugh – don't be so serious."

"I'm not being serious: I'm not *being* anything. I just happen to think it's a really dumb joke. That's the thing about you Alan: you play all Mr Holy when it suits you. But I don't think there's anything very holy – or clever – about making jokes of other people's religion."

He rolled his eyes.

"What are you doing that for?"

"Well what are you saying *this* for?"

"I'm saying it because I think it. I'm saying it because it's something about you that bugs the hell out of me and I've been thinking it about you for a while. You're just so sinc... sanc... what's the word..."

"Sanctified?"

"No."

"Not sanctimonious?"

"Yes that's it – you're just so sanctimonious sometimes. Big English word." He frowned. "You always think you've got the upper hand on me. Like I'm the child and you're the teacher. Let me tell you something. There's something you said to me one time. You were being all preachy about the Bible and we had this conversation about it and how you do your – what you call it – your 'Quiet Time' every day. And you said you couldn't understand how I don't do that."

"Well I don't."

"Shut up: I'm talking now and I'm making my point."

"Oh, sorry for having a thought."

"You said you don't understand how I don't do that. You said didn't I appreciate that people had suffered greatly – been burned at the stake and all of that to put the Bible in our hands and give us the freedom to read it? And no doubt you'd say burned at the stake by my sort as well."

"Well they were – that's just historical fact, I'm afraid. But you're casting *that* up. I didn't say that."

"I've not finished yet. You think you're the only person who understands things and you've got it all right down. You think you've suffered for your faith and you tell me all about the 'Scriptures' and people suffering for them. Well I can tell you all about that too."

"Where did all this come from?"

"Does it never strike you that I come from a place where people have endured *real* hardship for their faith? Not just the imagined stuff that you people have here. Have you never heard of communism and martial law or does none of that count because it never happened in poor old broken Ireland? Does it ever strike you that maybe the reason me and so many of my friends take our faith so seriously is that it was so nearly taken off us? I come from the land of solidarity: have you heard of that? There were elderly priests gave us the Eucharist in our chapel at home who did time in prison and labour camps because of what they believed in. And the Blessed Virgin was a comfort to them then. Try telling your dumb joke to people like that."

"Ok: point made."

"And all your moany friends. They're just the same as you: some of them they go on and on all the time. Like their take on suffering is some exclusive right. The world doesn't stop and start and…"

"Do you not mean start and end?"

"You know what I mean. You know exactly what I mean. Don't be so smart-arse. There's a whole big world out there of people who have also been through things and experienced stuff and feel passionately about their religion too because of all that. So next time you want to make a joke about what *I* believe – about what the woman who you say you love believes – remember that."

"I don't think there's any fear of me forgetting it…"

"You lecture me and lecture me: does it never strike you that if anything I have more right to lecture you?"

"This is an evening out dear, not a Presidential debate. Calm down."

"You see that's another thing. Politicians. You whine and you cry about your politicians. 'He's done this.' 'That one's done that.' 'They're all on the make.' 'They're only in it for what they can get out of it.' "

"Well they are. Sure Irish politics is as bent as the Duke of Kent."

"Well if you think they're all so crap why don't you get off your ass and go and make something yourself?"

"Make something? Like what? What would I make? Sure who would vote for me?"

"Well make a difference. You could try that, couldn't you? Sometimes you're just such a pig."

"Oh come on."

"No – I didn't mean that. I meant – what's the word?"

"Prig? You're not calling me a prig?"

"Yes, that's it. That's what you are: sometimes, anyway."

"Oh for God's sake woman, how did this start? I tell you a joke and the next thing I know I'm getting it in the neck because I'm not changing the world. I'll never tell you a joke again, if this is what I get. Sure why don't you stand for the anti-fun Party?"

"Well, hey, that would be great: I'd stand for something in the way that you stand for nothing."

"That's uncalled for."

"Maybe it is. But you see it's just another way where all you do is talk and talk and you think you have it all right down. I know how precious it is to be able to vote and change and shape things. When your mother and father were 18 could they vote?"

"Of course they could."

"Mine couldn't. They didn't have that privilege."

"Oh give it a rest now, will you? I mean let me hold and caress your moral upper hand and let's all make up."

"Why should I Alan? You tell me why I should. You're great and I love you, but I'm not like all the other girls."

"You can say that again."

"They might say to you: 'oh honey you're great and I wouldn't change you for anything in the world.' Well I'm not like that. I want love for the sake of love, not for the sake of reinforcement. You're smart and you're funny but you're clever and you're cynical. And you're not going to mould me to the image of what has gone before. I don't love anyone so much that I don't want them to change. That's not me. That's not the sort you've got on your hands now. If that's as plain as the nose on my face then what's the problem with you seeing it? It seems like I'm the one who gets it and maybe you don't."

There was a long pause before he punted the long shot of playing the little boy scorned. He sidled closer to her, leaning over to place his head and a suitably contrite face on her shoulder and looking hopefully into her eyes.

"Talking of… is there any… it's cold out here… you don't fancy a wee…?"

"Wee what…"

"…you know… wee cuddle?"

She opened the car door, smiled, and gave him a little less than lingering kiss on his lips. Then she left him hanging on for a moment before another quick kiss followed.

"Boys who want to get it need to start getting it, Alan. Sleep well honey, I'll call you tomorrow."

And at that he was left with nothing but the car door in his face.

26

Strangers in a strange land

Their new session saw them remain with Jeremiah and John decided at the opening juncture that he would read the passage himself this evening, "reading tonight from chapter 15 and verses 10 to 21.

Alas, my mother, that you gave me birth, a man with whom the whole land strives and contends. I have neither lent nor borrowed, yet everyone curses me.

The LORD said, "Surely I will deliver you for a good purpose; surely I will make your enemies plead with you in times of disaster and times of distress. Can a man break iron – iron from the north – or bronze? Your wealth and your treasures I will give as plunder, without charge, because of all your sins throughout your country. I will enslave you to your enemies in a land you do not know, for my anger will kindle a fire that will burn against you."

You understand, O LORD; remember me and care for me. Avenge me on my persecutors. You are long-suffering – do not take me away; think of how I suffer reproach for your sake. When your words came, I ate them; they were my joy and my heart's delight, for I bear your name, O LORD God Almighty. I never sat in the company of revelers, never made merry with them; I sat alone because your hand was on me and you had filled me with indignation. Why is my pain unending and my wound grievous and incurable? Will you be to me like a deceptive brook, like a spring that fails?

Therefore this is what the LORD says: "If you repent, I will restore you that you may serve me; if you utter worthy, not worthless words, you will be my spokesman. Let this people turn to you, but you must not turn to them. I will make you a wall to this people, a fortified wall of bronze; they will fight against you but will not overcome you, for I am with you to rescue and save you," declares the

LORD. *"I will save you from the hands of the wicked and redeem you from the grasp of the cruel."*

The scripture seemed tortuously juxtaposed to their moods: for the start of a new season they should have been exploring something light and upbeat – something encouraging. But little had changed in the world and words of Jeremiah.

"This passage" John said, as he looked self-consciously over the rim of new glasses "looks quite – eh – intimately at Jeremiah. It gets – shall we say – close up and personal to the man himself and his relationship with God. And that is the nature of the first question: 'what does this passage tell you about the kind of person Jeremiah is? What are Jeremiah's concerns in his prayer?'"

"Well I suppose" Adam suggested "– and I know this is a sort of contradictory thing to say – I suppose in a sense there's something very *encouraging* about how *discouraging* this passage is."

As Mike made his 'what's he on?' face to Alan, Adam continued.

"I mean Jeremiah comes across as being very human in it: a real man and not some plaster of Paris saint. So much of what is in this book is very difficult and it's good to know that he didn't find it easy either. He wasn't some mindless God-driven automaton who takes great delight in endlessly leathering into God's people, while God's people endlessly ignore him."

"Absolutely" Peter agreed. "I mean look at it: there's *real* despair in there. We've got to take this at face value: we've got to believe that the prayers of a righteous man before God are not exaggeration for dramatic effect. And when you're expressing anger about the very fact that you were ever born you're getting down as low as it's possible for a man to go. It's that reality of the inner and the outer life: isn't it? On the outside he is the man of steel who demonstrates immense character and resilience in putting across tough truth to God's people. But on the inside he's wrestling with some incredibly basic things about his belief in God. It's a plunging mood swing and because of that I think you need to be careful how much you read into it. Look at the way that he carries on. 'Avenge me on my persecutors'. I've been a good person and have tried to obey you and do what is right: 'I never sat in the company of revellers, never made merry with them; I sat alone because your hand was on me and you had filled me with indignation.'

I know we've been here before with this book but whenever you guys complain about the injustice of the Republicans – orchestrating their campaign of terrorism but in the end achieving their goal – you're only paraphrasing one of the most basic questions in God's word: why do the wicked prosper? There are shades of Jonah here in the resentment you can hear in Jeremiah's voice. It just seems to come up again and again the whole way through the bible – or the Old Testament anyway. I mean look at that verse there: he's so frank that he – he, the mere man – accuses God of failing. If someone said that today you'd accuse them of being heretical but that's in the Bible and it comes from a prophet."

It was at that stage that Willie gently lobbed a curveball. "You just never know: do you?"

"What?" John snapped.

"You just never know" Willie replied. "It was something my mother was very fond of saying. Perhaps her and my father would be talking about some other couple in our church – some quirk of personality or some small town scandal – and my mother would say that you just never know what goes on behind other peoples' doors, what goes on in their relationships. The same could be said of all of us: you just never know what exactly another person is thinking."

"I'm not a psychologist" Mike said "but I think that's perfectly natural. That's just the way things are. Some stuff is private and there are these wee circles of privacy that span outwards from just me, to me and the wife, to me and the family, to me and my friends and so on."

"You just never know" Willie muttered – as if on a different wavelength to everyone else – "what a butcher is giving you. You know, I went to the butcher's on Saturday as I've done for so many years. Sent off by Violet with the wee list of things that

I'm to request verbatim – a joint of beef to do six people; enough chicken to do four or whatever. And every time I go the girl behind the counter shows me the meat like it's some trophy and asks me: "there now – will that do?" And every single time I say outwardly 'oh yes, that's fine' while thinking to myself 'I haven't got the first clue.' You just never know…"

"But the question is" Adam asked "how much privacy is enough, and how much honesty is enough? There are things we talk about that we shouldn't talk about, but equally there are some things that might be better talked about but they never get aired. Maybe if I'd have had someone who I was really honest with – and that's a reflection on me rather than a reflection on my friends – my life mightn't have gone down the road that it did.

I know that as 'good reformed people' we shouldn't say this but I often think there's something appealing about the Catholic tradition of confession. I mean I know that we think the basic theology of it is flawed – that it's only God who has the authority to forgive sin and no person can pronounce forgiveness to another. But nonetheless there must be something very cathartic and humbling about physically sitting there with another person and verbalising your sin: not burying it and not pretending that you're as good on the inside as you are on the outside."

"But to me" Alan continued "it's just not in the culture of our Northern Ireland faith to be that honest. I mean even if you had been able to open up and tell other people the struggles that you were going through, is there any guarantee that *they'd* have been able to deal with it and would have known what to say?"

"Honesty too" Willie said "could be a very damaging thing. I mean I appreciate what you're saying Adam but I think if you're going to have lots of honesty you've got to be very careful about how it's managed. Honesty can be hurtful to the point of being cruel. Unrestrained honesty can be catastrophic. All of us have different personalities, so that to an extent the very basic act of day to day getting along with people is sometimes based on acceptable levels of dishonesty."

"You just never know" Adam muttered. "I kind of like that. So you just never know what all of us are thinking here: what goes on inside people." He seemed removed as he said this and wasn't addressing anyone in particular.

"You know – this is something I've never spoken to anyone about, but it might strike a chord, and then again it might not. I remember being a teenager and being at school in the mid-eighties and that was probably about the height of the troubles – there'd have been shootings or bombings every day. I'd come home every evening and the news would be on the TV in the corner of the lounge and it would almost invariably start with a report on whatever murder there had been the night before. I would never tell anyone this but I would always be – how can I put it – I suppose I would always be secretly *pleased* if it was a Protestant that had been killed."

John grimaced.

"Or – well – no, maybe pleased isn't the right word. But it was just better that way because it allowed me to be lazy about 'them and us' and it reinforced my mindset before I sat down to whatever my tea was that night. But if it was the case that a Protestant had shot a Catholic: well, that was a different matter. That had a challenge and a discomfort to it: easy to be the victim but a wee bit more to think about if one of your own is the protagonist.

And I was a really good, fine, young Christian person. Going to youth fellowships and on the SU committee and a school prefect, and marked out to do medicine with 'straight A's all the way, but inside – well, inside was a very different matter. Inside should have been young and angry and passionate and wanting peace. But inside wasn't terribly bothered as long as inside was the victim. Or at least as long as my side was sort of generally the victim because even if they were Protestants they were faceless to me. I was no war baby: it never touched me personally.

It's back to Sermon on the Mount faith, isn't it. It's murder being when you hate someone in your heart. It's being respectable on the outside but a bigot on the inside. The Sermon on the Mount tells the story of the last fifty years on this island. It sums up all the good living church going; all the moral uprightness; and all the veneer of respectability that masks sectarianism. Every time we think of a Catholic as a Fenian or Taig we murder them in our heart.

I remember being on a stag night years ago and I was getting a lift out of Belfast with these guys who I didn't know that well – we were all heading up towards Hillsborough for flour and paint and rounding off the evening. There were five of us in this car and the other four all knew each other but I knew none of them: it was just the way we'd divvied up at that point in the evening. So there I was crammed into the back of this wee Fiesta or something with all these strangers. We drove up the Westlink and through Broadway, and as we took to the M1 one of them asked 'What do you call Milltown cemetery?' And do you know what the punch line was: 'A good start'. And they all laughed and laughed at that. And these were good, supposedly God fearing, Christian people. What would Jeremiah have said about that?

It's like, do you remember that poor Russian who was poisoned in London years ago with some sort of radioactive material. I remember reading at the time – this just stuck in my mind – that there was so much poison inside him that they weren't sure if they could do a post-mortem on him for fear of the risk there would be to those carrying it out. You know: I'm just the same as that. For all my respectability, if you cut me open you would be repulsed. If you cut me open, you simply wouldn't want to know me."

There was no response. After some silence with only the ticking clock for company John thought that it was time to move on to the next question – but he couldn't help a revealing tut as he did so. "Jeremiah was extremely honest in his prayer to God. When do you find it difficult to be honest with God?"

"I think" Willie said "that a lot of it is just about the nature of the people that we are. I mean Ulster Protestants: we're kind of plain people who keep our heads down, and pull ourselves together. We're not inclined to wear our hearts on our sleeves: real men don't cry and so on. What is prayer: well some people would say that prayer is basically conversation with God, and if you're not inclined to be terribly vulnerable or open up to other human beings, well maybe it's inevitable that it follows through to your relationship with God.

Somebody once said to me that Northern Ireland people don't believe in the power of the Holy Spirit: they simply believe in 'the power to convict people of sin'. We're good at praying and longing for those outside of Christ to realise their need and be broken before God. But we're not quite so hot on the idea of Christian people being broken before God. Sure if one of us started to cry and weep now the rest of us wouldn't know what to do."

Alan looked reflective as he then began to speak. "OK then: here's some honesty. Now don't panic because we'll call it safe honesty. It's kind of philosophical rather than personal honesty. You know I've been thinking recently as I've been praying – I've been asking myself if prayer for this island actually makes *any* difference. Or maybe it's rather that it makes a difference but not in the way that I want it to. I suppose I'm living on my own…"

"Aye, but for how much longer?" Mike asked.

"We'll not get into that now" Alan replied, not even breaking his stride. "I'm living on my own and maybe I've more time to think than some of you other guys and that isn't necessarily a good way to be. But it's just that sometimes at night I lie awake and think and I have all these questions streaming through me. What if it really *were* God's will for Ireland to be united? We all sat in prayer meetings for years and prayed for there to be peace for Ireland: well what if the way that God has decided to bring peace to the island is by its unification?

But because of where I come from and what I've always been brought up to believe that idea is repellent to me. Look at the IRA and look at Sinn Fein and you have to ask: how could God do this to us? Does that then mean that God has failed? But God is God and therefore by his very nature He can't fail, so the extension of that question is that my view of God has failed. That I'm 34 years of age and the view of God that I have had all my life has failed. That I have had a *view* of God and what He ought to do rather than a genuine *faith* in Him. That hope has been hopeless."

"Don't be so hard on yourself" said Adam in an attempt to intervene, but now Alan was in a flow that was not to be broken.

"I'm bold as brass to question God but what does that mean? Is it strength of my faith that I question God or is it in fact a weakness? And then I go on and I ask myself – well – for all these things that I'm thinking, does prayer actually make a difference? Does God *ever* intervene: because I didn't want Ireland to be united and He didn't do anything about that?

Does prayer actually make a difference to the way that things turn out or is it just some imagined consolation for the way that things were going to turn out anyway? Sometimes I promise that I'll pray for someone – some friend going for a hospital appointment or a job interview – and then I completely forget about them. And a week later they thank me for my prayer and I feel so wick. And they have been in blissful ignorance thinking this effected the situation: is it the prayer that makes a difference to people or just the notion that someone was praying for them?

When I open the Psalms now is that just tea and sympathy from above: it's all very well having consolation in where I find myself, but could He not have made where I find myself different? I mean I'm sorry guys – but sometimes I just – *resent* it all so much. It's our country and it's where we live and now look at it… and I just resent it all. Why is that: why do I feel that way?"

"But that's alright" Peter insisted. "That's absolutely fine. Because look at Jeremiah and see the emotions that he is pouring out. And ask yourself what those emotions are if they're not resentment. Then listen to yourselves and listen to some of the things that you are saying about God. You all believe that He is holy and just and righteous and sovereign, yet you somehow question if He's fair and reasonable. Men: if He's all those former things then there's no way He can't be the latter things."

* * * * *

Peter

"Eh – time is marching on…" interrupted John in a hesitant manner "so we should maybe get on to the next question. What is God's response to Jeremiah's heartfelt prayer? Eh…"

"Oh stuff the questions" Peter exclaimed. "I'm sorry but – with the greatest respect – let's just stuff them! Don't you realise that we're right in the ring and we're wrestling. Never mind some nonsense of having to answer all the questions. This, gentlemen, is about hypocrisy: you don't have to be all polite and nice to God to his face when you come to Him in prayer, but nonetheless be thinking spiritual unmentionables behind his back. It's like – look – I tell you what, turn your bibles to Psalm 73 and let's have a look at that."

Nobody questioned. Everyone turned: quickly, as if they had regressed to sword drill days.

"When you read this Psalm what you discover is that it's like a journey. The first half of the Psalm is a struggle: a struggle that is full of honesty and has questions that bear an uncanny resemblance to some of the things you men are struggling with now. Read it with me: start at the first verse:

Surely God is good to Israel, to those who are pure in heart.
But as for me, my feet had almost slipped; I had nearly lost my foothold.
For I envied the arrogant when I saw the prosperity of the wicked.

That could be all of you, couldn't it? Surely God is good to Ulster: hey, wasn't for God and Ulster itself one of the maxims by which you lived. God and Ulster were joined: God had a relationship and connection with Ulster so how could this be happening? Now you find yourself envying the Republicans: now you believe that what you see is the prosperity of the wicked. You can't understand how a people who at times inflicted such cruelty on you have been allowed by God to take your inheritance. And then the Psalm goes on:

They have no struggles; their bodies are healthy and strong.
They are free from the burdens common to man; they are not plagued by human ills.
Therefore pride is their necklace; they clothe themselves with violence.
From their callous hearts come iniquity; the evil conceits of their minds know no limits.

How literally can you take all this? The Psalmist seems to be voicing a potent cocktail: the distorted paranoia of the victim mixed with the anger of one who has seen injustice. Much of this is the exaggeration that infuses the way so many people see their enemies. The reality is those diehard Republicans have problems like all the rest of us: the rain falls on the good and the bad. Haven't people even been saying recently that Gerry Adams doesn't look a well man?"

"Humph" John snorted: "sick in more ways than one."

"But to you it doesn't seem that way: to you it seems that they're breezing and cruising. You see them welcome the Pope and you see them march on Easter Sunday and it's as if they have their chests puffed out in the pomp and arrogance of victory. Were these unnamed villains in the Psalm as bad as the Psalmist made them out to be? Are they the object of anger or a subject of anger: who knows? If it were the truth and inspired insight about a people far from God, then God would hear that prayer. If it were just raw and madly charged emotion that had everything totally out of proportion, then God would hear that latter hurt just as much as the former. The fact is that Gerry Adams and Martin McGuinness are very probably not people who know no limits in the evil conceit of their minds. But the fact is equally that when you're defeated and when they're the other side, then hurt and imagination can be very powerful bedfellows. And so it goes and so it goes until it gets to the point that we all need to get to. Look at what it says in verse 16.

When I tried to understand all this it was oppressive to me till I entered the sanctuary of God; then I understood their final destiny.

That's where you're at: it's easy for me to see that because I'm outside of you and your situation. I know you and I love you but I'm not Northern Irish and I could *never* truly say that your loss is my loss. Because it just isn't. But I see that seeking to make sense of this is oppressive. I know that we've got to think this through and I know that the renewal of our minds can transform us. But I see you guys from afar and I think you've got to a point – I hear Alan talking tonight and I think you've got to a point – a point where you've just got to enter the sanctuary of God. I'm not saying you can manufacture a moment of God but it's your own choice to get into the sanctuary. Look at the words that we read from verse 21 onwards:

When my heart was grieved and my spirit was embittered, I was senseless and ignorant; I was a brute beast before you.
Yet I am always with you; you hold me by my right hand.
You guide me with your counsel, and afterward you will take me into glory.
Whom have I in heaven but you? And earth has nothing I desire besides you.
My flesh and my heart may fail, but God is the strength of my heart and my portion forever.

Look at that line there: that line there is surely the crux of everything: 'earth has nothing I desire besides you'. There is nothing – not even Ulster – that I desire besides Almighty God. The Lord gives and the Lord takes away: blessed is the name of the Lord.

There's a wonderful passage in the Old Testament where God speaks to Elijah through the earthquake, wind and fire. God asks Elijah what he is doing here and Elijah answers back with this depressing description of his plight and problems. And then God moves before him – then you get that earthquake, wind and fire. And then God asks him again what he is doing here and Elijah's answer is exactly the same – word for word – as it was the first time. And yet he sees everything so differently. You want the situation to be changed by God yet perhaps what God is saying is that the circumstances will remain exactly the same but it is your orientation that will be changed.

And it's not easy. I can see it's not easy. Because even after entering the sanctuary the Psalmist is still kicking and railing against it all. Still wanting his enemies to be destroyed – or a realisation perhaps that God is sovereign and just and all will work out for the best in the end. Right at the very end of the Psalm he is still talking of destruction and of those who are far from God perishing. Just like Jeremiah: no black and white neatness about it all. Jeremiah resented the people he was called to preach to just as much as you guys resent the Catholics – or the Republicans anyhow. We're just never going to understand all this: never in a million years. We're *never* going to understand: so let's get into the sanctuary."

27

John

John could not be sure of exactly how little sleep he had got. He was certain that he had seen one o'clock, two o'clock and three o'clock as the night passed by, but he supposed he never slept quite as badly on these occasions as he thought he did. He did know that between one and two he had gone downstairs to read some Psalms for twenty minutes, and between two to three he had descended again to make himself a milky drink. Now the little digital clock on his bedside table was telling him it was 5:47. He decided that if he turned over and tried to sleep more now, he would only make himself feel worse, so the best thing to do was be positive and just get up.

Not that he had much choice in the matter: for the last number of weeks he had been increasingly aware of an extremely vocal wood pigeon that resided in the trees opposite their bedroom window. Upon the basis of no foundation whatsoever he had started to put this down to some sort of sexual frustration on the part of the pigeon, but had little sympathy for its forlorn cooing. Had he still had his personal protection weapon he would gladly have put it out of its misery.

He was quiet over breakfast. Whilst not normally the most sociable of men in the early part of the day, he was starting to regret Gillian's and his decision to have their morning papers delivered to the house. The trend in the kitchen was increasingly that Weetabix meant Sudoku, but she only rolled his eyes at protestations that he was becoming a puzzle widow.

"Widower: you'd be a puzzle widower."

He didn't mind really but just this morning a little small talk would have been helpful to him. Gillian eventually resigned herself to a temporary defeat on her cranial challenge: she had two school refusers to educate, her first appointment being at ten o'clock. This left John to run a few messages before going to the Retired Men's Friendship Circle. "It's good for you: you need to get out and meet some new people."

She was soon on her way. He said he'd just be nipping to the bathroom and he'd be out the door himself in a few minutes. He shaved and cleaned his teeth and then he moved to the kitchen window to twitch the curtains and be sure that she had gone. That clearly being the case he went upstairs and changed into a suit, shirt and tie. He then went to the toilet – 'once more with feeling' – as a surge of trepidation raced through him and out the other side. He checked his watch: the journey from here to the town centre was so well rehearsed that he generally took it for granted, but he wasn't confident about the timing of it in this context.

He set off cautiously early but not being a frequent shopper he had forgotten that a Farmer's Market now took place in the High Street on the third Thursday of the month. The congestion this caused proved a helpful hoover of the excess time in his schedule, and he arrived at the police station just five minutes before his appointment.

He felt utterly alone as he sat in the stark and dank enquiry room, like a miscreant boy waiting to enter the headmaster's office. Many times he had stood behind such a reception desk himself: he had never comprehended just what uninviting places these were. Suspect; victim; witness; everybody was made to feel like a criminal here. Nerves did not detract from a momentary feeling of resentment and a conviction that he deserved better than this. The solitude was in part a choice he had made: had he wanted he could have brought a witness or even his solicitor with him but he was determined to see this through on his own. If he needed to let other people into this he could cross that bridge as and when was necessary: if not, then they need never know.

All in all he was in and out in just under forty minutes. Relief was palpable all through his body as he exited the entrance to the station. He had rehearsed any number of outrageous scenarios in his mind during the small hours of long nights. Of course – as was always the way on such occasions – reality proved less foreboding than imagination. As the adrenalin dissipated so tiredness kicked in. He felt almost dazed as he started to walk back up the street to where he had parked the car, and so was insufficiently alert to avoid Willie who was heading in the opposite direction.

"What are you doing here?" Willie said.

"Well I could very easily ask the same of you. Aren't you at the wee retired men's group?"

"Is that the group for retired men who are dwarfs or the small group of retired men?"

John didn't need this for what he'd just been through.

"Oh you know what I mean."

"No I decided not to go today. It was some man whose grandfather had been the local blacksmith today. I've got fed up hearing about local history. Sure I'm getting to the point where I'll soon be a piece of local history myself. And Violet and I will be at Gillian's meeting tonight as well – we weren't sure what to do but then we thought – well, sure 'we're all ecumenical now'."

Willie noticed that John's face was like a picture from a child's colouring in book: it had no expression or shade or life whatsoever. He was obviously restless to get away, and Willie had seen him coming out of the police station. He was not dressed in the manner that he'd expect his friend to be of a weekday morning and he felt that he should ask after him.

"Are you alright John?"

John looked down and mumbled unconvincingly that he was grand.

Willie placed his right hand on the top half of John's left arm.

"Are you sure now? You don't look alright: do you want to grab a coffee somewhere and have a wee yarn?"

John muttered that he was absolutely fine and didn't want to talk about anything. He looked for a moment as if he might even cry in the street on his friend. John pushed Willie's hand away and Willie knew that it was better now to let this drop.

Something was dreadfully wrong with John. As he looked up the street Willie felt like he was back in the old school corridor: he remembered times when he had seen weaker children bullied and tried to get near them, but the conventions of masculinity demanded that the teacher must be brushed away. As he watched his friend walk further into the distance he reflected that grown men are only bigger versions of small boys. And Willie thought too of prayer times at the end of their small groups where they would ask amongst each other of needs and problems to intercede for and rarely would anyone disclose a thing. 'You just never know' he thought 'what goes on behind other people's closed doors'.

* * * * *

Behind every man…

Gillian looked at the chairs in front of her. Should she arrange them in circles or should she put them in theatre style? And more to the point: just how many should she put out? If she put out too few she could always fall back on a cocktail of false modesty and make a self-depreciating comment about how she should have had more faith. But if she put out too many then the whole venture would start off utterly flat footed and she would have egg all over her face. She concluded that less was more on this occasion.

It had seemed so right on the Sunday after the protest to corner the Reverend Houston, and ask him what could be done to build on the occasion of togetherness they had just had. (He was a man who appeared fond of his personal space and tended to back off quickly if someone stood too close to him: for that reason he was not a difficult person to corner).

She had left the hall that Saturday high as a kite, on emotions she was sure came direct from the Spirit of God. Experience alone had not meant as much to her since the season of her life forty years ago when adolescent fervour had met with Pentecostal vigour. Now however – despite the fact that she had become a lady deeply suspicious of gut instinct – she was certain that this was a passing moment of God's own opportunity that must be quickly seized on before the holy vapour fades.

But this evening as she stood and looked at the empty hall before her, her body numbed with tension. What was a woman like this doing in a place like that? How was it that she now found herself in the dated and fusty décor of a function room at The Stone's Throw Inn? She thought the location horrible – it had no beauty of any sort, never mind beauty of holiness – but in practical terms there was little choice of venue.

Reverend Houston had agreed there would be no harm in a little bit of 'talks about talks' and had met with Gillian – and then with Father Byrne and Siobhan also – to try to tease out what shape such an exercise might take. "You have to bear in mind Gillian that if I look too far ahead of myself I'll only neglect to watch my back."

They decided to hold a public meeting which both shepherds would profile to their own respective flocks (it turned out to be a stated rather than an encouraged gathering). Such an event would allow them to explore the appetite for building on the initial activity. Gillian wanted to bring someone in with greater knowledge of such exercises to facilitate the evening but Father Byrne said he'd sooner they didn't run before they walked. Noel Houston said he would open the meeting with a short prayer but other than that it was agreed there would be no element of 'worship' at the event.

The gathering was held on a neutral venue – the pub being the church's proverbial safe place for a dangerous message. This was a matter of pragmatism as much as public relations: neither cleric wanted to nail his colours so firmly to the mast as to host the meeting, and it would stand a better chance of attracting a crowd if neither group needed to travel to an away ground. On sourcing the location Gillian was reminded of what it was that had started this, and was shocked at just how many restaurants and watering holes Davy Kyle owned.

She had left John to clear up after tea and had come down

early to prepare the venue. He had been quiet over their meal which disappointed her because he knew how nervous she was about the evening ahead, and just how much it meant to her. She suspected that he disapproved of what she was leading them into – it would hardly be unlike him given so much of what he'd come out with in the past. She resented him tonight – she found him uncommunicative to the point of rudeness and scored on a little mental abacus all the ways that *she* supported *him* – but she bit her lip. It was hardly in the spirit of reconciliation to row with your spouse before going out to a gathering such as this.

It was teeming with rain as she left home, and Gillian was drenched even as she entered her own upper room. It was the sort of downpour where mere moments in the outdoors could soak to the skin. This she thought was an ominous predictor: on an evening like this it would definitely be easier to stay in the house.

She had imagined that there might be some sort of demonstration outside their assembly and this prompted mixed feelings inside her. A part of Gillian would have revelled in that for she believed her community to be one where a picket was tantamount to an endorsement that one was doing something right. But such objections would lead to confrontation – and brave as she was rehearsing speeches to naysayers in the privacy of her own head, she would have been rather less confident facing down their protestations in the flesh. In the end there was no such presence outside the pub which she thought little of but was relieved about.

The meeting was advertised as being at eight o'clock, and by ten past eight there was a gathering of perhaps 25 to 30 in the function room. Gillian was encouraged that on a rough count the numbers at least appeared evenly split. She tried to cling on to the best Christian resilience of 'though our numbers are small' and 'where two or three are gathered together'. She was curious to see if Alan and his other half would show – and where they would sit if they did come – but they failed to put in an appearance. Peter came in a few minutes late and sat noticeably on the 'wrong' side of the room. 'No show without punch' thought John to himself.

Gillian had settled on arranging the room in four to five rows of seats with an aisle separating them in the middle. She quickly realised the folly of this layout as she saw the respective sides congregating with their own, the division between them all the more apparent from the vantage point of the top table. She was momentarily angry with herself for being so thoughtless, though their positioning seemed based on caution rather than animosity.

As the Reverend Houston rose to pray he was unusually lacking in fluency. Gillian soon felt that however much he was leading through the physicality of his being there, he offered little prospect of more meaningful direction as the night unfolded. Father Byrne – for his part – appeared as diffident at the front of the room as he had been at the rally some weeks ago. This disappointed Gillian because she had found him dry but chatty at the meeting they had held to arrange this.

('He's maybe alright when you give him the words of a Mass to read from a prayer book' said Violet 'but he doesn't look very comfortable in an unscripted situation. He's a bit furtive looking: I wonder if his bishop knows he's here').

Gillian convened the meeting with Reverend Houston sitting to the right of her, and Siobhan on her left, Father Byrne being in turn to the left of Siobhan. She made a brief presentation on what the scope of their group might be: how it could form simply on the basis of friendship, or how they could work to a more structured agenda if that was the preference of the members. It could all be as formal or informal as the group wanted it to be. There were people and organisations that facilitated cross-community gatherings and their skills could be brought in if that was desired. They could focus on history and sharing experiences and building understanding from the perspective of Nationalist and Unionist, or alternatively they could build their programme around aspects of Catholicism and the Reformed faith. It might even be interesting to visit one another's church buildings for insights into their respective traditions. They could meet on week nights once or twice a month and if there was sufficient interest they could even look at going away for a weekend together. These options being illustrated, she then opened up the floor.

The conversation took some minutes to warm up, but once it got going there was a steady if not abundant flow of ideas. A consensus soon emerged that faith rather than politics was a better – and safer – basis to begin with. All agreed that an external leader with relevant expertise was something they would benefit from, but it was way too soon to start thinking about a weekend away. Someone suggested that instead of going to their own churches it would be interesting to visit the two cathedrals in Armagh as a group together. One night a month was felt to be enough because people in churches could be running to meetings every night of the week and there had to be a cut-off point somewhere.

(Violet later complained about how modest she thought the contribution from the Catholics had been. 'I think it's a control thing, you know. They wouldn't be allowed too much opportunity to express themselves in their church so they don't know what to say on occasions like this').

Just after nine o'clock Gillian cut the conversation short: she did so on the vocal premise that it was a dreadful night and she didn't want to keep people too late, but in reality she wanted to conclude the discourse whilst it still had some flow, rather than have the embarrassment of it petering out. At the end she took an unplanned 'fit of the head staggers' and decided that before their cup of tea – instead of saying grace – they should all get up and move amongst each other and exchange the peace of Christ.

She falteringly took the initiative herself and first shook Siobhan's hand before reaching across to exchange the greeting with Father Byrne as well (she expected something limp but received something strong). Within seconds there was the beginning of mumbling and movement from the floor, and her heart skipped a little when Reverend Houston got up from the front and moved directly to the Catholic side of the room with his right hand outstretched.

"I hate doing that" John muttered to Willie as after a few minutes they all sat down. John had gone but had proved quiet all evening: there was no face of thunder or restless bum shuffling in his seat and he didn't appear unhappy to be there. But nonetheless he had nothing to say which surprised Gillian because he was usually 'fond of the sound of his own voice' on such occasions.

Afterwards the group shared a light supper of tea, coffee, and biscuits together. "There's something unusually horrible about hotel biscuits, isn't there?" Willie said to John as he reached ruthlessly for the only foil wrapped one on the plate. Then a small, bald and elderly man who had all the distinguishing characteristics of a farmer made himself known to John and Willie in a gesture of mixing. Having introduced himself this man then proved to be – in John's estimation – somewhat difficult to talk to. What was the point of initiating small talk if it wasn't something you did well?

"I suspect that Catholics who take their faith seriously aren't much fun" Violet whispered to John. "I think this is the Mass ten times a week and Pioneer brigade we have here. I think if it's a good night's craic you're after it's more the lapsed sort you want to meet."

Gillian was confused in her feelings as she settled the bill and headed to the car park. She had dreamed of this evening as something radical but it had felt nothing like that. Having gone out thinking that she and her friend might be able to change the world, she was returning home pragmatic that they wouldn't even change their town. She had wanted it to be something big and mighty and knew there were good things that had happened. Maybe she was just spiritualising tiredness but at this point it all felt a little feeble to her.

* * * * *

"Well that was a good enough start you made there. I thought you spoke well" John said, as he and Gillian entered their back door, turning on lights and discarding keys and coats in their kitchen.

"No it wasn't, it was nothing of a start."

"That's not true. It was fine. If it was *nothing* of a start, then what was it you were you expecting?"

"Well a fat lot of good you were!"

"What does that mean?"

"You know fine rightly what it means. It means that you were quiet to the point of downright ignorant all night. You might as well not have come. You could at least have tried."

"I'm not going to get into a whole row now."

"Not that there was anything new tonight, cause you've been pretty damn miserable to live with all round of late. What is it with you?"

"Nothing. I haven't been miserable: where are you getting that from?"

"I'm getting that from having breakfast with you and dinner with you and shopping with you and sleeping in the same bed as you. That's where I'm getting it from. What *is* it with you?"

"Nothing. What part of nothing do you not understand?"

"Oh don't come on like that. That makes it like talking to a five year old. That's the way the boys used to get on. 'Where are you going?' 'Nowhere.' 'What's that you've got?' 'Nothing'. That's just nonsense. Stop playing the strong and silent type. It's not mystery, it's only irritation…"

She paused for a moment of respite, as if counting to ten – though it seemed somewhat late for that now.

"Look I'm sorry I'm angry. It's been a long day – and I was so worked up about that tonight. But just tell me what the matter is."

"What are you throwing all of this up for? You did make a good start. It was a good start. You've done something, organised something, and made it happen. The longest journey begins with the first step and all that."

"Yes I know all that. I'm tired and it's late and you're right and I'm sure that in the cold light of day I'll see all of those very manly and sensible points you're making. I know *all* that. But that's not the point. Stop changing the subject and tell me what the hell is the matter with you. Is it me? Is it this? Have I done something to upset you?"

"No, of course you haven't."

"Then what is it?"

"Nothing."

She threw the car keys into the cutlery drawer and slammed it shut with a ferocity that surprised even her. She startled at that.

"Oh alright then. It's too late for games. I'm not going to drag it out of you if that's what you want. I've had enough – I'm going to bed – stew in your own stupid selfish juice if you want to."

He looked down in a hesitating manner of awkward shame. He was rubbing his hands from the top to the bottom of his face. It seemed bad. Maybe if she calmed he might just start with it at least. She spoke more softly now.

"What is it John? I love you very much. Nothing can be that bad. Please tell me."

He sat down at the kitchen table and she joined him. He rested both elbows on the surface and his hands covered his mouth. He was pensive, as if steeling himself, working out where to begin and digging for the courage to get started.

"Is it money?"

"No."

"You're not sick, are you?"

"No."

"You've not been seeing..."

"No don't be ridiculous, of course I haven't."

"Then *what*?"

She stared at him and placed her hand on his arm and he finally whirred into life.

"It's... it's... you know the historical enquiries thing that's been in the news lately. Going over old files and cases... what's this the politician said? 'We're looking for closure much more than we're looking to close files'."

"Yes I've heard of that. But what's that got to do with you?"

He sighed heavily.

"I got a letter... oh months ago... I had to go to Dublin. It was a summons. No ifs, buts or maybes: threats about pension rights and so forth if I hadn't gone."

"When was that?"

"I can't remember exactly."

"All of this has been going on and you never told me."

"I didn't know where to start. I wasn't hiding it from you."

"But you were. You have."

"It's not that I didn't want to admit it to you: maybe I just didn't want to admit it to myself."

"Admit what? So you went to Dublin – what happened there?"

"I went to Dublin and I must have spent... oh three to four hours being questioned and going over stuff... old statements and so on. And then... months and months and you hear nothing and you've no idea what's going on. And... well... this morning... I told you a lie Gill... oh dear Lord, it's been awful Gill."

He looked away from her to the kitchen wall but she rubbed his arm to encourage him to keep on going.

"I wasn't at the retired Men's Group. I had to go to the station in the middle of the town: had to go and see how it would all wash up."

"What? John: you still haven't told me yet. How would *what* wash up?"

"1994. Down won the all-Ireland football final in 1994. And you might remember that the night of the match, as all the celebrations were going on, there was this Catholic fella beaten up badly – savagely – in Banbridge. Only 18 or 19 – really just a child. He was a mouthy wee lad and he was absolutely blocked but his team had won and he was doing no harm. But he ran into the wrong sort – a whole pile of Rangers fans – and didn't have the wit to keep his mouth shut. Not

227

that that even begins to excuse what they did to him."

"I do remember that. Sure did they not beat him to within an inch of his life? But what does that have to do with you?"

"Well Banbridge was my patch wasn't it? And I was out in a car that night with Eddie Thompson. Well Eddie... I'm sure you remember me talking about him... Eddie was a tight man. And in fairness, not without reason: Eddie had his father and a brother who were both in the force and both of them were murdered by the IRA. The father was killed by a device under his car and I can't remember what exactly happened to the brother. I tell you: Eddie wouldn't have been one for Patton and modern policing...

So anyway, Eddie and I were out in the car that night and damn it, didn't we come across this thing just as it was all starting to unfold. Eddie was driving and he was in foul form all evening... and I remember me saying to Eddie that we needed to get out and do something. The wee lad had a Down top on: it was plain what he was. And Eddie said No there was five or six of them and it wouldn't be safe for us to intervene... and then I said well we'll radio for support... and he said..."

"And he said what?"

In none of this could he address his words to his life partner. He could only look straight ahead, detaching his confession from himself and his wife.

"He said 'No, just let him have it.' And I said 'Eddie, I can't believe you're saying that' and do you know what he said to me?"

"What?"

"Like I'm playing this out to you over minutes but it was something that happened in seconds. He says: 'well if you don't believe I'm saying it, sure no one else will believe it either. And then it's your word against mine John. Let the wee shit get what's coming to him. It'll teach him to keep his trap shut next time. It'll keep a few more like him in their place.'

And we just sat there and we watched it... And he was on the ground and they were punching him and kicking him and... dear God it was awful. Like I've seen a lot but that was grim. I think hearing the noise of it was uglier than the sight of it. And then… they all slope off and leave him there and then Eddie says 'right, call for an ambulance now then.'

"But you're alright. Where is Eddie Thompson in the middle of all this? You must just be a witness John?"

"Eddie Thompson is in Carnmoney cemetery: Eddie Thompson died of bone cancer in 2009 – apparently he had an awful end. There was a man walking a dog nearby and he came across all of this when it happened. He said he saw a police car nearby sitting with its lights off and the engine not running. Which of course we managed to keep quiet at the time… But now, well in this day and age and with these enquiries and all…"

"Oh John: well what was it that went on this morning? What happens now?"

"What happens in so many of these cases: I was given a formal reprimand this morning and it goes down against my file, but there are no charges or anything like that. It's not publicised: none of it goes in the paper, so at least we're spared that. And I had to sit and take all that this morning from some wee officious cub called Lynch from Dublin… some child who probably came straight out of University and got fast tracked into CID or whatever. A kid that knows nothing about nothing. Not that that's relevant… I mean that's beside the point."

"So is that it done and dealt with then?"

"No of course not. Because now in our modern, caring, sharing way of doing things, I'm going to have to meet the victim. I'm going to have to grovel and plead apology for what I've done. "

He didn't say this in an angry way. It was more self-pity. And he looked at her:

"That's it: there's nothing more. Over and out."

And then she found herself doing what she had least expected. She fell into his arms and she cried. *She* did the sobbing and the heaving and he… he just sat there. He comforted her physically – put his arms around her and stroked her hair – but he shed no tears of his own and gave her no connection. After a few minutes she got up and went to the sink. She ran the cold tap and cupped her hands beneath it, before rinsing her blotched face. She asked him if he wanted a warm drink and he said that would be lovely.

They talked and talked then in the effortless and unceasing manner of young love. They sat there for an hour or more but it didn't matter as they both agreed they hardly felt like sleeping. He shared with her all the angles of this that he had been endlessly exploring in his own mind. How remorseful he felt and how inadequate. Something deep inside his manly character had failed: cometh the hour there had been no courage. Who was he to judge others when he had been so weak? When the test came he had failed. And yet there was relief as well: he had carried this so many years, keeping it all close in to himself but at least now it was out. There was a certain catharsis in that.

He was wrong and now he had to face the consequences. He accepted that but there were things he could not accept. Look at the people who were in power… look at the things that they had done and yet people like him… people of integrity even if they were failed people of integrity, were to face this humiliation. He remembered that mercy is not getting what you do deserve, but he wanted to know also that grace is getting what you don't deserve. Was this then some perverted mercy and grace? For however much he knew that in this big bad world he should be grateful for not getting that which he deserved, he railed nonetheless at having to do that which he believed he did not deserve.

28

Peter

It was as Peter was reaching into the back seat of the car to get his scarf that the accident happened. The security light in the driveway had given up the week before and Adam had not got round to investigating it yet. He had picked Peter up from the railway station, and didn't see him put his hand back into the car as he shut the door behind him.

Slam! "Damn – you caught my finger" Peter winced.

"Sorry."

Adam fumbled in the darkness for the back door key and as they rushed into the house, the warm and numb feeling at the tip of Peter's index finger was beginning to give way to pain. He couldn't bear to look at it, and could feel blood throbbing out of it in time with his pulse.

"Let me see" Adam said. He sat Peter in a chair to take the weight off his feet after the shock, and stared intently at the injured digit. "No permanent damage there, bro. We'll get it cleaned up and see what I have to put a dressing on it. Hold that on it" he said referring to the water soaked and blood stained facecloth he had gathered round it.

He made Adam a sugary drink and they retired to the bathroom sink to wash it thoroughly. Summoning up the courage to look at the injury Peter was relieved to see that there was no fear of losing the finger. Soon the damage was being wrapped in a combination of germolene, gauze and micropore.

"Do you see what I'm doing?" Peter said. "It's quite biblical, really."

"What's that then" Adam asked – sounding sincere, but his eyes and hands focused on the task in hand.

"Well I'm doing what the people of Israel had to learn to do in Jeremiah's day. I'm turning to the source of my pain for him to be the source of my healing as well. I'm the children of Israel, which makes you…"

"God" said Adam, as he snipped some medical tape with a small pair of scissors and put the finishing touches to his repairs."

"You get it in the book of Hosea as well: 'Come let us return to the Lord. He has torn us to pieces but he will heal us; he has injured us but he will bind up our wounds.' Beautiful words but all a bit counter-intuitive: how many people are going to run to the one who's torn them to pieces for comfort?"

"Go easy on me Peter" Adam said. "I nearly took the end off your finger. I hardly tore you limb from limb."

"Oh absolutely" Peter replied. "I mean the finger… the finger's fine. But it's not natural is it? It's not logical for the healing and the injury to come from the same place. It doesn't tie in with the usual order of goodie and baddie as two distinct entities."

"I suppose not."

"Maybe it's a message for your people, Adam. God's dealt you all a blow and is apparently the architect of your loss, so the obvious response is to be angry: is to rail against Him and blame Him. Turn your back on Him in indignation at how He could have done this. But the word of God says they've got to resist every temptation to do this. That no matter how much they're hurting and they resent God, they've got to turn back towards Him and run and seek Him harder and keener than they've ever done before. But if God wants these loyal Ulster Protestants far more than they can possibly imagine – yet that's far less than they want Him – then it's hardly going to happen, is it?"

29

Alan

Inside every man is a pontificating pundit; a commentator who loves a soapbox. Alan Mackey's feet barely touched the ground between the car and the front door. He was bouncing from foot to foot with enthusiasm when the door was finally opened, like an excited toddler desperate for the toilet.

"Quick: let me in. Have you heard the news?"

"What news?" Adam asked: he had obviously not heard it. "I try not to have the TV on unless there's something I specifically want to watch."

"Well turn it on now because you'll want to watch this: Gerry Adams is dead."

Peter heard this news from where he was sitting in the kitchen. The three of them moved as a frenzied pack to the front room, and were soon lined up in front of rolling news. Adams had looked gaunt and drawn in public of late and rumours had been doing the rounds of his apparent ill health. He had appeared at events in the last month or two but had not spoken: he always seemed to be preposterously wrapped up against the unseasonably mild elements. He had taken to walking with a stick. The big man – "their big man as opposed to our big man" – was not a well man.

The newsreader reported that the President had been confined to bed in the last few days with a severe chest infection which developed into full blown pneumonia. His condition had deteriorated rapidly and doctors became sufficiently concerned to move him to a private hospital on the south side of Dublin. He had slipped out of consciousness in the very early hours of Thursday morning, and passed away at lunchtime the same day. He appeared comfortable and at peace, and had been surrounded by his family.

Now the screens and airwaves were full of analysis of what Gerry Adams' life had meant. Reporters did live pieces from outside the hospital – as if 'live' had any particular relevance to death – and there were pointless zooms to one particular window, which as Alan said "could be the Nurses' changing room for all we know."

Gerry Adams had died a statesman and was being afforded the kind of tributes made to a statesman. He had come from humble origins as a barman from West Belfast in a Northern Ireland where Catholics and Republicans were marginalised and mistreated. But he had died the President of a United Ireland that offered equality and opportunity for all. This was a man who had caught a vision and led his community to recognition and prosperity that would have been beyond their wildest dreams in the darkest days of the sixties and seventies. He was also the man who had taken his people out of armed struggle and took enormous risks within this community to broker peace and an agreed settlement.

Viewers were reminded too that in his private life the President had been a literary and a cultured man: he enjoyed the peace and tranquillity of his Donegal home and the surrounding countryside, and had been an accomplished writer. The tributes came from far and wide. From the former President Clinton and the current President Clinton; from the former Prime Minister Blair, and the current Prime Minister Milliband; and from an elderly former Taoiseach Reynolds, and the current Taoiseach Ahern.

"Well it's great to see a fair and objective coverage of events. It's so sepia your TV could be black and white." Alan said, talking to himself as much as to his friends in the room. "Well, I'll tell you something Gerry, something they're not saying in all the platitudes on prime time evening TV. I'll tell you what Gerry: Old Nick will have his poker well stoked for you! Ho-ho: you'll know all about Sinn Fein and the IRA being two separate organisations when you get a big hot poker rammed up your *solar plexus.*"

Peter didn't flinch but Peter didn't miss: "It's good to know that your view of Hell is *so* biblically grounded."

"Oh come on Peter: listen to it. 'One of the most significant men in Irish history!' Aye right: he's pretty significant to all the people who have grown up with no father or who have grown old as widows this past thirty or forty years. He's significant to people who are walking round today with prosthetic limbs. 'Doctors say he died comfortably with friends and family around him'. There wasn't too much peace or comfort for soldiers blown up in the back of their Land Rovers or policemen shot in the back of their heads. There's no part of Hell that's hot enough for him. Sometimes I have doubts about Hell, and how you reconcile that with the idea of a God of love. But it's good to know there's Hell for Adams. He was a bit of a contradiction was our Gerry: he liked to hug trees and write poems but he liked to see humans getting bombed and maimed too. It's good to know that he can't just shuffle comfortably off the hook in his peaceful ward in a private hospital."

Alan leaned forward enthusiastically.

"I tell you what Peter – here's an interesting boat to float: what would Jesus say to Gerry Adams? Have you ever heard one of those sermons? Things like what would Jesus say to Bart Simpson or George Best or whatever. What do you think Jesus would say to Gerry Adams?"

Peter

"Oh…" Peter sighed: "I'm not sure what Jesus would say to Gerry Adams. Hypothetical questions like that often end up being red herrings. What do you want Jesus to say to Gerry Adams? Stick his tongue out at him and go 'na-na-na-na-na, five minutes to Hell Mr Adams: who's a big man now?'"

"Well – yeh – sounds pretty good to me!"

"I mean I'm sure I could sit and reel off a whole lot of things that Jesus might say to Gerry Adams. He would inevitably talk about sin and righteousness and judgment: it seems that the man was involved in some despicable things, and like all of us he'll have to give an account of himself before God for that. God *would* be concerned about the murder and the pain: the blown off limbs and the coffins filled. And God would be concerned too about idolatry: about a man who apparently made Irish Republicanism his lord, when the Bible tells us that God and God alone should be our Lord.

But I'll tell you as well what God wouldn't do: he wouldn't treat Gerry Adams any differently because he had been an Irish Republican and his victims had been Ulster Protestants. What Jesus would say to Gerry Adams would be broadly speaking exactly the same as what he would say to Johnny Adair or Billy Wright. God is greater than the nations, and his judgment and justice are perfect. Gerry Adams isn't being judged by a great big Ulster Protestant clergyman in the sky: Gerry Adams is being judged by God – Yahweh – the Great I Am.

Anyway, as I said earlier it's all just pointless speculation. Who is to say that he wasn't saved? Who is to say God didn't burst into his life miraculously just as he was lying on his death bed? For all we know what Jesus might say to Gerry Adams could be 'welcome into your rest'."

"That's not fair" Alan said. "That's making it out as if I wouldn't want that to be the case. I'd have loved it if Gerry Adams had become a Christian." He stopped, and thought about that for a moment. "Well – ok, I'm not sure if I'd have *loved* it. But pretty flipping easy and convenient if he had come to faith that way: not too much taking up your cross in that. Anyway Peter: you're starting to string your holy hypothesising out to an absurd point."

"Well who started it? I mean, come on Alan: with the best will in the world, the problem with some of you people is that you're a bunch of Jonahs. You say that you would love for Gerry Adams to have become a Christian. But I reckon that if revival were to sweep up the Falls Road and the streets of Andersonstown, there'd be people in your community who would want to sit under a vine on the top of the Black Mountain and would say to God that it would be better for them to die."

Adam squirmed in his chair at his friend's exaggeration. "I think that's maybe pushing things a wee bit. I'm not so sure that it's a matter of judgment as much as it's a lack of faith. I think we might *pray* for people like Gerry Adams and Martin McGuinness to come to faith in Christ, but do we actually *believe* that it's ever going to happen?

It's all very well when we're sitting in church and we sing that line in the hymn: 'the vilest offender who truly believes, that moment from Jesus a pardon receives.' It's all very well to pray that Gerry Kelly or Pat Doherty might become 'trophies of grace'. But we haven't seen it happen and I'm not sure if that's because we don't want it *to* happen, or because we don't believe it *can* happen. Either way it's wrong and it's a dreadful heresy: we're actually limiting the Gospel and the power of what Jesus did on the cross.

Maybe one of the reasons we don't believe Gerry Adams could ever have become a Christian is that there was never any evidence of softening about him. I couldn't see any hint of remorse: he could wax lyrical about the fallen volunteers of his own armed struggle, but the British and Protestants who died just seemed to be faceless collateral damage as the Holy Grail of one Ireland was pursued."

Peter shrugged his shoulders. "Yeh but come on Adam: you don't know what the man thought in private. But in public he was a politician and he had a reputation to live up to. He was the leader of a movement."

Adam wasn't to be deflected. "Most of the people he called soldiers never fought a battle in their lives: all they did was carry out executions. What bravery was there in that? He was a politician alright: the peace process was all about tactics. It wasn't that they saw anything wrong with killing people: it was just time for a change of strategy. I suppose this is where we could start going down the very Protestant road of whether there can be forgiveness without repentance."

Peter interrupted at that point. "But you're just getting back into lots of theorising where you're kind of playing God. Surely the point and purpose of man is to attain to being like God: but we're never going to *be* God…"

"Well I know *that*…" Adam said defensively.

"Yeh of course you do: I know you do" Peter accepted. "But

I think we've got to get ourselves really rooted in a biblical view of judgment. Because so much of what we've been sitting and doing here is just judging this man. The single most important thing that the Bible says about judgment is that God is the judge and we as human beings simply have no place or right to judge. Think about so many of the obvious verses and it all hits home. Then think about Gerry Adams and the way that you've been talking. Firstly that really fundamental principle of do not judge: and in the same way that you judge others, you yourself will be judged.

And the second bit – "in the same way that you judge others" – really gives us food for thought. So if you *are* going to judge Gerry Adams on the rights and wrongs of how he lived as an Irish Republican, be prepared to be judged for the way you behaved as an Ulster Protestant. If good Christian Unionists are going to judge him for bank robberies and murder in pubs, then they should be prepared to be judged for petty sectarianism and casual bigotry."

"Ah, but – hold on there Peter" Alan said with a creeping smugness on his face. "Who is to say I can't judge Gerry Adams? Is there not a verse where Jesus tells the disciples that they will all sit with Him judging the twelve tribes of Israel? Is there not a bit somewhere where Paul talks about the saints judging the world?"

"There are verses like that" Peter agreed. "But what are you doing: you're plucking Scripture to bend it to your argument, rather than your arguments stemming directly from God's word. The Bible's a big book and it's full of contradictions: Christians have forever and a day argued from opposing ends of spectrums and both claimed the Scriptures are on their side. But I think the bulk of the weight is with me on this one.

I think it's pretty clear that the person who will do the judging will be Christ: it's a role entrusted to him by the Father. I mean it's one thing to say that we might do the judging, but surely what's indisputable is that we're *all* going to be judged. There's nowhere where it says that a select few will be fast forwarded to some Heavenly Club Class lounge and don't have to go through check-in. Man is destined to die once and face judgment.

And of course there are wonderful positives in that. Because you don't have to justify yourself to anyone Alan: as far as God is concerned there's no reason for Martin McGuinness to ever have to justify himself to someone like William McCrea. Paul talks about his conscience being clear in terms of what other people think of him, because it is the Lord who judges him. The judgment of God is meant to give us peace because we know that there is an ultimate place where justice can't be escaped: it's not meant to be a cause for gloating. It's very easy to fantasise about our enemies being judged, but there's not too many of us get warm and fuzzy thoughts about ourselves standing before the judgment seat of Christ. I mean, who is to say that someone like you won't be judged harder than the likes of Gerry Adams?"

"Oh come off it" Alan said. "You're away with the fairies! How do you work that one out?"

"Well, I work it out quite easily. Think about Peter when he talks about judgment beginning with the family of God. Think about the sheep and the goats, and think about the parable of the talents. I think it's arguable that Christians might actually be judged harder than non Christians: because they have a lot less excuses in terms of knowing what the ground rules were. Gerry Adams grew up in Catholic West Belfast and people like you love to point out that he would never have been told the truth of the Gospel. But you were brought up in a good Christian home and you've known what God has done for you, and how He would have you live, from you were knee high to a daisy. So it stands to reason that God might give you a tougher time at the judgment.

But look: remember ultimately one of the statements of Jesus. He did not come to judge the world but to save it. The character of God is just but it is also utterly loving: we haven't once talked about grace tonight. It's fanciful speculation to say that Jesus might be inviting Gerry Adams into his rest. But it's a sure-fire bet that Jesus would far rather be welcoming Adams with open arms than condemning him to eternal fire. We take

239

vindictive pleasure in the thought of our enemies being judged: but God is about the nature of being Holy rather than the business of settling scores. God wants all men everywhere to come to salvation."

A loud and embarrassing rumble gurgled out of Alan's stomach. Adam looked at him: "have you had anything to eat?"

"Oh thank God for that" he replied. "I thought you were never going to ask."

"Oh right" Adam said. "Do you want me to fix you something? I could do you a toasted sandwich, if you like."

"That would be great. And while you're at it, I'll use your loo if you don't mind: my bladder's playing havoc with my concentration."

A short while later, as they supped and munched, Adam posed a question. "I suppose you could always ask whether Gerry Adams and a lot of the terrorists could particularly help themselves."

"Could you?" Alan replied in a snap of disagreement.

"Well: I'm playing devil's advocate here…"

"Which in the case of Gerry Adams is a *very* appropriate way of putting it…"

"Oh do stop it" Peter snapped. "Let the man make his point."

"What I'm trying to say" Adam continued "is that for a lot of people there must have been a certain amount of… let me call it *situational inevitability* about getting caught up in violence. Were they bad people who did what they did because they *were* bad, or did they just fall into it because of the combination of all that was going on: the deprivation, and the inequality, and the civil rights, and internment and so on?"

"Not a bit of it: that's way too easy to say" replied Alan. "I can only speak for myself but I would have had principles: if it was me and I had been in that situation, I wouldn't have let myself get caught up in it."

"Are you really so sure of that" Peter asked. "I think – with the greatest respect – it's very easy for you to say that yourself. From the comfortable middle class upbringing that you have had – with all its privileges of family and church and education and so on – it would be explicably not the thing to do to get involved in terrorism and unrest.

But what if you're 16 and immature and finding your way in the world? And you've been brought up from infancy to imbibe the bitterness of your community. And you've no qualifications and no job and your parents and your brothers and your cousins have no jobs, and life is dead end and directionless. You have no prospects whatsoever and the man in the next road along who is rumoured to be the leader of the local terrorist cell walks tall and seems unimaginably glamorous in the small world of the back streets. Don't get me wrong: I'm not defending it, but you can see how it happens."

Adam responded. "People have surely been debating these person versus situation arguments from time immemorial. But can you let people off the hook because they morally sleepwalked into terrorism? I hear what you're saying Peter, but I have to disagree with you because you're only telling half the story. For some young people, deprivation and social circumstances must have played a part in them getting involved. But that wasn't the case for everyone. If there were so called volunteers who were foolish and impressionable, then who was leading and exploiting them? This wasn't Gerry Adams and his band of merry men, jauntily robbing from the Prods and giving to the Catholics. This was a premeditated, well resourced and highly organised killing machine. It didn't happen by accident and it wasn't just about a lack of jobs and bad housing either: poisonous ideology had a lot to do with it too."

"I think as well" Alan continued "that you need to strip away the veneer of glory they tried to cover themselves in: all Gerry's ethereal claptrap about armed struggle and freedom fighting. Intimidation and bragging rights in your own community – beating to death an innocent man in a pub and then closing ranks – that has nothing to do with freedom fighting. Robbing the Northern Bank: that has nothing to do with armed struggle on behalf of the Nationalist community.

Criminality has nothing to do with achieving equality for your own people. I'm sorry Peter, but get real about the sort of people we're talking about here."

"You're right, you're right..." Peter conceded in an effort to gain a foothold back into the debate. "But look – shades of grey too – I'm right up to a point, as well. And you know as well as I do, that the Loyalist paramilitaries did terrible things as well. We could just as easily be a pile of Catholics with the shoe on the other foot, having the very same conversation about loyalists. It wasn't all one sided..."

"We're not saying it was..." Alan replied.

"You're not" Peter agreed. "But you've got to be willing to see the thing from the other community's point of view. What you must accept is that God would never have sympathised or endorsed the armed struggle and the bloodshed inflicted by the Republicans, and yet at the same time He must have felt a compassion for the circumstances of their broader community. And guys 'do unto others as you would have done unto you'. The terrorists travelled journeys themselves and a lot of it can't have been easy for them. Whether you're a God fearing Christian, or whether you're an IRA man, counter cultural is still counter cultural. When you're kith and kin all blindly hate the police imagine how brave you have to be to advocate that people from your community should join it.

And even if their strategies weren't always entirely pure – motivated by tactics rather than righteousness – is it not a reason for thanks to God that these things happened? There are hundreds and hundreds of people alive and well and with their full complement of limbs who would not otherwise have been that way, were it not for the ceasefires. Paul said that whatever the motives – whether they are good or bad – he rejoiced when the Gospel was preached. And I think it should be the same when terrorists give up their guns and decommission: whether that be out of repentance and awakening, or out of sneak and strategy, it's still marvellous that it happened.

Dare to see the grace of God at work in your history. The problem with you people is that you only see grace when you've got the Prince but you forget that the beast became beautiful when he was loved in his ugliness. God is just as much at work in the decision of a terrorist to abandon the armalite and pursue the ballot box, as he is in the moment of decision when a person responds to Christ at an altar call."

Adam

"Look" Adam said with a hint of exasperation: "we could sit and talk about this all night. But we're never going to get to the bottom of it. We don't have the answers. One way or another Gerry Adams is going to stand before God and be judged, and whatever it is that God says to him and does to him, God is perfect and holy, and Adams won't be able to say that the outcome is unfair.

I come down on the side of individual human responsibility. We all of us have choices to make. Think about that verse in Joshua: it more or less says to choose for yourselves this day what it is you want to be and what it is you are about. But as for me and my household we will serve the Lord. The Lord: not Ireland; not the Union; but the Lord comes first. Think about those verses at the start of Psalm 1. First of all you walk in the counsel of the wicked, then you get a bit comfortable and stand with the sinners, and before you know it everything is cosy and you're sitting down with them. It's all about decisions that we have to make.

Every moment is a choice. The same goes for terrorism and murder and intimidation and criminality. Every human being – I believe – is responsible for his or her behaviour. I'm sure it wasn't easy for a lot of people in our community but saying that 'well it was West Belfast, and the late 1960s, and my people were under pressure, so I joined up' is just too much akin to saying that I ate the apple because the woman told me it would be tasty. The first words of the devil to Eve were 'Did God *really* say?' Was it *really* so bad to join the boys with the guns and the balaclavas given all that was going on? It's in the nature of human beings to take something that is black and white and try to find grey ground in the middle to justify their actions to themselves.

And I do believe in a devil – and I don't believe that he's Gerry Adams either. He's far bigger than that. Think about the soldiers who were savagely beaten to death when they inadvertently drove into the Republican funeral. Think about blowing up the soldiers along Carlingford Waters and then having another bomb timed to go off when help arrives at the scene of devastation. Think about detonating explosives on a Saturday afternoon when people are popping into the chippy for a fish supper.

Think about who planned these things: I don't believe you can do things like that unless you fundamentally like to maim and hurt and torture. Some of it was because of what they wanted for Ireland and some of it was because they enjoyed it. I believe that at one level the problems of this country have been about two communities unable to reconcile their differences. But I also believe in a devil prowling around Ireland like a lion and looking for people and communities to devour."

It was pitch black outside now, and Alan got up and moved over to the window, where he pulled blinds and drew the curtains.

"Hard to argue with any of that" Peter said. "You know, there is one thing the Bible says about judgment that I forgot about when we were talking earlier. It's the concept of getting wound up about the speck of sawdust in your brother's eye and paying no attention to the plank in your own. The problems of this land – as far as I can see – all exist within a pyramid of sin, and whether we're at the top or the bottom, we're all in the pyramid."

"What do you mean?" Alan asked.

"Well it's quite simple" Peter replied. "At the top of the pyramid are the terrorists and the diehards: those who are pure in ideology and won't give an inch. They're prepared to take up weapons and beat and shoot and so on. In the middle of the pyramid are those who are to the extremity of their community: they'll vote Sinn Fein and they'll be in residents groups opposed to Orange marches. They'll sing sectarian songs in kick the pope bands and block public highways for the sake of getting up the Garvaghy Road. The people in the middle might not do the things that those at the top would do but they give support and legitimacy to the top level.

The people at the bottom are decent and middle class and respectable. But they wonder where a stranger went to school and they mutter inwardly when he says he's called Dermot or pronounces a 'h' with a 'haitch'. They believe it's as wrong to worship with a Catholic as it's wrong to smoke or drink a glass of wine. They are passive rather than radical, and they will always curse the darkness rather than light a candle. And the people at the bottom, in their own inert way, give legitimacy and add support to the people in the middle. In short, you are all a part of it.

Northern Ireland – and the whole island of Ireland – has enormous sin problems that need to be addressed. When Cain killed Abel he was told that his brother's blood cries out to God from the ground. It is as if the sectarianism and the divisiveness of Ireland almost cry out from its land: in the land like the toxic pollutant of people and communities that it is.

It's too easy to ask what Jesus would say to Gerry Adams. What – if we're honest –would Jesus say to any of us here? There's a beautiful verse within the Nativity story where we read about Simeon and are told that he awaited the *consolation* of Israel: that's an absolutely wonderful concept, the thought that a whole land can be consoled. That is what Ireland needs but perhaps it is too trite and easy to talk only about consolation. Because there is just so much sin of division and fracture and bigotry: and it exists at oh so many levels. And we are all going to be judged. We need the consolation but we need to be honest and have conviction as well. That's what people like us should pray for: the conviction *and* the consolation of Ireland."

30

John

The appointed time for John's apology to that victim of a beating so many years ago, turned out to be a sunny Friday morning in October. He had only got two weeks notice of it which he thought a good thing because it reduced the anticipation of it, which he believed would be worse than the actual reckoning.

Two days after his revelation to Gillian, he had phoned Willie and asked if he could take up that offer of a listening ear. He had cut his friend off in the town that morning and felt he should explain himself. Perhaps there had been too much dishonesty – too much dishonesty all round. He held nothing back and laid it all out to Willie in a fluent and reasoned manner: the interviews with the police and the all too recent confession to Gillian had made him effortlessly articulate in the telling of this story. Willie listened much and spoke little. John said he was particularly embarrassed at the fact that he was the leader of the small group: here was the man who had sat so holier than thou and led all sorts of studies and prayer times down through the years. He felt he had been so inauthentic. But Willie said that they couldn't all be wearing their souls inside out all of the time: forgiveness doesn't require humiliation in a public space.

Gillian gave John no option as to whether or not he would make the trip on his own, being adamant that she would accompany him. The deliberateness of their travel plans lead them to arrive forty-five minutes early so they took advantage of the sunny weather and took a stroll in the grounds of the plush Belfast hotel where the encounter was to take place.

At half-past ten they were received first of all at a reception desk by Sergeant Lynch from Dublin, who required that John sign some formal paperwork to confirm that he had been true to his word and had showed for this encounter.

"There you go" he muttered to Gillian: "another notch on the bedpost of peace and reconciliation."

Then they were then taken into a small ante-room where they met a middle aged American woman who introduced herself as Judy. She explained how she would be sitting in on their meeting that day: nothing would be taped or recorded and her role was merely that of a witness and facilitator.

The victim – whose name was Damien – would speak first and give an account of his experience and how it had affected him. Then John would speak and explain his perspective of the events and give an apology. During neither of these statements was one to interrupt the other. There was no time limit on this: it was to take as long as was necessary. She asked if John had any questions and he shook his head. After that there could be some more free exchange if both parties were comfortable with such discussion. Her manner was formal but she was not judging. A smile would have been nice – and he felt that his wrongdoing was being 'processed' – but at no stage did John feel she was forcing him to wallow as a perpetrator.

The rules of engagement having been established, Judy disappeared for a short period of time, before returning and inviting them to accompany her to an adjoining room.

Damien – a callow teenager on the night of the beating – was now a man of nearly forty, balding and sporting a tight crew cut to disguise the impact of his hair loss. A small stud earring sat in his left ear and he was wearing a new looking suit in which he appeared distinctly uncomfortable. He too was accompanied by his wife and together they had a hard but careworn and nervous appearance. Gillian thought that this lady's eyes were so bloodshot it was a wonder she could see anything at all.

Judy made some brief introductions and invited Damien to speak. Damien hesitatingly started to explain in broken sentences and a grinding accent how he had not even known the police car was there that evening – he vaguely remembered stumbling across the pile of Gers fans, but had been too drunk to recall any of the details of the night.

In the middle of this account he faltered and reached to open a bottle of water in front of him, but his hands were sweaty and he struggled with the screw cap. John reached over and took it from him, opening it with ease and returning it to Damien. John thought that a kind of olive branch but the gesture was not acknowledged.

Damien went on to explain that however little he recalled of the night in question, he had strong recollections of what came afterwards. He might have been as good as anesthetised when he was being beaten, but that was as nothing to what followed. He didn't just suffer for one evening: he suffered for months that lead to years. There was what seemed like an endless cycle of operations and hospital visits and physiotherapists and even now he still takes medication relating to that night. John and the other policeman intervening wouldn't have changed the fact that he was badly injured but they might have lessened it a bit. Throughout this he looked at the table rather than John, but his wife's eyes were fixed on John and Gillian all through his testimony.

John momentarily thought that he was in some way getting off lightly before Damien explained that actually the attack had a greater effect on his family than it did on him. His mother had died of a heart attack eight months after the beating: and whilst she was hardly in the best of health, everyone was in no doubt about what it was that caused her to go in the end. The strain had been too much for her, and then seeing the impact that all of that had on his father had only made things even worse. His older sister used to say that it only took one encounter on one night to tip a domino and look how the whole lot came falling down.

Every sin is like this, thought Gillian: just because we do not see the consequence does not mean it doesn't exist. It's not what this man has been through that is so un-normal: it is having to listen to the out workings of your husband's actions that are so bizarre. Human beings are moral polluters: there's no escaping that.

Damien said he had done his best to put it all behind him: his father said that he was too young not too and that he had the whole of the rest of his life in front of him – that advice had always stuck in his mind. But he'd be lying if he said it didn't affect him: he was anxious about the places he went to and didn't even like to go out and walk the dog on his own at night. He was always looking over his shoulder.

Then it was John's turn to speak: he apologised profusely and did not excuse himself or hold back in any way. Although he thought himself in some Christ-like manner to be sitting where Eddie Thompson should have sat, he did not in any way diminish his own complicity and sins of omission. He said little because so much conversation had already been spilled on this in the past weeks: this occasion was about saying sorry and was about Damien. It was not about John and his guilt and his regret and yet he had to make it clear that if he could do anything to turn back the clock and go back to that night he would have seen to it that things turned out very differently. Damien nodded and gave other non-verbal ticks of acknowledgment as John spoke, but at no stage did he speak to explicitly confirm any acceptance of the apology. There was no further discussion: neither side wanted to prompt or probe.

As Gillian looked around her and listened to all that was going on, she became conscious of how ill-judged the venue for this meeting had been. It was meant to be plush and neutral but Damien and his wife appeared ill at ease in such luxurious surroundings. It might have been the height of comfort but it certainly did not help *them* feel comfortable.

John observed the edginess of Damien and his wife – she was never introduced which seemed odd – but thought of it a different way. He experienced the encounter as an example of how giving is more rewarding than receiving. Maybe it was a class thing or a social thing or even a spiritual thing, but he was surprised at his conviction that he was getting more out of this than the victim was. He felt pain at the realisation of the impact the events had on an entire family and yet he felt too the relief of a burden lifted. Damien looked as if he didn't want to be there, yet by rights it should have been John who felt that way. Is digging into all the detail of something that happened over twenty years ago really wise for anyone to do? Was this really helping this man? At the end John stood up and stretched out a hand which Damien accepted.

Afterwards John and Gillian had planned to go and start some Christmas shopping in the city centre: they thought that might have been a welcome distraction but now that notion seemed tasteless and neither knew how they could even have countenanced the idea. John looked at Gillian as they headed out of the hotel reception together and she smiled reassuringly: there was a clear understanding that they were going to go home now.

John looked pale as he reached the car keys out of his pocket and Gillian held out her hand to say that she would drive on this occasion. The traffic was tediously heavy that day and it took them an hour and fifteen minutes to make their journey. And neither of them said a word.

* * * * *

Alan

Alan was bored and Alan was frustrated. Both of these feelings were related at the current moment to his work but they felt like a metaphor for the wider morass of his circumstances. This Friday lunchtime found him struggling to find inspiration in pulling together concepts for the first annual report of the *Irish Interpretive Society of Loughs and Lakes*.

The society's Chairman had been on the phone half an hour ago: he reiterated to the designer his heartfelt conviction that the formation of the new body was one of the most exciting developments in Irish Freshwater circles in the past fifty years. Alan was so sick and tired of these words and more: 'new' and 'premium' and 'innovative' and 'exciting'. All of them had ceased to mean anything: they needed to be replaced by something... well... new. He stared at his Mac and longed to be in a different time and place where exciting meant something different: a place where it was substituted and you said – and felt – electrifying or titillating or thrilling instead.

But then again... maybe not. He had had an electric moment the night before but there had been nothing good about it. Nadia had come round to the house for tea and whilst in the process of making it, he came to a flustered point in the recipe where he suddenly realised he needed fresh cream. She was in the bathroom having a shower after her shift at the chip shop: he called through the door to tell her where he was going. On the way out he realised he'd nothing smaller than a fifty euro note, and knowing how much that irritated the 'scary woman' at the corner shop he thought he would rummage through Nadia's bag for her purse and some smaller change.

He furrowed through assorted bits and pieces: mobile phone; hair clips; keys; IPod – the purse seemed to be at the bottom: it's always the way in furtive moments. And just as his hand was about to reach the furthermost depths his eyes fell on a long piece of paper. He took it out and quizzically examined it up and down. It looked like the end of a till roll from the chip shop and in descending rows were written two words over and over again: Nadia Mackey. He grimaced as his eyes fell down the scroll: he was no expert in the interpretation of handwriting but panic convinced him that as you got further and further down the script became what he would later describe to Mike as 'flouncier and bouncier', the scribe clearly enjoying herself more and more.

"Oh holy moly" he muttered to himself – how could she... what made her think... he couldn't see any way that he'd thrown her lines or sent signals to suggest that *this* was coming... What was it with women and this obsession they had with there being some sort of endgame? He never thought that way: what was wrong with living for the moment and that alone? He had dated more girls than he cared to remember, and had fantasised more than he cared to repent, but weddings just never entered into the image projector of his mind.

He stuffed the flotsam of her handbag back where it

belonged and fled to the shop like he was running from some scene of crime, not from his own back door. *Marriage*: what was she on? And then his pulse revved again to its red line as dread of matrimony moved him on to the notion of children. Man joined to woman equals offspring. Now there was a thought: generally he regarded himself as the sort of man who didn't mind children so long as they weren't his own. But what if they ever got that far: would she be more a procreation than a pleasure sort of girl and would they wind up with a football team of kids around them? A little voice inside him was saying "contraception: sure you know what Catholics think of that."

He had gone on to sleep badly that night which wasn't helping his creative block at the current moment. As his head hit the pillow he had been beset with grim and far fetched imaginings of what a Polish wedding might be like. He visualised himself in traditional Eastern European dress, with women in white blouses with braces, enormous multi-coloured skirts and clogs egging him up the aisle. He wondered if there was any sort of equivalent of the Jewish thing of plate smashing that they went in for in Poland. Would he have to chase a wild goat around the village and capture and tether it to prove his virility? Would he have to demonstrate his worthiness by eating a traditionally enormous sackful of fermented potatoes the night before the nuptials?

This first torrent of anxiety in the middle of the night had then given way to a wave of guilt. He pondered how much he despised snobbery when he was at the bottom of its pile in a conventional home-grown experience of the sentiment. But now he was overcome by feelings of 'I'm as bad as they are'. The third phase of his dark night was a simple and glum stillness, as resignation and feelings of being trapped set in. He had bitten off more than he could chew and dug one mighty hole for himself, and now here he sat in the consequence of his choices: bloated and nauseous at the bottom of a deep black pit. The last time he saw the clock beside his bed it was saying 3:37.

And as his eyes returned from the office window overlooking the city centre, to the screen of his computer, a foreboding sense of callousness and self-preservation took over. This relationship had now gone way beyond the point where he could still regard it as 'exciting'. When you're soaring very high in love all you see is blue sky and your dreams have a tendency to blot out all good sense and reality. Drop a little lower than your dreams and even then you still just have your head in the clouds, deluded and unable to see a clear path and direction to take. So the hard truth is that what is called for is to drop lower still, and that's where he was now. He was at a sufficiently low altitude to properly sense the big picture and could finally see enough to realise that it was getting to the time where he'd have to pull the rip cord.

Tired and jaded words were just the same with all his good living Christian friends. Over time – he reasoned – you can become immune to the proper meaning of 'lamb' and 'salt' and 'sword' and 'world' and 'light' and 'fruit' and 'good news'. They're safe in their sanctity but eventually become lost in translation of relevance. They make the church a foreign language to those beyond its borders. He so wanted love to mean love but it's pointless if that's just another way of saying blind stupidity. The moment had come when truth was going to have to mean hard talking. Kindness – in the long run – would leave him no option but cruelty.

31

Peter

Peter was finishing his tea one evening, when he made the announcement. He was mopping sauce with bread and after wiping it round his plate he held it up before biting into it. "I've got something to tell you."

"What's that then?" Adam asked.

"Well" Peter continued – before pausing to finish his mouthful – "things have gone really well with the university this past year, and they've offered me a permanent position. A mix of teaching and seeing how we can get the research moved on a bit more."

A look between delight and despair spread across Adam's face.

"Don't worry" Peter said. "I'm not expecting to stay here. I wouldn't: you've been more than good, but I wouldn't impose myself on you any more. You're bound to want your space back. I'm going to buy my own place."

"You're going to *buy*?"

"Yep: I've already been looking about."

Peter shrugged as he finished the glass of wine in his hand.

"Well I suppose it's something of a buyer's market here, right now" Adam said.

"Absolutely" Peter replied. "I'll probably stay till Christmas or just before, and then I'll go back to Jo-burg for a month or so and sort out my affairs. And then I'll be back." He paused at the sound of his own presumption. "I mean: if that's alright with you. You don't mind having me till Christmas, do you?"

"Oh no it's grand." His response was genuine: he was already thinking how empty the place was going to feel when his friend was gone.

Peter put his knife and fork together, set them on his plate and pushed it away from in front of him. "I'm going to buy a house and I'm going to call it Anathoth."

"Anathoth?" Adam exclaimed. "Where do you get that from?"

"It's biblical mate: from the book of Jeremiah. It's a sign of my belief in this place: it's a sign that I believe the only way for Ireland is up."

"Right" Adam replied, sounding unconvinced. "So how does that work then?"

"Well it goes back to the point in the story when the Babylonians are closing in and besieging Jerusalem, and Jeremiah has been confined to the royal court. Things are grim: Doomsday is approaching. As guys round here would say 'the end is nigh'."

Adam rolled his eyes.

"It's fire sale time: it's time to get out, to cut and run. And Hanamel – Jeremiah's cousin – comes to him and says 'buy my field at Anathoth: it's your right and duty.' It's like a kind of family first refusal thing."

"So Jeremiah buys it."

"Jeremiah buys it: which seems like lunacy. The king and the court are about to fall and the cream of society are going to be murdered or driven into exile. And Jeremiah weighs out his seventeen shekels of silver and decides it's time to do a deal? Why?"

"Why indeed?"

"Because God told him to: because the word of the Lord came to him. Things seem bad and bleak but Jeremiah says it isn't always going to be this way: 'houses, fields and vineyards will again be bought in this land'. The people can only see the destruction at the end of their noses: they don't have the vision to see the possibilities for how God will – in time – redeem the situation and rebuild the land."

"And is that why you're going to call your house Anathoth, then? Has God been speaking to you as well?"

Peter broke away eye contact then and his voice became softer.

"I wouldn't go so far as to say that. I mean we're pretty rational sort of people, aren't we. It seems a bit loopy to go and buy a house because God's told you to buy a house. It's like something you'd expect me to say on a one phone call a day out of the asylum. But I really believe in this place and in some weird way that I struggle to explain or understand I think God wants me to be here. God's not a wrecker – God's a builder up. I think God's the same now as he was in Jeremiah's day: I think God sees the future for this place far brighter and clearer than the people do. I think God wants to do things here: and I want to be about to see them."

32

Adam

Adam had no particular expectation of how many people there would be at the morning's service. He discussed it about a week beforehand with Peter and they agreed it would be interesting for them to go. This being the case Adam felt almost voyeuristic about their planned attendance: he could not claim any direct need to be there; but this year – for the first time that he could remember – he was conscious of a compelling sense that this was something he ought to do. He owed this to somebody somewhere. And so it was that he and Peter found themselves ensconced in winter coats and standing at the town's small war memorial to await the act of Remembrance at eleven o'clock.

"Maybe it's the small 'b' 'Britishness' in me: or maybe it's just the fact that I'm getting older; and in the process of that there's a growing awareness of tradition and things that ought to be continued. It's a sobering thought that so much of that which is important to me is only a generation away from dying out – imagine that – a generation away."

"Did you never come at all, then?" Peter asked. "You're not telling me this is the first time you've been to one of these, is it?"

"Oh no, of course it's not" Adam replied. "I mean there would always be a service in church, and I'd have been to that in the course of Sunday worship, but I'd never have gone out of my way to come down *here*. I mean I never lost anyone directly in The Troubles: no uncles or cousins or even close family friends or anything like that. And as far as I'm aware there were no Cupples cut down in the trenches at the Somme or at the beaches at Normandy. I wish I'd asked my dad a lot more about the old family history, and written a whole lot of it down, but I'm sure if there had been things like *that* he'd have told me."

Adam put his hands up to his cheeks to determine their precise temperature and decided it sufficiently cold to reach into his pockets for some gloves. He unpacked more thoughts as he threaded his fingers and thumbs.

"I was never particularly sure of the services we had in the church itself: I always felt like an outsider looking in. I suppose I'm what you might have called dissenting in outlook: I could never have said that what happened was wrong, but I just felt very uncomfortable about it. A service of worship to God and there in the middle of it you had flags and old soldiers and medals and the National Anthem being sung and all.

Gosh, I remember one year the Minister forgot to do the National Anthem – it was always announced with great and simple gusto as 'The Queen' – and everyone would stand up with fervour to belt it out. After the service some wee woman – I can't remember her name – cornered me and complained about this – as if it was somehow something to do with me – and I foolishly said in an off the cuff manner that it was hardly the end of the world. I tell you what: famous last words. She lit into me: one accidental omission set her against that Minister for life. I suspect she might have had some personal story to tell, but it was a fascinating microcosm of the depth of feelings that are out there. That was years ago: I wonder what happened to that wee woman..."

Peter shrugged his shoulders. "Probably dead and gone from the way you describe her."

"Probably. Like I've said before: most of the time, the church chose to deal with The Troubles by – well – by not dealing with them. You would have had prayers said for the protection of soldiers and police in times of intercession but that was about the height of it. Heaven forbid that the Minister would ever do something as unseemly as straight on preach a sermon about the mess of a divided society and the relevance to all that of the Gospel of Christ. And in the midst of all this inertia, there was this sense that in an unspoken way The Troubles entered our worship on Remembrance Sunday, as the little service within a service confirmed the Unionism of the congregation.

The other thing that hammered home our Britishness was the Minister praying for the Royal Family. The old boy who was there before Noel Houston used to be particularly into that. He used to pray with deferential frequency that the Queen would be protected and given wisdom. And I used to sit there and think to myself that given the privilege and luxury of royal life, and the fact it was actually the Prime Minister who ran the country, this was all a bit pointless. I suppose he'd have cited that verse about praying for kings and those in authority, but I think it was as much to do with identity as anything else. I don't expect there were too many priests at Sunday Mass who prayed for the Queen."

"Oh relax" Peter said. "The past was a different time and place and it wasn't all good just as much as it wasn't all bad: people shouldn't have to flagellate themselves for history they mightn't even have been a part of."

"You're right" Adam muttered. "But you know, I think it would be tremendous if this modern Irish state could keep hold of the heritage of Remembrance Sunday. One of the things the Irish tend to be bad at – on both sides – is taking a very narrow view of the world that revolves around the history of their land."

He held out his arms wide apart and then brought his hands to almost touching.

"It's as if they cast aside all the histories that have ever happened: depending on who you are, the Unionist story of Northern Ireland sold down the river is the most important one there is to be told, or the Republican tale of poor old downtrodden Ireland is the definitive version of history. Nothing was ever such a crafty betrayal as the British breaking the Union, and no one was ever as oppressed as Irish Catholics. The communities here don't think of the greatest story ever told: they think of the only story to be told. But Remembrance Sunday reminds us that's not the case: it reminds us that the world is a far bigger place."

And at that he took his arms back out wide again.

"Broadly speaking, what people have fought for in this

place, is the right and privilege to fly a particular flag and claim a certain identity. But there have been wars within this continent in the past century where what was at stake was the fundamental freedom of humanity. On the Richter scale of historical suffering the Holocaust was a great big mighty earthquake, whilst what Irish Catholics went through is a wee tiny tremor that would hardly register.

Putting on my doctor's hat, I'd say the people of Ireland have a very masculine approach to the pain they've been through. Men have a very different threshold to pain than that of women: some men can't cope with a nasty cut but women can have children. The people of Ireland are all men: in the grand scheme of world History they have had at worst a bad cold, but they've convinced themselves it was a terrible disease that scarred them for life."

"Yeh but come on Adam: some individuals have suffered terribly."

"I agree with that Peter: I agree entirely. Those who have suffered injuries that have left them in wheelchairs, women widowed at a young age, children growing up without parents: it hardly bears thinking about. But I'm not talking about individuals: I'm talking about the community as a whole – the collective psyche.

Think about the Holocaust. Think about Hiroshima. Think about Apartheid and what your kith and kin went through. Think about the genocide in Rwanda. Think about the Tsunami. Think about Nine-Eleven. Think about places like Burma and North Korea. Then think about how utterly self-absorbed and up themselves the politicians of Ulster were about whether they could find it in themselves to get power sharing up and running again.

Irish Republicans saw themselves as fighting to free the six counties and called it their 'struggle', but that was as nothing compared to the struggle against fascism in the Second World War. One of the great things that I think Remembrance Sunday could do in a modern Ireland is encourage us as a nation to look back in a way whereby we take in a more outward looking view of things: do a wee bit of vision catching." At that he paused. "Hey up: here's a familiar face."

Whilst they were talking John had ambled up behind Peter and towards Adam, seeing as he did a familiar face in the small gathering. Peter turned round and greeted John.

"Well John: how's about you? What are you doing here?"

John looked back at Peter and simply rolled his eyes. "Listen: just you look at me and then you look at yourself and then look at where we are. More to the point: what are *you* doing here?"

"Well..." Peter mumbled.

"Oh for goodness sake man: be quiet. I'm only winding: I know what you meant and I suppose you've as much right to be here as anyone." And then he leaned into his friends to make a more important point. "But seeing as you're asking I'll tell you what I'm doing here: I'm here to honour the spirit of *don't let the bastards grind us down.* That's what I'm doing here." And at that he added to his words a proud nod.

* * * * *

As the Act of Remembrance took place, the dwelling stopped and the history started: in the end it is all about people rather than ideology. It brought home the simple importance of remembering the few and what they had done for the many.

John managed to get through the short service, but there were moments during it when his bottom lip edged noticeably proud of his top lip, and he appeared clenched and drained in stoicism. He said nothing the entire way through, but edged himself between Adam and Peter, as if he was glad of them being there. At the end of it all, the three friends seemed to flap about a bit, unsure of the direction in which they should go: as if the church were one way but some sort of wind was blowing them back. Peter voiced his thoughts.

"I've a feeling that this is a great morning to go for a walk: church can wait and I think God understands. Does anyone else agree with me?"

His friends' heads bobbed in agreement and there was little said as they headed off in that direction. Heading into the park it was Peter who broke the silence.

"Are you doing alright now?" John looked up slightly and nodded shyly that he was, because it was clearly to him that the question had been directed. And Peter carried on talking.

"I suppose it's easy for old emotions to become confused at times like these. You know one of the things that people are very inclined to get caught up on is this silly need to make a link between forgiving and forgetting. You hear people say that, don't you: "oh I can forgive but I can't forget." Personally I think there's absolutely no connection between the two: just because you forgive doesn't mean that you can automatically wipe things that have happened from your memory. You must have seen some dreadful things John – especially in the course of your work – and if anger or sadness returns with an event like today, there's not a single thing wrong with that.

The Bible seems to me to take a view that's the opposite of forgiving and forgetting: whilst it places tremendous importance on the significance of Christ's gift of forgiveness – and the forgiveness that we are in turn to show others – it also gives weight to the matter of remembering. No good was ever achieved by trying to sweep past realities under the carpet. It has to be an honest thing."

Adam appeared bemused at his friend's views. "I don't think I agree with that. I think the Bible is absolutely all on for forgiving and forgetting. God forgives our sins, doesn't he?"

Peter and John nodded.

"But God also forgets our sins, doesn't he? He puts our sins behind Him – isn't there some place in Scripture where He says He will remember our sins no more. So God forgives *and* God forgets. Surely the point of being a Christian is that God's behaviour is our aspiration as much as our salvation: surely *we* should forgive and forget as well. Forgetting kind of makes it the real deal: to forget the sins of your enemies – wow – that really takes some grace. Look at what happened in South Africa.

You've got to forgive but also move on – surely you get that better than either of us."

John began to speak but he did so with his head and eyes remaining firmly fixed on the straight ahead, just as his hands were plunged deep in his pockets. He sounded a little distant in the rehearsal of his thoughts.

"You're absolutely right" he said, before repeating that as if to teach himself something: "you're absolutely right. But the past was a different country, wasn't it? That's a silly phrase that people use, but now it's really true. Not that I can complain: my father used to take me for walks in this park and then I took my own children here. You're quite right to say that I've seen some dreadful things, but then life has also given me many wonderful memories as well."

Peter began to develop his earlier strand of thought. "The problem with the Bible is that it's full of seeming contradictions: there are urges to forget in it yes – I accept that – but there are also constant instructions not to. One of the most interesting examples of remembering in the Bible is the story of the Passover. At the same time that God himself passed over the nation of Egypt in order to free his own people, He took the time to create and build into Israel's heritage a sacrament that would help the community to remember this act.

And it says something as well that he built it into the family unit. Wouldn't that be a wonderful thing to do today: wouldn't it be great if the church was to announce one Sunday morning that we shouldn't come to worship that evening but instead we should stay at home as families and have meals together to celebrate the good things God has done for us?"

Peter looked at Adam who appeared pained and was saying nothing, and then realised just what he had said. Adam smiled gently to assure that this didn't matter. He carried on in a slightly more cautious manner.

"But you see the point I'm making, don't you? The Passover was all about symbolism and means to remembering: something that generations and generations are to celebrate into the future. And when your children ask you why it is you're doing all of this, you can tell them that God passed over and struck down the Egyptians but we were spared and given divine passage to leave. And of course it was just the same in the New Testament when Jesus gave us the Lord's Supper to remember the night He was betrayed.

But it's not just in those sacraments where the Bible puts importance on remembering: there are many occasions in the Old Testament where the children of Israel look to the hope that the best evidence of how God will behave in the future is how He has behaved in the past. Sometimes that is a source of celebration and on other occasions it seems to be clutched like a desperate straw. Think of how the Psalmist implores that what God has done must be written for a future generation, that those not yet created may praise the Lord.

I was looking at some of the Psalms the other night and a fantastic example of that are the ones from 105 to 107. You have this great exaltation of all the wonderful things that God has done in the history of Israel: all this proof of the faithfulness of God. The covenant that God made with Abraham; the redemption of Joseph's life after he was sold into Egypt as a slave; the deliverance of the children of Israel out of Egypt; and so it goes on. And the refrain in the midst of all these things is that the only response can be to praise God.

One of the greatest things about these Psalms is their honesty: they're warts and all. It's not like some communist state historian writing the official biography of the land and its supposedly great leader. When you remember before God you remember everything: the golden calf and the grumbling and the terrible way in which compromises were made with false religions and false idols. Very often when we remember we tend to glorify the past but there's no sense in the Bible of missing and hitting the wall."

"I suppose" Adam said, "that sometimes we tend to take a glib view that the only things we need to remember are the good things Christ has done for us. That's very worthy, but can also be convenient in its narrowness. Sometimes you hear people in prayer meetings here and it almost put years on you to listen to them: they're heaping scorn and unworthiness on themselves for all their past sinfulness, and yet I find myself thinking that God has told them they are holy and blameless in his sight.

It's as if they're beating themselves up beyond a point that God would ever want to beat them, when the Gospel is all about grace. But the thing about it is that it's all so individual, that it's incredibly rare to hear communities confess in this country."

"Absolutely" Peter added. "Absolutely. There's a frighteningly stark passage in the book of Ezra where the people are confronting their sinfulness in how they have interacted with the exiles, and the word used is that Ezra and the people of Israel sat before God 'appalled' at what they have done. I've seen a lot of your people kicking out against God for what has happened in Ireland, but I haven't seen a whole lot of you being appalled at your own actions and attitudes.

The other thing about history and remembering is that the Bible seems to link together the behaviour of different generations of the people of Israel. God says that however much he is slow to anger and abounding in faithfulness – forgiving wickedness and sin – nonetheless he will not leave the guilty unpunished. God says in fact that he punishes the children and their children for the sin of the fathers to the third and fourth generation. I've sometimes wondered how that works. I'm not sure if God – who is after all meant to be a God of justice – is saying that in a vengeful and a holy way He himself is tangibly going to pursue punishment on and on through generations. Or maybe it's simpler than that: maybe God is just stating the obvious fact that actions beget consequences, because where sin really has its way in nations such as Ireland and South Africa and Yugoslavia and so on, it obviously leaves legacies of hatred and division and folk-myth bitterness. That's how it goes on and on to impact on the future generations"

"But what does God mean for me?" John asked.

"What?" responded Peter.

"Well – this is all very high minded – what about 'so what'? What does all of it actually mean to me and us standing here today?"

Peter appeared a little taken aback and stumbled over some attempted words of response, but then Adam cut across him with clarity borne of being local.

"Well I suppose there has to be real honesty about what the past was truly like in this country. Jeremiah at times appeared to be almost brutal in laying before the people their sinfulness and the extent to which they'd strayed. But a lot of that was all about attempting a wake up call *before* the people went into exile. Now that we are where we are, I would hope that God would speak to us more compassionately. But there needs to be realism about the way that the past was. I think that's especially true for us because as a generation we're over 25 years clear of the IRA ceasefire and we're 40 to 50 years on from the very worst of the violence. A lot of it is modern history that my generation and my father's generation lived through, but that the likes of your wee grandson will need to be taught from scratch. There's a lovely little phrase in the Bible where individuals of great wisdom are held up as men who 'understood the times'. What we need to have in Ireland are Christian people who understand past times: we need to have prophets of God who will interpret the past and not the future.

How many people are about now who remember really well the 1960s and the start of the Troubles? There needs to be an acceptance by Protestants that Northern Ireland in the 1950s and 1960s was in many ways not a fair place for Catholic people. It was all too often a Protestant place run in the self interest of Protestant people. And it's particularly depressing to reflect that much of this injustice occurred in an era that Christian people reminisce about as a wonderful time of church going and flourishing evangelical congregations. I know I didn't live in those days, but as far as I can see all the apparent Biblical Christianity didn't seem to do much good socially. What does that tell you: that true faith in Christ might be transformational, but religion makes damn all difference to anyone or anything? Jeremiah would have had us lot well sussed."

"Don't tell me it was all bad" John retorted. "Religion was good for me. I might have had Bible verses and Catechism hammered into me and resented it at the time, but I'm glad of it now. It did me plenty of good."

"I'm sure it did. And equally there needs to be an acceptance by the Catholic people that horrific things were done in the course of the Troubles: that violence left a dreadful legacy. I think that's something their community needs to work particularly hard at, because of how things have turned out. The Second World War is a good example of that: the history that we knew as British people was that of the defeat of fascism and the evil of the holocaust. But because the British were amongst the allied winners it's all too easy to overlook the cruelty of events such as the bombing of Dresden and other German cities, and the terrible loss of life of German civilians.

Ireland needs to have a very balanced history: because the Republicans have won there's a terrible danger that the North will be burned into Irish memories as a place of miserable Catholic oppression, whilst the terror of Republican violence is conveniently glossed over. If you've won there is an automatic tendency to assume that your victory must therefore have been just, but that isn't necessarily the case. Sometimes Republican leaders used to express frustration that Protestants weren't prepared to trust them and take leaps. After all that our community had been through it would have been more surprising if we *had* been prepared to trust them. They just didn't seem to get the fact that if you wage a campaign of terrorism against a community then it affects prospects for building a relationship with that community for generations."

John had been quiet up to this point, but was obviously deep in thought, and now he spoke. "I used to have a wee theory that one of the problems in this country is that the Protestant people only want to look back but the Catholic people only want to look forward. Protestant people always seemed to be on the defensive, whilst at every juncture the

Republicans seemed to be stepping forward and making more and more gains. So the Protestants just licked their wounds and failed to catch any sort of vision for the future: whereas the Republicans… well, I suppose if you were the political wing of a terrorist campaign that until recently had been pushing a bloody campaign, then you had a very vested interest in talking endlessly about the future.

"You know" Peter said: "I think so much of this is down to what you believe the character of God is: having a deep confidence in the future trust of God is related to how you view the past. The fact is that our memories of years and generations gone by are bound to be confused and twisted when the future is something to be feared. But depending on your view of who God is, the future is something to look forward to. God is a God who has given us so many promises: that all things work for good; the promise that he hears our prayers; the promise of the Holy Spirit.

Somebody once observed to me that we have been crucified with Christ and that a crucified man can only look forward. You cannot influence the past but you can influence the future. I think you have to mix together the Old Testament and the New Testament in our thinking: the Irishman in you has to be realistic in looking back and the Christian in you has to be hopeful in looking forward. Amongst all the stuff that we talked about God and the way he wants us to remember, there is *one* thing that He does not remember. Like Adam said earlier: the Bible states that God will forgive our wickedness and He will remember our sins no more."

33

Alan

Alan Mackey had been a man stewing – if not bubbling – in his own juice all day: and it was a state he could bear no longer. He had not seen Nadia on Monday evening because one of her house-mates was going home, and together a group of girl-friends had thrown a party for her. Then tonight she was working, and tomorrow night was the small group with the guys. How much more of this could he take? He felt compelled that he would have to do the deed tonight: lance the boil and have it done and dusted.

He spent the day imagining the scene and rehearsing the softest and most cushioning of soliloquies he thought he could string together. But every time he settled on a form of words he had second thoughts: each mental run through the act saw some notion of stage-fright on his part. He'd spent an agonising evening flicking from watching football to praying to removing all the books and CDs from his shelves and rearranging them in alphabetical order.

The shop closed at ten but it was generally half past the hour by the time staff had the equipment cleaned down. He moseyed over to the door and called to greet her just as she was coming out. Nadia was surprised to see him but nonetheless delighted, which did not get him off to the best of starts.

First he had to calm that pleasure in her: he did that through giving off his mood with a fretful face and pushing his hands up and down in weak motions indicating to her to 'calm yourself'. Then he explained that he had come over to meet her because he had something to tell her, and he was afraid it wasn't good news. That seemed to startle her so he had to explain that nothing was wrong... well something was wrong... but not... "Well... not like that... don't worry... nobody's died or got run over or got some awful disease or something…"

And then he looked at her and in a moment – after all the preparation and dry runs to the kitchen wall – she just got it in one and looked away, to hide her face and compose herself.

He had expected it to be different and had psyched himself up for more than this. He thought she would call him for everything: that had happened often enough in the past. Perhaps in some masochistic way he actually wanted it to be much less smooth. He tried to catch her attention and danced around her in the street. She seemed to spin in circles like a toddler refusing to be told off: every time he moved to position himself in front of her she turned her back on him again. And all the time she was looking down, as if to keep herself doubly covered.

He said it was off. Every time he'd done this in the past it had been because he couldn't see the relationship going anywhere. This time it was for exactly the opposite reason. It was due to the fact that she and it had more direction and purpose than anything or anyone he'd ever known before that he had to call it a day. Tying the knot would be just that: tying the pair of them up in endless irresolvable knots. They would be kidding themselves to think it could be any other way.

She still wasn't looking at him. Reggie who owned the chip shop knocked at the window and scowled a face as if to ask Nadia if everything was ok. They motioned together – as if they were dance partners – that it was absolutely fine before returning to their moves.

Alan knew now that he loved her. He'd fallen for her sort rather than a real person at the start: for the looks and the smile certainly, but really for the notion of going out with who she was and what she was. It was as if she'd been the latest passing object in a shop window. Week after week and then day after day he had walked past her – imagined himself going for meals with her, going for walks with her, kisses and cuddles with her, trips to the cinema together – maybe even taking her to church with him. She had been to him a kind of gadget of desire, different in ways he hadn't tried before, and he was overcome by the notion that he had to have her. He hadn't bargained for loving her – not that he was that callous – well, not this depth of love anyway...

She wasn't surprised, she said. She was disappointed and she'd hoped for something more. She had been reading all the signals for a while: had sensed him shifty and quieter than usual. She then started to talk under her breath in Polish the way that she did when she was angry, but nothing more than that: she was holding it together. He got the distinct impression that more than anything else; he had simply let her down. He couldn't be sure that he had broken her heart. That figured: there was no hardness about Nadia but there sure was toughness.

It was quiet in the street, and in an instant they startled when distant caterwauling punctured the silence: some hisses and spits and then calm again. This was the coldest night of winter so far, and as they had now been standing for several minutes he was starting to feel the chill. His parents were on holiday so he had his mother's car. He offered her a lift, but she said she didn't want that: she always preferred the fresh air and the stillness after the grease and the rush of the shop. He was conscious of the lateness of the evening, and that being the case he at least insisted that he would walk her home. There was no traffic about but he was sure to have her on the inside of the pavement all the way.

It was a mile and a half's walk to the house she rented on the far side of the town: aside from the odd nocturnal dog walker there were no souls about, and neither of them spoke a word the whole way. Turning into the corner of the street she suddenly – but quite deliberately – took his hand in hers. They approached her home and she squeezed it hard. But she didn't look at him – not a glance or linger or anything in between – she simply walked away.

He watched her go to the door, fumble for her keys, and let herself in: she didn't look back. Did that mean she didn't care? Was she going inside to curse him up and down, or would she slump immediately with her back against the door and sob her eyes out? Such thoughts seemed voyeuristic, so he shook his head and grimaced and turned to start his return journey. He allowed himself a little sigh and skip of relief as he headed out of her street, but realising what he had just done he quickly recalibrated his mind to a repose of remorse.

He had barely got to the end of the road when it started to rain. There were only little spots at first but soon they came thick and fast and before he knew it there was the sort of downpour that requires just moments to leave its victims soaked to the bone. He didn't believe in Karma but he thought nonetheless about those bits in Psalms where people are cursed to get all that they deserve.

Heading round the final corner to the road where he had parked the car, he felt a strong wind blowing directly into his face. As he reached for the keys his sodden clothes were sticking to him and it was then that he heard the chime of a text hitting his phone. He clambered into the shelter of the car and clumsily clicked digits to find that it was from Nadia.

"I love u anyway Alan. U knows it all but u get nothing – why am I left with the crap that u deserve? That's u all over – u and grace – u r all in 2 your God taking what u deserve, and u being 4given. Handy that – I suppose you've said your prayers about me already. So you do the confession and me the penance? But I love u anyway. Xx."

* * * * *

Strangers in a strange land

"Peter" John said. "Seeing as this is your last night with us – at least at one of these gatherings – I think it would be good if you could read the scriptures for us. Tonight's reading is from Jeremiah chapter 29 and verses one to 14." Peter smiled to confirm that he would be delighted to do so.

"This is the text of the letter that the prophet Jeremiah sent from Jerusalem to the surviving elders among the exiles and to the priests, the prophets and all the other people Nebuchadnezzar had carried

into exile from Jerusalem to Babylon. (This was after King Jehoiachin and the queen mother, the court officials and the leaders of Judah and Jerusalem, the craftsmen and the artisans had gone into exile from Jerusalem.) He entrusted the letter to Elasah son of Shaphan and to Gemariah son of Hilkiah, whom Zedekiah king of Judah sent to King Nebuchadnezzar in Babylon. It said:

This is what the LORD Almighty, the God of Israel, says to all those I carried into exile from Jerusalem to Babylon: "Build houses and settle down; plant gardens and eat what they produce. Marry and have sons and daughters; find wives for your sons and give your daughters in marriage, so that they too may have sons and daughters. Increase in number there; do not decrease. Also, seek the peace and prosperity of the city to which I have carried you into exile. Pray to the LORD for it, because if it prospers, you too will prosper." Yes, this is what the LORD Almighty, the God of Israel, says: "Do not let the prophets and diviners among you deceive you. Do not listen to the dreams you encourage them to have. They are prophesying lies to you in my name. I have not sent them," declares the LORD.

This is what the LORD says: "When seventy years are completed for Babylon, I will come to you and fulfil my gracious promise to bring you back to this place. For I know the plans I have for you," declares the LORD, "plans to prosper you and not to harm you, plans to give you a hope and a future. Then you will call upon me and come and pray to me, and I will listen to you. You will seek me and find me when you seek me with all your heart. I will be found by you," declares the LORD, "and will bring you back from captivity. I will gather you from all the nations and places where I have banished you," declares the LORD, "and will bring you back to the place from which I carried you into exile."

"There's that verse" Mike said. "The flighty feel-good one that people used to give to each other: and probably still do."

Alan nodded in agreement: "ah the things we did when we were young." The rest of the group looked at Mike quizzically.

"What on earth are you on about?" John asked.

"It's Jeremiah 29v11, isn't it?" Mike replied. ""For I know the plans I have for you" declares the Lord, "plans to prosper you and not to harm you, plans to give you a hope and a future." That's the flighty verse: that's the sort of verse that people write in peoples' Bibles when you're all adolescent and inclined to ask people to write verses in the back of your Bible for you. It's good for throwing into prayers as well" Alan nodded again, only harder this time. "Wonderful stuff."

"Well that's all very interesting" John said in a somewhat disingenuous tone. "Now do you mind if we get to the study? The first question asks what the situation is into which Jeremiah sent his letter? What is the essence of Jeremiah's instructions in verses 4-9?"

"Well" Willie said. "It's the exile, isn't it? Jeremiah is giving this message to the children of Israel in the context that they've just gone into exile. I suppose it's interesting that the instructions seem to be practical rather than spiritual. It's not all about holiness and holding on to your religious practices amongst these strange people. It says nothing about their Sabbaths and festivals and all the Jewish ways of religious separation.

It's all about building and houses and settling down: laying roots and expecting to stay instead of go. Marry and have sons and daughters and expect to see yourselves build as a community in this particular place. Get involved and seek the prosperity of the country, because if it is a good place to be, that in turn will be a good thing for you. I suppose what's so striking about it – particularly when you think of us Protestants – is the way it's so positive rather than defensive. It talks about the people prospering and yet we've always had a mindset of digging in deep to hold on grimly to what we have. I don't think that as a people we've ever thought of ourselves as prospering: the greatest victory there could have been was maintaining the status quo."

"You're spot on" Adam agreed. "It talks about integration and pitches it in a very upbeat tone. Whereas we all too often choose to live apart from those who are different from us: think of all the towns across the North that have their Catholic 'ends' and their Protestant 'ends'.

It's like that area on the far side of town that takes you

out to the Lough: those town lands where so much housing has sprung up like Drumnalee and Drumnagallon. I remember a few years ago going for a walk one Sunday afternoon down near the Lough and when I was driving home there was some road diversions set up: for water main laying or the like. And I drove round all these different roads and developments and so on. You know, for all that I knew and recognised you could have parachuted me into the middle of Dorset or Cumbria or wherever because I hadn't the first notion where I was. And I remember thinking – 'but I'm only a few miles from home' – isn't that a terribly damning indictment on this country."

Willie shook his head. "I'd be the same: if I tried driving round there I'd just get lost."

"You got a whole lot of it in Belfast as well" Adam continued. "North Belfast just emptied in the sixties and the seventies as the nice middle class Protestants shipped out to safe enclaves like Jordanstown and Whiteabbey. And then you would hear people talking about how Catholics move into places and buy houses and 'come in and take over, because that's what Catholics do you see, they take over.'"

"But when you think about it, it's all common sense" Peter suggested. "I love the concept of our prosperity being bound to the prosperity of the community in which we're living. What is it that would be a modern take on that? The reality is that Northern Ireland is gone and now you should all want plain old Ireland to do well: if modern Ireland is vibrant and booming and confident, then you in turn should do well.

But I don't think this message was just one of God telling the people to be shrewd and canny for the sake of economic self-interest. I think that for them then – and for you people today – there is also a sense of God speaking into their emotional well being. I think God was urging them towards a serenity to accept the things they could not change. You will actually be far happier if you accept your circumstances rather than continually questioning them and wishing for something that plainly isn't going to happen. The Union is gone: Ireland is

275

here. There's no peace in continually railing against that. Accept it: get on with it."

"Get on with what?" Mike retorted. "Get on with meekly rolling over! Hardly!"

"Ah but that is where your promise comes in, isn't it" Peter replied. "Christianity is not having your cake and eating it: it's having your meat and two veg and eating all of that up, as well as getting your cake. You can't have the promises of God if you're not prepared to accept the commands of God. Nobody said the exiles that had come from Jerusalem had to *like* this: but entwined with the promises that God knows the plans He has for them – plans to give them a hope and a future – is their side of the deal. And their part of the deal is a humble agreement with the plans of God – settling down and forming businesses; making relationships and raising families – doing their utmost to build good lives for themselves in the place where God has put them.

Actually have the trust to increase in number in this place. The future of you people in this land doesn't have to be one of a small Protestant rump that shrivels and diminishes to less and less every year: consolidating in number and education and retreating to wherever it is that you choose to live. You go out and do what God told the exiles to do: get good educations; enter the professions; be part of civic life – things like forming parties and electing councillors.

How can you expect to have any belief as a people if you don't have a belief in God? Not just a belief that Jesus died for your sins and rose again and if you believe all of that you can get to Heaven and avoid going to Hell. But something that is arguably bolder and more exciting than that: that God is not just someone who in your limited imaginations confines himself to the little salvation of little people. Believing that this God is the maker of time and history and can sweep to redeem a whole confused community: accepting that Northern Ireland is taken away but knowing that Jesus Christ is Lord and that can *never* be taken away."

"Aren't you getting a bit carried away?" John said.

"But that's the point" Peter replied in exasperated enthusiasm. "What if I'm the one who *is* getting it – who *is* getting God in this situation – and you folks are the ones who are not?"

"How dare you!" John snapped.

"How dare I what?" Peter asked. "How dare I ask the next question? Look at the page in front of you. Go on: read it."

"Don't talk to me like that – you've been trying to take this group over since you first came here. Don't: don't talk to me like that."

"Like what? I'm not talking to you like anything. I've no desire at all to lead your group: you're great at leading the group. I'm saying 'read the question'. Seize the moment. The Bible isn't a nice book to read before breakfast for ten minutes every morning and then put it away until the same time the next day. This is the Word of God relevant as never before. Live like it actually *is* truth. Just look at what it says…"

"Oh shut your preaching" said John disdainfully.

But Peter read it with his voice raised and trembling and his accent in stark contrast to all around him.

"Why do you think Jeremiah found it necessary to give this message? What parallels do you see between the Jews who were exiled and your life as a Christian? How do these verses encourage you as you try to remain faithful to God in a strange and change-filled society?"

Willie held his hands up to his head. "Gentlemen – please" he said. "No one… this is not what we come together to do. At least not like this… not in this way. Let's just… John: why don't we have another round of tea and coffee? Sure come you into the kitchen with me and the two of us will make it."

The Protestant in John was stung; the leader in him felt humiliated; and the Christian in him was utterly disorientated. He gladly accepted the offer, his tail between his legs. Peter said it seemed warm in the room and decided that he would go outside for five minutes for some fresh air. Adam felt that he should join him. Alan didn't say anything for a minute or two but then rolled his eyes and suggested to Mike that they could sneak John's TV on and see what was happening in the football.

* * * * *

John

John stared hard into his cup: the tea in it was good and was giving him warmth. When he spoke it was as if he was speaking simply to himself.

"It's strange that I'm the one who is so stubborn about all of this. Sure I've only to look within my own four walls to see my own wife and how she lives: her friendship with Siobhan. We're *talking* about it but she's *doing* it.

But I don't want to do it. I just don't. I'm not *full* of years like the Bible puts it but I have a lot of years in me, and I'm at a stage in life where – for what I've seen and what I've done – well, I just don't want to change. If there's a wall between the present, and a future that is like the passage in this Bible, then I don't want to go over that wall."

"But there isn't a wall" Peter said intently. "The only walls are the ones built in your heart and mind. And nobody but nobody is going to force you to go over them."

John shook his head with vigorous certainty. "I don't want to go over that wall."

"I'm not sure we have a choice" Adam replied. "I've thought about this a lot lately, probably because I've been thinking like you John – about where I've come from and where I'm going. The world is getting richer and faster and warmer and people don't seem to hate each other any less. I think there has to be change. I'm not saying we all have to go off and marry and settle down with Catholics and have children with them..."

"That could be you mate" Mike said, butting in. He nodded over at Alan. "*You* could lead the charge there."

"Oh no I couldn't" Alan replied, flustered. "No, no, it wouldn't be right. And it's not going to happen now, anyway. What were you were saying Adam?"

"You've not gone and..."

278

"I've not gone and done anything. Not now Mike: Adam is trying to make a point. Please."

"So you're in a hole and I stop digging?"

"Yes. Adam – what were you saying there?" He then mouthed an out of sight obscenity at his so called best friend.

Adam looked puzzled. "I can't remember."

"Short term memory's the first to go" Alan warned.

"The world is richer and faster and warmer" Peter said.

"Oh yes – eh – I'm not saying we settle down and marry Catholics but I do think that fundamentally we need to get down to the business of relating to them and understanding them – and loving them. I think it used to be the case that cross community stuff was alright for a few woolly people: the Prod lefties with their beards and their patterned jumpers and their wee weekends in Corrymeela and so on. I don't believe that anymore.

Too many people today only care about me and don't give a toss for community. The couple who live in the big detached houses in the sprawling upper class developments are living in social castles that they barricade themselves into every evening. As long as they're getting two or three holidays a year and there's shopping centres and restaurants to go to at the weekend and the new Audi is in the drive they're quite happy enough, thank you. They don't care for this country and all its problems. They don't bother to vote because they somehow think they're above it. They don't give a damn about Iran or North Korea or Africa or whatever: but in detaching themselves from society they get around them the society they deserve.

I remember many years ago talking to an elder in the church: I think it was the 1980s and if I'm right it was probably 1987 and Neil Kinnock was running Maggie Thatcher close in the polls. The subject of the election came up and I asked him who he thought would win – or maybe I asked him who he wanted to win. Do you know what his answer was? 'I'm really not fussed as long as there's less tax taken out of my pocket?' Is that a Christian attitude to politics: that as long as I'm ok myself I really don't care about any bigger picture?"

Peter shook his head. "Fool – I tell you: there's not too much right-wing economics in the Bible I read."

"Ohhhh" Mike winced. "You're starting to sound very integrated yourself man. That's a real good Northern Ireland head you've got on." He stuck on a strong accent for effect. "That's like 'there's no praying to Mary in the Bible I read' or something like that."

Adam was irritated and itching to make himself heard. "I actually think we've got to a point where absolutely every so called Christian should be getting their hands dirty with a cross community agenda. Maybe if that had happened thirty of forty years ago, the country wouldn't be in the mess it's in. There's no point in being concerned with the wearing of ripped jeans in church and moving a service of worship from eleven o'clock to half past eleven if a Catholic is not a person to you but is just a Taig or a Fenian."

"Oh be reasonable: I never said I thought like that" John said.

"I know you didn't: but you can't disengage brother. It's not as simple as saying you just won't go over the wall. What if it's God's will that we all go over the wall? We tend to think of offending God being all about obvious sins: the easy and the external things like gambling and drink and pornography and so on. Well let's be honest: we're all basically good men and we don't do that. And there's plenty of sinners and tax collectors who don't do that either. But what if grieving God and letting God down is about just detaching and disengaging with one half – not even a half, it's about three quarters now – of all the people who live around us. That will just impoverish us and it will impoverish them as well."

"You said something earlier that struck me" Alan said – addressing Peter – "what was it? Something about knowing that Jesus Christ is Lord and the reality that *that* truth can never be taken away. I think that's the challenge. It's a Prod thing yeah, but it's about a lot more than that. It's not just about climbing some abstract wall so that Catholics and Protestants don't matter anymore.

I think there's a challenge to us to be distinctive and attractive because of Christ. Not just because we're Protestant so we're a bit quirky: we still wear Sunday best; and we have no interest in GAA; and we don't blaspheme because that's offensive to us. Going over the wall is about more than leaving the Protestant and Catholic thing behind. It's about leaving money and cars and the best of fashion and careers and all those things behind as well. Not being conformed to the culture of the day but being radicalised by Jesus Christ."

"You've changed your tune all of a sudden" Mike said. "Mind yourself when you sit back there, in case you do damage to your wings."

"I know, I know" Alan replied. "It all sounds so ethereal sitting here, and I don't know how it works either. I don't know if I'll ever be terribly different from all the people around me. You know the way you sometimes wonder about detergents – whether they're actually any different or if the washing up liquid and the dishwasher tablets and the bathroom spray are all just the same things in different containers. Sometimes I think that about people: sometimes I wonder if the Christians are really any different at all. Horrible notions that we can't change things and there's nothing we can do. But maybe there just isn't anything we can do."

"Maybe not" Peter ventured. "Maybe the truth is that what has happened to your history and your people in the past couple of years is not a bad thing. Maybe it's absolutely the best thing that could have ever happened…"

There was an obvious sigh of exasperation from John…

"No – listen – hear me out" Peter continued. "Just look back to the passage again and see what it says. 'You will seek me and find me when you seek me with all your heart.' You see – with all of your heart. There's no Union and no Britain any more because that is gone. And so other than in a forlorn and a grieving way *that* can't have any of your heart: you have to let it go and accept its loss.

But you find God when you seek Him with *all* your heart: I think it's a cruel truth that it's only now that a lot of your community can give God *all* their heart. Now that you're a minority rather than a majority you have a much greater sense of need *of* God and faith *in* God. All of the distractions are stripped away and there's a far greater sense of what really matters. Were previous generations of Protestants in Ulster confident because they were God fearing and filled churches up and down the six counties? Or were they confident because they were the majority and the lesser community was kept well and truly in its place? But now you're like the biblical concept of the remnant: reduced to a low ebb before God can begin to do anything with you. So you may not be at an ending: where you are now could in fact be a brilliant beginning."

"It's a very un-Protestant notion" Adam said. "There is something really fascinating about God's statement that 'I will be found by you' rather than our assumption that God always takes the initiative: the basis of our faith that we are chosen and found by God. But faith does not just happen to us: we ourselves – according to this – can make it happen.

That's why the analogy of the wall is really quite frightening: because God is not going to come running over the other side and grab you and carry you over the wall Himself. God's not going to force us. We are much less passive in the grand design of God than we think: we can choose to wallow where we are in 32-county Ireland or we can choose to find God."

"Exactly" Peter affirmed. "God works in mysterious ways, His wonders to perform. That which seems to be your very lowest point could be the greatest moment in the history of your faith."

There was silence of the depth where every noise is audible: ticking clocks; radiators gurgling with hot water; and restless bums shuffling in seats. And then there was one startlingly big noise as John crashed both his hands down decisively upon his thighs.

"It's like born again" John said. "OK... I'm in. I haven't a clue what it means, but I want to go over the wall."

34

John

John often thought that churches can be peculiar places: where grace should so easily abound, it is often the case that pettiness abounds more. But at Christmas – he thought – that all goes out the window: however much people may be different and find it hard to get along through the year, everyone can love each other in church on Christmas morning.

This year appeared to be no different from any other. Men wore new jumpers and were contentedly long suffering of them: wives wore new coats and were evidently delighted with them. In the pews, children – who were conditionally welcome upon the rejoinder of "bring a *quiet* toy" – were restless but justifiably indulged. Teenagers sat mesmerised and stared in sullen concentration at tiny handheld consoles.

At the front the Reverend Noel Houston had forsaken his dog collar for a sports casual look as was his festive wont. His wife this year had put him in a brown corduroy jacket and dark blue chinos: he would have looked more comfortable in a monk's habit. But contemporary fashion somehow made him appear more vulnerable and that in turn caused him to be more likeable. Also appealing was the manner in which he never grew bored of doing his little Christmas auction: starting off with who had been got up out of bed at seven o'clock and then willing up the bids of excitement to the likes of children who had woken in the middle of the night. He seemed to love this.

Church on Christmas morning was as ever a mixture of the always here and the long gone: sons and daughters who have gone away to make new lives for themselves and each year return with a little more prosperity on their backs but age upon their faces, the growing children or even grand children in tow.

John looked around at people such as these: he supposed that it was nice to see the visitors but the pleasure really was in seeing his long standing friends enjoy having their families around them. This was normally just another part of Christmas, but this year the awareness of those returning home was more marked in a way that did not smell or seem of togetherness: those coming back for the first time that had departed for less foreboding territory just a year earlier.

The tension was just below the surface. John looked around him and he thought of Jeremiah and the Scripture he had studied with his friends. He thought about engaging and the challenge of going over *that* wall. And then he looked around him and he felt a smouldering and judging sense of revulsion. He saw old acquaintances around him and he wanted to be casual and relaxed on the birth day of his Lord. But he could only be angry at these people who were glad to come and be among his brethren on a special day like this, yet had made it so clear that really for the rest of the time they would sooner be out of here and living somewhere else. He had loved these people and thought them his kith and kin in faith and Union: now his disappointment with them could not be contained. Christmas might be better if these people were not here, if he was sharing it only with those who had proved the truly faithful.

He noticed across the rows of pews that Kenny Turkington was coming into church now, with Susan – wasn't that Kenny's wife's name – and the kids in tow. Kenny had been on the committee with John a few years back, and John remembered him embodying all the good and the bad of a 'tight wee man'. Kenny was a butcher and the last John had heard he had gone to somewhere in South Wales and got a job in a big supermarket there.

He could see Kenny walking past Bertie Robinson and going to sit in the pew behind him: and whilst not wanting to stare John had to check twice to see that this was really happening. As he went to sit in the pew Kenny started as if to greet Bertie, but Bertie totally blanked him. Bertie stared straight ahead and just ignored him. Now John felt guilt and misgivings at what he had thought just moments earlier: this was church on Christmas morning; this was wrong surely. Twelve months ago he'd have thought he'd have been right there with wee Bertie, but now he was not so sure: just as he was unsure of so many things now.

In a few days anyhow he and Gillian would be going over to Scotland to spend New Year there with Peter and Ruth. It would be good to get out of the country for a short while. That being the case David and Vicki had come down from the North Coast to spend Christmas with John and Gillian. John was delighted that they had all volunteered to come to church together. He wanted to believe that it meant something – some thawing or thinning – but he knew really that it was just that church was nice to go to on Christmas morning, and David understood how much it would please his Mum. And as he sat with people milling and buzzing around them, John felt a tremendous pride in little JP. He thought a little more of the people who stopped to admire his grandchild, and a little less of those who didn't. He was anxious too that people would talk to David and Vicki, for he had absolutely no confidence that the believers would be friendly to the strangers.

They had come early to be sure to get a seat and now John found himself drifting into thinking time. He gazed wistfully at his grandchild and that took him away in his thoughts. People simply didn't appreciate the child the way that he did: he heard every gurgle amplified and saw every smile stretched. When tiny dimples momentarily appeared he wanted to look around and bask in all the appreciation of this child, but other people simply didn't notice: to them it was just another baby. He found himself feeling pangs of regret too: he looked at the tiny hands and feet and he tried to recall how he'd felt about Peter and David when they were this age. He felt deep love for the grandchild but he felt guilt too because he suspected he loved it more than he had loved his own children when they were that small.

He wondered why that was: maybe he was just older and wiser and could appreciate these things more now. Maybe it was easy to romanticise the grandchild whereas with his own there'd been all the nappies and the spoon feeding and the broken sleep, and that had made him ambivalent. Then he saw Violet a few pews in front peering quizzically over bi-focals at a watch that appeared to be a Christmas present, and he decided there was a lot to be said for not thinking too much at all. And then it all seemed to come together, in a way that it very rarely did for John. He thought then of another old man – of Simeon in the Temple – taking the baby Jesus in his arms and praising God. John looked down at the little boy beside him in the portable car seat, and he thought he realised in a moment a bit of how God might have felt to view the Christ in the manger. This was a heart thing and not a head thing and that was most unlike John.

He wondered what the life of this little child beside him would hold in store. His heart swelled with pride but then hadn't God himself said when Jesus was baptised that this was his son who he loved and was pleased with. That was more like a Daddy God speaking than a Father God and John understood that now. So many boys grow up to be sheepish about their dad: reticent about the things they do and all too often awkward in their relationships. Dads are fundamentally not cool. But it wasn't like that at all with Jesus: Jesus was always going on about the Father this and the Father that and how great the Father was and how He'd be obedient to everything the Father told him to do. John wished he'd felt that way about his dad but he didn't: he was sure he'd been a disappointment to his dad, and he'd have so loved to turn the clock back now with his own boys. He questioned what exactly the baby at his side was thinking: but then David was 28 and he didn't have a notion what was going through his head either.

Mary – it was said – pondered things and treasured them up in her heart. Sure – thought John – doesn't every parent do that, at least to some extent? The baby's face was smooth and perfect in every way. But it wouldn't always be like that: of course it would get spotty and pimply and those hands and legs would fall over and be marked with cuts and bruises. But that's as nothing to knowing that your child will go to the cross and all that it entails: the flogging and the nail pierced hands and feet and the crown of thorns. He saw his grandchild and understood that he would never understand the full depth of the love of God.

Now the Reverend Houston was flapping about a little anxiously at the front: tapping at his radio-mike and darting nervously amongst a few people who would play a part in the service. John looked over and saw that Kenny Turkington was now looking down and seeming lost in church on Christmas morning. That wasn't right: he decided that he'd have to go and make a point of talking to Kenny and shaking his hand at the end of the service. He knew that he was Irish and he didn't like it: Kenny he supposed was English now but they were both in church and that made him his brother. After all he reckoned: we're all just human beings at the end of the day, and that – ultimately – is the most important thing.

* * * * *

Peter

"They didn't seem very happy, did they?" Adam said.

"Well that's hardly a big surprise now" Peter replied. "I mean Egypt isn't exactly a happy place to be when you've gone for all the wrong reasons. I mean England…"

"Egypt. Are you losing your mind?"

"No, it's just that, well… for England read Egypt."

The two friends had been to church together and returned to Adam's home where they were gathering presents before going their separate ways. Peter had been invited to spend Christmas Day with Willie and Violet, whilst Adam was going to his parents' home, where his kids would join him in the evening. Peter unwrapped his obscure remark as he zipped his coat up and proceeded to its buttons.

"For England read Egypt. When the Babylonians invade Israel, the response of many of the Israelites is to flee to Egypt.

Jeremiah tells them not to: they're going to the wrong place for the wrong reasons. They're fleeing to a land that will be comfortable and where life will be easier for them, but also a place that can never provide the authenticity of living and faith that home can. These were people who thought of their Lord as the God who brought them out of Egypt and yet here they were bolting to Egypt of all places when the going gets tough. Go figure."

"Well there's nothing new under the sun, is there?" Adam replied. "It's not a million miles away to viewing the English as the people who sold you down the river, yet England's the place you run to when you need to run away."

Adam rummaged through carrier bags on the sofa to make sure he had everything. "I think it's particularly hard though for those folks who are more mature in years. It's one thing taking a wee sapling out of a pot and planting it in the garden, but when you're forty or fifty years old and all your roots are here and deeper, moving is bound to be a whole pile tougher."

"If you can't stand the heat, get out of the kitchen" Peter said. "If you're not a strong enough character to stay here and stick it out, why should you expect to be big enough people to go and make a new life somewhere else and be happy. People who crave an easy life don't do challenges well."

"That's a bit hard, is it not?" Adam asked, stopping his sorting to look up at his friend. "I'm sure they all had their reasons."

"Life is hard" Peter replied. "They made their choices."

"But they did what they did because... I don't know... because they wanted to do the best for their children and their families. They didn't think this is a place to raise their kids. It's not their fault England is so different that people like them don't fit in easily."

"Yes but what did Jeremiah say about the flight to Egypt. 'If you stay in this land, I' – that is the Lord – 'will build you up and not tear you down; I will plant you and not uproot you.' And then he goes on to say that in Egypt 'you will be an object of cursing and horror, of condemnation and reproach'."

"That was then but this is now Peter. Two different times and two different places. I just don't think you can say that."

"Maybe not" returned Peter, wrapping his scarf around himself. "But they can't expect to have their cake and eat it. On the one hand they don't have the faith and the confidence in God to stand their ground when the time of trial comes, but on the other hand it's God's fault when the bolt hole has a leaky roof and draughty windows. I don't think that's how trust in God works, mate."

35

Alan

As Mike Matthews stood in the corner shop with a large pile of mushrooms, bacon and sausages in his arms, perusing with wide eyes the offers on soda farls and potato bread, an other worldly voice started to speak from behind him:

"Stop! Think! What's that you're going to eat? Have you really *thought* about the impact of those fatty foods on your arteries and the scales? A moment on the lips but a lifetime on the hips..."

He knew who it was immediately.

"Go away Alan. It won't go on my hips anyway. It'll go on my bay window."

He turned to greet his friend and continued talking to him.

"I've got the worst sort of middle aged spread you can have: the Mr Skinny type."

"The what?"

"The Mr Skinny type. You'd hardly know it: it must be a few years since you've read Mr Skinny. He's all anxious about his weight and how thin he is, so he goes to see Dr Plump and Dr Plump sends him to live with Mr Greedy for a few months to get fattened up. And at the end of the story he's just the way he was at the beginning – stick thin up and down – except that he's got this absurd little tummy in the middle of his body. That's me man: I'm turning into Mr Skinny."

"Well sure: at least you're still married to Little Miss Sunshine."

Mike rolled his eyes and Alan continued.

"How is the hen? Have you all had a good Christmas?"

"Oh aye, cracking, no complaints there. I was going to give you a ring actually. We were thinking of having a wee party on New Year's Eve: it was so *grim* last year, and we're all a year older and wiser now and it's hardly been as bad as anyone thought it would be. The men still work and the women still cook and clean and the children still play. God's still in his Heaven. So we thought it would be good to have a few friends round: are you doing anything?"

"Sorry: I'd love to but I can't do New Year's Eve."

"Oh right: the free and single man about town. Have you got a better offer?"

"Absolutely: I'm seeing Grace."

"What!"

There was a pause for a moment as Mike failed miserably to disguise his thoughts before carrying on.

"Are you seeing her or *seeing* her?"

"Oh ho: I'm *seeing* her. It's all back on: I'm going round to her place on New Year's Eve."

"You dirty dog: when did that happen?"

"Christmas Eve. Rodney had a party for those of us who aren't at the leaving Santa and Rudolf a snack stage. And lo and behold I ended up in a wee corner with her... and the lights were dim and there were logs on the fire... and the old sense of humour you know: it never fails." He jigged from side to side to emphasise the coolness of the charm.

"Good grief. You didn't waste your time then."

"Absolutely, and no presents or anything with the shops and all closed."

"Well: you got caught so badly last year, and then there's all the other ghosts of Christmas past: you must be due a Jubilee year by now!"

"You know how it is Mike. Women: you can't live with them and you can't live without them."

"What do you mean you can't live without them? Sure you've never actually got as far as *living* with any of them in your puff: how would you know? And Grace is still on for it: after – I'm not sure what to say – after all the water under your collective bridge?"

"Oh absolutely. I think in a way she's maybe even keener than she was the first time round."

"Which is another way of saying maybe you deserve each other. When I think of the way you moaned to me about her…"

"Sure you could argue we're both going into it with our eyes wide open now. Maybe in a way absence makes the heart grow fonder."

"But what about Nadia?"

"What about her?"

"No I don't mean that: I mean I know it's off and that's that. But what about the fact that it all happened and it was so… well… different. This thing with Grace: you normally hover for such a long time before you swoop. You don't think you're doing this for the wrong reasons, do you?"

"What, you mean on the rebound?"

"Aye."

"Not at all: anyway, I think rebound is more a female thing myself."

Alan was starting to wonder if Grace had been out with anyone in the past year but he didn't even want to go there. His friend carried on.

"I think in a way it's all quite poetic. From Nadia to Grace: we could be an article in *Life Times*. Big picture spread of us and all: he walked on the road to Rome but then he discovered grace."

"I'd have thought *Life Times* would have wanted you married and posing in the soft furnishings of your expensive new home before they'd run the story! Saved by God, furniture by Fulton's, hair by David International: that would be your style." Anyway: there's nothing gracious about it!

"What!?!"

"Well there isn't! If pigs could fly you'd be a squadron leader."

"That's not fair: I've seen the grass on the other side and I know it isn't greener. I've learnt my lessons the hard way…"

"Not as hard as for the other people involved…"

"… and I've decided I'm better off where I am."

"No you haven't! You've done nothing of the sort. You're doing what suits you until something else suits you better.

You'd be better not coming round on New Year's Eve: I'll have to drag Wendy off you when she hears about this."

"Oh listen to James Dobson, will you. You're meant to be my friend: I thought you'd be pleased for me."

"With your ego looking after number one, you hardly need friends, do you? Now where do they keep eggs in this place?"

36

Strangers in a strange land

The place where Adam had his home computer was beside the window in his upstairs study. This was not ideal as light and glare was prone to shine in upon the screen. But Adam didn't mind really: he loved natural light and could never understand why anybody might choose to keep it out. If ever he entered a room in the middle of the day and there were curtains drawn or blinds pulled, he would open them immediately if it was at all in his control. Always let the light in, he thought: why would you not want to?

He also enjoyed the view from this room which was located at the side of the house: glancing sideways allowed you to view the street and all that was going on. He liked the fact that he could see so much without himself being seen. Life on his own now was so quiet, and occasionally there was company to be had through the distant noise of children playing outside. This was where he found himself on a Friday afternoon in January, sitting in front of his flat screen to see what had tumbled into his inbox in the last few days.

It was great in some ways to have the house back to himself again, but he missed Peter more than he cared to admit. He understood a little of what David had meant when he lamented Jonathan and said that his love for his friend was more wonderful than that of women. Two weeks had passed since Peter's return to South Africa to tidy up his affairs, and in that time nothing had been heard from him. But there – when Adam double-clicked – was an email from his soul companion. It began by rehearsing routine sentiments of asking his friend how he was whilst assuring Adam in turn that he was keeping well. A timetable was given on the forecast progress of his affairs, which he expected would see him back in Ireland in six weeks or so. Then he shared some thoughts he'd been having since he'd gotten back to Johannesburg.

"I've been working through the Psalms this last week or so, and I came to some that made me think of Ireland. The first one that made me think of you folk is Psalm 136: it starts off stating some attributes of God, but then becomes a list of many of the good things that God did for Israel throughout the nation's history, and between each line is the refrain 'His love endures forever'. He struck down the firstborn of Egypt and His love endures forever. He brought Israel out from among them, and His love endures forever. And on and on it goes in this vein. One interesting aspect is that it seems to focus solely on the ups rather than the downs: some Psalms contain passages of lament and repentance, where there is regretful honesty about the episodes where the Israelites strayed from God and failed Him, but not this one.

It made me think about the way that you and others in your community have responded to what you've faced over the past year or so. Do you accept that the love of God endures forever – whatever the circumstances and despite what you have been through – or do you link it to your history so that like this Psalm seems to suggest, it's easier to believe that God's love endures forever when your enemies are being routed and the Union is in its place. That's a simplistic and selective way for me to think, but then the Psalm also seems to be selective, and it's right there in the Bible.

But what makes it even more fascinating is that you get to Psalm 137 – the very next Psalm – and you find yourself reading of distress and how the people wept when they remembered Zion. The contrast with what has just gone before – which is like a propaganda song for how God has blessed a nation – could not be starker.

This is not a case of the Lord gives and the Lord takes away, but blessed be the name of the Lord. This is a case of how can we sing the songs of the Lord whilst in a strange land: how can we sing praise to God when we don't want to be here? And unlike so many Psalms there is no chink of light in this one:

there's no sense of the sun breaking through the clouds at the end with the Psalmist suddenly roused to give some praise to God and remember His love and kindness. Rather it ends with the desire that in revenge for what the Babylonians have done, their infants would be seized and dashed against rocks, which is an absolutely horrific image. And again, it's right there in the Bible.

One Psalm is relentlessly upbeat and then the next is relentlessly downbeat. Is that the way it's meant to be: are Catholics in Ireland who love and fear the Lord now left to sing Psalm 136 and Protestants who love and fear Him left alone with the sentiments of Psalm 137? Is there no in-between? Surely there has to be, and I suppose the two passages prove that even the Psalmists were mere sinning flesh and blood, who got caught up in moments of trusting their emotions rather than trusting God. But the fact is that they're both there in scripture and are each one a legitimate response to God. I don't suppose this helps very much Adam, but when I read them, I just couldn't help thinking of you all.

One more thing: losing things is dreadful; nobody wants to lose things. The Israelites didn't want to lose Zion; the Rich Young Ruler didn't want to give up his possessions; and you people didn't want to lose Ulster. The story of so many in this world is of holding on to the wrong things for the wrong reasons, but not embracing that which is most precious, that which God has given us. When the Rich Young Ruler asked Jesus what he had to do to be good, Jesus told him to obey the commandments: don't murder; don't steal; honour your father and mother and so on. And right at the end of what Jesus told him, was the injunction to love your neighbour as yourself. Maybe that sums it up Adam: let Ulster go, and love your neighbour as yourself. Think what could happen then. And it's only obedience: it's only what's commanded of you."

Adam looked outside to rest his eyes from the VDU and to give his mind a break. But when he turned his gaze to the street he was disappointed to see a girl – she looked to be in her mid-teens – who at just that moment was walking sulkily up the street in her school uniform. It was a girl: but it could just as easily have been a fleece or an angel. Because she was obviously a Catholic – you could tell it just by looking at the uniform. His mother used to say proudly that Protestant schools always had much more classy uniforms: nice greys and blacks and dark blues. But she complained that some of the Catholic uniforms were truly desperate: all greens and browns and beige and 'really Fenian looking'. What Adam saw pass his window was just one of those: a dark brown uniform with a distasteful yellow blouse and tan coloured tights: he supposed it did look pretty awful. There were more and more of them moving into the area now. 'Because that's what they do: they come in and they take things over.'

He looked back towards the high-minded sentiments on the screen before him and felt disheartened that just one girl in just one street had made him think the way he had. An Ulster Protestant was simply what he was: these interpretations were wired deep inside him. Like the African who sees black and white, or the Moslem who sees Shiite and Sunni, he felt them unconsciously. And he believed that no victory could be enough to make him think differently.

The bigotry he did not want to think was exactly what he was thinking. And yet he thought he was right: he couldn't let go of being right. If the life of faith is a journey – as people were fond of saying to him – why did all the travelling and repenting and examining had to be on his side only? If it were all as halcyon and dreamy as Peter in the safe distance of Johannesburg would say it is, would the other half not know their own awakening and come to meet them half-way? Paisley said he wanted them to wear sackcloth and ashes and he was lambasted for it. But he was right: for what they have done so they should be repenting in sackcloth and ashes.

Peter was one who went on and on about the journey thing: that we are all works in progress, that we will never be the finished article. He knew Peter was sensible in such pragmatism, but it made him feel empty: it was such an easy cliché. He worried that he had become to believe more in the journey – in his own sinfulness and mess and stumbling – than in any eventual destination. But as someone had once remarked saints are sinners who keep on trying: and he knew there were beliefs and convictions inside him that transcended moments like these. He would persevere and finish and indeed he was determined he would finish well. Maybe, he thought, the other half doesn't need to meet the Protestants half-way: maybe we just need to travel our own road and resolve our own issues, and let them worry about their road themselves.

He moved to shut down his PC and as he did so his eye was caught by the small Celtic cross that hung on the wall behind the desk. Carolyn had bought it for him from a little pottery they'd visited together on a holiday in the west of Ireland. That must have been twenty years ago. It wasn't an ordinary cross... it was an Irish cross... it was a cross – he pondered – for Ireland. No – he thought – that's just nonsense. I've got to snap out of this: the Great I am has love wide as an ocean. He's not some little trickle whose every tributary flows towards poor old Ireland and all her naval-gazing sins and woes. The cross was for everyone and everyman and every sin. It's easy, Adam pondered, to talk in the language of Jesus dying for 'my sins'. The cross is just the cross – nothing added and nothing taken away. The journey was the only one there was: there were no other options that he wanted to entertain. Northern Ireland was gone but heaven and earth would never pass away.

References

Chapter 1
All Scripture quotations are taken from the HOLY BIBLE, NEW INTERNATIONAL VERSION, NIV, Copyright 1973, 1978, and 1984 by International Bible Society.

Chapter 2
The actor who made the statement about God having Chinese people yelling at him was Mel Brooks.

Chapter Four
The bible studies from Jeremiah that the men study in their cell group are based on those in Run with the Horses, by Eugene Peterson, published by InterVarsity Press, 1996.

Chapter 8
Some of the points about Daniel are based on a talk that Stephen Cave gave at Belfast Bible College in Autumn 2005 as part of a series on 'Jesus' heart for his people'.

Chapter 16
The idea of the challenges that are posed to God by contradictory prayer requests is explored by Philip Yancey in his book Prayer (Hodder, 2006). The musings of Adam whilst on his walk were inspired by a section of this book.

Chapter 26
Glenn Jordan did a class at Belfast Bible College on Praying the Psalms, and a particular class on Psalm 73 was helpful in forming some of the ideas in this chapter.

Chapter 29

The idea of pyramids of influence is not entirely my own: it was drawn from some deep recess of memory and I think can be attributed to the Rev Dr John Dunlop.

Lightning Source UK Ltd.
Milton Keynes UK
UKOW040822151112

202185UK00001B/23/P